HOOD RAT

K'wan

HOOD RAT

St. Martin's Griffin ☙ New York

This is a work of fiction. All of the characters, organizations, and events portrayed in this novel are either products of the author's imagination or are used fictitiously.

HOOD RAT. Copyright © 2006 by K'wan Foye. All rights reserved. Printed in the United States of America. For information, address St. Martin's Press, 175 Fifth Avenue, New York, N.Y. 10010.

www.stmartins.com

Library of Congress Cataloging-in-Publication Data

K'wan.
    Hood rat / K'wan.—1st ed.
      p. cm.
   ISBN-13: 978-0-312-36008-5
   ISBN-10: 0-312-36008-8
   1. Street life—New York—New York (State)—Fiction. 2. Gangs—New York (State)—New York—Fiction. 3. Hip-hop—Fiction. 4. African Americans—New York—New York (State)—Fiction. 5. Harlem (New York, N.Y.)—Fiction. I. Title.

PS3606.O96H67 2006
813'.6—dc22

2006045570

D 20 19 18

Acknowledgments

Well, at this point I think I've pretty much thanked everyone, but let me run through it again just to be sure.

I'd first like to thank God and my mother. My mother, for blessing me with this gift, and God for empowering me with the good sense to do something with it. It was not so long ago that the three of us sat down and spoke about my stepping down because I felt that my time might have run its course. Then you unlocked yet another dimension within me and I came to understand what it was you required of me. I used to try and shut out the voices, but now I embrace them. Thank you both for creating such a powerful vessel.

What can I say about my scholar (Ni Jaa) and my actress (Alexandria)? Even if I were to sell millions of books, you two would still be my greatest accomplishments. Not only do I love you more than I can put into words, but you represent something that I can never get back, innocence. For as long as there is breath in my body, I will do any and all things necessary to see that you hold on to yours as long as possible. My life for yours.

My grandmother, Ethel "Nana" Foye, and my aunt, Quintella "Tee-Tee" Harris. Neither of you will probably ever comprehend the amount of love that I have for you. We butt heads from time to time, but it's not because I'm ungrateful, it's because just as my mother's was, mine is a spirit that cannot be caged. Since I was a shorty, with no direction and more anger than my little body could contain, you both have always been loving and patient with me. Even when I didn't want me, you did. If I don't do anything else, I'm going to make sure that you both know at least a little happiness in this lifetime.

The whole Foye clan: Les, Darryl, Frankie, and especially my Uncle Eric. You already know, so I ain't gotta say it. See you same time next week.

Charlotte . . . hmmm . . . I watched you nearly bleed out on the table bringing Ali into the world, yet the desire to be here for our child kept you with us. Now that's GANGSTA!!! We've had some ups, downs, and sideways, yet the bond only grew stronger. You even managed to tame the untamable. Apparently Kismet is more than just a word.

Denise. Right about now you probably expect me to say something off the wall or belittling of you. Nah, it ain't even that serious. You birthed my oldest mischief maker, and I love her unconditionally. Besides, the world is so much bigger than that. Making sure my daughter receives equal love from the both of us outweighs any petty squabbles we can't seem to put to rest.

I'd like to thank Monique Patterson and the staff at St. Martin's Press. Your professionalism and strategies have been most enlightening and each passing year teaches me something new about sharpening my swords. Six books in and still producing like a champ. Trust in my talent enough to let me take the gloves off and I will show you storytelling in its truest form.

You had to know there was more:

Tony and Tyrone Council; they took my arms, but I'm still out here fighting. I would hope that by the time this book drops, all the drama will have worked itself out and y'all niggaz is on the street with me, but only time can tell that. Still, we press on and try to keep fighting the good fight. But for all the friendship that this world has brought and will surely continue to bring us, I have but one request.

Will the real niggaz stand up and the bitches lay down? When you lie to save your own ass it affects more than just the people you point fingers at.

Vickie Stringer, keep reaching new heights and handling business. Haters will always have their say, but the truth always makes itself known in time.

My man Derek Vitatoe. I know it took a minute, but you thugged it out and now your book is tearing up the shelves. We might be small, but we can walk with our heads held high because larceny doesn't dwell anywhere in these ranks. I, as well as everyone affiliated with BLACK DAWN, INC., am glad to have you on the roster. Once someone helped me out and I'm glad to have been able to do the same for you.

Mark Anthony (Q-Boro) and Nakea Murray (As the Page Turns) you both get special shout-outs. I asked a million and one questions when I was structuring the publishing division of Black Dawn, but you guys always made time to answer them. You didn't do it because you wanted something in return, but because you wanted to see me do well with my project. I got nothing but respect for y'all. Thank you.

For my folks:

All the kids. There's *too* many of y'all to add, but you know who you are. This is the blueprint for something way bigger than anything I'll accomplish in this lifetime. We're entrusting you with the world, so make it count!

Young Koo-Koo. It's a damn shame that as old as you are you don't have any ID. But you know what, you still my dude. From out the trunk to the *New York Times,* lets get it! Party Tyme, I'm glad to see you on your way to the big check we always talked about. Now hurry up and cash it so we can party it up like we used to do! Cousin Mark, stop acting like that. Billy Greene (my pops), Cousin Shae, cut it out. Killa Free, it ain't ya fault, son. I was there from the cookie days. Tommy Greene, the Jefferson crew, Young Star, Shaq, Val Castro. Page, aka Wild Out. The entire Douglass projects (Monster Island), at least the stand-up cats. My dude Eric Gray, one day they're gonna stop sleeping on you. Anthony Whyte and Jay from Augustus, Treasure

Blue, Shannon Holmes, Tracy Brown, Tu-Shonda Whitaker, what a brilliant author. T. N. Baker, Danielle Santiago, Keisha Ervin Kashamba Williams, Daryl King, and the rest of T.C.P. Brandon McCalla, get your head in the game!!! Roc Wells (Brolick), L. A. Banks, Miesha Holmes, Jamise Dames, and the few other authors who I rock with, but might have missed. I hope you all continue to be successful and lay the ground word for those who will come behind us. Dirty Boo, White Al, you got more soul than most brothers I know. Mighty Budda, lil Mexico and Sean, all my peoples in Delaware, Philly, Detroit, Baltimore, and every other town I've touched. Can't forget the bookstores, book clubs, vendors, and distributors who've helped to make the movement what it is. I told you I was coming!

An extraspecial shout-out to the readers who have been holding me down since '02, as well as the ones who are just getting up on game. Thank you so much for keeping my heart in the game with your kind letters, e-mails, and support. I do this for you.

It wouldn't be right for me not to thank all the women in my life now, or in days long gone, who gave me the inspiration to write this novel. Good or bad, you or your actions have had enough of an impact on me to make me sit down and spin this comical, yet very tragic tale. Don't take it personal, it's only a story . . . hahahaha.

A Word to the Readers

When I first toyed with the idea of creating this novel I was tentative about the concept. With the influx of urban fiction swooping in on us, did we really need another story about young women with no aspirations or dreams of doing much other than just existing? The answer to this question was yes. In my life and travels, I have encountered many women like the ones depicted in this novel and as amusing and entertaining as the story may be, the situations are very real. It saddens me to see a species of creatures who possess such strength slowly lose sight of who and what they are. I feel that this is due to a lack of educating our young sisters and low self-esteem, partially caused by men. I watched my mother, grandmother, and women of their generation overcome hurdles and struggle to raise their children on their own, only to give way to a new strain of femininity, the hood rat.

Now, ladies, I am in no way saying this applies to you all as a whole, but there are a growing number of hood rats sprouting up all over the country . . . pardon me, the world. Women who have lost or never been taught what it is to be women. Strong, independent, and proud.

There are so many women in the world who, instead of concerning themselves with nurturing and enlightening our children, are more worried about what they can get from the child's father. To make matters worse, they use children as pawns or tools of spite. If you have a man who wants to be in his child's life, don't deny him that because you two aren't getting along. If you have a man who isn't doing what he's supposed to for his child, take him to court instead of trying to trick another nigga into doing it. A baby isn't a paycheck, or bargaining chip, it's a life. A life that will emulate what he/she learns from his/her parents. Watching through the stained window of ghetto reality, I can't help but wonder what went wrong, and as men, how much of a part did we play in the decline.

Ladies, you are queens, tillers of the earth and keepers of the most cherished gift, the gift to create life. But what so many of our women seem to forget is that it doesn't stop there. It is our duty as parents and guardians of the future to insure that we thrive and flourish. These kids are like sponges and emulate what they are exposed to. Take this novel not as a slight, but a wake-up call. You gotta go out and get it because no one is gonna give it to you.

Enjoy the story,
K'wan

Black Dawn, Inc.
c/o K'wan
P.O. Box 1728 Lincolnton Station
New York, NY 10037

Part One

I'll Bet You Know Somebody Like This

1

That's right, nigga, fuck this pussy!" Yoshi grunted as she threw it back. The muscles flexed in her toned arms as she gripped the semiclean bed sheets of the motel room. Her back arched and flattened with the motion of his stroke, making slapping sounds as his thighs hit her ass. The young man cursed and rained spittle on her back as he went for broke on the fine light-skinned girl. From all the noise she was making, you'd have thought he was wrecking it, but it was all a show on her part. She learned early in the game how to get into a man's head and make him blow his wad. Two minutes later, it was a done deal.

"Damn, Yoshi. That shit was the bomb!" he huffed, flopping on his back.

She brushed a strand of her jet black hair from her forehead. "Yeah, daddy. You laid it down."

"Yo, I was thinking," he said as he slid a little closer to her, "maybe if you're not doing anything Saturday, we could get together. My uncle is having a cookout and—"

"Nah, don't think I can make it," she cut him off.

"Well, maybe Sunday? We could go to dinner or something."

Yoshi reached over to the nightstand and removed a Newport from the half-empty pack. She lit the cigarette and casually blew the smoke into the air. "Check this, Rel. You're cool, but it ain't that serious. You knew what it was before we laid down, so don't try to make it more than that."

Rel was glad the room was dark so she couldn't see his facial expression. He felt like someone had cocked over and took a shit in his mouth. Rel had met Yoshi at a strip club where she danced the weekend prior. All his boys had kicked shit on her name, but he believed in giving everyone a chance. He had gone back to the club on several occasions, just to see the yellow tender, and try to get close to her. After having a few drinks and a few dollars, he decided that she was cool peoples. His man had told him not to get roped up with the fast chick from Harlem, but Rel allowed his heart to lead him. Sure, she was a stripper, but he dug her as a person. His theory was, if he could show her a different way to live, they might have a chance at building something. Now he realized that he was panning for fool's gold.

"Damn, it's like that?" he asked.

She blew rings into the air. "It ain't like nothing. That's what I'm trying to tell you."

"I don't fucking believe this shit." He angrily slid his jeans and T-shirt back on. "Here I am trying to show you love and you're shitting on me."

"Love ain't got no place in my world, boo-boo. I ain't looking for a man, Rel, just a come-up. You can leave that bread on the nightstand."

Rel pulled some bills from his pocket and tossed them at her. "You're a cold bitch, Yoshi. I should've known you can't reform no ho!"

Using her leg, she swept the bills closer to her. "Call me what you want, nigga, but you won't call me broke. Don't let the door hit you in the ass on the way out."

Rel glared at her, contemplating kicking her ass and taking his money back, but figured he'd be worse off for it. When they had begun undressing, he peeped her stashing a .22 under the pillow. Clenching his jaw, he stormed out the door, slamming it so hard that one of the dime store portraits on the wall fell and broke.

Yoshi never even flinched. She took her time counting through the bills, making sure he hadn't shortchanged her. Folding the bills and placing them in her Coach bag, Yoshi placed the bolt on the motel door and headed into the bathroom. It was only 1:45. If she hurried, she could make it back to the club in time to catch another trick. Time was money.

Reese stood on the corner of 135th and Fifth Avenue, tapping her foot impatiently. She was five foot four, with brown skin and hair that stopped just below her earlobes. Reese had a nice ass and healthy breasts, but her face wasn't all that. She wasn't an ugly girl, but lost points for her wide nose and crooked teeth. Word on the streets was what she lacked in looks she made up for in skills. Reese had the reputation of being a head specialist.

Glancing at her watch, she noted that she had been standing there for almost a half hour, twenty-five minutes longer than she should have. Her boo told her that he would be there and once again he pulled the bullshit. You'd have thought that as much as he did it she'd be used to it by now. She decided that if he didn't arrive within the next five minutes she was leaving.

No sooner than Reese had the thought, a silver Benz pulled up to the curb. The car's tints were so heavy that the onlookers were probably not only wondering who was in the car, but how they were able to even see out the window. Reese pushed the ill thoughts she had had a few seconds prior out of her head and hopped in.

"Hey, baby." He kissed her on the cheek, scratching her with his beard. Teddy was a heavyset cat with cocoa-colored skin and pearl white teeth. He was a working-class dude in his early forties who had taken to messing with girls half his age to feel like he was still in the loop. Most bitches only dealt with him because he was a trick, but Reese actually liked him.

"Ted, you know how long you had me out here waiting?" She clicked her gum.

"Stop acting like that, you know I be in the mix." He waved her off.

"So fucking what, you still could've called my cell phone!" she barked, holding up the Motorola he had bought her the month before.

"Look, I just had to go through some shit with Penny and I really ain't in the mood to hear it from you," he told her.

Reese slit her eyes at him. "I should've known."

"What the fuck is that supposed to mean?"

"It means that I'm about tired of her cutting into my time. Every time I turn around you're late or pulling no-shows because you had something to do for her."

Teddy ran his hands across the top of his waved-up fade, as he often did when he was frustrated. "Reese, don't start this shit. You already know what it is."

"Yeah, I know what it is and I'm about sick of it," she said. "Why the fuck do I always have to take a backseat to that bitch?"

"Ain't no need to be slinging names, ma. You need to hold your head."

"Hold my head?" she asked as if the statement was offensive. "Teddy, how long have I been holding my head? This shit is getting tired."

"Reese, what do you want me to do? Penny is my wife."

"And I'm supposed to be your girl!" she snapped. "How long have you been promising me that you were gonna leave her?"

"It ain't that easy, ma. I can't just go home and say, 'Penny, I've fallen in love with someone else. It's over.'"

"Why not, Teddy? You claim you love me, so why do I have to keep waiting around for you to tell this bitch what the real deal is?" Reese had been seeing Teddy for a little over four months. At first she didn't know he was married, but by the time she found out, she was already hopelessly in love with the man. When she confronted him, he fed her a story about how the marriage was already on the rocks and how he was about to file for a divorce from his wife of ten years. Though her brain screamed he was a fat fucking liar, and she should cut him loose, her heart vetoed it. Teddy had his fucked-up ways about him, but for the most part he was good to Reese. He spent money on her and made her feel beautiful. Though in her heart she knew there was more to love than that, it was enough for the moment.

"Reese, a situation like this requires tact. Penny is an emotional woman. If I break it to her like that, there ain't no telling what she might do. I'd feel like shit if I found out she killed herself 'cause I left her," he said, flattering himself. "I promise, baby." He stroked her cheek with the back of his hand. "Just give me a little more time and it'll just be me and you."

"Whatever," Reese said, pouting like a child.

For the next five minutes they drove in silence. Teddy fumbled with the radio while Reese busied herself looking out the window, watching the blur of faces. When they reached 125th Street, Teddy made a right instead of busting a left to head to the east side.

"Teddy, where are you going? Madison Avenue is the other way," Reese pointed out.

Teddy kept his eyes directly in front of him as he navigated through the busy traffic and turned left on Seventh Avenue. "I know, boo, but I gotta stop by the spot right quick."

"Come on, Teddy, I wanna get to the store before they run out of my size in those new Dior shoes."

Teddy pulled in front of a building on 124th and Seventh and parked the car. "Baby, them shoes ain't going nowhere. Big daddy got you." Without giving her a chance to protest, he hopped out and began walking toward the building.

On the third floor, Teddy led her into what he liked to call his Honeycomb Hideout. It was a sparsely furnished studio apartment that he kept in Harlem, unbeknownst to his wife. Reese had been there a few times, but he kept her visits limited and wouldn't allow her to have a key. The reason for this was he claimed to have work on that block, but didn't want the niggaz from around there getting too familiar with anyone he cared about. Teddy had a bullshit story for every occasion.

"Teddy, please don't take forever," Reese said, leaning against the wall.

"Baby girl, you're too uptight," he said, kissing her gently on the forehead while palming her ass. "Why don't you let daddy work some of that tension up outta you?"

"Cut it out." She pushed him away. "I ain't trying get all sweaty with you up in here."

"Reese, I know you ain't gonna deny me. I ain't tasted that sweet fruit in like a week," he pleaded.

"That's because you were laid up with your wife," she shot back.

Teddy ignored her comment and continued kissing her on the neck and lips. "Lets not talk about her, this is our time. Come on, baby, let daddy get a little something."

"I told you I ain't trying to get all sweaty and end up having to go home and change. You better go see Penny about some pussy."

"Yo, you know how sexy you are when you're trying to be mad?" He cupped her breasts. "Reese, you don't know how bad I want you right now."

Teddy placed his hand behind Reese's head and began to kiss her passionately. As much as she wanted to pull away so they could get back outside, she found herself helpless under his strong touch and on-slaught of kisses. Gradually he started pushing down on the top of her head. Reese knew what time it was and didn't resist. Dropping down on her knees, she proceeded to undo Teddy's jeans. She pulled his thick penis out and examined it.

"That's right, baby," he said, prodding her head further. "Do that for daddy."

Reese looked up at him and thought for the umpteenth time how full of shit he was. That was okay, though. When they got to the Dior store he would pay like he weighed for that blow job. Reese began by gently licking around the head of Teddy's dick. Something tasted different, but she really didn't have time to dwell on it before he was trying to force himself in her mouth. She ran her tongue up and down his shaft to get it good and slippery, then proceeded with the magic trick. Reese took all of Teddy into her throat, drawing a low moan from him.

"I can't take this shit," he said, snatching her to her feet and damn near dragging her over to the couch. Teddy roughly slung her over the arm of the couch and started pulling at her pants.

"Nigga, these is Seven jeans. You rip 'em, you bought 'em," she warned.

"Sorry," he said, panting and continuing to pull at her jeans. Finally he got them down and admired Reese's ass. Seeing her in jeans, you could tell that she had a little something, but when they came down you could appreciate the whole union. Fumbling with his short, fat penis, Teddy began trying to penetrate her from behind.

"Damn, hold your horses!" she shouted, slapping his hands away from her hips. "You got a condom on?"

"Come on, ma, don't start tripping off that shit. You know how me and you do," he said, continuing to force himself inside her vagina.

Reese had always had a problem taking Teddy inside her. Though he didn't have the longest dick in the world, it damn near had the girth of a miniature salami. She tried to tell him to take it slow, as she wasn't wet yet, but he ignored her and kept pushing. Reese felt like she was getting rug burns on the inside as Teddy crammed himself inside her. Gripping her hips, he began pumping away, obviously not bothered by the dryness of her. The worst part about it was that by the time she had gotten wet and was ready to enjoy it, Teddy came.

"No the fuck you didn't?" Reese looked back at him disgusted.

"My fault, ma." He was still panting. "Yo pussy is so good that a nigga couldn't hold it. I'll make it up to you, though." When he pulled his dick out of her, cum ran down her inner thigh and landed on the back of her jeans. Reese wasn't sure if she was more pissed at the fact that he had cum prematurely or the fact that he had fucked up her jeans.

"I don't believe you came on my jeans," Reese said, using the overhead mirror on the passenger side to try and fix her hair.

"Reese, I said I was sorry. Fuck you want me to do, buy you a new pair?" he asked sarcastically.

"I'd appreciate that," she said as if he had been serious. Teddy looked over at her like he wanted to say something, but his cell phone cut him off. He listened for a while, said okay, and hung up. Reese didn't like the tone of his voice while he was on the phone and she liked the way he was looking at her afterward even less.

"Baby, we've got a slight change in plans," he said solemnly.

"Oh boy, what is it now? Penny break a nail and need you to take her to the fucking emergency room?"

"You know, one of these days I'm gonna bust you in your smart-ass mouth," he warned her.

"The moment you feel like losing that same hand you raise to me, be my guest," she said defiantly. "Now, are we gonna sit in front of this fucking building all day or are you taking me to Madison Avenue?"

"That might have to wait till later on."

"Teddy, I know you ain't about to pull this bullshit on me. I waited for you all damn morning and now you're telling me we ain't going?"

"Yo, it ain't my fault," he said, running his hands across the top of his fade. "Penny was supposed to go pick Sha up, but now she's talking about something came up so I gotta do it." Sha was Teddy's eight-year-old son. Reese had met him on more than one occasion, but couldn't honestly say she spent any great length of time around him.

"Oh, is that all? Why don't you just snatch him up and bring him along. It'd be nice for me and Sha to finally get to spend some time together."

"Nah, you know how Penny be tripping. If she found out I had our son around another bitch she'd kill me *and* you."

"So that's all I am, another bitch?" she asked defensively.

"You know what I mean, Reese. You're *my* bitch." He reached out to touch her face, but she moved back. "Tell you what," he said, peeling off a fifty and a twenty from his bankroll and handing it to her, "use this money to jump in a cab from here and get your mind right. Get yaself a bottle and some smoke, and when I finish with Sha, I'll hit you back and we can see about catching the store."

Hearing that he would be coming back to scoop her, Reese's face softened a bit. "Teddy, you better not be playing with me." She took the money and got out of the car. "If you have me waiting around and you don't show up, it's gonna be on and popping."

"Ma, I got you," he said, smiling like the cat that ate the canary. Reese went to say something else, but ended up getting a mouthful of exhaust as he peeled off down Seventh.

"Pooh, get your ass out here and get the sneakers out of the middle of my living room! If I fall and break my neck, I'm gonna break your ass!"

Rhonda was dressed in a pair of denim shorts that were trimmed along the back, showing off her ass cheeks. The tank top she wore drew attention to her double-D breasts, but did nothing to hide her slightly protruding belly. She was a short woman with a large ass and oversize breasts, but as small as she was, she had the mouth of a giant.

Rhonda made her way through her cluttered living room, mock-sweeping up the cigarette butts and beer bottle tops from the night before. Rhonda wasn't a dirty woman, but her house always looked like a whirlwind had swept through it. It was due in part to the card parties she often threw. Being that Rhonda was one of the few girls who had her own crib, the girls were always coming through partying. On weekends, Rhonda sold plates to everyone in the hood to have some extra cake to stack on top of what she was already getting from the government.

Though Rhonda wasn't the most book smart of her friends, she was a master hustler. She was getting checks from all branches of the aid system. The state gave her a little cash and food stamps for her three children, but the big payoff was Social Security. Rhonda had swallowed some of her own stool when she was born, so the doctors said there was a chance she might develop a learning disability. Though there was nothing wrong with her, her mother went to the state building and told them there was. Rhonda's mother had been getting checks for her since she was four years old, and when Rhonda turned eighteen, they came in her name. The hustle was so sweet that she used her son's ADD condition to get one for him, too.

"Alisha." Rhonda turned to her thirteen-year-old daughter. "Get off my goddamn phone and go iron P.J.'s clothes."

Alisha rolled her eyes. "Hold on," she said into the phone and covered the receiver with her hand. "A'ight! I'll do it when I get off the phone."

"Bitch, who you yelling at?" Rhonda tossed a shoe at the child. "Don't make me whip your little pissy ass! You just do like I say."

Alisha hung up the phone, with a suck of her teeth. When she passed Rhonda, she mumbled, "I hate you."

"What the fuck you just say?" Rhonda grabbed Alisha by the shirt. "Say it again, so I can kick your little ass." She shoved Alisha roughly toward the bedroom.

Alisha wanted to cry, but she wouldn't give her mother the satisfaction. All her mother ever did was yell and curse at them. All of the kids' mothers yelled, but not like Rhonda. There were things that Alisha wanted to confide in her mother, as every little girl did, but they didn't have that type of relationship. She longed for the day when she was old enough to move out. When Alisha got to the back of the apartment, she slammed the door roughly.

"Don't be slamming no doors in here!" she called after Alisha. "I gotta pay for that, and I got your little funky ass for free." Rhonda's tirade was interrupted by her phone ringing. She looked at the caller ID, but couldn't tell who it was because the batteries were dead. "Hello!" she answered in her best hood rat tone.

"Bitch, you can't answer the phone no better than that?" the caller replied.

"Don't play with me, Billy. What's up?"

Billy was one of Rhonda's closest friends. Though she was younger than Rhonda, they had lived in the same projects a few years back before Billy's mother had gotten them out. She hadn't known Billy as long as Yoshi had, but over the years they had developed quite a friendship.

"Nothing, 'bout to go to Kingdome and see what's going on," Billy said.

"Shit, I ain't been there all summer," Rhonda recalled. "I need to go with you. Who else is going?"

"Me, Reese, and Jean."

"Jean? Billy, what's really good with you and that bitch?"

"Don't be funny, Rhonda. You know me and Jean used to play for Brandeis together."

"Umm-hmm. Tell me anything," Rhonda said suspiciously. "Let me find out you eat at the Y."

Billy sucked her teeth. "You know what, y'all better stop playing with me. You and Reese kill me with them slick-ass dyke comments."

Billy's sexuality was a sore spot for her. Growing up, she had always been a tomboy. She didn't play with dolls or do other things that little girls would. Billy felt more comfortable playing sports. Before her father was killed, he had taught her to play basketball. From the time Billy was five until right before she entered junior high school, he would take her to the park every day to work on her game. By the time

Billy was twelve, she could give any of the older boys on the court a run for their money.

Her friends always clowned her about being so boyish, but she was quick to defend her femininity. She had had several boyfriends through the years, but always felt like there was a void being left unfilled. Being around like-minded girls in the sports circuit all her life, it was only natural that her curiosity was peaked. Billy didn't consider herself gay because she didn't have a girlfriend, nor did she consider herself bi because she only got involved with guys. Oh, she had experimented a few times, but had yet to find the bitch to turn her out properly.

"Well, maybe if you wasn't so hard, people wouldn't think it," Rhonda continued.

"Rhonda, just because I don't run around with my tits and gut out like you doesn't mean I'm not sexy."

"Please," Rhonda said, "I got three muthafuck'n kids. This gut is a badge of honor. Besides, niggaz love to suck these titties." She groped her breasts, as if Billy could see her through the phone.

"Speaking of your big-ass titties, I seen Paul the other day," Billy taunted.

"Fuck him!" Rhonda snapped. "I ain't stunting his square ass."

Billy sucked her teeth. "Yeah, right. You be on that nigga like a fly on shit."

"You can't be serious. All Paul can do for me is take care of P.J. and make sure my pockets is right."

"You ain't got no shame," Billy said.

"Shame, my ass! My son has his last name, and that means I'm tied to that muthafucka for the next fourteen years. Membership has its privileges," Rhonda said smugly.

"Now ain't that some larcenous shit," Billy remarked. "Rhonda, just because you and Paul have a baby together doesn't mean he owes you. His job is to take care of his seed."

Rhonda moved the phone away from her ear and stared at it for a minute before she resumed their conversation. "Willamina, you've been my girl for a long time, but you must've fell and bumped that peanut-ass head of yours. I was on that table for twenty-six hours pushing that big-head little muthafucka out my ass. The least Paul can do is make sure I look just as good as P.J. does. *You lay, you pay.* Those are the rules, sweetie."

"Whatever. So you going or not?" Billy changed the subject.

"Gimme like an hour. I gotta throw something off and get rid of these bad-ass kids," Rhonda said.

"Why don't you bring them with you? The kids could play in the park, or watch the game. The fresh air would do them good. Besides, I haven't seen my girl Alisha in a while anyway. How is she?"

Rhonda huffed. "That little bitch is trying to make me kill her. I told her little ass to iron P.J.'s clothes and she acted like she was feeling some kind of way. Slamming doors and shit!"

Billy snickered. "Stop playing."

"I'm dead-ass. She don't know, I'll lay her to rest, early!"

"You need to stop talking about them kids like that."

"I brought the bitches here, so I can take 'em out. You just make sure y'all come get me."

"Just have yo trick ass ready when we get there!" Billy shot back, but it was too late because Rhonda had already transferred her to the dial tone.

2

Paul Dutton was the middle child of three boys. His mother worked as hard as she could to raise them after their father decided that a piece of sixteen-year-old trim was worth more than the wife he had uprooted from humble roots in Ohio, and the children they had bore. When the girl's parents found out their relationship, they didn't hesitate to sic the law on him. He was currently in the eighth year of a ten-year sentence.

For all of their mother's efforts, and the multiple jobs she worked, her children still managed to be swayed by the call. Paul's oldest brother, Boo, managed to make jail his home. He had been in and out of different correctional facilities since he was thirteen. He was on the last leg of a three to nine, and looking to come home by the following summer.

His baby brother Jahlil, or Jah, as he had taken to calling himself, was a loose screw. All of the Dutton boys had a touch of the devil in them, but Jah was just evil. He had taken to running with a pack of young kids from the Polo Grounds. They were behind several murders and strong-arm robberies. The old heads gave them a wide berth, and in return they let them be. Anyone who didn't fall under the umbrella was food.

Paul wasn't a career criminal like Boo, or a sociopath killer like Jah, but he was no angel. Paul's game was the con, and his weapons of choice were words. He had learned it from a dope fiend named Bub who used to hang on his block. He started out hitting up cee-low games and switching the dice. This held him down as a youth, but when he became a teenager, his need for dough increased. He saw the things that hustling friends had and wanted to keep in step, but he didn't have the stomach for the risk that came with it. He would rob with words, as opposed to iron. Paul talked his way in and out of various department stores and other businesses using smoke and mirrors to fleece them of their goods.

The boost game was sweet, but Paul's greed pushed him to bigger and better scores. He got in good with this bitch who worked for the post office as a casual and kicked his hustle game up. Shorty would snatch credit cards and mail order checkbooks, bringing them to Paul to get off. Now instead of coming off with a few stolen pieces, he could simply walk in and purchase what he needed. He had even set up online accounts via the 'Net, making his job that much easier. Everyone in the hood was checking for Paul to cop the newest and flyest shit at half price.

This went well, until the girl he was dealing with got greedy and tried to get over. She had come up on a Visa charge card, but her dumb ass didn't know the difference between a debit and a credit card. All that week she had been shopping and eating at expensive restaurants. One she had particularly taken a liking to was an Italian joint called Bella's. She was becoming a regular there, always ordering expensive wine and meals she couldn't pronounce. On her fifth day of fun, the curtain finally fell. It didn't take long for the account holder to notice that someone had been making sizable dents in her account. The feds noticed multiple charges to Bella's on the account and were waiting in hopes that the thief would show. Sure enough, her trick ass showed up.

The police took her down without much effort. Paul couldn't be sure when it happened, but he had been told she started talking before they even got downtown. She fed them a bullshit story about how Paul was the mastermind, and he forced her to help him. With her bogus story, the deck looked stacked against Paul. His saving grace was that they only found merchandise at his house, no sales receipts. He was handed eighteen months and five years' probation for his part in the capers. This brought his hustling days to a slow crawl.

Paul sat in the middle of his studio apartment, wearing only a pair of jeans and a stocking cap. His chocolate-colored body was splattered with paint from the dripping brush that he held in his hand. On the easel in front of him was a five-by-five-foot canvas, assaulted with colors. The image wasn't complete, but you could make out angles and white clouds. These kinds of portraits were Paul's favorite to paint. Though he wasn't a religious man, he found a certain joy in the images.

In school, Paul was one of the most talented artists in the city. He was blessed with an artistic eye without having ever taken a lesson. He was offered scholarships to several schools, but none ever panned out. He let his need for cash overpower his common sense, and chose the streets over education. Years later, he found himself a starving artist, hustling here and there to make it and trying to take care of his son.

A knock at the door stopped him midstroke. A mixture of blue paint and egg whites dripped from the tip of the brush and made splatter patterns on the wood floor. He wondered who it could be since he hadn't expected anyone to come by. He inched toward the door, careful not to step on the loose floorboard. Looking through the peephole, Paul sucked his teeth. He wiped his hands on his pants and opened the door for his childhood friend, Larry Love.

Larry was a portly young man, with a belly like a honey jar. He wore his hair in zigzag braids that day, tied off by black rubber bands on the end. Larry and Paul had been friends since grade school, both running in the same circle of troublemakers. While Paul was serving time for credit fraud, Larry had managed to square up and get a job. Though he still sold weed in the hood, loading UPS trucks was his reportable income.

Larry brushed past Paul, giving him a friendly pat on the back. " 'Sup, nigga?"

"Larry, how many times I gotta ask you about not popping up at my spot?" Paul frowned. "For all you know, I might've been in here with a bitch."

"Bullshit." Larry flopped on the sofa. "That might've been a possibility a few months ago, but you ain't built like that no more."

"And what's that supposed to mean?"

Larry pulled a sack of weed from his pocket and a Dutch. "Come on, son. You ain't gotta front for me. Ever since your ass got with Marlene, you've developed a tender dick."

"Fuck outta here." Paul dipped a larger brush into a tray of green paint. "I'm still the same old G."

Larry looked at Paul disbelievingly, crushing some buds up into the now split cigar. "Paul, you know Marlene got you like that."

"Marlene ain't got me like nothing, Larry. I can still get outta here and pull any bitch I want."

"I'm sure you could, my man, but the truth of the matter is, you ain't got that fire in you no more. Its cool, though, it happens to the best of us. Just not a true player like me."

"Man, fuck you!" Paul spat.

"The truth is the light, dawg," Larry responded. "If you got a soft spot for these hos, then you got a soft spot."

"I ain't got no love for a bitch, kid. My heart pumps straight ice water."

"Ice water, my ass. Paul, every time you get with a chick who seems okay, you wife the ho. I know you, kid. Look at Rhonda."

"Here we go with this shit. Why don't you leave that alone, Larry?"

"Because it's a prime example of what I'm talking about. When you got with her, we all told you to hit it and quit it, but you didn't listen. You catch feelings for her and ended up hit. When she got pregnant, I told you to make her have an abortion, but you wouldn't listen. She starts kicking that pro-life shit in your ear and you fall for it. Don't get me wrong, I love P.J. like my own flesh and blood, but you got caught up, man."

Paul became defensive. "I ain't trying to hear that shit, man. Rhonda is a bitch and a half, but the kid is innocent. I love my seed and I'm gonna make sure he's good."

"And I applaud you for that." Larry lit the blunt. "But the downside to having a kid with a bitch who ain't about nothing is you're bound to her and her bullshit."

"Man, what Rhonda eats don't make me shit. She has her life and I have mine. We don't fuck with each other like that."

"And that still ain't stopping her from throwing a monkey wrench in your shit every chance she gets. How many times have you been trying to get your quality time with Marlene and Rhonda blows your phone up?"

"Man, what am I supposed to do, ban her from calling my phone? It could be something with P.J."

"Paul, you know that chick calls your phone just to piss Marlene off. She's on the other end of your jack twenty times a day, whether it's about P.J. or not. She's just a royal pain in the ass. If you analyze it, you know I'm right."

"Thank you, Maury. Any more relationship advice?"

"I just call 'em like I see 'em, Paul."

"Fuck you. What the hell are you doing here anyway?"

"I came by to see my dude." Larry passed the weed off. "Figured you might like to come out of the dungeon for a while and have some fun."

"What you trying to get into?"

"Hit a few blocks and see what's good in the hood. I hear there's a game at the Kingdome today. You know it's always bitches out there, kid."

"Oh, hell yeah!" Paul said excitedly. "Give me a few minutes to wash this paint off and get dressed."

"That's my nigga. Make it happen."

Paul went off into the bathroom to start getting ready, leaving Larry in the living room, smoking. He paced the tiny living area, examining the different works that Paul had on display. Larry always marveled at how talented his friend was. Though he was from a world of ugliness, same as everyone else, he still managed to find some beauty in it. Paul had really thrown himself into his art since P.J. was born. He wanted to provide the life for his son that he had been so long deprived. The job market wasn't offering him much above minimum wage, so it was vital that he succeed with his artwork. If he could manage to break into the circuit by selling a few paintings, just maybe, P.J. would have a chance.

Larry's attention was drawn by the ringing phone. He was going to let the machine get it, until Paul called from the back and asked him to pick it up. He took the cordless off the base and looked at the caller ID. When he saw the name on the little screen, he again thought about just not picking up.

"Hello," Larry said into the receiver.

"Who is this?" the caller asked with much attitude.

"What's up, Rhonda."

"Who is this, Larry? What you doing answering Paul's phone?"

"He's in the bathroom. Something I can help you with?"

"Nigga, you can't do nothing for me but put Paul on the phone."

Larry sighed. "Rhonda, I told you he's in the bathroom. I'll have him call you back when he comes out."

"You know what, Larry? You're turning into as big a liar as Paul. He's probably sitting right there, telling you to feed me this story."

"Rhonda, that's my word, the nigga is in the bathroom. I ain't got no kids with you, so I ain't gotta lie to you."

"Oh, so you're admitting that ya boy be lying to me?" she asked suspiciously.

"I didn't say that, Rhonda . . . look, I'm not going through this shit with you. Either I can have him call you back, or you can wait on the line until he comes out," Larry said sarcastically.

"I'll wait," she shot back.

Larry looked at the phone and shrugged his shoulders. He placed the phone down on the coffee table and went into the kitchen to raid Paul's refrigerator.

Fifteen minutes later, Paul came out of the back wearing denim shorts and a white T-shirt. Larry was lounging on the futon, drinking a Red Stripe and flicking the channels. Paul was used to his friend's mooching ways, so he didn't bother to say anything. He glanced at the coffee table and noticed that his phone was on.

He snatched it up and clicked the off button. "Larry, you couldn't turn the fucking phone off after you used it?"

"I didn't use it." Larry took a gulp of his beer. "You had a call."

"Well, did they leave a message?"

"Nah, Rhonda didn't leave no message. She was still on the line the last time I checked."

Paul looked at his friend. Because of Larry's bullshit, he knew that he'd have to hear Rhonda's mouth. Before he could press the issue, the phone rang. As soon as he clicked it on, shouting came from the other end.

"You muthafuckas better stop playing with me!" Rhonda barked. "Got a bitch on hold for forever. Y'all be on some bullshit."

"Rhonda, don't be calling my house yelling and shit, all right?"

"Fuck you, Paul. If you didn't want to talk, you should've said so. You ain't gotta have Larry lie for you."

"Rhonda, what the hell are you talking about? Never mind. What do you want?"

"I was calling to tell you that your son needs some sneakers."

"Sneakers? Didn't I give you the money for a pair of sneakers two weeks ago?" he asked.

"I had to go tap into that. These muthafuckas at the welfare fucked up on my food stamps, so I had to use cash when I went shopping. We gotta eat, don't we?"

Paul let out a long sigh. "Rhonda, how many times do I have to tell you about budgeting?"

"Budgeting? Paul, you seem to forget that I got three kids. Welfare don't hardly give me shit, so I gotta make due with what I got."

"Rhonda, you get welfare and Social Security. What the fuck do you do with your money?"

"Me and my kids got expenses. You know how much Pooh's sneakers cost? That little muthafucka is wearing grown man sizes now. Let's not forget how much it cost to clothe us all. You know I don't put my kids in no cheap shit."

"Rhonda, you know this job I got ain't really paying shit, so the money is tight. When I give you something for P.J., you gotta stretch it."

"Stretch it?" Rhonda asked nasally. "Shit, you act like you be setting it out like that. That little bit of money you drop off ain't really nothing. I got three kids."

"Yeah, and I only have one," he reminded her.

"Oh, I forgot how you do it. Paul is only concerned about P.J. Fuck the rest of us, huh?"

"Rhonda, don't make it like I don't hit you with bread for all of them when I have it. I don't see you calling none of your other babies' fathers singing them the same bullshit story."

"That's because they ain't shit. Them niggaz ain't never do nothing for my kids."

"So I gotta suffer because they're fucked up?"

"You know what? Forget it, Paul. You ain't gotta give me shit. I should've listened to my mother and put P.J. on my budget. That way I wouldn't have to ask nobody for shit. That's okay, though, I'll just talk to my worker in the morning."

"Why you always gotta fuck with me?" Paul asked heatedly. "You know damn well I ain't letting you make my son no welfare baby. As long as I can get out and work, P.J. ain't going on no damn welfare. It'll be just my luck, I'll finally sell one of my paintings and welfare will want their cut for some shit you put together. It ain't gonna happen, Rhonda."

"You ain't my man, or my daddy, Paul. You can't tell me what to do. If I put P.J. on, my stamps and cash will go up. Shit, it's gotta be better than the little bit of change you call yourself dropping on me once a month."

"You know you're playing yourself. I take care of P.J. all year-round, and still give your sack-chasing ass money. Give me a fucking break."

"Oh, I'll give you a break. If I take P.J. and move away, you won't have to worry about it. Stop fucking with me, Paul. You already know P.J.'s size, so I ain't gotta tell you. 'Bye, nigga!"

"You fucking bitch!" Paul screamed into the phone, but the line was already dead.

Rhonda hung up the phone and enjoyed a devilish giggle. There was something about plucking Paul's nerves that brought her a sick joy. She tried to act like she was truly over him, but it was a lie. Paul had been the best thing to ever happen to her. He might not have been the most romantic cat, but he took care of home. He always made sure Rhonda and her children didn't go without, even before P.J. came along. In the end, it was her own laziness and greed that drove him away.

Paul had moved on to greener pastures. He was rebuilding his life, and even had someone new. Rhonda had met her twice, and could honestly say that she couldn't stand the bitch. She paraded around in her little business suits and pressed hair, making Rhonda want to choke the life from her. It wasn't that Marlene had ever done anything wrong to her, Rhonda was just hating.

She had tried on several occasions to get back into Paul's good graces, but always ended up coming up short. She thought it was because of Marlene, but the reality was that Paul was just fed up with Rhonda's shit. He no longer had the patience for her or her ways.

It didn't matter to Rhonda, though. He could have his happy life and everything in it. As long as she had P.J., Paul would be bound to her. He might turn her away now, but there would come a day when he would give in to her advances.

A knock on the front door brought Rhonda out of her plotting. Alisha came out of the back room to get it, but Rhonda beat her to it. She opened the door and a dark-skinned kid, wearing a fitted Yankee cap and a white T-shirt, strode in.

"Alisha," Rhonda said and turned to her daughter. "Take P.J. and Pooh outside. I'll be down in a minute."

"Why I gotta take them?" Alisha whined, and was rewarded by an open-hand slap.

"Don't be asking me no fucking questions. Just do what the fuck I tell you," Rhonda scolded.

Alisha clutched her face and scampered to the back of the apartment crying. A few minutes later she came out with the two boys in tow. She shot Rhonda a look, but didn't dare open her mouth.

When the children were out the door, Rhonda turned back to the young man in the cap. "What's popping, daddy? I missed you."

The young man just smiled, showing off his tobacco-stained teeth. He sat on the couch and undid his jeans, letting his dick rest against his thigh. He stroked himself with his left hand and beckoned to her with his right. Without hesitation, Rhonda dropped down and blessed him.

Larry shook his head and relit the blunt. "I don't know why you even get yourself worked up, man."

"This bitch is always playing with me, Larry." Paul tossed the phone on the futon and sat in the computer chair opposite Larry. "I do what I'm supposed to as a parent, and I still get the short end of the stick."

Larry shrugged and handed Paul the blunt. "That's your own fault."

"How do you figure that?" Paul snatched it. "I'm wrong for being a good father?"

"Nah, you the man for that. You wrong for getting crossed up in that in the first place. We tried to tell you about Rhonda, but you didn't listen. Now you got this bitch in your head, driving you up the wall. You're doing what you can, kid. Don't stress it."

"How can I not stress it, Larry? That's my seed."

Larry leaned forward and became serious. "Paul, let's take the gloves off for a minute. You come home from your bid, and Rhonda's waiting on you with a bundle of joy. Keep in mind, you had no idea what the fuck she was doing out here unless one of us told you. Even when we did bring certain shit to your attention, you downplayed it. When I told you to make her take a paternity test, you let her talk you out of it."

"Man, I know that's my seed."

Larry raised an eyebrow. "Do you? Paul, I know you and Rhonda had some good times, trust me, I do. You was laying up in her crib, eating good and tapping that ass, but do you really believe you're the only one that was hitting it?" Seeing anger flash across his friend's face, Larry softened his approach. "Paul, you know you're my nigga from now till the end of this, but we all knew Rhonda was scandalous. I'm just keeping it real with you, my dude."

"Well, you ain't helping." Paul huffed, killing the blunt roach.

"Man, fuck this depressing-ass shit. Let's hit the streets and see what's up with these hos on Twelfth."

"That's what I'm talking about. Let's do the damn thang!"

Paul headed for the front door, followed by Larry. The big man stopped short and walked back to the coffee table. He downed the rest of his beer and followed his friend out the door.

3

Billy sat behind the wheel of her mother's '95 Saturn, glancing at her watch periodically. They had been parked in front of Rhonda's building for almost twenty minutes, but there was still no sign of her. All three of the girls in the car were annoyed, but Reese was the one who voiced it.

"What the fuck is taking this bitch so long?" Reese sucked her slightly crooked teeth.

"You know how slow Rhonda is," Billy said, twirling a strand of her dark hair around her finger. Of all their crew, she and Yoshi were the prettiest. Billy was statuesque, standing at five foot ten in flats. Her skin fluctuated between honey and reddish brown, depending on the season. Billy had the look of a model, but sports was where her heart was.

"That's why I can't fuck with her. By the time we make it out there, the park is gonna be packed," she continued, cradling her cell phone to her ear. She had been trying to call Teddy for the last hour and was having no luck, which shouldn't have surprised her. That coupled with Rhonda having them waiting in front of the building in the heat only added to her aggravation.

"I didn't think it would matter to you, Reese. It ain't like you're going to watch the game," Billy teased.

"Yeah, Reese is trying to catch a baller," Jean added.

"Fuck you, Billy. And Jean, you know I don't really fuck with you like that, so take is easy."

"Why you getting mad at her?" Billy asked. "She ain't said nothing that ain't true. You know you go to the games to check for the niggaz."

"I can't even front, it do be some fine niggaz at the Kingdome." Reese chuckled. "But y'all hos wouldn't know nothing about it."

"Oh, so you got jokes now?" Jean sat up. "Ain't no shame in my game. I don't mind a stiff dick, but ain't nothing like a wet pussy." She rubbed her meaty hands together and looked hungrily at Reese.

"I don't know what the fuck you're looking back here for. I'm strictly dickly." Reese glared at her.

Billy laughed. "Jean, please stop playing with this girl, with her homophobic ass."

"I ain't homo nothing. I just don't play that shit. Y'all keep them kind of games to yourselves."

"What do you mean, 'y'all'?" Billy asked defensively.

"You heard, Billy. You're damn near as hard as this heifer." Reese thumbed towards Jean.

"Reese, you need to quit."

"Quit, my ass. Billy, when is the last time you wore a skirt?"

"I wish you could hear yourself, Reese. So you mean to say that because I wear jeans most of the time, I'm not feminine? You sound like my mother."

"You need to listen to her."

"Whatever, bitch. I know who I am, regardless of what anyone says."

While Billy and Reese continued to debate her sexuality, Rhonda finally brought her ass out of the building, with the young man in the Yankees hat a few paces ahead. He pulled his cap low and made hurried steps toward the avenue.

"Damn, why don't you slow down!" she called after him. He slowed down, but didn't stop walking. "You in a rush or something?"

"Something like that," he replied. "I got some shit I need to take care of."

"A'ight. So, am I gonna see you later?" She leaned in to kiss him, but he stepped back.

"Yeah, hit me up later on, shorty." He gave her a weak smile and walked off.

Rhonda felt played, but she didn't show it. She was feeling the young man, but she knew he had a girl and he had made it quite clear that he had no intention of leaving her. They both agreed that it was just a fuck thing, but Rhonda had other ideas. He might've had game, but she was a professional gamer and he would learn it soon enough.

"That's what took your tramp ass so long," Reese said to Rhonda as she approached the car.

"Fuck you, Reese. You always hating on somebody," Rhonda shot back, climbing into the car beside Jean.

"Yo, that kid looks crazy familiar. Don't we know him from somewhere?" Billy asked.

"Probably. He fuck with Sonia from Forty-third and Eighth." Rhonda smiled triumphantly.

"Hold on, dark-skinned Sonia?" Reese turned around in her seat. "The same Sonia that does your hair?"

"Yep."

"Rhonda, you ain't shit." Billy shook her head.

"Please, she don't know what to do with him," Rhonda said. "If she did, he wouldn't be creeping out of my house."

"That's some cold shit." Jean shook her apple-shaped head. "I thought Sonia was your friend?"

"We cool, but we ain't like that. She does my hair, but we don't hang out."

"Ain't you got no shame?" Billy asked.

"Shame don't live here, boo. Besides, that nigga could gag a bitch with all that meat he's swinging. I had to taste that!" She gave Reese a high five.

"Shameless bitches," Billy mumbled, putting the car in gear.

On a crisp afternoon in July, Lenox Avenue was popping. Both sides of the strip, between 112th and 116th, were packed with people. Some were on foot, while others were slow coasting in their rides. Shorties were out wearing next to nothing, trying to attract the next up-and-coming ghetto superstar, or style on old flings.

The Kingdome games always drew crowds, mostly because you were liable to bump into people you hadn't seen in a while or could check out who was up and coming on the scene. It also allowed some of the city's most skilled ballers to come out and showcase their skills. This particular day, the park was especially crowded. Everyone wanted to see the evening game. A squad from out of Brooklyn came through to challenge Harlem's reining champions for bragging rights. It was one of the most anticipated games of the summer.

Paul was posted up on the corner of 114th and Lenox, watching the parade of chickenheads. He had stopped a tender young thing, rocking a too-short tennis skirt and flip-flops. Her perky breasts peaked out from beneath her baby-doll tank top. His cell phone rang in the middle of his mack game, putting it on pause.

"Excuse me for a minute, ma. I gotta take this," he said, looking at the caller ID. When he was safely out of earshot, he answered the call. "Hey, boo."

"Hey, baby. What you doing?" Marlene asked.

"Nothing much, just chilling."

"Well, while you've been busy chilling, did you make it over to see P.J.?"

"I was gonna go earlier, but Rhonda started her shit, so I'll probably swing by there later."

"Lord, what was she beefing over now?"

"Something light. P.J. needs a pair of sneakers."

"Already? Didn't you just give her some money to buy him sneakers?"

"Mar, you know she tapped into that," he said as if she should've known.

"Paul, if you know she's not gonna do the right thing, why do you keep setting yourself up?"

"What, I'm not supposed to take care of my seed?"

"Slow your roll, partner. You know I would never allow you to half step," she checked him. "All I'm saying is that you and Rhonda need to get your shit together and come to some kind of understanding."

"Oh, you don't think I've been trying to do that?" Paul asked. "There's no reasoning with that girl."

"Then take it a step further," Marlene suggested. "If Rhonda wants to keep playing these fucked-up games, then let a lawyer sort it out."

Paul sucked his teeth. "I ain't trying to go to court over this shit."

"Why not?"

" 'Cause that's for white people. How many black dudes do you see going to court on some custody shit? You know we don't rock like that."

Marlene pinched the bridge of her nose. "Paul, you are such an intelligent man, but sometimes you say the stupidest shit. So you mean to tell me that instead of going to court and handling this the proper way, you're going to keep tolerating Rhonda's bullshit?"

"I'm trying to be the bigger person about this, Mar," he defended. "If I take Rhonda to court it's only gonna get uglier than it already is. Don't worry, Mar, it'll blow over."

"When, by the time P.J. graduates high school?" Her tone was becoming heated. "Paul, when does enough finally become enough? For as long as we've been together, Rhonda has been doing the same shit. She blows your phone up, she's always asking for money, and she plays games with P.J. I could understand it if she had a valid reason to be a bitch, but she's doing it out of spite."

"Marlene, I'll take care of it." He sighed.

"Paul, you've *been* taking care of it," she reminded him. "Sweetie, I love you, but love only goes so far. This is seriously fucking with my peace of mind."

"So what are you trying to say?" he questioned.

Marlene felt herself becoming emotional, so she took a minute to gather herself. "Baby, all I'm saying is that I wanna be happy. We can talk about this another time."

"Yeah, a'ight," he said with an attitude.

"So, where are you guys?" she asked, changing the subject.

"In the hood," he replied. "Me and Larry about to go watch the game at Kingdome."

"Don't be out there fucking with them bitches, Paul."

"Baby, you know I ain't on it like that. I only got eyes for you."

"Tell me anything, Paul."

"Never *anything*, boo, only the truth."

"Aww, my baby is so sweet. But like I fucking said, don't be out there fucking with them bitches."

Paul sighed. "Marlene, why you always think I'm out fucking with some other hos?"

"Because I know how you and that fool Larry do when y'all get together. Y'all probably out there ogling them stank-ass bitches like everyone else," she told him.

"Whatever, Mar. I ain't trying to argue with you."

"We aren't arguing, Paul. We're talking, right? That's what adults do. Anyhow, you coming to see me tonight?"

"I'm not sure just yet," Paul said, watching a big-butt female stroll by, shaking what her mama gave her. Paul winked, but didn't dare call out to her while on the phone with Marlene. She could be as sweet as she wanted to be, but get her started and you'd find yourself in a bad way.

"What do you mean, you're not sure?" she asked.

"That's what I said, ain't it? I got some shit to take care of out here and I'm not sure what time I'll be done."

"Whatever, Paul. It's funny that you can put everyone and their mamas before me," she said.

"Here we go with this shit," he grumbled.

"What shit?"

"Marlene, why we always gotta go through the motions?"

"Listen, Paul. What you call 'the motions,' I call effective communication. I believe in expressing myself to my significant other, to prevent confusion of certain shit. You should be glad that I bring things to your attention, instead of seeking comfort elsewhere."

"What the fuck is that supposed to mean? I know you ain't trying to get fly," he accused heatedly.

"No." She sighed. "Paul, all I'm saying is, when couples feel like they can't communicate, one, if not both, of them ends up turning to others for that understanding. Baby, I love you too much to have our relationship turn into a *Lifetime* movie."

"Yeah, okay," he said, still unconvinced.

"Let's not fight, baby." She softened her tone. "You know I love you, and cherish the time that I get to spend with you. Look, do what you need to do in Harlem, and if you can't make it, I'll understand."

"I'm gonna try, Mar."

"That's good enough, *for now*. Love you."

"Love you, too, baby."

Click.

4

"That had to be the sweetest shit I ever heard," a voice called from behind Paul. Larry was standing there, wearing an ear-to-ear grin and clutching a black liquor store bag.

"Fuck you, Larry," Paul said playfully.

"I love you, too, baby," Larry repeated. "Youz a good dude, Paul."

The two men's ribbing session was broken up when a ten-speed bike rolled to a squeaky stop next to them. The rider's face was young, but his eyes held untold years behind them. He was of medium build with light skin and a nappy afro. A Dusty knapsack was slung over his shoulder with unidentifiable stains on it. The small boom box on the handlebars pumped a muffled tune that no one was really familiar with. The bike rider gave Paul and Larry a warm smile that caused them to sigh. Eight was in the building.

Crazy Eight was a cat from 110th and Columbus. He had always been a little out there, but had never been as bad as he was now. Eight had a learning disorder and his mother sought to come up off his disability. She applied for SSI, but was ordered to put the young boy on medication in order to prove the validity of the claim. In her greed, she gave the boy the medication without thinking about the long-term side effects of medicating a child who didn't need it. The chemicals ended up having an irreversible effect, causing brain damage. It seemed like the older Eight got, the worse his condition became. He was functional enough to move around in the streets and try to pass for normal, but anyone who spoke with Crazy Eight could tell he wasn't all there.

"Peace God!" Eight shouted, giving Paul a pound. He tried to dap Larry up, but the big man looked at him as if he couldn't be serious. "A'ight, a'ight," Eight said, and nodded at Larry, then turned his attention back to Paul. "Yo, I just got finished pressing up these CDs, God." Eight held up a CD case with a hand-drawn image on a folded sheet of notebook paper that served as the cover.

"That's what's up, my dude. Congratulations," Paul said sincerely.

Eight put down the kickstand to hold his bike up and went to stand beside the two men. His eyes held a vacant look as he continued talking to Paul. "Word, God, I'm 'bout to blow up out here, word is bond!"

Larry looked at Eight as if his very presence was an offense. "Yo, what's up with you and this 'God' shit?"

"Son, I just came into the knowledge," Eight said as if it was common knowledge. "I be the God Wise. Wise words spoken by as wise man," Eight almost sang.

Larry and Paul looked at each other. Every other week Eight came outside on some other shit. One week he might be a born-again Christian and the next week he might be a stick-up kid. All the medication he'd taken caused him to live in several different realities. Eight kind of knew he was off kilter, but he didn't mind too much. The $675 a month that he got from the government coupled with his other hustles insured that he didn't have to worry about a job where he would be asked to think anyhow.

Larry had finally gotten tired of listening to the man. "Yo, you're straight up full of shit. Don't nobody wanna hear your plan of the month, Crazy Eight. Get up outta here, you're scaring all the bitches away."

Eight looked at Larry as if he wanted to cry. "Why you gotta come at me like that?"

" 'Cause don't nobody wanna hear that stupid shit you're kicking."

"Leave the nigga alone, Larry. You know Eight ain't got it all."

"That's a'ight, fam." Eight gave Paul a pound. "It's all love." Eight's eyes suddenly took on a maddened glare as he spun to face Larry. "Yo, y'all niggaz better watch how the fuck you talk to me! On the real, I'm 'bout to start putting niggaz in wheelchairs."

"What?" Larry moved closer to him with balled fists.

Eight cringed and became sane again. "I wasn't talking to you, my dude, we fam. I was talking to them bitch-ass niggaz over there." Eight nodded at a group of men who hadn't so much as looked in his direction. "Them niggaz be trying to play me like I'm soft. I got love on these streets, feel me?" He held his hand out and Larry looked past it.

"Yo, bounce, Eight," Larry said seriously.

Eight looked like he had something on the tip of his tongue, but whatever it was, he kept it to himself. "Yo, I'm mobile," he said, riding a loop around them on his ten-speed. "Y'all niggaz stay up."

"A'ight." Paul waved. He waited until Crazy Eight had ridden off before questioning Larry. "Yo, why you always treat that nigga like that?"

"Fuck that crazy-ass dude. He ain't nothing but a con artist anyhow."

"What's he ever done to you?" Paul asked.

Larry looked at the fleeing form of Eight and turned to answer Paul's question. "Check it, about two or three months ago, I bump into this piece of shit, sitting on the curb in the rain. He gets to telling me how he's down on his luck and hungry. I offer to buy him something to eat, but he has a better idea, 'Loan me a hundred dollars so I can get a room, and when I get my check next week I'll give you two.'"

Paul let out a snicker. "Larry, tell me you didn't go for that shit?"

"Man, that's Little Harv's older brother, so I gave him a play. I didn't think he was gonna beat me for my bread. Anyhow, a month or so goes by and this nigga is ducking me. When I finally catch him, he feeds me a song and dance about how he got robbed and was too ashamed to tell me. What a fucking liar."

"So did he ever give you your money?" Paul asked.

"You damn right, he did!" Larry said triumphantly. "I took his ID and held it hostage. When he went to the check-cashing spot, I was right there with him."

"Guess you'll know better next time."

"Damn right, I will. He's lucky I didn't fuck his ass up."

A '78 Caddy slowed to a stop right next to Paul and Larry. It was painted sky blue with brown angels and red devils, warring for the pearly gates of heaven airbrushed on its hood. A short chick, with an ass made for a horse, stepped from the passenger side wearing a tight black leather skirt and heels. She opened the rear passenger door and a miracle stepped out.

When he stood to his full height, he was at least six foot two. His midnight black skin almost blended into the black silk button-up he was wearing. He carefully shook the creases of the dark blue jean shorts he was wearing, and placed a size-twelve Jordan on the curb.

Black Ice and Paul had known each other for quite some time. Ice used to deal with Paul's brother back in the day, so it wasn't unusual to see him in the hood. The thing about Ice, though, was he didn't sell drugs. He bumped a little weed here and there, but his main source of income was pimping. Ice was a young nigga with a good-size stable and respect from the old heads on the track.

Paul smiled proudly and extended his hand. "Black Ice, what da deal, my dude?"

Black Ice slapped his palm and gave him a diamond-toothed smile. "Taking it light, cat. You know how I do it."

"I see that paint job is holding up." Paul admired the car.

"Yeah, you put the God hand on it, son."

Black Ice's car was one of Paul's masterpieces. When Ice had initially restored the ride, he'd put it through a series of face-lifts. Everything from paint and tire color, to rims and grilles. It was hot, but Ice still felt it wasn't flashy enough. This is where Paul came in. Back then, he was just airbrushing jackets and T-shirts. Ice was telling Paul about a car he had seen in Cali and asked if he could do it. Paul stepped to the plate and did a wonderful job. Ice hit him with a nice chunk of change and promised to keep him in mind for future jobs.

A motorcycle roared by, drawing everyone's attention. It was a nice bike, with a custom paint job, but the main attraction was the girl on the back. She was wearing a leather corset, with denim shorts that left hardly anything to the imagination. Her plump but not oversize ass was cocked up on the back of the bike, nearly causing several traffic accidents.

"That bitch had a phat ass!" Larry shouted.

"Yeah, she's a fine little bitch." Ice rubbed his hand over his chin whiskers. "I've been trying to get Yoshi under the wing for a minute now. Damned renegade bitch knows how to get a dollar."

"That was Yoshi?" Paul squinted. "That bitch is getting thick!"

"I'll fuck the shit outta Yoshi, B." Larry rubbed himself.

"Yeah, she a'ight. But my new little bitch ain't no slouch. Spice," Ice called over his shoulder. "Come out here, and let these square niggaz see what a sporting bitch is supposed to look like!"

The girl who slid from the back of Ice's Caddy was stunning. She had long legs, connected to a perfectly round ass. Her skin was banana yellow, with a tinge of honey. A long black wig flowed down her back and dropped slightly over her arched brow. She gazed at Paul with cat-like green eyes, making him turn away after a while.

"Shit, Ice." Larry stared openly at the woman.

"You know I only fuck with the best, man." Ice patted Larry on the back. "For a few dollars, you can spend some time with her. What do ya say, baby." He turned to Spice. "You think you might be able to handle my man Larry here?"

Spice walked over, slow and seductively. She ran her hands from the top of Larry's head down to his chest. With her other hand, she gently caressed him through his jeans. "Yeah, I might be able to do something with him."

"What ya know about it, nigga?" Ice crossed his arms over his eighteen-karat gold cross.

"I wish I could, Ice. But I ain't got the kind of money to cover one of your bitches," Larry copped out.

"Come on, nigga. Since you and Paul is peoples, I'll let you get the family discount. Give me a buck and you can take this bitch somewhere and nasty up her pussy."

"Next time, daddy."

Black Ice shrugged his thin shoulders. "Suit yourself. Get back in the car, Spice." The young whore did as she was told. As she was climbing into the back of the car, her short skirt rode up, exposing her entire pussy to the three men assembled. Paul just sighed and tried to ignore the erection in his pants.

• • •

Rhonda, Jean, Reese, and Billy strolled through the park, talking shit and sipping nut crackers. They had originally planned on going to the liquor store, but decided that it was too warm to drink hard.

"These shits ain't even strong," Rhonda complained, swishing the ice around in her cup. "That bitch is falling off."

"Shit, mine is strong enough," Reese said, sipping her drink.

"I need something harder than this. Let's go to the liquor store like we planned. I need some Hennessy in my life."

"Rhonda, you must be out of your mind. I ain't trying to drink nut crackers and Henny back to back," Billy said.

"Youse about a punk bitch, Billy." Rhonda waved her off. "With four of us on a pint, we'll only get buzzed."

Crazy Eight pedaled over to the girls and looped them once. He had a crusty-looking blunt tucked behind his ear and a half-smoked cigarette dangling between his lips. "Ladies," he sang, skidding his bike, "what's good?"

"Definitely not your silly ass." Rhonda sucked her teeth.

"Stop acting like that, ma, and recognize game when you see it," Eight said confidently.

Rhonda looked at her girls to make sure her ears weren't playing tricks on her. "Is this nigga serious? Crazy Eight, you need to get your bootleg CD-selling ass outta here before it be some shit."

"Laugh all you want, boo, but a nigga is on his way to doing big things," he said, removing one of the CDs from his dirty knapsack. "I'm selling these shits for ten dollars a whop, but since you ladies are so lovely, I'll let it go for five." He gave them a yellow-toothed smile, which caused all the girls to laugh.

"Eight, we don't wanna buy no CDs," Billy said politely.

"A'ight, so I'll set 'em out for three," Eight negotiated.

"Nigga, we don't want no CDs!" Rhonda barked.

Eight's eyes took on a great sadness, then anger. "Word, you ain't got no love for my work? Bet you'll be on my dick when you see me at the Grammys." He gave her the finger and pedaled off.

"Fuck you, you dirtball muthafucka! You need to go wash your ass!" Rhonda tried to go after him, but Billy and Reese restrained her. "I hate that muthafucka."

"Yo, it's some bad bitches out here!" Jean proclaimed, not seeming to realize that Rhonda was about to go on the warpath seconds prior.

"Hold that shit down, Jean. If you wanna chase pussy, take your ass to the other side of the park. Don't bring that kind of attention over here," Reese warned her.

"Look, somebody walk with me to the liquor store," Rhonda said.

"I wanna catch the game," Billy said.

"Me, too," Jean added.

"I'll walk with you." Reese cut her eyes at the two girls.

Rhonda started toward the park exit with Reese and called over her shoulder, "Don't look to put you nasty-ass mouths on the bottle if you ain't trying to walk."

They had just about made it to the corner when Rhonda's phone rang. She looked at her caller ID to make sure it was someone she felt like speaking to, then answered, "What's up, bitch?"

"Shit, out here on the ave," Yoshi responded on the other end. "Where y'all at?"

"Kingdome, trying to see what's up with these sorry-ass niggaz."

"I'm out here, too. I rode down with Scooter on his new bike."

"I don't know how you fuck with those things. I'm scared to death to get on a bike," Rhonda told her.

"Shit, if you was fucking with a nigga who handle bread like Scooter, you'd be on a bike too, bitch." The two girls laughed. "But yo, check this shit. I just seen that nigga Paul."

"Where you seen him at?" Rhonda asked, trying to hide her excitement.

"On Fourteenth. He right in front of the liquor store with Larry and Ice. I ain't know Paul fucked with that pimping ass nigga like that?"

"You know Paul know some of everybody, girl."

"Yeah, he's real popular these days. You should've seen how Ice's hos were smiling all up in his face," Yoshi taunted.

"Fucking jump-off-ass nigga. I'm 'bout to walk over there."

"A'ight. Let me see what's up with this nigga, and I'll probably walk over there. Give me about fifteen minutes. If you're gonna get stupid, call my phone."

"I ain't gonna get stupid, I'm just gonna get him to buy the bottle."

"Oh, Lord. If that's the case, I'll be there in ten."

Paul was leaning against a parking meter, discussing a mural that Ice wanted him to do on his living room wall, when his phone rang. When he heard the lyrics to Three 6 Mafia's "Baby Mama," he knew who it was without looking. Letting out a long sigh, he picked up the phone.

"Hello."

"What's good, Paul? Where you at?" Rhonda questioned.

"I'm in my skin," he said, not bothering to hide his irritation.

"Don't be fucking funny, nigga. I was just calling to see what you were doing."

"Me and Larry are kicking it. What's up?"

"Nothing, just wondered if you felt like chilling?"

"Nah, I'm good. Besides, I ain't coming through the projects till later on. I'm handling some business right now."

"How're you handling business, standing in front of the liquor store?"

"What the fuck, are you spying on me?" He looked around nervously.

"You know I always got my eye on you, baby daddy." She blew him a kiss and hung up.

"That girl is asking for trouble," Billy said, shaking her head.

"Yo, ya friends be on some real chickenhead shit," Jean said.

"Don't be trying to dis my girls, Jean."

"It's the truth and you know it, Billy. That boy is over there minding his business and Rhonda is gonna fuck with him for no reason."

"Well, that's between her and her baby daddy. Rhonda and Paul have always had a love/hate relationship."

"I'd hate that bitch, too, if I was stupid enough to have a baby by her," Jean told her.

"Well, you don't have a baby by her, so mind your business. Now, let's see if we can catch some of this game," Billy said, heading into the projects.

There were people for as far as the eye could see. Some were watching the game, but most were just getting their stunt on. Over near the end of the parking lot, Billy spotted a familiar face. Teddy was leaning against the gate talking to a girl who looked like she couldn't have been more than sixteen.

"Oh, shit." Billy tapped Jean and nodded in Teddy's direction.

"Who's that?" Jean asked.

"That old married nigga that Reese is fucking," Billy replied.

Jean frowned. "Married? Does the bullshit ever end?"

"I'm 'bout to call Reese and let her know what the hell this snake is up to," Billy said, pulling out her phone.

"That might have to wait. She's got her hands full right now." Jean pointed across the street.

Billy looked over by the liquor store where a small crowd was gathering and all she could say was, "Damn!"

When Rhonda and Reese got across the ave, Paul was standing by a tricked-out Caddy, talking to Ice and two of his girls. Her anger immediately welled up, seeing him out there smiling with the two pretty girls. Though she wasn't with Paul, she couldn't stand to see him around another female. She decided to crash the party and make her presence felt.

"What's good, y'all?" Rhonda said, stepping on the curb.

When Paul turned around and saw her, his whole mood changed. He tried his best to be cool with Rhonda for the sake of P.J., but they never could sit horses.

" 'Sup," he said, uninterested.

"Shit, hello to you, too." She stepped right into his and Ice's space, disregarding the conversation they were having. "You ain't gonna introduce your baby mama to your little friends, Paul?"

"Ain't nobody here that you got a reason to meet, Rhonda. I'll get with you in a little while." Paul turned his back on her and tried to resume his conversation with Black Ice.

"Nigga, don't be trying to style on me for these hos!" Rhonda raised her voice.

"These Harlem bitches got me fucked up!" Passion spoke up. She was another of Ice's hos who were present. "Who is this little black bitch talking to?"

"If the dick fits in your mouth, suck it, bitch!" Reese spat.

"Oh, I got your bitch right here!" Passion said, advancing on Reese. Passion was about five foot eleven and weighed 170-something, so it took the combined efforts of Ice and one of his other women to hold her back.

"Why don't y'all go somewhere with that shit," Paul said, stepping between the warring parties.

"Fuck you, Paul. That bitch shouldn't have come out her mouth!" Rhonda shouted, way louder than she had to.

Paul turned to Ice. "Yo, I'm sorry about this shit, Ice. I'll talk to you later."

"Ain't nothing, baby. We're all gentlemen here." Ice brushed his shoulder off.

Paul looked at Rhonda and had to restrain himself from saying something vicious to her. Instead, he tapped Larry and motioned for them to keep it moving. He got about three feet and Rhonda was right on his heels.

"Nigga, don't be walking away from me!" She ran up on him.

"Rhonda, I ain't trying to do this with you. Just leave me alone."

"See, that's your problem. You can't take me, and that's why you couldn't fuck with me. Tell the truth, Paul. I was too much woman for you, huh?"

That drew a few snickers from the onlookers, but Paul didn't feed into it. "Rhonda, why don't you go play in traffic?" Paul turned to walk away, but she wouldn't have it.

Rhonda grabbed him by the neckline of his shirt. "I said, don't walk away from me!" Using both hands, she tore Paul's shirt clean off his back.

The whole corner roared with laughter. Paul looked like a complete ass, standing there in his tank top, with strips of his shirt hanging off him. Rhonda stood there smiling, but her face went slack when she saw the fire raging in his eyes. As quick as lightning, Paul slapped the shit out of Rhonda. She spun around twice and collapsed, holding her cheek.

"Bitch, what the fuck is wrong with you? I'll murder your chickenhead ass out here!" he bellowed. He tried to move in for the kill, but Larry grabbed him about the waist.

"Be easy, my nigga," Larry whispered in his ear.

"Fuck that, Larry. I'm tired of this bitch!"

"That's my cue to leave," Ice said, shooing his women back into the car. "I'll get wit' you, cat daddy. I don't need this kind of heat." Ice hopped into his Caddy and spun off.

"Nigga, why you hit her like that?" Reese jumped in Paul's face. When she saw the madness in his eyes, she backed up.

"Fuck you, Paul!" Rhonda screamed, while Reese tried to help her up. "That's the last time you're gonna put your fucking hands on me. I'm taking P.J. and leaving. You ain't never gonna see your seed, muthafucka!"

"You threatening me, bitch!" Paul struggled against Larry's grip, but he held fast.

"Reese, why don't you take your friend and get up out of here?" Larry pleaded.

"Fuck that, he shouldn't have hit her!"

"That's a'ight, nigga. You gonna get yours," Rhonda threatened, wiping her clothes off.

"Get whoever you want, bitch. When I'm done with him, I'm gonna put something hot in your ass!" Paul snarled.

"Watch your mouth, kid, there're people out here," Larry warned. He looked up the block and saw two uniformed cops making their way through the crowd. "Time to go." He tapped Paul and nodded up the block. Paul was angry, but he wasn't stupid. The two of them made hurried steps across the street and disappeared into the projects.

"What the fuck was that all about?" Billy asked.

"Paul clocked her again," Yoshi volunteered.

"What the fuck set him off?" Billy handed Rhonda a paper towel.

"Yo, I was just going to the liquor store and this nigga started spazzing," Rhonda lied. "He was out there trying to stunt for Larry and that pimp-ass nigga Ice."

"If I was you, I'd call the police on that muthafucka," Reese said. "I wouldn't have no nigga putting his hands on me."

"Reese, why don't you stop instigating," Billy said. "You wasn't talking that shit when Bone used to put his foot in your ass."

"Fuck you, Billy. This ain't about me."

"You know damn well Rhonda and Paul will be fighting today and friends tomorrow. Don't try to add fire to the shit."

"Nah, I ain't gonna call the police, but I'm gonna fix that nigga," Rhonda plotted. "Paul is gonna learn just what kind of bitch his baby mama is."

5

The sun had dipped below the shoreline of the Hudson River, bringing the temperature down with it, but that still didn't stop the action on the busy streets of Harlem. The popular avenues, such as Lenox, Seventh, and Eighth, were still buzzing with people, and police. The Beast always patrolled Harlem in the summer, like tourists on the boardwalk, trying to catch somebody dirty or harass someone minding their own business in search of the all-demanding quota set forth by the mayor and his henchmen.

On the side of the bodega on 142nd and Lenox, a group of young men stood around shooting dice. Open containers sat on the ground and atop cars, with the sweet smell of weed smoke lingering like an unseasonable fog. Though all the players wore smiles and laughed good-naturedly, there was plenty of larceny present, each man wanting to relieve the others of whatever cash, or in some cases jewels, that they were willing to play for. A few buildings over sat the governing chickenhead council of those parts, doing what they did best: killing time.

Yoshi, Rhonda, and Reese sat on the stoop of a slightly dilapidated building, drinking cognac from foam cups and swapping stories with some of the locals. The excitement of that afternoon had come and gone, giving away to the anticipation of what the night might bring. If you played the hood long enough, you were bound to see something noteworthy.

"Yo, my ass is sore as hell from riding that motorcycle all day," Yoshi said, massaging her thighs.

"Either that, or letting Scooter pound you in your shit box," Reese snickered.

"Fuck you, Reese. You always got some slick shit to say. Don't act like you ain't never take it in the ass, bitch."

"That was only once and I didn't like it, ho," Reese lied. Truth be told, she took it in the ass from time to time, depending on whom she was with and what she thought the act could get her. Reese knew that she wasn't as pretty as Yoshi or Billy, and hardly as cunning as Rhonda, so she had to get it however she could. Young men traded stories about her on a regular basis, but she chalked it up as taking one for the team.

"Where the hell is Billy?" Rhonda asked, taking a huge gulp of her drink. The liquor caused her eyes to water, but she held it like a true soldier. Rhonda could outdrink all of her girls and a few guys they knew.

"She was supposed to be dropping Jean off downtown and coming right back," Yoshi said.

"They're probably somewhere licking each other's asses," Reese said scornfully.

"Yo, y'all really think Billy get down like that?" Yoshi asked.

"I wouldn't be surprised," Rhonda answered. "She sure as hell dresses like a dyke. When is the last time you seen her slide with somebody or heard about a nigga hitting that?"

"I ain't seen Billy with a dude since Sol, God bless," Reese said.

"She ain't been the same since that nigga got killed," Yoshi recalled.

Sol had been a local knucklehead who they had gone to school with. He fashioned himself a pretty boy and his mind was constantly on his paper. He and Billy had hooked up during high school and had a romance straight out of a music video. They could often be seen hugged up on the block or shooting hoops in the park. One night after Sol had dropped Billy off in the projects, some stick-up kids approached him and demanded his chain. Sol, being a true soldier, refused to part with the showpiece. For his insolence, they put two in his melon and took it anyway. Billy wore black for damn near six months after his murder. She hadn't been quite the same since.

"These Harlem niggaz ain't nothing but trouble." Reese shook her head.

"Speaking of trouble." Rhonda nodded up the block.

The young man who was heading in their direction had a baby face and a slim build. His hair was nappy and wild, but freshly shaped up around the edges. He had a confident swagger and murderous eyes. Young Jah was the type of kid who your parents warned you never to bring home. He was a good dude to those he was cool with and a headache to those he wasn't.

"Ladies," Jah said in a voice that was almost that of a man, but still had a childlike squeak to it. "What's good?"

"You." Yoshi looked up at him.

"So I've heard." He smiled. "What y'all doing?"

"Sipping on something light." Rhonda showed him the bottle.

"What's popping, Rhonda? How's my nephew?"

"Bad as hell. Between him and your stupid-ass brother, I can't even get my mind right."

"I heard y'all got into it earlier." Jah placed a Nike on the stoop.

"This nigga be on some bullshit, yo. All I was trying to do was have an adult conversation with him and he starts flipping out."

Jah just looked at her. He knew his brother and he knew Rhonda. He had seen them go through the motions for years. Rhonda would do or say something stupid and Paul would lose his temper. They would go through it at least once a month. Jah didn't think it was right for his brother to put his hands on Rhonda, but you'd have to know Rhonda to understand it. She knew all the right buttons to push to get a rise out of him and did it on a regular basis. Her theory was, as long as his attention was on her instead of anything or anyone else, she was happy, even if it meant slapping her ass around. Women like her were under the misconception that if a man didn't knock her upside the head every so often, they were either weak or didn't care.

"Anyway." Jah waved Rhonda off. "What y'all sipping on?"

"A little Henny." Yoshi raised her glass as if toasting the air.

"Let your boy get a li'l of that." Jah reached for the empty cup that was sitting on top of the bottle.

"Nigga, please." Reese snatched the bottle away. "You hustle, go cop a bottle. We chipped in for this."

"Word, a nigga can't get a drink?" Jah screwed up his face.

"Reese, stop acting like that." Yoshi snatched the bottle from Reese and handed it to Jah. "You know Jah is peoples."

"Yeah, my little brother done came through and got us right plenty of times," Rhonda added.

Reese sucked her teeth, but knew better than to say anything to Jah. Even though he was young, Paul's baby brother was one of the hood's most dangerous cats. Jah poured a shot into his cup and toasted Rhonda and Yoshi. Reese raised her glass, but he ignored her. Turning the cup upside down, he downed the fiery liquor. He made a funny face, then tossed his empty cup into the street.

"What you know about that dog, nigga?" Rhonda laughed.

Jah wiped his mouth with the back of his hand. "I don't know how y'all can drink this shit twenty-four seven. Give me an ice-cold forty and I'm good."

"This here is for grown folks," Reese said, swirling ice chips around in her cup.

"Then what the fuck are you doing with it?" Jah spat, drawing snickers from the people. Reese just rolled her eyes.

A lot of people couldn't understand why Reese didn't like Jah, but they knew just what the beef between them was. The previous summer, Reese found herself at the ass end of a crush on an older cat from the neighborhood. He wasn't known as one of the more high-profile cats, but he kept himself fresh and had a nice ride. More importantly, he carried himself like a gentleman more often than not. After some coaxing, Reese found herself in the staircase of the projects giving him head. Jah happened to be coming down the stairs and busted them. He demanded that Reese bless him, too, but she refused. Jah, being young and still having that mentality, went and ran his mouth. Unfortunately, the word got back to the kid who was claiming Reese as his shorty. Needless to say, the relationship ended badly. Reese had cursed Jah as a big-mouth little boy and things hadn't been the same since.

"Jah, I know you holding. Put it in the air." Rhonda tapped his pocket. She knew Jah was a notorious pothead and could often be found holding some of the best weed in town.

"You know how I do it," he said, pulling out an already rolled White Owl. "This that shit right here." He dangled the blunt in front of Rhonda and snatched it back when she reached for it. "Easy, shorty. We 'bout to get ski high off that Diesel."

"Damn, nigga, that shit is hard as hell to score. Jah, how come you always seem to get your hands on shit that no one else can?" Yoshi asked.

Jah gave her a perfect smile, equipped with dimples. "It pays to know somebody who knows somebody. Jah get you what you need, boo."

"Nigga, stop trying to mack and light the weed!" Rhonda broke the mood.

The four of them sat on the stoop, passing the blunt of potent weed and talking shit. Though Jah was definitely gangsta with his, when he was in good spirits he was a funny dude. Even Reese managed to unscrew her face and laugh at some of the off-the-wall shit he said. The strange thing about weed is its ability to bring people together. If you got high enough in the right company, you could forget what you were pissed about in the first place. At least until you came down.

When the blunt was about three quarters of the way done, Jah's eyes took on a funny glare. He was fixed on the dice game as if he was just noticing it. Yoshi and Reese seemed oblivious to it, but Rhonda knew what time it was. He was scheming.

"I'm about to get up outta here," he said, stepping off the stoop.

"There you go, on your bullshit already," Rhonda said.

"Nah, I'm just going to see if I can come up right quick," he said oh so innocently. With his small frame and funny voice, Jah seemed harmless enough, but he was full of shit. Rhonda knew he was about as harmless as a baby viper. Bidding the ladies good-bye, Jah bopped toward the corner.

"That nigga is always scheming." Reese said when he was out of earshot.

"You know how he do it," Rhonda said.

"That li'l nigga can get it," Yoshi added. Rhonda and Reese both looked at her as if they had heard wrong. "What y'all looking at me like that for? He *can* get it."

"Yoshi, you need to quit. You know that little boy ain't even in your league," Rhonda said.

"Yeah, I know. But I might still fuck him one day. There's something about that little bad-ass muthafucka that turns me on."

Yoshi's observation of Jah was broken up by the heavy bass of a car stereo. A red Hummer coasted slowly down the block, rattling windows in its wake. The windows were tinted so heavy that you couldn't see who was in the ride. The girls didn't need X-ray vision to recognize one of the hood's most infamous stars, Don B.

Don B.'s was a true rags-to-riches story. He was born and raised in the Drew Hamilton projects, on the Eighth Avenue side. As a youth, he had distributed more cocaine and slugs to niggaz on the street than the police. Over the years, he had been shot seven times, stabbed twice, and even strangled while he was locked up. Through it all he had managed to deny the grim reaper his due time and again. People would always joke that with all the shit he had lived through, God must've put him on earth for a purpose. The running joke had come to reality when his record label, Dawg Food Entertainment, managed to secure a multimillion-dollar distribution deal with Sony. Don B. had two singles on the *Billboard* charts and was fast on his way to becoming a star.

"Now, there's a nigga who can get it." Rhonda licked her lips. "Don B. might not be the handsomest muthafucka, but his money is way long."

Reese sucked her teeth. "He ain't all that."

"Bitch, stop acting like you wouldn't fuck him. All he'd have to do is drop a few dollars on you and say the word, and you'd probably suck his whole squad off."

"Rhonda, you must be fucking crazy. There's no way in hell I'd suck his whole team off for no paper. Maybe him and his right-hand man, though." The three of them burst out laughing. Their jovial moment was shattered when shouting reached the stoop. They turned their attention back to the dice game just in time to see Jah pull his hammer and blast some kid in the chest. While the rest of the players took cover, Jah snatched the money off the floor and vanished.

Reese just shook her head. "I told you he's always on some bullshit."

Forty minutes after the shooting, the police escorted an ambulance through the cramped block to load the wounded man and cart him off to the hospital. They tried asking anyone if they had seen or heard anything, but only drew blank stares. Figuring it'd be easier to talk to a female than it had been a male, the two uniformed officers walked over to where Rhonda and her friends were sitting.

"Evening, ladies," the dark-skinned cop said, tipping his hat. "We were wondering if we could ask you a few questions."

"We ain't seen shit . . ." Yoshi began.

". . . Ain't heard shit . . ." Reese picked up.

". . . Don't know shit," Rhonda finished it off.

"How the hell do you girls expect us to do our jobs when no one wants to help out?" the white cop asked. "The only way we can protect these neighborhoods is to get these animals off the streets."

"Your job." Rhonda chuckled. "That the funniest shit I heard all day. The only time you muthafuckas even come through this block is to harass niggaz and collect bribes. Fuck outta here wit that job shit!"

"You'd better watch your mouth, miss," the black cop said.

"And you better watch your ass, *Tom*," Reese added. "How the fuck can you sleep with yourself knowing that the people you work with don't give a fuck about the people you *live* with? That shit ain't never made sense to me."

"Listen, sis," the black cop began, switching up his tone to make himself sound more down. "Ain't nobody trying to give you a hard time, we just wanna catch the punk muthafucka that popped shorty.

Now, we know y'all be on this stoop twenty-four seven, so don't act like you don't know what happened."

The dark-skinned cop kept his face serious and his eyes sincere. He talked a good one about wanting to protect the neighborhood, but all he really wanted was a gold shield and possibly some sergeant's bars. He looked at Rhonda's face and seeing her bottom lip begin to quiver, he thought he might've been making some progress. That all changed when she doubled over laughing.

"You hear this nigga?" she asked Yoshi, slapping her on her exposed thigh. "If I didn't know any better I might've taken this muthafucka seriously. Nah," she said, turning back to the cop, "we don't know nothing."

"You know we could run you in for obstruction of justice."

"Yeah, and spend all night doing paperwork," Yoshi said. "Why don't y'all take that stupid shit down the block? Maybe one of them bum-ass bitches from Seventh will tell you what you need to know for a case of Pampers." Yoshi clutched her stomach, laughing at her own joke.

The white cop wanted to slap the pretty light-skinned girl to the ground and throw his dick in her mouth to see how funny she thought that was, but there were too many people watching. "Come on, Ed." He tapped his partner and started back in the direction of the squad car. Before getting in, he had one last jewel to drop. "You know, one day you might need to call on the law and you better pray to God I ain't the one to answer the call, bitch!"

"Go lick out ya mama's ass!" Rhonda shouted.

"Remember Louima!" Yoshi added. They stood there ranking on the cops until they had finally cleared off the block. No sooner than they pulled off, Teddy's Benz came creeping down the block.

"Look what the fuck the cat drug in." Rhonda nodded toward the car.

"Ain't that the fat Gerald Levert–looking nigga you fuck with?" Yoshi asked Reese.

"Yeah, that's that nigga," Reese said, fronting like she didn't wanna hop off the stoop and run to the car. "Let me see what the fuck this nigga wants." Reese slowly made her way in the direction of the Benz.

Teddy pulled up by the fire hydrant and kept the engine running. Usually he would've hopped out to holla at her, but this time he chose to stay in the car, only making Reese angrier.

"Oh, that's the kind of shit you on, Ted?" she barked, but got no answer. "Fuck do I look like . . . ?" The rest of Reese's sentence died in her throat as the tinted window rolled down and it wasn't Teddy behind the wheel, but his wife, Penny. Not really sure what to do, Reese paused.

As Reese stood there trying to figure out what her next move should be, a soda bottle came flying out of the car window. Being that Penny was sitting, making the throw an awkward one, Reese was able to sidestep the bottle. When the glass hit the ground, Reese smelled that it wasn't soda or beer in the bottle, but bleach. "Stay away from my husband, you fucking hood rat!" Penny shouted before peeling through the red light.

6

Paul got off the bus and adjusted his backpack. He hated taking the long ride from Harlem to Long Island City, Queens, but it was a necessary evil. After hitting the corner bodega for a six-pack of Corona and a Dutch Master, he began his nine-block hike. He could've stayed on the bus for another ten minutes and gotten off closer to his destination, but Paul enjoyed walking. It allowed him to clear his mind and take in the feel of the area.

During his walk, he observed the sights and sounds of the foreign land and couldn't help but think how different Queens was from any other borough. Though Queens was a part of New York City it was only so in name. It lacked the grittiness of Brooklyn or the historical feel of Harlem. The bowels of Queens were more or less like the neighborhoods of any other city, but the farther out you went, the more it was like being in the suburbs.

Marlene owned a three-bedroom brick house in Long Island City. He walked through the little iron fence and up the driveway to the varnished front door. After taking a moment to listen, he let himself in. On the outside it didn't look much different than the other half-dozen houses on the block, but the inside was laced. Big-screen televisions, marble floors. Marlene had gone all out with the decor.

He placed his bag by the front door and removed his shoes. Marlene had this thing about tracking up her floors and was quick to bark on violators of the no shoes rule. Descending the few steps past the foyer, he made his way to the kitchen. Everything in the kitchen was steel, giving it a hospital/cafeteria feel. Taking a beer from the box, he placed the other five in the refrigerator and headed into the living room.

The dim lights shining on the white furniture highlighted the fabric's specs of gold. The fifty-inch television was on CNN, but the sound was muted. Crossing the plush living room, and passing through the glass doors, Paul entered what Marlene liked to call her sanctuary. It consisted of a desk, a small television, and an entertainment system. The soft sounds of Faith Evans hummed through the speakers as he passed them. Jasmine filled the air, with a hint of chronic underlying. As soon as he smelled it, he knew what time it was. Marlene only smoked when she was stressed. On the Italian leather recliner, dressed in a bathrobe, with her hair freshly wrapped, sat the lady of the house.

Her copper skin glowed under the light of the candles, which were the source of the jasmine fragrance in the air. She was sitting with one leg dangling over the side of the recliner and the other propped to expose just enough of her shapely thigh to cause a slight bulge in Paul's jeans. Though she rarely ate meat anymore, she had ass and hips that could've only been born of pork. Marlene was fine as wine and twice as sweet, generally.

She and Paul had met right after he was released from prison. He had been picked up for having weed on him and she was the public defender assigned to his case. The prosecutor wanted to send Paul back to jail on a parole violation, but Marlene convinced him otherwise. Since the police had illegally searched Paul and whipped his ass in the process, she threatened to go public with it. After what had happened with Louima and Diallo, the city didn't need any more bad press. The charge was knocked down to a misdemeanor and a fine.

Paul was so grateful that he offered to take Marlene to dinner as a way of thanking her, since he didn't have to pay for her services. Normally,

Marlene wouldn't have dreamed of dating a client, but there was something about Paul that moved her. He had a thug's exterior but the poise of a true gentleman. As Marlene got to know the man behind the case file, she found herself falling for him. Nearly two years later, she found herself a star defense attorney for a high-profile firm, and madly in love with the man she'd saved.

Paul crept silently over to the recliner. Marlene had her head back and her eyes closed, but he knew she wasn't asleep. She was probably just waiting for him to take the initiative, as usual. Marlene often subjected Paul to these subtle tests. He didn't know if it was to piss him off, or because she was really that insecure. Whatever the case, Paul dealt with it.

Leaning over the back of the recliner, Paul placed a kiss on her heart-shaped lips. She cracked a smile and kissed him back. Her lips tasted like honey and her breath smelled of mints. Yes, Paul was truly a lucky man.

"I missed you," she said, casting her soft brown eyes up at him.

He snaked over the arm of the chair and sat beside her. "I missed you, too, sweetheart." Paul took the joint from the ashtray on the end table and relit it. After taking two long tokes, he handed it to Marlene. "So, how was your day, counselor?"

She expelled a thin puff of smoke. "Jesus, I don't even know where to begin. We got a case today involving a young man who had been accused of murdering another guy over some drugs. When I questioned him, he admitted to shooting the other boy, but claims it was in self-defense. He and the other boy were arguing over who had the right to hustle on that corner. Things got a little heated and he reached inside his jacket, that's when my client shot him."

"Damn, was the other kid strapped?" Paul asked.

"Yeah, they found a gun on him."

"So, what's the big deal? Shorty was just trying to protect himself."

"Yes, it's easy to look at it like that on the streets, but in a court of law it's a whole different ball game. To them its not a boy trying to protect himself, it's a drug-related shooting. If I can't convince them otherwise, they're gonna try and fry that kid."

"Sucks to be you," Paul said offhandedly.

Marlene got up from the recliner so fast that she almost knocked Paul on the floor. "I don't see the joke, Paul. There's a young man's life at stake here."

"Come on, Mar. You know I didn't mean it like that. All I'm saying is, you and I know how it can be in the hood, but these crackers that run the show ain't got a fucking clue. Now, what if your client hadn't hesitated? He'd probably be deader than all hell, and it'd be the other boy who got prosecuted. It's like you can't win with these pricks."

"You're telling me." She walked over to the entertainment system and switched the CD. Lyfe Jennings's "Must Be Nice" replaced the first lady of Bad Boy. "Sometimes I wonder what the fucking point is. Who knows, maybe Monday morning I'll just go in and quit."

"Who the fuck are you kidding?" Paul swigged his beer. "You love your job too much. Besides, if you were to quit, how would you keep up the mortgage on this little mansion here?" He looked around the room.

"I'd manage. I've got some money tucked away for a rainy day, and I could do legal consulting. Besides, you'd take care of me, wouldn't you?"

"Of course I would. I ain't got much, baby, but whatever I have is yours," he said seriously. "You're my beginning and my ending. Whatever you need, you have but to ask."

"Glad you feel that way, Paul. So when are we moving in together?"

Damn, walked right into that one, he thought to himself. "Come on, Marlene."

"Come on? Are we going somewhere?" she asked sarcastically.

"You know what I mean," he said, pulling the wastebasket to rest between his feet while he split the Dutch over it. "Why do we have to go into this now?"

When Marlene peeped the move, she knew she had him on the ropes. Whenever Paul didn't want to answer something honestly, or couldn't think of a politically correct response, his hands started moving. Normally, he would start sketching or mixing paints, but he didn't have either within arms' reach. The blunt would be his buffer.

"Paul, how come every time I wanna talk about something that's important to me, you don't?" She moved to stand in front of him. Even sitting, he almost reached her five foot two. "You make me feel like the things that move me aren't important to you."

"You know it's not like that with me, Mar. Of course the things that are important to you are important to me." He tried to reach out and pull her closer, but she stepped out of reach.

She fixed her eyes directly on his, to make sure she had his undivided attention. "You don't act like it. Paul, let's keep it funky," she began, which bothered him because she rarely used improper English. "We've been together for a while now, and what have we accomplished?"

He put the finishing touches on his blunt and glared up at her as if she'd offended him. "What the hell is that supposed to mean? You left the city and went with a private firm with more perks, and I've given up scamming to go legit. I know I haven't sold a painting yet, but I'm creating a buzz. Soon it'll be on and popping!"

"Paul, I think you've misunderstood me," she said seriously. "Both of us have accomplished a great deal of noteworthy things individually, but what have we done together?"

He responded by lighting the blunt.

"That's the kind of shit I'm talking about." She threw her hands up. "I say things to you and they go over your head!"

"Marlene." He exhaled the smoke. "You ain't gotta be yelling. I can hear you just fine from here."

"Sometimes it seems like that's the only way to get a reaction out of you. Do I have to scream like a fool for you to understand that I love you?" she asked, eyes threatening rain.

Paul felt that familiar tug at his heart, telling him to be more attentive. He knew where Marlene was coming from, because he often did it to himself. It is often said that artistic people live in a world unto themselves, and whoever came up with that observation must've shared a room with Paul as a child. He could articulate himself through art with an almost magical fluidity, but saying exactly what was on his mind was like a circus trick. His mind said one thing, but his words and actions mispronounced the verses. More often than not, he chose silence as his defense.

He fought back his sharp retort and decided to bend. "Marlene, I know you wanna do it real official with a nigga, but its gonna be some time. I wanna be able to take care of my family on the constant basis, not in spurts."

"Sweetie, you know it's never been about money with me," she said, taking the blunt from him and sipping from the stream of smoke trailing it. "I did it before you, and during. You know I'll go out and get it without coaching. It's just that, more often than not, I'm lonely."

"I know." He stood and kissed her on the forehead. "Soon as I sell one of these joints. I promise." He tapped her once more on the tip of her nose and left the sanctuary.

Marlene watched him leave, dangling his half-empty Corona. Even while upset with him, she couldn't deny the fact that there was a sex appeal to him, in an innocent yet wicked way. Marlene, who would be turning forty the following month, was more settled and focused on what she wanted from life and what she was going to make it give her.

When she had first discovered the young felon, she knew he was something special. He was still really a little boy, yet with grown people's responsibilities. The gangsta part about it was that he was handling it. She could recall countless stories about her friends' baby daddies and them dipping out on the kid. Paul handled his with a high head. Even though his baby's mama was a royal pain, he kept the bond with his seed strong. That was rare in this day and age.

Paul was damn near perfect, except for his reluctance to let go of his past. He had more than a great deal of potential, but no one to give him that extra bit of direction. That's where Marlene came in. She had already resigned herself to the fact that he could cop or blow.

7

It was 1:00 A.M. and Billy still hadn't gone back to join her homegirls. On her way to drop Jean off, Jean convinced her to make a stop at Mt. Morris Park. Some people she knew were supposed to be having a big barbecue for a homey that just touched down from doing a bullet. Billy wasn't in too much of hurry to get back to her friends and their stoop antics, so she agreed to stop through for a few minutes. The next thing she knew, almost two hours had passed.

The hosts of the event had been more than generous with the entertainment for the night. There were gallons of liquor and at least a half pound of weed floating around the park. It seemed like every time Billy handed one blunt off, another one was being passed to her. Billy had considered calling her girls to invite them to the event, but didn't feel like hearing their mouths. It was mostly a bull and queer event and she knew their homophobic asses wouldn't have been comfortable.

Sometime during the event a trio came through. The first girl was cute, but hardly as attractive as the other two. She wore pleated linen pants and a sleeveless blouse beneath a linen jacket. The second girl was beautiful, with golden skin and catlike green eyes. She had a Dominican look about her, but Billy wasn't absolutely sure. Her eyes were partially slanted on her doll-like face, with a crown of auburn curls atop her head.

The third member of the party was so handsome that he danced on the line of being pretty. The young man wore a silk shirt, unbuttoned at the top, showing off his well-built chest. His skin was the color of milk chocolate, and when he smiled, perfect white teeth flashed in the moonlight.

Jean introduced the trio to Billy as Rose, Cat, and Marcus. Rose nodded, but didn't bother to extend her hand in greeting. Cat, on the other hand, was very friendly, holding onto Billy's hand a little longer than necessary. There was something about her green eyes that made Billy uncomfortable. Marcus was a different case. When he greeted Billy, he bowed slightly from the hip and kissed the back of her hand. When his lips made contact with her skin, Billy felt a chill snake up her back.

She watched the trio from a distance for some time, trying to figure out what the connection was between them. At first she thought that the two girls and Marcus were gay, but something about the way he moved made her think different. He had a charming effect on all the ladies, even the gay ones, and the two girls he was with hung on every word he said, especially Cat. On several occasions, Billy caught her pinching his rear and running her hands through his long braided hair. From what she gathered, Marcus belonged to her, or vice versa. She looked over at the striking young man from time to time, but didn't allow her eyes to linger too long. She knew how territorial women could be about their men and didn't want to cause any problems at the barbecue. Nonetheless, something about Marcus intrigued her.

As the night went on, people started branching off into groups. Billy was posted up off to the side, smoking a clip and sipping a Guinness when Cat approached her. She slithered over in her flared mini and thigh-high boots, wearing a smirk, as if she had a secret that she wasn't going to share. Cat made it a point to occupy Billy's vicinity, but not quite her space.

Billy felt like she was being stalked, but she didn't let Cat know she was uncomfortable. She kept tapping her foot, mouthing along with the Don B. song blasting from someone's speakers. Billy turned around and was surprised to find Cat staring at her. For a long while there was just silence, with both of them staring. Finally Cat said something.

"I hope I don't sound too thirsty, but do you mind if I hit that," Cat said, eyeing her hungrily.

"Excuse me?" Billy shot back.

"The blunt." Cat smirked. "Oh, you thought I meant . . ."

"Sorry," Billy said, a little embarrassed. She passed the blunt to Cat and watched her take deep sensual pulls.

"It's fine. I'll bet you've had a lot of girls come on to you today," Cat said in a matter-of-fact tone.

"What makes you say that?"

"I dunno." Cat shrugged. "A pretty girl at a barbecue full of dykes, call it an educated guess." She expelled smoke from the corner of her mouth and handed the blunt back to Billy.

"Yeah, I've had a few offers," Billy said, puffing on the el.

"So, you chose one yet?" Cat asked innocently.

"Sorry, not quite my cup of tea," Billy replied.

Cat raised an eyebrow. "Is that right?"

"Yes, that's right," Billy said defensively. "Listen, Cat, if you figured you'd come over here and test your luck, I didn't come here for that."

"Sorry, I didn't mean it like that, Billy. I didn't come over here to push up. I don't chase women."

"Oh, so you don't swing?" Billy looked at her suspiciously.

"Oh, I do pussy with a side of dick from time to time, but I don't chase women. They're usually chasing me," Cat said seriously.

"Aren't you the confident one?"

"Just telling you what I know, Billy. But like I said, I didn't come over here for that. I actually wanted to ask a favor."

"A favor?" Billy looked at her. "What kind of favor?"

Cat dipped into her small purse and produced a Phillie and a bag of weed so bright that it was almost yellow. "I saw you blazing and figured you wouldn't mind rolling this up for me, if I shared it with you? Sadly enough, I can't roll very well." She gave Billy a schoolgirl smile.

Billy popped the small plastic bag open and inhaled. The weed smelled like freshly cut grass, glazed in sour apple candy. She knew that whatever Cat was holding was some bomb shit. Seeing that Cat wasn't trying to press her, she relaxed a little. After rolling the blunt, she and Cat sat off to the side getting higher than a "no money down" interest rate. It didn't take long before they were laughing and talking like two old friends.

Cat was very open with Billy about how she had moved to New York with her mother and brother from Baltimore. It had always been her dream to become an actress, but she'd only found low-paying jobs and a high cost of living. Trying to stay above the poverty line, she took a part-time job as a dancer. After a while the money got so good that she found herself doing it full-time.

Cat paused for a minute as if she were deep in thought. "Billy . . . I was thinking. Well, I don't know if you do the club thing, but, maybe you'd like to come by and check out the show?"

"I don't know," Billy said.

"Come on," Cat urged. "It's a straight club, so it'll be a mixed crowd. The spot is pretty classy, too. Not one of those hole-in-the-wall joints. After my set, we can get drunk and admire some of that prime beef they have running around in there."

Billy let out a giggle.

"I wanna laugh, too, what's the joke?" a smooth voice called from behind Billy. She turned around and was surprised to see Marcus standing behind her.

"Damn, you're nosy," Cat said, playfully kissing him on the chin.

"You know I gotta keep you outta trouble," Marcus responded, twirling one of Cat's curls around his index finger. "Did I interrupt something?" he asked Billy.

"Oh, we were just smoking," Billy said nervously. Marcus was giving her the same look that Cat had been a few minutes prior. Something about being in their combined presence made Billy feel like the main course at the Last Supper.

"I see you've taken a liking to my Cat," Marcus said, shifting his gaze from Billy to Cat and back again.

"Oh, nah, it ain't like that. We were just smoking," Billy told him.

"It's okay, Billy, women come on to Cat all the time. I'm pretty used to it by now," Marcus assured her.

Not liking the way the couple looked at her, Billy got defensive. "Hold on, par. I think you got the wrong idea. I don't do women and I wasn't pushing up on your girl."

Marcus raised an eyebrow. "My *what*?"

"Aren't you and Cat together?" Billy asked, not really catching on.

Cat burst out in laughter. "Billy, we came together, but not *together*. Marcus is my brother."

The pieces finally fell into place. Those same graceful motions, the predatory glare, it was all in the genes. She felt like a real chickenhead for not getting confirmation before she opened her big-ass mouth. "Sorry, I thought . . ."

"No need to explain," Marcus spoke up. "This happens to us more often than not. We've got different fathers, that's why her eyes are green and mine are just nigger brown. Cat and I have done some freaky shit, but we've never gone that far."

"Damn, I feel stupid," Billy admitted.

Cat eased back into Billy's space. "You shouldn't. The idea is actually kind of tempting. What do you think, Marc?" She glanced at her brother. "Could we split a Billy sandwich?"

"I don't think so," Billy said sternly.

"Cut it out, Cat." Marcus stepped between them. "Billy, she was just playing with you."

"Cat!" Rose called from over by the grill.

"Oh God, she probably thinks Billy is over here putting the moves on me. Marc, why don't you see if you can keep Billy entertained while I'm gone." Cat winked at Billy and sauntered off to see what Rose wanted.

"Your sister is mad aggressive," Billy commented.

Marcus flashed a smile. "Its genetic."

"So now I'm gonna have to back you down, too?"

"Nah." Marcus raised his hands in surrender. "I'm aggressive, but not extra. I like to let a woman realize that she wants me on her own."

"I hear that."

"So which side do you play for?" Marcus asked very bluntly.

Billy's eyes flashed. "Excuse me?"

"No disrespect, sis, but considering what kind of party we're at, I gotta ask."

"Well, I could ask the same of you. Are you a catcher or a pitcher?" Billy looked him up and down.

Marcus gave her a throaty chuckle. "Good one, ma. Nah, don't fuck around. I'm strictly hitting pussy. My sister dragged me down here. I heard a free meal and some drinks, so I rolled out. I didn't know it was gonna be a rainbow parade. No offense."

"None taken, 'cause I don't do same sex, either," Billy said.

Marcus stared at her for a moment before speaking. "So what do you think has landed two straight people at a barbecue like this one?"

Billy looked around at the people in attendance and shrugged. "I don't know, a slow summer night?"

"Indeed." Marcus nodded. "Yo, if you wanna get out of here, we could—"

Billy raised her hand and silenced him. "Slow ya roll, par. Just because I don't do pussy doesn't mean I hop on every dick. We just met, my dude."

"Pardon me, gangsta, I ain't mean no disrespect," Marcus said in a mock-thug tone. This got Billy to smile a little. "But for real," he said seriously, "I just wanted to get to know you a little bit."

"That's a better way to put it," Billy said, crossing her arms. She cocked her head to the side, letting the moon catch her sparkling eyes.

Marcus watched Billy's every move, as if he'd be tested on them at the end of the night. Though she was way thugged out, Marcus found himself attracted to her. She had a defiant air about her that he wasn't used to seeing in women. Most of them turned to mush under his confident stare and boyish good looks, but Ms. Billy was hard. Not hard in the sense that she reminded him of one of the barbecue dykes, but the kind of hard that would make a man stronger. Billy definitely wasn't having it.

"I can definitely respect your directness, and I'd like to get to the bottom of it." Marcus removed a business card from his back pocket and handed it to Billy. "Why don't you come down to the spot for a drink one night? On me, of course."

Billy read the car and frowned. "This is the same club your sister dances at. You a stripper, too?"

"Nah, my clothes only come off behind closed doors. I do a little bartending and help out around the club when they need me. There'll be a lot of ass floating around, but it's nothing either of us haven't already seen before."

"What're you trying to say?" Billy asked.

"I ain't trying to say nothing. Just you need to come down and holla at me," he said, closing her hand around the card, as if it would blow away.

"I'll try." She nodded.

"You'll do more than try," he said, backing up and turning to rejoin his sister. "See about me, Billy," he called over his shoulder.

Billy watched Marcus walk away and melt back into the crowd by the grill. For the rest of the night he smoked and mingled with the partygoers, never bothering to glance back in Billy's direction. Something in her moved when Marcus spoke, something that hadn't moved in a while. Glancing at the slightly crumpled business card in her damp palm, Billy decided that she'd give some serious thought to Marcus's offer.

Paul sat in the basement of Marlene's house, perched in front of an easel. Marlene had converted the basement into a makeshift studio where he could come and work when he was there. There were canvases and poster boards of all shapes and sizes at his disposal. Her thoughtfulness was just one of the many reasons why he was sure she was the one. Chicks in the hood weren't built like his boo.

When he had first planted himself there, hours prior, it had been a blank, white canvas. Now it was host to blunt angles and vivid colors. Painting was something that always helped to sooth his nerves during tense times and Marlene definitely had him tense. She just couldn't see why Paul was so reluctant to move in with her. He knew she meant well, and would gladly share all that she had with him, but that's not how he wanted it. He had promised himself a long time ago that he would never have to lean on a woman.

When Paul was locked up, he had no choice but to depend on the kindness of others to help him get by. Larry would send him a letter or a few dollars every so often, but he knew that the man had his own life to live. The person whom he had expected to hold him down didn't measure up.

When he had gone away, he and Rhonda were somewhat serious about their relationship. Though they didn't have any kids together then, he had held her and her children down until the day they put him behind the wall. Rhonda would come up to visit sometimes or send him the occasional kite, but as far as keeping it gangsta, she had no idea what the phrase meant. Instead, Paul utilized his skills to get the things he needed. He did tattoos for those who wanted them and made holiday cards for inmates and COs. It wasn't as lucrative within the prison as drugs or prostitution, but it beat the hell out of starving. Ever since then, he vowed to do for himself.

Dipping his index and middle finger first into a jar of orange paint, then a yellow one, Paul traced an arc over the top of the canvas. The effect was that of the noonday sun across the New York City skyline. Since he was a child, painting with his fingers had always been one of his favorite methods. The feeling of the paint in different stages did something to him, which was translated to the canvas. It was as if making direct contact with the paint made him more intimate with it. The finger paintings were some of Paul's best abstract work.

As he continued to work on the painting, the floorboards behind him creaked. Marlene came up behind him and placed her arms around his back. He could feel her small breasts pressing against his bare back, and it sent shivers up his spine. She began kissing him on the neck and made her way down to the small of his back. Turning around on his stool, he pressed his cheek against Marlene's stomach, careful not to get the paint on her. She took his wrist in hers and raised his hands. She used his still-wet fingers to trace colorful lines around her nipples. Paul swallowed, watching her face contort with ecstasy.

Marlene placed a leg on either side of him and began to straddle his thigh. Even through the denim, he could feel the heat pulsing from her. As delicately as he could, he kissed her on the lips. Marlene immediately swallowed his tongue and part of his bottom lip. Her passion was like a vacuum threatening to suck the life from Paul's very lungs. He wanted to be inside of her so bad that his penis scraped against the fabric of his jeans.

Paul tried to get up to wash his hands, but she pushed him to the ground roughly. Ripping away the buttons on the nightshirt she was wearing, Marlene stood above him, ass naked. As she descended on him, he tried to direct her while undoing his belt. Again she pushed him away, letting him know who was in control. Marlene slid her wet pussy up his chest and brought it to rest on his chin. Paul darted his tongue across her clit, sending shock waves through her. With a thrust, his mouth was embedded in her pussy. Paul slurped at it like a man dying of thirst. He wasn't the biggest fan of pussy eating, but he didn't mind going down on Marlene. Her pussy always smelled fresh and clean, even on the wake-up.

Paul's paint-stained hands gripped her ass as she gyrated her hips. The motion made little colorful swirls on her skin. After the appetizer, Marlene slid down for the main course. When he entered her, it was like a five-alarm fire. She pumped slowly at first, getting the feel for his hardness, and gradually built up speed. Soon Marlene was bouncing up and down on Paul, becoming more turned on as he made faces beneath her.

Feeling himself about to cum, Paul flipped her over on her stomach and penetrated her from behind. Her pussy was so wet that it made a sloshing sound every time he pumped. In the heat of the moment he tried to grab her hair, but she moved her head out of reach. She had paid too much money getting her 'do right to have him getting paint in it. They went at it for just under an hour, exchanging control every so often. Marlene was lying on her side with one leg propped on his shoulder when he finally exploded inside her. When it was over, they lay on the floor in a spooning position, listening to the sound of each other's breathing.

Damn, I love this bitch, he thought to himself.

8

The sky was a sickly pink when Reese finally crossed Seventh Avenue en route to the projects. Yoshi had a slide, so she dipped off before everyone else. Billy never came back to the block, so Rhonda and Reese had to walk home. During the walk, Reese tried to call Teddy about twenty times. Of the twenty calls, she left fifteen very nasty messages. Billy had told her what she saw in the park and Rhonda was not happy about it. First he embarrasses her in front of her friends by talking to the young slut, then his punk-ass wife tried to blind her. Somebody's ass was gonna be grass.

When they got to 135th and Lenox, Rhonda headed east while Reese went west. It was just a short walk between their two homes. Just about everyone had gone home, save for a few hustlers trying to make their quota before the end of their shift. Reese spoke to a few cats, but didn't stop to hold a conversation. When she got to 133rd, she decided to stop at the corner store and get a blunt. They had blazed theirs and everybody else's trees all night, but Reese managed to hold on to a few buds that she was going to take to the face. As she was standing at the window waiting for her purchases, the notorious red

Hummer pulled to a stop on the corner. Reese's heart skipped a beat when the back door opened and someone stepped out.

The young man was in his early twenties, rocking a white do-rag beneath a fitted Cincinnati Reds cap. His pants hung slightly off his ass and were cuffed over a pair of black-and-red Jordans. He walked over to Reese and just stared at her without speaking.

"Can I help you?" she asked, fingering the box cutter in her purse.

"Sorry, miss, I ain't mean to scare you," the kid said, backing up a step. "My man in the ride would like to know if he could get a minute of your time?"

"What, his legs broke? Tell that nigga if he wanna holla, get his ass out the car." Even as Reese said the words she couldn't believe her luck. There was only one nigga in Harlem who had that custom red Hummer. She just hoped that it was actually Don B. that wanted to holla and not one of his flunkies. The kid walked back to the Hummer and said something to one of the passengers in the back. After receiving a reply, he stepped back to allow the back door to open. Standing on the corner of 133rd and Seventh, looking like a rock star, was Don B. himself.

Don B. was a typical Harlem nigga. Fitted cap, a white thermal shirt, and a fresh pair of burgundy Gore-Tex boots. The only difference was, his neck and arms looked like Christmas tinsel. The diamonds on his chain were nothing compared to the ones in the piece. The B hung crooked from the chain, and stopped at his belly button. The stones in his ears were so big that they made her wonder how his lobes supported them without ripping. As Don B. approached her, she could feel her mouth go completely dry.

" 'Sup, shorty," he said in a raspy voice.

Reese's brain said "speak," but her mouth said nothing. She finally gathered her wits enough to reply, "Nothing."

"So, I'm saying though . . ." Reese didn't hear much after that. The next thing she knew, she was in the back of Don B.'s hummer, on her way to only God-knows-where.

About forty minutes later, Reese was sitting in the penthouse suite of the Marriott in Times Square. She was hoping that it would be just her and Don B., but unfortunately there were a whole slew of people running about. Don B. led her to a small love seat in the far corner of the room, where bottles of champagne were already lined up. A few quick words from the kid in the Cincinnati hat, whose name was Jay, and the people that had been occupying the seat cleared out.

Don B. filled all their glasses and instructed Jay to roll a blunt. As they sat there sipping, Don B. began to touch Reese playfully. Normally, she wouldn't have really been for a nigga touching on her in front of his boys, but this was Don B., so he was allowed special privileges. She allowed his hands to roam over her ass and thighs, but drew the line when he tried to grip her pussy.

A girl who looked like it was taking all of her concentration to stand up straight shambled over to the area where they were sitting. She was balancing a silver dish, with a mound of white powder atop it. Reese began to get a sinking feeling in her gut when the girl placed the platter in the center of the table.

Jay pulled a ten-dollar bill from his pocket and folded it like a shovel. He scooped some of the powder onto the bill and snorted it off the tip. Using both nostrils, he cleaned the bill and pinched the bridge of his nose. Reese could tell by the way his eyes were watering that it was some grade-A shit.

The bill came around to Don B., and he eagerly accepted it. Scooping up nearly twice as much as Jay, he shoveled a scoop into each nostril. Don B. made a piglike snorting sound as he sniffed up the powder. His eyes suddenly went glassy as a dumb smile appeared on his face. He slid the tray over to Reese and handed her the bill.

She looked at it, dumbfounded. Getting bent wasn't the issue with Reese. Her and her girls smoked and drank every day and even dropped a little acid or E from time to time, but coke was way out of her league. She knew a lot of people dabbled with the white lady to get their buzz on, but had never imagined herself doing it. She had heard too many horror stories about people trying it once and becoming hooked. Another habit was the last thing she needed.

"What's the problem?" Don B. asked, looking like he couldn't understand her reluctance.

"I've never done it before," Reese admitted.

"Oh, we got us a virgin, huh?" Jay smirked. "Go ahead, baby, its just a little sniff. It ain't like you're doing crack."

Reese looked from Jay, to the plate, to Don B. He was looking at her, waiting for a response, while she weighed her options. Apparently, this was Don B.'s thing, and if you wanted to stop with the big dogs, you had to roll with the punches. She thought about refusing, but the look on his face suggested that he would be very disappointed. When his eyes began to wander to the other scantily clad girls in the room, she knew she was losing ground.

"Real bitches do real things," Jay said, nudging the plate closer to her.

Reese took a deep breath and figured, what the hell. "You only live once," she said, taking the bill. She scooped just over a fingernail full of the cocaine on the bill and stared at it. Feeling the heat on her from the others assembled at the table, she inhaled the snow. She immediately broke into a sneezing fit.

The cocaine felt like gunpowder in her nostrils. When the sneezing had passed, there was a dripping sensation in the back of her throat. She tried to clear it, but that only made it worse. The back of her tongue felt like she had a half-dissolved aspirin sitting on it. To make matters worse, her head started spinning at a hundred miles a minute.

Reese tried to stand, but her legs almost gave out on her. Before she could crash back to the couch, Don B. caught her by the arm. The faces around the room were distorted like something out of *The Twilight Zone*. Then as the dizziness passed, she began to feel good all over. The cocaine was like someone had wired a battery to her ass. For the first time she realized that there was music playing. The sounds of Don B.'s latest, unreleased single came through the speakers, causing everyone to get to their feet.

The girl who had brought the cocaine out was dancing in the middle of the floor. She dropped into a half split and began popping her ass to the bass of the song. Someone pushed Reese from behind and the next thing she knew, she was standing in the middle of the floor with the girl. The coked-out girl grabbed Reese by the hand and made her slap her ass, while the men in the room cheered. Don B. started grinding on Reese from behind, shoveling more coke into her nose.

She tried to turn her head, but lacked the coordination to dodge his hand. Something about the whole setup didn't feel right, but she was having too much fun to process it.

Don B. ran his finger along Reese's lip and slipped it into her mouth. The way she was sucking on his finger, he hoped to God that she sucked dick just as good. As the song played on, Reese began to feel more and more alive. The room grew extremely hot, causing her to sweat. Don B. handed her a glass of champagne, which she thirstily downed. She was so zonked that she never noticed the unusual debris floating in it.

By the third song, Reese felt like her heart was going to shoot from her chest. Trying to catch her breath, she leaned against the wall for support. Don B. placed a gentle hand on her back, then guided her into the plush bedroom. He gave his man Jay a wink over his shoulder and stepped through the door behind her. Before the door was even fully closed, he was on her.

Reese let Don B. run his hands all over her, snatching off articles of clothing as he went along. Reese's whole body felt like it was on fire. Everywhere Don B.'s hand touched her felt like he left a warm print. She didn't know if it was the cocaine or the wine, but she was ready to let it all hang out.

Once Don B. had her completely stripped, he tossed her on the bed. Reese, still feeling the effects of the drugs, ran her hands up and down her body. Her skin felt like silk as she stroked her breasts with one hand and her clit with the other. Don B. smiled greedily as he anticipated what her insides would feel like.

When he mounted her, he didn't even bother to take his clothes all the way off. He kicked off his boots and stepped one leg out of his jeans. Reese looked at the throbbing hulk that was Don B.'s penis and found that she had trouble arranging her thoughts. One side of her brain screamed for him to get inside her and beat the pussy, but the other side of her brain told her to slow her roll. Without giving her time to decide, he penetrated her raw.

Don B.'s dick felt like a stone pillar when he entered her. Reese screamed like a wild woman, drawing cheers from the next room. Every time Don B. pumped, it felt like he expanded a little more.

Crawling off his dick, Reese took him into her mouth. She sucked on him like a ten-cent Blow Pop, dripping saliva from the shaft of his dick. Don B. fucked her forward and sideways, with her screaming for more the whole time.

He flipped her over on her stomach and began savagely pounding her. She felt him explode inside her, then cum drip down her leg. When he pulled out, she tried to turn around, but he held her down and told her to hold that pose. Reese fingered herself and waited for Don B. to reenter her. When he did, there was something that felt different. The length was there, but the width wasn't. Even the hands that gripped her sides didn't feel as big. She finally managed to pull her face from the pillow and turn around. To her suprise, it was Jay, not Don B., who was hitting it.

She tried to squirm away, but he was latched onto her thoroughly. She knew what was going down was wrong, but the fire in her body only intensified. Every stroke brought her to new levels of pleasure. After Jay bust in her, another man came to replace him. At that point, it didn't even matter who was inside her. All that mattered was the fire.

9

Rhonda sat on her sofa, watching BET and sipping a wine cooler. "Slap Ya Self," the new video of the song from Don B.'s group Bad Blood, was playing on her forty-inch television. When Don B. got his company up and running, he immediately started snatching up the hungriest young niggaz in the hood and taking them under his wing. They all had aspirations of becoming stars, but so far Bad Blood had shown the most potential.

The group was composed of five young men, each representing a different borough. Lah and Jynx were from Queens and Staten Island, respectively. They were just two pretty boys that Don B. put down with the group for marketing purposes. They had all the young girls in the hood going crazy over them. The heart of the group was True, Lex, and Pain.

Lex was the gold-toothed Brooklyn kid with the extra-hard bop. Before joining the group, he made his bread stealing. He fashioned himself a modern-day cowboy by carjacking and robbing subway trains. Lex would wait until the train went through a long tunnel, like the one running from 110th and Central Park North to Ninety-sixth Street, and hit as many cars as he could before dashing off to another station. He knew Pain from high school and occasionally made trips to Harlem.

Pain was from the Bronx, the Gun Hill projects to be more specific. He had been in and out of detention centers and jails since he was thirteen. When he wasn't out trying to extort dealers, you could find him in the boxing gym, destroying heavy bags or opponents. Pain's name fit him to a T, because that was all he ever caused or gave out, pain. One Christmas when his mother was asked by a relative what she wanted, she replied, "For my son to receive a lengthy jail sentence so this evil will be removed from my house."

True was the glue that held them all together. He and Don B. had grown up in the same hood, so he knew the young man as well as he knew himself. True had gone from a snot-nose kid, slinging stones hand to hand, to a ghetto superstar. At the age of seventeen he was able to purchase his first Mercedes. Realizing that fast money might end up leading him to a bullet or a bid, he jumped on the chance to become one of Don B.'s protégés. The ironic part of it was that he was actually nice on the mic. All of the members of Bad Blood were talented, but True was a born celebrity.

Being that the group hung around the same blocks Rhonda did, she knew them all, but she and True had a history. Back when Rhonda only had two kids and True was still hugging the block, they used to mess around. It was never that serious, just a situation where they would occasionally see each other at a spot and slide off afterward. When Rhonda became pregnant with P.J., True fell back, but they kept in contact. When they would see each other, it was always love, but had never gone beyond a friendship until recently.

One day while at Rucker Park, Rhonda had bumped into True. Being that he and the group had been on tour for most of the winter and spring, no one had really seen him, so when he popped up on the scene he had to make a grand entrance. His smoke gray Roadster crept up Eighth Avenue, looking like a remote-control toy. He just nodded and smiled, looking every bit the triple-platinum rapper that Don B. was pushing him to be.

Rhonda and Reese just happened to be standing on the corner that True pulled up on. They immediately greeted each other with hugs.

They stood there kicking it for a minute, but the wayward groupies that kept popping up were putting a serious cramp in Rhonda's game. The two of them exchanged two-way info and agreed to hook up. Rhonda waited for almost a month before hitting him up. It just so happened that True was in New York at the time. She enticed him into coming over with the promise of a home-cooked meal. Being on the road didn't allow too much of that, and he eagerly agreed. The fact that she'd reminded him of how tight her head game was didn't hurt. Now, three days later, she sat in her spotless home waiting for the arrival of her guest.

When the phone rang, Rhonda almost killed herself trying to get it. Breathlessly, she answered it, only to be disappointed that it was a kid named Von and not True. Von was Rhonda's latest victim. He was originally from Yonkers, but currently resided in Virginia, where he slung birds. She had fucked him one night after leaving the club, but after sampling her fruit, he found himself turned out.

Von came to New York at least twice a month and always came bearing gifts. He had laced her and her kids with all kinds of fly shit. His dick game was whack, but the way he threw his money around made up for it. Rhonda didn't mind letting him hit it from time to time in exchange for paper, but that day she wasn't feeling him. Her pussy had True written all over it.

"What's good, ma?" he asked in his heavy voice.

"Hey, daddy, I was just thinking about you," she replied, faking excitement.

"Did the people deliver your shit?"

"Yeah, it came this morning. Thank you so much, Von, really."

"It's a small thing to a giant, baby," he said confidently, knowing that he'd be sick when the bill came for the high-priced entertainment system.

"You're the biggest nigga I know." She repressed a snicker. "When you get back up top, I'm gonna show you how much I appreciate it."

"That's what I like to hear. Yo, a nigga in the city, so let's do something. I'll be by there to pick you up in like an hour."

"Sorry, can't do it today. I got some things to take care of, so I'm trapped in the house," she lied fluidly.

"Okay, well, maybe I can come by there?" he pressed.

"Nah, my aunt is staying with me for a few days and I really don't want her in my mix like that. How about we get together tomorrow or something?"

"A'ight, ma," he said, in a defeated voice. "I really wanted to see you, but I ain't gonna come between you and your family B.I."

"Okay, daddy," she said, relieved.

"Yo, you better not have another nigga up there in my pussy, neither," he said seriously.

"Daddy, you know I'd never play myself like that. This pussy only curves to your dick."

"Muthafucking right! Holla at ya, boy . . ."

Before he could finish his sentence, Rhonda had hung up. Picking up a Dutch and a bag of weed from the table, Rhonda began twisting a blunt. No sooner had she put fire to the end of the blunt when there was a knock at the door. Adjusting the belt of her robe, she went to the peephole and looked out. A broad smiled crossed her face as she began the process of unbolting the door.

True stepped into the apartment with a real Harlem nigga swagger. The gold star hanging around his neck resembled something you'd see on a Christmas tree. The way his jeans were hanging off his ass, Rhonda knew that his wallet had nothing to do with it. Though True was on his way to big things, he was still a street nigga at heart, and operated according to the laws that governed them.

Rhonda rebolted the door and hugged True tightly. "Nigga, what's good!"

"Same old, same old. Trying to get that," he replied.

"I know that's right. Y'all niggaz is ringing bells all over the place. Every time I turn around some new bitch is on y'all dick."

"The life of a superstar," he said arrogantly as he plopped on the sofa. "Looks like you've been doing okay for yourself." He looked around, admiring her entertainment system.

"You know I'm a chick that likes to have things." She sat beside him and crossed her legs. When she did, her robe slid up, exposing her thick thigh. True tried to act like he wasn't looking, but Rhonda knew he was. She planned it that way.

He wiped his hand over his thick lips and chuckled. "So I hear."

"What's that supposed to mean?" She sat up.

"Come on, Rhonda. Don't act like because I ain't in these streets no more my ear ain't to 'em. Word is, you and your girls got Harlem on lean."

Rhonda got up off the couch and folded her arms. "See, that's why I hate the hood. Niggaz ain't got nothing to do but gossip. Yeah, I fucked a few niggaz in the hood, but that ain't no secret. Ain't no shame in my game, True, you know that."

"Be easy, ma. Ain't no need to get all excited." He leaned back, crossing his legs at the ankles. "I know how the hood can twist shit around, so I don't put much stock in what I hear. I deal with people based on how they deal with me."

She smirked. "And how do I deal with you, True?"

He pulled her down on the couch beside him and kissed her on the cheek. "In true G fashion." True's hands slid under Rhonda's robe and cupped her ass. When he ran them around to the front, he was pleased to find out that she wasn't wearing any underwear. Rhonda let him slip his finger inside her before pulling away.

"True," she said, and slid off the couch, "there'll be time for that later. I gotta go check on your food."

"I knew something smelled good in this piece." He rubbed his hands together. "What you got for a nigga?"

"It's a surprise," she said, and disappeared into the kitchen. Rhonda rattled a few pots and checked the contents of the oven. As she closed the oven door, she felt a pair of hands ran up her back. "Come on, True," she said, and giggled.

When True turned her to face him, she saw the hunger in his eyes. "Be easy, ma. You know a nigga miss that. Set it out." Without giving her a chance to protest, he grabbed her by the waist and sat her up on the counter.

Rhonda reached down and caressed his penis through his jeans. "True, we can't do it in the kitchen."

"Why the fuck not," he rasped. True reached in his back pocket and removed his Glock .40. Placing it atop the refrigerator, he began to lick Rhonda's neck. One hand slid her robe completely open, while the other fumbled with his belt. He was so hard that he almost couldn't get it out. Seeing that he was having some trouble, Rhonda got it out for him. It had been so long since Rhonda had him inside her that she was soaked from anticipation. Scooting her ass off the countertop, she slipped him in. True's penis throbbed against Rhonda's walls, causing them both to let out a moan. Just as she was about to get into her groove, he pulled out.

"What's the matter?" she said, panting.

He fumbled around in his pocket until he found a condom. "Chill, boo. Let me strap up first."

"True, you've known me since forever, I'm clean. We don't need no condom."

"No glove, no love," he said, rolling the Magnum on. True and Rhonda were tight, but he knew what she was about. Rhonda was about a dollar and fertile as hell. The last thing he needed was to get her pregnant and fuck his whole swagger up. He'd heard of the drama she was known to put niggaz through and wasn't going to subject himself to it.

Rhonda was tight, but she was too seasoned to show it. She hadn't tasted that dick in a while and she wanted to feel it inside her. She also reasoned that getting him to hit it raw would only have him more open. Rhonda had spent many years studying her vagina and could manipulate it far better than most young women her age, making her pussy one of her most effective weapons against men. She knew if she pressed True enough, he would cave and run up in it, but the risk of her plan backfiring and him leaving wasn't worth it.

When True reentered her, it still felt good, but it wasn't like that skin-to-skin action. He beat her from the front, pulling her to him every time he pumped. Flipping her around, he entered her from behind and went for broke. They went at it in several positions before he finally came.

Rhonda stood there, hands braced against the counter, legs trembling. Her inner thighs were damp and sticky, but something about it felt good. She looked back at True, whose caramel face held a relaxed smile. She knew she had him.

After giving him a cloth, Rhonda went about the task of finishing her meal. When he came out of the bathroom, a plate topped with cheese eggs and a porterhouse steak was waiting for him. True sat and devoured his meal while Rhonda hopped in the shower. When she came out, they puffed two blunts of haze and went at it again. By the third round they had run out of condoms, but she had him so worked up that he jumped out the window and hit it anyway.

Rhonda sucked him, fucked him, and licked his ass. She made it a point to take it in her mouth when he was ready to pop for the last time. True emptied all that he had left down Rhonda's throat and she greedily took it. She wanted to make sure that he remembered just who the fuck she was. The groupies he met on the road didn't have shit on her when it came to being nasty. When it was done, all he could say was, "Damn!"

After two glasses of water and a Heineken, True lounged on Rhonda's couch, smoking a Newport. Rhonda moved throughout the living room, wearing nothing but a thong and tank top, straightening up the mess they'd made. Rhonda spotted a loose weed bag that she'd missed on the first sweep of the living room. Instead of bending over to pick the bag up, she dropped it like it was hot, letting him see that phat-ass jiggle.

True rubbed his groin and continued to watch her go about her routine. If his boys knew where he was right now, they would surely clown him. Everybody knew that Rhonda was a scandalous chick, but they just knew what the streets said. He and Rhonda had grown up on the same block under the same conditions. Rhonda had five gladiators for older brothers, and at one point or another had gone toe to toe with each. Her mother let them rule the house, so what they said was pretty much the skinny. It was a hard-knock life, and Rhonda had to fight for her respect.

Once she got out on her own, she realized how hard knock it really was. She quickly understood the jungle creed of the strong must feed. And feed she did. Rhonda didn't really have any life skills to speak of, but she was living better than most employed people. Though she had body she wasn't the best-looking girl out of the group, so she got it the only way she knew how, through game.

10

Rhonda stood at her bathroom mirror singing Trina's "Da Baddest Bitch," fixing her hair. It had been fun, but eventually True broke the news that he had to leave. Rhonda had expected as much, so she wasn't tripping. After throwing on some sweatpants and a T-shirt, she offered to ride him downstairs.

While they were descending in the elevator, he handed her a small fold of bills. She quickly fanned through them, guesstimating about two hundred dollars. Rhonda felt funny about taking the money from True because she genuinely liked him, but it didn't stop her from stuffing the money into her pocket. True was a good dude, but he had it and she needed it.

They exited the building into the afternoon sun. True's BMW 540 was parked right in front of the building, so he didn't have far to go. As he and Rhonda started walking down the path toward the car, Pooh and Alisha came jogging up to the building. They were both draped in their school's mandatory white tops and blue bottoms.

"What's up, True?" Pooh said, punching True in the arm.

True threw a few phantom punches at Pooh. "Look at you, ya little bad muthafucka. Get outta here before I slap you," he joked.

"I seen ya new video," Alisha said, playfully pushing True. "Why y'all always gotta look so mean?"

"We gangsta rappers, shorty," True replied.

"Yeah right, True." She placed her hands on her tiny hips. "You'd have to have shot somebody to be a gangsta rapper. Shine shot some people, so he's gangsta. You, you're just a nigga from the hood."

"You better watch your fucking mouth." Rhonda swatted at Alisha, but the preteen danced out of her reach. "I'm gonna bust you in your smart-ass mouth if you keep running it. Apologize to True for being disrespectful."

"It's cool, Rhonda. I know Lisha don't mean nothing by it," True assured her. "She's just her mother's child."

"Yup." Alisha smirked at her mother.

"You know what? Take your little ass upstairs before I kill you, Lisha," Rhonda snapped.

Little Alisha sucked her teeth and stormed toward the building. "Come on, Pooh."

Pooh looked from his sister to his angry mother and decided to bow out gracefully. "Later, True." He dapped the young rapper and hurried to catch Alisha.

"Bad-ass kids," Rhonda said offhandedly.

True pushed her playfully. "Stall her out, shorty. You know Alisha ain't no worse than you were at that age. I can remember your brothers chasing your fast ass up the block back in the day."

"Nigga, please. I wasn't nothing like that little heifer. She's gonna fuck around and make me do something to her."

"You're still crazy as ever. But check it, I'm outta here. I gotta go meet my niggaz and hit the studio. Hit me up, though," he said, holding his two-way in the air.

Rhonda hugged True and stood in front of the building, watching him swagger to the car. Halfway to the curb, he was approached by a young lady whom Rhonda knew by sight. Rhonda thought about checking the little bitch, but she didn't want to play herself. True wasn't her man yet, and she had no right to cock-block. True smiled and said a few words to the girl before signing a paper bag for her and continuing his walk. *Groupie bitch*, Rhonda thought to herself.

At the same time True hit the alarm on the Beamer, a black SUV pulled into the spot behind his. She didn't recognize the car and was too far away to get a good look at the plates. When the driver's side door opened, all Rhonda could mutter was "fuck," as Von stepped out.

True saw the light-skinned kid stepping out of the truck, but didn't pay him a whole lot of attention. He was drained and tired. The only thing that was on his mind was getting back to the crib and taking a nap before the group's show that night at Club Exit. Halfway to his car, True was cut off by a familiar face, riding a ten-speed.

"What's the science, God?" Crazy Eight asked, riding circles around True.

"Crazy Eight." True greeted him with a smile and a pound. Back in the day, Eight's little brother Harv and True had made a few moves together, so he had a soft spot for Eight. "What da deal, yo?"

"Nothing much, God, you know how I do it. Yo, I'm glad I caught up with you, son. On the real, I got the hottest tape on the streets right now. Let me kick something for you."

"Eight, I was kinda in a rush . . ."

"Check it, God: *I hold the block with my nine, and kill swine. Can't stand a pig, they don't want us to live . . .*"

Eight went on for almost ten minutes and still wasn't saying nothing. True wanted to take his hammer out and bang himself, but he settled for a more subtle approach. "Yo, that shit was hot, kid," True lied.

"Word up, True. I'm out here putting it down for all my sons in the struggle. But on the real, you need to listen to my demo."

"Hit me wit' it later, I gotta roll," True said, continuing his walk to the car.

"Nah, I got it right here!" Eight called after him, catching up on his ten-speed. "You just check it out, my dude."

"A'ight," True said, getting in the car. To his surprise, Eight opened the other door and was about to load his bike into the backseat. "Eight, fuck is you doing?" True looked at him sideways.

"I thought we was about to burn the road up and listen to the CD, God?" Eight asked seriously.

True didn't say it, but the look he gave Eight let him know that he was going too far. "My dude, I got something to do."

Eight placed his bike back on the curb and stepped away from the car. "Okay, True. I respect it, fam. Listen to my joint and get back with me."

"A'ight," True said as Eight closed the door.

The man watching True from the truck was a big-lipped kid, with a slightly receding hairline. The whole time that True rounded his car to get into the driver's seat, he kept his eyes glued to him. Since becoming semifamous, True was used to cats staring at him, but there was something in the kid's eyes that he didn't like. Right after Crazy Eight had gone he placed his .40 cal on his lap as he started the engine.

In the rearview mirror, True saw the big-lipped kid get out of the truck and head in his direction. True's heart began to pound in anticipation of what was about to pop off. He didn't know the kid's face, so he was pretty sure he had never crossed him, or given him reason to want to harm him, but with hating-ass niggaz operating the way they did, a reason wasn't necessary. As the kid drew nearer the driver's side window, True checked to make sure there was one in the chamber of the Glock.

Von clenched and unclenched his fists as he approached the car. Whoever the kid was who was hugged up on Rhonda was about to get himself checked. Von was sure the kid saw him approaching in the rearview, yet he didn't move. Von figured that he was probably shitting his pants, which only made him feel even bolder. He opened his mouth to say something smart, but the words got stuck in his throat when he saw the hammer resting on True's lap.

"Can I help you?" True glared up at Von.

For a minute Von just stared, dumbfounded, until eventually he was able to find his voice. "Oh, my fault, yo. I just wanted to say ya new video is dope."

True just nodded and repressed the urge to laugh at Von's cowardice. "Thanks. Cop that album, son," True said, putting the car in gear and peeling off on Von, who stood there looking like a clown.

Von must've raised hell for almost a half hour. He pressed Rhonda with questions as to who the cat in the Beamer was, and made accusations and threats about what he would do to him. Rhonda knew how True rocked, so she saw right through Von's lie. He was trying to make it seem like he was the one who was pulling the G moves and not the other way around.

She insisted that he was just a friend from the block, but was careful not to divulge his name. Rhonda mock-pleaded with Von not to kill her childhood friend, knowing damn well if he went looking for True, he'd likely be out of her hair forever. Though it was tempting, she didn't want to be the cause of Von getting murdered, or True going to prison. After whispering lies about how she respected his gangsta too much to play him dirty, Von eventually calmed down.

After jetting upstairs to check on the kids, Rhonda came back down and got in the truck with Von. They hit a few spots in Harlem so he could check on a few things and see some people he knew. Rhonda didn't mind, because the longer they stayed cruising, the less likely he was to ask for some pussy. As if reading her mind, Von suggested they get a room.

"Von, you know I can't leave my kids in the house by themselves. I've been gone long enough," she protested.

"Come on, baby. A nigga is backed up," he pleaded.

Rhonda saw the thirst in Von's eyes and decided to play on it. "Nah, Von. We can't do that. I've got to cook dinner for the kids and I gotta meet somebody later on."

"Who you gotta meet?" he asked.

"Nobody," she replied.

"Rhonda, don't fucking play with me. Its bad enough I come around and find you hugged up with some supposed friend, now you got a date and shit."

"It's not a date, Von."

"Then what is it?"

Rhonda didn't respond. Instead, she busied herself looking out the passenger's window. Through reflective glass, she could see the insecurity in his face. She let a few dramatic seconds pass, then turned to face Von. "Listen, daddy, if I tell you where I'm going, you have to promise not to get mad."

"Stop playing and tell me," he demanded.

"Okay, this is the deal. Welfare is supposed to have been paying part of my rent, but I got a letter in the mail saying they fell behind with the payments. I've tried calling my worker, but keep getting the voicemail. If I don't come up with the balance, they're gonna try and put me and my kids out."

Von's eyes got wide. "What? Why didn't you tell me you needed some bread?"

"Von, you know I don't like to come to you like that. You do enough for me as it is."

"So what's up with this person you're supposed to meet?"

"Well, I know a guy who works at this strip club. He says he'll let me tend bar there a couple of nights a week so I can make a few dollars. The thing is . . . I have to tend bar topless."

"Oh, hell nah," Von almost shouted. "You say you can't come to me, but you'd go to a pimp for the money?"

"He's not a pimp, Von. He manages a club."

"Same shit, Rhonda. Listen, boo, I'm getting too much bread in Virginia to have my shorty shaking her ass at a club. How far behind in the rent are you?"

Rhonda tingled with excitement. She hadn't intended on hitting Von in the head again so soon, but he had put himself out there. She didn't allow other men to just pop up on her, and he sure as hell wasn't an exception to the rule. She had to teach him a lesson, so she blurted out, "Twenty-five hundred."

Von winced when she said the figure. He had just spent a grip on her entertainment system, now the bitch needed another two grand to pay her back rent. Rhonda was turning out to be the most expensive lay he ever had. He couldn't blame anyone but himself, though. He wanted to play the roll for the young Harlem chick, so he had to play it to the end. Reaching in the glove box, he pulled out a roll of bills and handed them to Rhonda.

"Pay ya rent, and use the rest to buy you and the kids something," he said.

"Oh, thank you, daddy." She hugged him.

"It's a small thing, boo."

Rhonda smiled devilishly. "You know what, daddy? Since you've been so good to me, I'm gonna be good to you."

"Oh yeah? What you got in mind?"

"Don't worry about it, just drive."

Von pulled out into the afternoon traffic wondering what the hell Rhonda had up her sleeve. Three blocks later, he found out as she pulled out his small, fat penis and put it in her mouth. Von leaned his head back against the headrest and moaned as Rhonda took him to another world.

11

Yoshi stepped from the cab on the corner of 147th and Convent with the grace of a jungle cat, meaty thighs pressing against the fabric of her capris pants. She wore a tan hat with a wide brim, to try and protect her from the ever merciless sun, letting her dark hair low from beneath it. All eyes were on her as she headed up the block.

As she entered the walk-up apartment building, she literally bumped into Jah. When she braced her hands against his chest, she could feel the heavy vest strapped to him. Jah looked like he was about to reach for something until he realized who it was. Letting his hand fall easily back to his side, he smiled at Yoshi.

"Damn, nigga, where're you going in such a hurry?" Yoshi asked.

"My fault, Yoshi," Jah said. "I had to see my man, and I ain't wanna be on this block like that dirty. Jumpouts all up and down this shit. What you doing over here?"

"Gotta go check my grandmother."

"Word, I ain't know you had family on this block."

"There's a lot you don't know about me." She gave him a seductive wink.

Jah moved closer, invading her space. "Then you need to let a nigga find out."

"Cut it out, Jah." She pushed him back to a comfortable distance. "What am I supposed to do with your young ass?"

He smirked, as if he had been waiting for her to ask that very question. "Let me show you how a real man treats a lady."

Yoshi sucked her teeth. "Oh, so you're a real man?"

"Let me tell you something, Yoshi," Jah said, becoming serious. "I might be young, but I'm a young dude with purpose. I'm gonna blow up or throw up out here, ma. Think on that one and get back with me." Jah winked at her and hotfooted it down the block.

Yoshi waited until he was a good distance away to smile. Yoshi had spent more time around Paul because he was Rhonda's baby daddy and closer to her age, but she had known Jah since forever. She watched him grow from a bad-ass li'l nigga on the block to a young cat on the come-up. Jah was known as a nigga who was down to do whatever. It didn't matter if it was slinging stones or hitting a nigga up, if there was paper involved, he was with it.

"Thug-ass nigga," Yoshi said, and laughed before heading into the building.

Jah hit the block feeling like he was on top of the world. The sun was shining and he had a hundred sack of Sour Diesel stuffed in his sock. When his man from uptown had called and told him he had come up on some Diesel, Jah wasted no time coming to see him. A lot of cats claimed to have the rare buds, but only a few had the real deal. His man was one of those few.

Crossing 145th and Lenox, he spotted young Tech posted up in front of the bar with some cats. The bar usually didn't open until after dark, but something must've been going on that day. The owners were known to adjust their hours, depending on what was happening and who made the request. Jah knew most of the faces, but one he didn't recognize right off. The dark-skinned man, sporting a bald head and a bunch of tiny gold chains, had a familiar face, but Jah couldn't seem to place it. As Jah approached, the cat's eyes locked on him and he couldn't help but wonder if it was someone he may have wronged along his travels. If that was the case, he was glad he brought his .40 out with him.

"What's good, Jah?" Tech beamed. Tech was a few years younger than Jah and headed down the same path. At age fifteen, he was already building up a lengthy rap sheet. Tech was always down to put in work, whether it be pulling a heist or going hand to hand on the streets. He had visions of being the next Nino Brown, but at the rate he was going he'd most likely be dead before he hit drinking age.

"Jah? Is that li'l-ass Jahlil?" the stranger asked in a voice that sounded like he smoked way too many cigarettes. As soon as he opened his mouth, Jah placed his face.

"What up, Dollar?" Jah asked very unenthusiastically. Dollar was a former money getter from 144th and Seventh. Back in the day he had the streets on smash, but it all fell apart because he couldn't keep from dipping into the poison he was selling. About eight years prior, he had gotten knocked in one of his crack houses. Dollar was so high at the time of his arrest that he didn't even realize he was in jail until his arraignment three days later. After almost a dime behind the wall, he was back on the streets.

"Man, I ain't seen you in what, eight or nine years?" Dollar slapped him five.

"Eight," Jah reminded him. "When did you touch down?"

"Two or three days ago. I'm just coming through, making sure everything was how I left it," Dollar said with a grin, showing off his gold teeth.

"Same shit, different day. It was good seeing you, Dollar, but I gotta bounce," Jah said, trying to walk off.

"Hold on, man." Dollar grabbed Jah by the arm, ignoring the murderous look the young man was giving him. "We was about to go inside and have a drink on some welcome home shit. I know you got time to drink wit' ya nigga?"

"Dawg, it's a little too early to be drinking. Maybe later."

"Oh, you done got too big to break bread wit' a cat?" Dollar asked in a challenging tone.

"Dollar, you know this li'l nigga ain't old enough to drink," Booby said mockingly. He was a local shit bird who jumped on the dick of anyone who he thought was holding a few dollars.

"Bullshit. My li'l homey is good wherever I say he is. Come on, Jah," he said, throwing his arm around the youngster's shoulder. "Just have one with me and you can go back to snatching purses or whatever the hell it is you're up to these days." Dollar steered him toward the bar and Jah grudgingly allowed it.

Even in the middle of the day, the interior of the bar was pitch black. A withered old man wearing a gangsta suit stood behind the bar cleaning glasses. When he noticed the men enter, he gave a half smile and waved them to the seats with a crooked finger. Booby took a seat at the end, leaving a stool available on either side of Jah. Tech took the right, while Dollar plopped on the left, inches from his .40.

"Jackson, give us a round of my usual shit. For the next hour I don't wanna see a dry glass in the room!" Dollar barked. There wasn't a damn soul in the bar other than the five of them, but Dollar said it like it was a packed house.

"You got it, Big D," Jackson said, pulling a large bottle of Jack Daniel's from beneath the bar. He raised the bottle, but stopped short, zeroing in on Tech. "Hold on, man. You boys are good, but I ain't serving the kid." He thumbed at Tech.

"Come on, yo, I can hold my liquor. Why you acting like that?" Tech protested.

"I don't give a good goddamn what you can hold, I ain't losing my license over some wet-behind-the-balls teenybopper," Jackson said, squinting at Tech.

"All right, give the young boy a soda then, and set that fire out for the rest of us," Dollar said, patting the bar top. "So Jah, I hear you're out here on your real thug shit?" He turned to the young man.

"You can't believe everything you hear," Jah told him.

"Come on, Jah. You ain't gotta front for me, yo. I ran into a couple of heads from 'round the way while I was locked down. They say you out here doing ya one-two."

Jah shrugged. "I'm just trying to see tomorrow, kid."

"You hear this nigga?" Dollar asked Booby, who just shrugged. "Spoken like a real *made* nigga," Dollar said sarcastically.

"Yo, niggaz know what time it is wit' my dude out here," Tech said, supporting Jah's notoriety.

"Shut yo young ass up!" Booby shouted from his perch.

"Damn, Jah, you even got cheerleaders?" Dollar elbowed him. "You came a long way from the shorty I knew, snatching chains for bread."

"I don't snatch chains anymore," Jah said easily as he sipped his Jack. He cut his eyes to the door as two young women came in, escorted by a dude wearing rhinestone-studded sunglasses.

"So it seems." Dollar sneered. "Say, do you remember when we used to run you up outta the game room? Shit, you were always trying to hang around the big boys and pop your li'l cherry. I used to give you dollars for going to the store for me," he said loud enough for the new trio to hear. Booby slapped the bar laughing, only making the situation worse.

"Times have changed," Jah said with a chill in his voice. "I don't go to the store for dollars."

"I can respect it with you being all grown up." Dollar downed his drink. Fishing around in his pocket, he pulled out a five-dollar bill. "So why don't you take this and go get me a pack of cigarettes!" Dollar roared as if he had made the funniest joke of the century.

By the time Dollar had turned to tell Jah he was just joking, a glass was being broken against his face. Jah followed with a left hook, staggering Dollar. The older man tried to right himself, but the knee Jah slammed into his gut doubled him over. With the wind knocked out of him, Dollar crumpled to the ground. Booby slid off the bar, but Jah already had the drop on him with his .40.

"Booby, that's my word, if you try me I'm gonna paint that fucking jukebox behind you," Jah warned him. Booby thought about it and sat back down. "Look at me," Jah said, lifting Dollar by the front of his shirt. "I know you've been away for a while, so maybe you haven't gotten the wire. I'm a beast on these fucking streets, son. The next time you come at me like that, you better be ready to murder something, faggot!"

Everyone in the bar was silent, waiting to see what Dollar's fate was to be. Jah dropped him back to the ground and looked around cautiously. "What happened?" Jah asked Jackson, pointing the .40 in his direction.

Jackson raised his hands in surrender. "Shit, not a damn thing, blood!"

Jah backed out of the bar, keeping his pistol down, but ready. He kept looking from the front door to the people assembled in the bar, ready to pop off at the first sign of trouble. Booby was shooting him a murderous look, but he knew better than to challenge Jah. Dollar had been getting him high all day, but they weren't cool enough for him to go against a hammer.

When Yoshi got to the fifth floor, the first thing she heard was the blare of music. Daddy Yankee's "Gasolina" vibrated through the walls of apartment 5F. Yoshi let herself in and immediately smelled the pungent odor of marijuana. At the end of the hall she could see her cousin Selma *ass popping* in front of the living room mirror.

Selma was fifteen years old and dying to catch an STD. Like Yoshi, she was a mix of Latin and black. The difference was Yoshi's father was Puerto Rican, while Selma's was Salvadorian. They both had long dark hair, but where Yoshi stood five foot five, Selma was only five feet even.

Selma was the type of impressionable young girl who believed what she saw in rap videos. Yoshi or one of her cousins were always chasing Selma from one set or another, trying to keep her from the wicked things that lurked there. It was said that a few niggaz had tasted her fruit, but she wasn't totally out there. Selma had G to be so young, but without guidance, she would be carrion to the vultures who stalked the New York underbelly.

Selma was standing in the middle of the living room, going through a series of moves she had picked up somewhere. The denim shorts she wore barely covered her tight little ass, letting just a hint of cheek show. On the front of her tight T-shirt was a quote from the Pussy Cat Dolls: *Don't you wish your girl was a freak like me?*

"Look at you," Yoshi said, coming into the living room. "This is what you do with your free time?"

"Don't start, Yoshi," Selma said over her shoulder, never breaking from her routine.

"Girl, you're only fifteen and trying to drop it like it's hot." Yoshi slapped her on the ass playfully.

Selma turned around and planted one hand on her hip. "Ain't nobody dropping nothing. I'm just staying on top of what's up."

"You need to stay on top of school instead of them trick dances," Yoshi said, flopping on the couch.

"I know you ain't preaching. Don't you strip?" Selma shot back.

"I'm an exotic dancer, not a stripper, smart mouth."

"If it walks like a ho," Selma said slyly.

"You keep playing if you want to, Selma. When I punch you in the fucking mouth, I guess you'll be satisfied. Besides, I'm grown and you're still a child. You need to try acting like one."

"Whatever, Yoshi."

"Where's Grandma?"

Selma sucked her teeth. "Obviously she's not here."

"Keep running your mouth, and I'm gonna slow it down for you," Yoshi warned her.

"I thought I heard your mouth, Yoshibelle," Vivian said, coming out of the bedroom. Selma's mother was a thick woman with sharp features. She was only thirty-three and had held together well after childbirth. Motherhood had slowed her roll, but once Selma got older, she'd picked up where she had left off. It wasn't unusual to find her at the club, or other happening events, getting her swerve on. Though this sometimes irked Selma, Vivian didn't care. She was a woman enjoying her life.

"What's up, Aunt Viv?" Yoshi gave her a high five.

"Trying to live. What're you two out here arguing about?"

"Selma's smart-ass mouth." Yoshi shot the teen a look.

Vivian turned to her daughter. "Selma, what did I tell you about respecting your elders?"

"Please, what elder?" Selma rolled her eyes. "Yoshi is only a few years older than I am."

"She's still your older cousin, so respect her."

Selma turned her scornful glare on Yoshi. "You're always starting, Yoshi. Sometimes I can't fucking stand you."

"You watch that damn mouth, Selma!" Vivian snapped.

"Why do I always have to get yelled at? I hate this house!" Selma shouted and stormed into the bedroom.

Vivian flopped on the sofa, worry lines etching her brow. "That girl is gonna drive me to the crazy house."

"Selma is off the hook," Yoshi said, eyes still on the path of Selma's exit. "What's gotten into the girl lately?"

"Smelling her ass. It seems like the older she gets, the harder she becomes to deal with. I've tried everything from being hard on her, to trying to deal with her like a friend. She rebels against it all."

"You need to try going upside her head," Yoshi said seriously. "Selma is getting beside herself."

"You're one to talk," Vivian said, raising her eyebrow. "Yoshi, you weren't exactly an angel."

"True, I wasn't, but I waited until I was at least out of high school to start acting a fool."

"Yeah, right, Yoshi. You waited until you were out of high school to start being blatant with it. You might have fooled your mom, but not me. I always suspected you were up to no good." Vivian giggled. "But seriously, when are you going to get it together?"

Yoshi sighed. "Come on, Viv, don't start this again."

"I'm serious, Yoshibelle. There's no future in the way you're living."

"I can't tell. I got money and my own crib."

"But look how you're getting it. Yoshi, you think you can make a career out of stripping?"

"I'm an exotic dancer," Yoshi corrected her.

"That's just a fancy way to say 'stripper.'"

"Aunt Viv, why are you so down on me for dancing? You used to do it."

"Yeah, and look what it got me. I ended up being young, pregnant, and on my own. My life ain't easy, Yoshi."

"Well, neither is mine. No offense, Auntie, but I ain't trying to get caught up with none of these niggaz on some kid shit. I'm strictly about my bread. By hook or crook, I gotta get it how I get it. If stripping is what's gonna pay my bills, then that's what I'm gonna do."

Vivian shook her head sadly. "Yoshi, you can't make a career out of stripping. Take it from someone who knows. It'll only be a matter of time before your breasts begin to sag a little, or your ass isn't as firm as it used to be. Then what are you gonna do? You're the shit now, but that's until something younger comes along."

"Well, by then I'll have my own club," Yoshi said, as if she was being witty.

Vivian touched Yoshi's face. "Baby, how you gonna run an establishment with no type of skills? It takes more to run a club than overseeing the employees. There's a whole flip side to the coin that you're not seeing."

"Listen, Aunt Viv, I'm running in the fast lane and I ain't gonna slow down until I reap all the benefits of life. If this stripping shit was to dry up today or tomorrow, I'm still gonna get money."

"How, by continuing to sleep around the way you do?" Vivian asked, a bit more sharply than she had intended.

"You don't know what I do!" Yoshi snapped.

"Yoshi," Vivian looked at her seriously, "who do you think you're talking to? The streets talk, mami. Your name is ringing in the hood."

"Auntie, you need to stop listening to what people say. These muthafuckas don't have anything better to do but gossip."

"I know what you've been up to, but you're grown, so I'm not always on you about it."

"Auntie . . ."

"No, Yoshi. Just listen to me for a minute. You are a beautiful and intelligent girl. You have your youth and your health. Why throw it away running around like a piece of trash?"

"I don't have to listen to this shit." Yoshi tried to walk off, but Vivian grabbed her by the arm.

"That's your problem, Yoshi. You never wanna listen. Baby," she stroked Yoshi's cheek, "I see girls like you every day at the clinic. Beautiful young women of color, poisoned by these streets, and too bullheaded to know their own worth. I don't want that to happen to you."

"That's *not* gonna happen to me."

"That's what we all say when we're out there. Do you know how many girls I see come in on a regular basis who are either pregnant or getting treated for STDs? There are some things that a shot won't get rid of."

"I'm careful," Yoshi said.

"That's the same thing my sister said," Vivian reminded her.

Though they were only words, they hit Yoshi like a physical blow. Like all the women in their family, Yoshi's mother Carol was beautiful. Unlike Vivian, Carol wasn't the party girl. She was quiet and kept to herself. Yoshi's father was the first man she had ever been with, and though he didn't stick around past Yoshi's fifth birthday, it didn't stop Carol from shouldering the load of both mother and father. It was she and Yoshi against the world.

It was years after the breakup with her first lover before Carol had healed enough to take another. Let her tell it, Cash was the beginning and the end. At six foot three with light skin and curly hair, all the women went crazy over him, and Cash reveled in it. People always suggested to Carol that he was sleeping around, but she turned a blind eye to it. She convinced herself that a man was just going to be a man and let it go. As long as he held her number one above everyone else, she tolerated it.

About a year into the relationship, Carol had come down with a terrible case of the flu. She thought it would pass, but a month later it was still there. After some coaxing, she let Vivian take her to the doctor to run some tests. When they got the results back, the doctor revealed that she was HIV positive.

The news brought Carol's whole world crashing down around her. Cash, of course, denied giving it to her, but she hadn't been with anyone else. The bastard even packed his things and took off after infecting her. For loving this man, Carol had condemned herself to death.

The first few weeks were the hardest for Carol and her family. With the help of the doctors, they tried to convince her that there was life after the HIV virus, but all she could think about was how she wouldn't be around for her daughter. Though Yoshi was young at the time and didn't really understand what it meant to have the virus, she understood that it was fatal. She tried to be there as much as she could for Carol, but nothing seemed to move her anymore. Yoshi would sometimes listen to her mother cry herself to sleep between shots of Jack

Daniel's. They say alcohol numbs the pain, but it didn't do much to ease Carol's.

After a while she seemed to be coming out of it. She had quit drinking and gone back to work. Everyone was glad to see her coming out of her stupor and getting on with life. This lasted until right before Yoshi graduated from junior high school. She came home one day and found the house flooded with water. She called out to her mother, but got no answer. Making her way to the back, she found the source of the flooding. Someone had left the water running in the tub.

She figured her mother had done it by accident and went into the bathroom to shut it off and begin trying to clean up. It was there that she found her mother. Carol had settled into the tub and slit her wrists. The water was pinkish from the blood that still ran from Carol's veins. Yoshi threw up almost a half-dozen times before she was finally able to call 911. The image of her mother's prone, nude body as the ambulance carted her away was something that would stick with Yoshi for the rest of her days.

"Yoshi," Vivian continued, "I'm not trying to hurt you, I swear I'm not. I just want you to see what you're doing to yourself before it's too late."

Yoshi looked away so her aunt wouldn't see the tears forming in her eyes. "I'll be okay."

When she made to leave, Vivian stopped her with an embrace. "You just don't see it, do you?" she said, with tears in her eyes. "I love you, Yoshibelle."

Yoshi could feel the lump forming in her throat. "I gotta go," she said, grabbing her purse off the couch. "Tell Grandma I came by." She didn't even wait for Vivian to answer before she made hurried steps toward the front door. By the time she got across the threshold, the tears had burst from her eyes and were soaking the front of her new blouse.

12

Marlene sat within the confines of her plush office, listening intently to the woman across from her as she explained her situation. For the last five years she had been used as a punching bag by her husband. She told the attorney how the man would go into drunken rages and proceed to beat her and her son. When asked why she didn't go to the police about the abuse, the woman informed Marlene that her husband was a respected officer of the Thirty-second Precinct. The beatings finally stopped several days prior when their son had taken the man's gun and shot him. Her sixteen-year-old son was now being held in the Tombs awaiting his court date.

"I've talked to several different lawyers and they either want to charge me a fortune or try and convince my son to take a plea bargain," the woman said, sobbing. "The police turned a blind eye to one of their own breaking the law. Now my poor son is sitting up in the system for trying to protect his mother. Ms. Tate, I really don't know what to do."

Marlene studied the woman. She was a bit on the chubby side, but hardly fat. Her yellow face still bore traces of the bruises inflicted by her husband. Some were so deep that Marlene doubted they would ever heal. She felt for the woman, not because the NYPD was trying to twist another tragedy to take the heat off them, but because she, too, had been a victim of abuse.

She was fresh out of law school and living in Montclair, New Jersey. It was while working at a small firm out there that she had met Michael Brown, the firm's junior partner. He was young, fine, and on his way to doing big things. In no time at all, Michael had managed to sweep her off her feet, and Marlene found herself abandoning her roommate to move into Michael's condo. Her mother advised against moving in with the man so quickly, but Marlene was a girl in love. Michael played the roll of loving spouse for the first few months of the arrangement, but then came the old adage, You never really know someone until you live with them.

Marlene hadn't noticed at first, but Michael drank quite a bit. Granted, there was no harm in having a beer after a hard day's work, but Michael would often down a six-pack at a time. Normally, Michael was a sweetheart, but when he drank he became someone else. He would curse Marlene and shove her around if the house wasn't cleaned to his standards or his dinner wasn't hot enough. He had even slapped her a time or two during really heated arguments.

Marlene was never one to take abuse, but she was stuck on Michael, so she convinced herself that they would work it out. Over time, the drinking got worse and the physical abuse became more frequent. Marlene had finally had enough and notified Michael that she was leaving. His response to this was a black eye and two bruised ribs. Michael made it very clear to Marlene that the only way she would be leaving him was in a box.

Michael became very possessive, clocking Marlene's every move. She wasn't allowed to leave the house unless it was with him, and they worked together so there was no escape there. Marlene became a prisoner of love.

The mental and physical abuse went on for quite some time before Marlene finally got up the courage to leave. While Michael was passed out drunk, Marlene loaded the majority of her things into the back of her car and stole away. She had planned to put New Jersey and everything associated with Michael behind her. Before she left, she placed two phone calls, one to the firm and the other to her cousin Shank down in Philly. Michael was fired from the firm and slapped with an assault charge, but not before Shank and a few of his boys beat him damn near to death. Marlene managed to break the cycle of abuse, but it took years of therapy before the scars even began to heal.

"Don't worry about it, Mrs. Johnson." Marlene patted her on the hand. "We're going to do all that we can to get your son out of jail."

"I don't have a lot of money saved up, but I'm willing to work off the debt," Mrs. Johnson said seriously.

"Don't worry about the bill, Mrs. Johnson. I'm taking the case pro bono."

"Bless your heart." She sobbed, kissing Marlene's hand. "I'm gonna put you in my prayers."

"You do that, Mrs. Johnson, and we'll call it even."

"Hello?" Reese answered the phone in a sleep-ridden tone.

"Bitch, I know you ain't asleep!" Rhonda said on the other end, her voice sounding like a sonic boom.

"Rhonda, what the hell are you calling me so early for?"

"Early? Reese, its almost twelve o'clock. The sun is out, let's not waste the day."

Reese turned her heavy eyes to the digital clock on her nightstand. "Damn, I didn't even know it was this late."

"You must've had a hell of a night. What did you do after you left us?" Rhonda asked.

Reese yawned. "I had a slide."

"I should've know, with your dick-thirsty ass. Was it anybody I know?"

"Don B.," Reese said timidly.

"Bitch, you lying!" Rhonda squealed. "You know you gotta give me all the nasty details."

"Listen to you, nosy."

"Nosy, my ass. You know you wanna tell it."

"Maybe, maybe not," Reese teased.

"Well, if you tell me about your night with Don B., I'll tell you about my morning with True," Rhonda bartered.

"True? When did he come back into town?"

"A few days ago. Girl, it was some serious drama over here, but I'll tell you about it when I see you. Get your stinking ass up and get dressed. I'll be over in an hour to give you the play-by-play."

"Okay, I'll see you when you get here," Reese said, then hung up. Closing her eyes and taking a few deep breaths, Reese slid out of the bed. When she stood up, her legs felt like noodles. Her pussy still throbbed from the wild night she had had at Don B.'s suite. Due to all the drugs and alcohol she had ingested, she could only remember bits and pieces of what had gone on.

As the haze lifted from her brain, images of what she had done flashed through her mind, causing her to hang her head in shame. Don B. and his squad took turns pounding her pussy well into the morning. She knew she had played herself, but the coke and whatever else they had given her had turned her into someone else. It was as if she was watching the whole thing from the front row as opposed to being center stage. Afterward, he had offered to take her to breakfast, but she could barely walk, let alone eat. He dropped her off in front of her building and promised to call her later. Whether he would actually keep his word or not was another story.

Reese half staggered into the hallway, where her nose was immediately assaulted by the smell of her mother's cooking. Normally she would've reveled in the delicious aromas, but in the condition she was in, all it did was upset her stomach further. She had barely made it to the bathroom before the liquor and fast food she had ingested the day before came spilling out. Reese continued to throw up until her stomach was empty, then waited out the dry heaves. The cool porcelain of the toilet against her head made her feel a little better, but did nothing to help with her nausea. When she was finally able to stand, she climbed into the shower.

The water was so hot that it threatened to boil her tender skin, but she forced herself to stay under the scalding stream. The steam helped ease the throbbing in her vagina, but it would probably be a while before she was able to have sex again. She washed herself over and over, but still felt dirty.

When Reese turned the water off, she heard someone pounding on the door. Living with five people and only having one bathroom didn't allow for a whole lot of self time. It seemed as if every time she got in the bathroom, someone else had to use it. She sucked her teeth and ignored it, while she began the task of drying herself. The banging continued, followed by the high-pitched voice of her younger sister, Sharon.

"Reese, I know you hear me!" Sharon shouted.

"I'm using the bathroom, what the hell do you want?" Reese shot back.

"Someone's on the phone for you."

Reese took a moment and leaned against the bathroom door. Her head was spinning and she felt sick as a dog. The last thing she wanted was to talk to someone on the phone. Pulling her towel around herself, she opened the door.

Sharon stood there, looking like a miniature version of their mother, hair braded into two pigtails. She was a plump preteenager, with big brown eyes and smooth chocolate skin. Of all her siblings, she and Sharon butted heads the most. It was probably because their personalities were so similar. Much like Reese, Sharon thought she knew everything.

"You know how long I've been knocking on this door?" Sharon asked, holding the phone out to Reese. Reese took the phone and slammed the door without even acknowledging her sister's question.

"Hello," Reese said, placing her still-wet ear against the receiver of the cordless.

"What's up, baby," a masculine voice said. Even if she hadn't heard the commotion in the background, she'd have known who it was on the line. Of all the people who could've called her that afternoon, Bone was the one she wanted to speak to least.

Bone was Reese's on-again, off-again boyfriend. He was a notorious knucklehead who was always looking for the big score. Bone and Reese had a relationship that was built on familiarity more than anything else.

They had known each other since junior year in high school, and from the gate it was a love-hate relationship. He treated Reese fairly well, but couldn't manage to keep his hands to himself. On more than one occasion, Bone had kicked her ass. It wasn't unusual for her to pop up on the block with a busted lip or a pair of designer sunglasses to hide a black eye. When Bone got locked up, it was both a gift and a curse for Reese.

He was currently sitting up on Riker's Island, waiting to be transported upstate to serve out a three-to-nine for possession with intent to sell. He had made the foolish mistake of running a red light with two ounces of cocaine in the trunk of his car. Unfortunately for Reese, she happened to be a passenger in the car when he got stopped. She got a slap on the wrist and probation, but because of Bone's record, they slammed him. She had to report to a probation officer once a month, but she had finally managed to get a break from the relationship. Reese bit back the curse that was trying to pop out and found her voice.

"Hey," she said dryly.

"Damn, you don't sound happy to hear from a nigga," he said.

"Sorry, I'm just going through a lot right now."

"You must be, because I ain't seen you in almost two months. You don't miss a nigga?"

"It's not that, Bone. Coming out to the island is an all-day process, and I be crazy busy. I'm gonna make it out to see you this week."

"That's the same thing you said last week, and the week before," he reminded her.

"Bone, I told you that I be busy."

"Reese, I don't know what the fuck you got going on out there in the world, but you better get your shit together and start showing a nigga some love."

"Bone, don't start this shit today. I'm really not in the mood for it," she snapped.

"Bitch, I know you ain't trying to get fly."

Reese held the phone away from her ear and looked at it before delivering her response. "Bone, you've got some nerve calling my house with this dumb shit. Nigga, you must've fell and bumped your head. I got a felony on my record fucking with you, yet I still keep money in your commissary and go through the headache of coming to visit you on the island."

"Reese, that's your job!" Bone said in a very indignant tone. "I'm your man, so you're supposed to hold me the fuck down while I'm in here."

"Bone, you seem to keep forgetting that I'm not the one who put you there. I have a life, and it doesn't revolve around taking care of your grown ass. Press your mama about a damn visit."

"If I was on the streets you wouldn't be popping that shit, 'cause I'd bust your fucking head open!" he raged.

"Well, that's something I won't have to worry about anytime soon," she taunted.

"Reese, I'm gonna kill your ass!"

"Bone, you ain't gonna do shit, but try and keep one of them bulls from running up in your little shit box, you crack-slinging, jailbird muthafucka! Lose my number." In the midst of Bone's profanity-laced tirade, Reese pushed the phone's off button. No sooner than she'd sat it down on the edge of the sink, it rang again.

"Muthafucka, can't you take a hint?!" Reese barked into the phone.

"Damn, what he fuck did I do?" another male voice asked.

"Teddy? Oh, I know damn well you ain't on my line."

"Baby girl, let me explain . . ."

"You ain't got to explain shit, you child-molesting muthafucka. My girl told me she saw you hugged up on that little bitch in the park."

"Ma, that was my li'l cousin," he protested.

"You must think I was born on Stupid Avenue. Teddy, you a foul nigga. Oh, and while I'm thinking about it, tell your fat-ass wife that I'm gonna bust her shit when I catch her, since she wanna be throwing bottles at bitches. The only thing that saved her Slim Fast–drinking ass was the fact that she ran through the red light."

"Reese, I didn't have anything to do with that."

"Teddy, you had everything to do with it. But you know what? I can't blame anyone but myself," she admitted. "I'm holding on to your fat ass like you about something instead of doing me."

"Don't even play like that, you know you're my girl," he said, trying to soothe her.

"What the fuck ever, Teddy. I've been blind this long, but now I can see the light. You ain't shit, so you and that fat bitch can have each other."

"Yo, you talking real greasy right now."

"Yeah I am, but in a few minutes I won't be able to talk at all. I got a real nigga over here about to put his dick in my mouth. And you know what? Since I am a bit thirsty, I think I'll let him cum in my mouth," she taunted him.

"Bitch—"

"I ain't no bitch, you're the bitch, Teddy. I hope you and your wife will be very happy together at fat camp. Go play in traffic, you bird-ass nigga!" Reese clicked off the phone. The conversation with Bone had had her uptight, but she felt much better after kicking Teddy's ass to the curb.

Rhonda made her way up Lenox Avenue with all three of her children. Pooh skipped ahead, occasionally stopping to kick a can or a stray piece of trash. Rhonda called after him several times to slow down, but he paid her no mind. Alisha walked a few paces behind her mother, holding P.J.'s hand, who was struggling to keep up. Rhonda continued on her way, paying little attention to either of them.

When they rounded the corner of 142nd, they bumped into a neighborhood girl named Verna. A black scarf was wrapped around her head, covering her shoulder-length hair, which she kept pinned up. Verna's large ass was even more visible under her pajama pants because she wasn't wearing underwear. She had the body of a porno star, but that was about all she had going for her. Her face could've been considered cute if it weren't for the scar running from her temple to her cheek, and the lingering bruises that never seemed to heal from her many fights over the years. Verna was notorious throughout the streets of Harlem for her brutal knuckle game. There weren't many chicks on the block who were foolish enough to try her.

"What up, Rhonda," Verna greeted her, sitting her grocery bag on the ground with a clank.

"Damn, what's all that?" Rhonda asked, nodding toward the heavy bag.

"Shit, I had to go get some milk for Star. I missed my WIC recertification, so I gotta pay for this shit until they make me another appointment."

"Damn, I remember them days," Rhonda recalled. "I'm glad these little muthafuckas ain't infants no more, I remember how high that milk was."

Verna lifted the bag. "You ain't lying. These shits is five dollars a can. I can't do much more of this."

As Rhonda and Verna continued their conversation, two girls came walking up the block, with a familiar-looking young man trailing them. From what Rhonda could tell, the young man was pleading with them about something, but the girls were ignoring him. One girl wore an indifferent face, while the other's was twisted in anger. Rhonda had no idea who they were or what their intentions were, but Verna seemed to.

"I know muthafucking well this nigga ain't bring these bitches through my hood," Verna whispered to Rhonda, tightening the grip on her plastic bag.

"Who the fuck is they?" Rhonda asked, ready to ride out with her homegirl.

"Don't even worry about it, Rhonda. You got your kids with you. I got this."

"Ay yo, bitch. I need to holla at you!" the angry one barked.

Verna tilted her head. "Bitch? Little girl, who the fuck do you think you're talking to?"

"I'm talking to the bitch that's been tipping with my man," the girl shot back.

"I ain't gonna be too many bitches, yo," Verna said seriously.

"Why don't you cut this shit out," the young man said, finally catching up.

"I'll deal with your ass in a minute," the girl shouted at him. "Like I was saying," she turned back to Verna, "I heard you've been creeping with my man."

"Did he tell you that?"

"It ain't important who told me that, what I'm trying to figure out is if you got a death wish, bitch."

Verna flexed her jaw. "You got one more time to call me a bitch and we're gonna have a problem."

"Let me tell you something, bitch . . ." That was as far as the girl got. In a flash, Verna clobbered her with the bag. Cans of baby formula scattered all over the street as the girl staggered back. The second girl looked like she wanted to do something, so Rhonda caught her with a two-piece. Seeing the blood that was now running from her nose, the girl took off running before Rhonda could swing again.

Verna picked up one of the loose cans from the ground and walked over to the angry girl, who was now lying on the ground, clutching her head. "You little bitches is always coming from up on the hill talking shit." Verna hit her in the face with the can, breaking her nose. "You think about this ass whipping the next time you put your mouth in grown people's business." She whacked her again. "The dick was wack anyway."

"Yo, Verna, why you wildin'?" The young man snatched her up off his bloodied girlfriend. Without uttering a word, Verna spun on the young man and smashed the can into his jaw. The young man was out cold before he even hit the ground.

"What the fuck was that all about?" Rhonda asked, panting.

"Young bitches not knowing how to act over a piece of dick," Verna said, gathering her cans of formula.

Rhonda, not wanting to be around for the fallout, bid her friend good-bye and took her children up the block.

By the time Rhonda got to her mother's building, news of the fight had already reached the stoop. Resting in a lawn chair, recounting an exaggerated version of what had happened, was Ms. Lulu. Lulu lived on the first floor, where she spent most of her time perched in the window smoking Camels. Not much went on that she didn't see and relay to her seniors crew on the stoop.

"Hey, y'all," Rhonda greeted everyone on the stoop.

"Hey, Rhonda." Bernadine smiled, showing off her coffee-stained teeth. Bernadine didn't live in the building, but spent most of her time sitting on its stoop.

"Was you in that fight down the block?" Ms. Lulu squinted. She had horrible eyesight, but that still didn't stop her from trying to catch any and everything that went on, and getting it all ass backward.

"No, Ms. Lulu," Rhonda lied.

"I heard it was that Verna girl," Ms. Yvonne added. Her wig sat at an odd angle on her head, but no one said anything. Even standing ten feet away Rhonda could smell the Captain Morgan rum on her breath. It wasn't even midafternoon and the old woman had been sipping. It was what she, Ms. Lulu, and Bernadine did to pass the time.

"I seen her whip two girls and a *po*-lice officer," Ms. Lulu said.

"You need to quit yo lying, Lu. You ain't seen no such thing," Bernadine disputed. "That cheap-ass wine you was sipping for breakfast got you seeing things, wit' yo drunk ass."

"If that ain't the damn pot. If I recall correctly, yo thirsty ass was sitting right beside me sipping."

"I had one damn drink and that was only half a cup." Bernadine and Ms. Lulu went on like this all the time. When they'd been drinking, they were always going at it. On several occasions, they had even come to blows. But once sobriety hit, they continued as if nothing had ever happened. Rhonda caught a chill envisioning her and her crew in their places.

"Anybody at my mom's?" Rhonda asked.

"I don't know, I'm just coming out," Ms. Yvonne said.

"Ya sister Kelly was round here a while ago, but I ain't seen ya mama today," Ms. Lulu said.

Rhonda immediately felt the urge to leave. Ever since they were teenagers, she and Kelly hadn't gotten along. They were only two years apart, but had personalities like night and day. Kelly had gotten good grades and gone on to attend Spelman College before landing a job at a marketing firm downtown. She looked down her nose at Rhonda for the choices she had made in her life and made it a point to publicize it.

"I see you got the children with you." Bernadine smiled down at the trio. P.J. said "hi," and Pooh waved, but Alisha just scowled. "You ain't speaking today?" Bernadine asked Alisha.

"I said hi," Alisha said dryly.

"Umm-hmm," Ms. Lulu grumbled, staring at the child. She wanted to hop up from her chair and slap the shit out of the grown child, but she knew she couldn't blame her too much. Children only knew what they learned from their parents, and Rhonda had been the same at that age.

Trying to save face, Rhonda grabbed Alisha by the arm and shook her. "You better respect your elders, do you understand me?" The pre-teen nodded, but the anger in her face was apparent.

A young man dressed in a lavender Polo shirt and denim shorts came walking out of the building. The sun danced off his waved-up black hair and bronze skin. A gold pinky ring adorned his left hand. The piece wasn't gaudy, but tasteful. Pushing his blacked-out Prada sunglasses up on his nose, he gave the ladies on the stoop a radiant smile.

"Hey, Kelvin." Ms. Lulu touched his tattooed arm.

"Hey, ma. How you doing?" Kelvin replied in an almost musical voice.

"Where's that nice car of yours?" Bernadine asked.

"I had to get it serviced. I'm riding with a friend today." As if on cue, another young man came walking out of the building. He was about nineteen if he was a day, with cherrywood skin and shiny black curls. He smiled at the women on the stoop and walked out to the curb.

"You ain't speaking today?" Kelvin asked Rhonda.

"What up," she said, very unenthused about seeing him. Kelvin was Rhonda's younger brother and Kelly's twin. For the most part, he and Rhonda got along, or at least better than she did with Kelly. She had asked herself time and again where they went wrong with him. She loved her little brother, but didn't agree with his lifestyle. Now, Kelvin was a real street cat; she had even heard that he had a little spot on the Hill. Cats respected him in the hood, no matter what his "tastes" were.

"Uncle Kel, let me get a dollar." Alisha put one hand on her hip and extended the other one in anticipation.

"Damn, I don't even get a hello," Kelvin joked, pulling out a knot of bills. He handed each of the kids a ten and rubbed Alisha's head. "What you came to do, your usual?" he asked Rhonda sarcastically.

"Don't be funny, Elton John," she capped. "Let your sister hold something."

Kelvin rolled his eyes, chuckling. "There you go."

"What?"

"Rhonda, you stay hitting a nigga up for bread. The worst part is, I know you're out here catching 'em."

"What're you talking about, Kel? I'm out here chilling."

"Rhonda, you act like I don't know True is back in town. Your freak ass probably already hit him off."

"Forget you, Kel. You don't know what you're talking about." Rhonda brushed him off. "So you gonna let me hold something or what?"

"What you need?"

"Like a hundred."

"You bugging, I ain't giving you no hundred dollars."

"Come on, Kel. I gotta get the kids some sneakers."

"Tell their fathers to get them some sneakers. I buy the kids stuff all the time."

"A'ight, then let me hold fifty until I get my check," she bargained.

"Here, man," he handed her a bill, "don't bother me no more."

Rhonda kissed him on the cheek. "You know you love your sister."

"Here come Rita," Ms. Lulu said, pointing up the street.

Rhonda's mother was walking up the block, carrying two shopping bags and a large purse. She bore a resemblance to Rhonda, but didn't have her body and had Kelvin's bronze skin. Her hair was cropped short on the sides and feathered on top. From behind her rimmed glasses, she examined Rhonda and Kelvin.

"What y'all doing, loitering on my stoop?" Rita asked.

"Ain't nobody loitering, Ma. I was on my way out," Kelvin said, joining his friend and heading toward their ride.

"Why we gotta be loitering? I brought your grandkids to see you." Rhonda smiled.

Rita put her bags down and folded her arms. "Rhonda, you're full of shit. I ain't baby-sitting no kids. I just got off work and I'm tired as hell."

"Ma, I never ask you to watch them. I need to run to Two-fifth right quick. I'll even bring you something back."

"Rhonda, I don't need nothing, and you hardly ever ask me to watch the kids because you leave 'em anyway. I went through all that hell to get you and them kids out of my house for nothing, because you're here all the time anyway."

"The kids miss you, Ma," Rhonda said, pushing P.J. toward his grandmother. "Just for an hour or two, Mommy." Rhonda stepped off the curb and flagged a cab.

"Rhonda!"

"No more than two hours, Ma. I promise," Rhonda called over her shoulder, climbing into the cab.

No sooner than the cab had rounded one corner, Alisha rounded the other one. Rita stood there with P.J. holding her pant leg and Pooh looking up at her. Ms. Lulu, Bernadine, and Ms. Yvonne looked at Rita sympathetically and shook their heads.

As was their ritual, Marlene and her coworker Audrey met in front of their office building for lunch. They wove past the hot dog and gyro vendors, making their way to a little strip mall a few blocks away. Their choices for food were limited to a Chinese restaurant and a deli. They had about exhausted themselves with the $4.50 lunch specials and decided to go with sandwiches.

Between telling the young man making her sandwich that he wasn't putting enough mayonnaise on it, Audrey went on about the latest office gossip. Marlene only half listened as she stared vacantly at the wall menu.

"So you think the girl who does the liens is fucking Freddy?" Audrey asked, taking her cup to the fountain and selecting her grade of soft drink. "They try to cover it, but I think something is going on. What do you think, Mar?"

"Uh-huh," Marlene said distractedly.

Audrey touched her arm. "Girl, what planet are you on today?"

"Sorry," Marlene came around. "I've got a lot on my mind right now."

"I can tell. You've been like a space cadet all day at work."

"Audrey, I feel like I'm constantly in the trenches," Marlene said, pausing to order a ham and Swiss. "If these clients don't drain me," she continued, "Paul and his baggage will."

"Told you about fucking with them young boys. You lay a taste of some seasoned pussy on 'em and they lose their cool."

"It ain't even that, Audrey. It's his reluctance to take control of his life and the things in it."

Audrey raised an eyebrow. "You mean people, don't you?"

"Let's not even go there." Marlene rolled her eyes.

"Homegirl still crashing the party?"

"Nah, she's gotten better, but I still can't stand the bitch. Rhonda acts like she can't go a day without imposing her presence on Paul and his relationship with me. I can almost feel when she's gonna call or pop up somewhere."

"Pop up? You holding out on Rhonda stories, Mar?" Audrey asked.

"What, you mean I didn't tell you? Paul and I were having ourselves a nice dinner at this soul food spot in Harlem about three weeks ago. He had been telling me about this joint for a minute, so I was like, 'cool.' Audrey, by the time I was halfway through the appetizer, guess whose loud ass walks in?"

"Marlene, you need to stop lying on that girl," Audrey insisted.

"Lying? That's on everything I love!" Marlene slapped her palm on the counter to punctuate her statement. "Rolled in with the whole little ragamuffin crew, dressed in their cheap-ass Sunday rags. This bitch actually had the nerve to act like it was a coincidence."

"You know them hos don't eat nothing outside of McDonald's and Chinese food," Audrey added.

"That's what I'm trying to tell you. She tried to get me to step out of character, but I held it together, 'cause a classy bitch always holds it together." Marlene raised her hand and Audrey slapped her palm.

"Yes, Lord," Audrey agreed.

"Paul got ready to break fool, but I made him let it roll. That's all I would've needed is him and his baby mama causing a scene in public. Needless to say, I had lost my appetite, so I got the check and we rolled. The whole way to the door, I could feel her beady-ass eyes on me."

Audrey grabbed the tray holding their food and led the way to an empty table by the window. "I would've whipped her ass if I were you."

"You know, I like to consider myself a lady and avoid the bullshit. But at the rate she's going, it's gonna come to that."

"What does Paul have to say about it?"

"He's checked her on her bullshit a few times, but the effect is always temporary. I feel like pulling my fucking hair out."

"Shiiid," Audrey began, sliding into the chair, "then your ass is crazy. If I were you, I'd kick Rhonda in her ass and tell Paul to pull hisself together and come up to your level or keep it moving," Audrey said bluntly.

"Come on, Audrey, you know Paul is my boo."

"Boo, my ass, Marlene. Time is too precious to be wasted on someone who ain't with the program. Baby, these are the glory years and we ain't got a lot of 'em." Audrey sipped her Coke.

That's why Marlene liked talking to Audrey. She was a straight shooter who would let you know exactly what it was. In a sense, she was right. They were approaching their glory years and the thought of them passing them by and still not getting life's plan right was a dreadful one. No one wanted to die an old maid, but at the same time, she knew that Paul would be a work in progress when she got with him. She saw something in Paul that he didn't yet see in himself and she sought to shape him. Unfortunately, it was taking a little longer than she had planned. Paul was a brilliant young man, but at the same time he was so fucking ghetto. Still, he was her young'n, and she'd give him enough rope to hang himself.

13

Deep within the recesses of Shooter's gentlemen's club was a door. It was a thick wooden door, reinforced with a two-inch-thick steel plate. Behind the door was the main office. Though not the biggest, it had a very comfortable feel about it. Soft carpet lined most of the floor, with polished tiles peeking out from the edges. The rear wall was covered in video monitors that covered every foot of the club and the surrounding block. Hunched over a steel desk directly in front of these cameras was Marcus.

Dressed in a black T-shit and black stocking cap, he looked every bit of a cat burglar, but the gold-rimmed glasses sitting on the bridge of his nose threw the outfit off. Most people would never know he wore glasses, because you hardly saw him with them on. They irritated his face and made him feel stupid, but when it came to making sure his paper was straight, all that shit flew out the window.

Marcus looked up from his desk at the sound of the manager's door creaking open. Only two people had the key to the office, so there was no need for him to grab the twelve-gauge that was resting against the desk near his leg. The man who walked in looked to be between the age of sixty and sixty-five, but Marcus knew for a fact that he had been on this earth for nearly eighty years. His black shirt was worn open, exposing the gold cross nestled in a bush of graying hair. Though his body had begun to wilt some years ago, he still emitted the same aura he did at the age of twenty-five. When in the presence of men like him, you had no choice but to show respect. Yes, he looked very much like a typical older man, but Shooter was one of the last real gangstas.

"Boy, don't you never go home and sleep?" Shooter asked, standing in front of the desk.

"This place ain't gonna run itself, Shooter," Marcus replied.

Shooter shook his head. "Man, I had a buddy like you back in 1961. He was always working at his print shop, trying to tighten shit up, never placing any of the weight on his employees."

"Shooter, do we have to go down memory lane right now? I'm trying to get this done."

"Boy, don't cut me off when I'm talking." Shooter unsheathed the blade he carried strapped to his forearm. "You show some damn respect before I open you up in this bitch, hear?"

Marcus sighed. "Yeah, sorry, Shooter."

"Now, that's more like it. As I was saying, my buddy would sometimes work from sunup to sunup, running this damn company. One morning the manager came in and found his ass keeled over one of them printing machines. Seems he had a heart attack and fell over in it. He had the number forty-eight stamped on his face 'bout fifty, sixty times, 'cause that was the page he was printing when he died."

Marcus put his ink pen down. "Interesting story, Shooter, but what's your point?"

"My point is, you need to let that gal we pay to handle this type of thing do her job, before somebody finds your ass dead from exhaustion."

"Work now, rest when you're dead," Marcus shot back. "I gotta keep this joint popping, man. You don't want me to look like I'm slipping with my club, do you?"

"*Your* club?" Shooter squinted. "Li'l nigga, need I remind you whose name is on that marquee?"

"Nah, Shooter, I ain't mean it like that," Marcus said.

"Then say it how you mean it, dammit." Shooter slapped his cane against the table. "Just because I let your li'l ass help me out round here don't make it yours. I'll kick you and the funky piece of money you put up on the damn streets. Can ya dig it?"

"This is your club, baby, you got it," Marcus said, trying to hold back the laughter.

Shooter was usually a sweet old dude but could be as mean as a rattlesnake. Years ago when Marcus was trying to come up on the fast track, Shooter had become somewhat of a mentor to him. He watched Marcus go from a petty thief to a businessman, and was proud to say he had a hand in it. Shooter had been the one who'd taught Marcus the importance of stacking his bread.

Shooter had owned the spot for a number of years, but when he first opened it was just a bar. He had some good years with it, but as the neighborhood changed, so did the people. The bikers from Hell's Kitchen had started coming down and causing all kinds of conflict in the black establishment. This was where Marcus came in. At the time he was still on the grind, so Scooter enlisted him and some of his boys to do security at the bar. During the next conflict, two people were placed in the hospital and one was never heard from again. Word soon got around that Shooter wasn't someone you wanted to mess with.

The arrangement worked out, so Shooter wanted to keep Marcus and his boys as permanent bouncers, but Marcus had other ideas. With his mind always being on new ways to generate income, he immediately saw what Shooter wasn't seeing. They were in a prime spot to open a gentlemen's club. With the garment district a few blocks away and easy access to New Jersey, they couldn't lose. Approaching Shooter with an idea and fifty thousand dollars of his own money, Marcus and Shooter soon became partners and completely redid the place. Thanks to Marcus, Shooter now had one of the hottest spots in New York City.

"How was the barbecue?" Shooter asked, lighting a Winston.

Marcus shrugged. "It was cool; too many homos, though."

"Shit, you knew that before you left." Shooter blew a ring of smoke out. "One of them sissies try to grab your ass?" Shooter teased.

"Never that," Marcus assured him. "But I met a girl."

"Boy, what kind of girl you meet in a room full of faggots? You ain't got nothing she can use."

"She's straight, Shooter."

"That's what they all say, until you find 'em trying to get their fingers in your ass to see if you're open to it. I knew this young bitch back in '53—"

"I get the point, Shooter."

"What I tell you about cutting me off?" Shooter waved his blade. "So is this a nice young gal or what?"

"She seems to be."

"Last girl you went after seemed to be, too. I told you not to plant roots with that skank, but you wouldn't listen to old Shooter. Your head is as hard as a bowling ball."

"I know, Shooter, that's why I'm not trying to jump out the window with this one. I mean, I ain't in love or nothing, but I do like her."

"I sure hope not. It was no easy task, picking up the pieces of your broken heart," Shooter said.

"I wanna see where her head is at first. I think she's a nice girl, but only time will tell that. You ain't gotta worry about me falling victim again."

Shooter sat on the edge of the desk and said seriously, "You're a good kid, Marcus, so don't go laying around with trash and letting that pecker of yours convince you that you're in love. If she's a good girl, then you make sure you do right by her. But if she's a dog, treat her like the tramp bitch she is, and when you're done with the pussy, let old Shooter have a taste." Shooter and Marcus both bust out laughing.

After dealing with the morning drama, Reese was finally able to get dressed. It was hot out, but her body was way too sore for anything tight. Reese opted for a pair of Nautica sweats, a tank top, and a pair of Air Max. She thought that the drama for the morning had ended with Bone, but as soon as she stepped into the kitchen, her mother started in.

"Didn't I ask you to stop having that boy calling my phone?" her mother said, pouring a glass of Kool-Aid. Reese's mother Pat was in her midforties, but was still trying to hold on to her lost youth. She was wearing a pair of spandex pants that did little to hide the lumps in her ass, or control the gut that lapped over the waist.

"Sorry," Reese mumbled, opening the refrigerator.

"I ain't playing with you, Shareese. My phone bill is high enough without getting them damn collect calls from jail."

"He's on the island, Ma. They use clicks, so it's not a collect call."

"Clicks, my ass. It's my phone and I don't want that nigga calling," Pat said with finality.

"It's your phone, but in Sharon's name," Reese mumbled.

"What you say?"

"Nothing, Ma," Reese lied, and carried her glass into the living room.

Reese's younger brother, Mel, was sitting on the couch with one of his friends, playing the newest edition of Madden. She could tell from their bloodshot eyes and the empty cookie packages on the coffee table that they were high as kites.

"Damn, do you do anything besides play video games?" Reese asked, flopping on the love seat.

"Do you do anything besides mind people's business?" Mel shot back, drawing a snicker from his partner. "As long as we're in conversation mode, was that Don B.'s Hummer I saw you getting out of this morning?"

"Wha . . . Mel, I know you ain't spying on me."

"Nah, sis, I was making a blunt run and I peeped duke's ride bend the corner. So what's the deal with y'all two?"

"Ain't no deal. You need to mind your business."

"If it 'ain't no deal,' why you getting all defensive?" Mel taunted her.

"Look, Mel, I'm a grown-ass woman and I don't have to answer to my little brother," Reese said sternly.

"She tight, son," Mel's friend said, then laughed, thumbing the controller.

"Fuck you, ya little burn-out muthafucka," she addressed him. "Mel, you need to be more selective about the company you keep."

Mel paused the game and gave Reese his undivided attention. "I know you ain't talking, with your Rat Pack-ass crew. Fucking Yoshi and Rhonda, give me a break!"

"Son, you talking about Yoshi from One Forty-seventh? Yo, I heard that bitch got some mean head," Mel's friend spoke up.

Reese slammed her glass down and stood up. "I can't even sit here with you disrespectful muthafuckas." Reese headed for the front door, but on a parting note she told them, "If you no-class li'l niggaz knew how to treat a bitch, you might be able to get some pussy without paying for it." She slammed the door in her wake and left the two boys stuck on stupid.

No sooner than Reese stepped out of the building, she saw Rhonda coming up the block. Unlike Reese, who had chosen to go conservative, Rhonda was dressed for the muggy weather. Her white tennis skirt was hiked up on her ass, threatening to show cheek, but never raising quite high enough. On her face she wore a smirk, letting Reese know she came bearing new gossip.

"What happened now?" Reese asked as Rhonda approached.

"Yo, you missed it. Me and Verna whipped these two bitches out on Forty-second!" Rhonda exclaimed.

"You and Verna? How the hell did y'all end up as tag team partners?"

Rhonda went on to recount the story to Reese, making sure she exaggerated her role in the scuffle. Reese listened intently, feeling her heart begin to speed up as if she had been one of the combatants.

"She beat the bitch with a can of Similac?" Reese asked disbelievingly.

"On my kids!" Rhonda declared. "I thought she was gonna kill the bitch."

"Verna stay gettin' it popping. That's why her ass is all chopped up now."

"Reese, you should've been there. After we stomped them bitches out, we gave it to that bird-ass nigga she fuck with from Forty-fifth."

"Your ass is too grown to be out there scrapping. The whole block probably seen your black ass," Reese teased her, tugging at the bottom of Rhonda's skirt.

"Bitch, it ain't even get that hectic. You know your girl is a knock-out artist." Rhonda threw two phantom punches. "Now, what's this business with Don B.?"

"Damn, you're nosy."

"Don't even act like that, bitch. You know you wanna tell it. So inquiring minds wanna know, how big is Don B.'s dick?"

Reese blushed. "Rhonda, you ain't got no couth."

"Fuck that, I wanna know."

Reese paused for a minute, building the moment. "He was hung like a horse!" The two girls exchanged dap and hugs, while Reese recounted the adventure. She excluded the parts about her letting Don B.'s squad hit it and her neglect to use a condom, but built up she and Don B.'s escapade. Rhonda hung on every word, so as to be able to repeat it verbatim when she put it out in the hood.

"My bitch done finally came up," Rhonda said proudly. "So how much did he hit you with when it was over?"

Reese immediately felt like someone had superimposed a jackass's head over hers. For what she had subjected herself to to sleep with the celebrity, there hadn't been a dime in it for her. The night she had slept with Don B. and his crew, she had been too high to remember the first rule of thumb: Cash for ass.

"I'm saying, he was so much of a gentleman that I didn't even crack for no paper. I'm setting him up for the long con," Reese fronted.

"Reese, this is me you're talking to," Rhonda said seriously. "I'm your bitch, so I'm always gonna keep it funky with you, and I hope you'd do the same with me. Girl, you can't even spell 'long con', let alone pull it off. You probably got in there with Don B. and got starstruck, that's why you didn't crack for no paper."

"Rhonda, you got some nerve. You act like you're the only one who got game."

"Reese, everyone has got game in them somewhere, but if you can't apply that shit to your life, it don't count for nothing. I tell you bitches all the time that it's all about execution. These niggaz gotta pay like they weigh, ma."

"Whatever, Rhonda. Contrary to what you believe, everybody ain't out to sell their pussy. Why can't I just fuck a nigga 'cause I like him?"

"Contrary," Rhonda repeated, chuckling, "I like that one. Not for nothing, while you're trying to sound educated, you're still moving like a fool." Rhonda saw anger flash in Reese's eyes, so she explained herself. "Reese, me and you been tight for too long for me to try and sugarcoat shit to try and spare your feelings. You and I both know what Don B. is about, so don't go thinking that through some miracle that he might consider wife'n you. He's just like the rest of these niggaz out here, trying to get a nut. Niggaz like him expect to spend paper for a shot of that, so we're only doing what's right by demanding our due."

"All you ever think about is the come-up."

"You muthafucking right. If I'm gonna lay with a nigga that's not my man, please believe he's setting it out. Like my girl Lil' Kim said, 'Fuck niggaz, get money.' That's the real anthem. It's not like he's a regular Joe, that nigga is a platinum artist!"

"Anyway," Reese said, letting Rhonda know she didn't want to talk about it anymore, "I wasn't the only one with a celeb, what popped off with you and True?"

"You know I did me, ho. Rhonda gets hers. But the funny shit was how Von rolled up while True was leaving."

"Stop playing!"

"Reese, that's my word. I was walking True out the building and Von pulled up to the curb. I thought the shit was gonna get ugly, but it ain't go down like that."

"Von ain't flip?" Reese asked.

"Nah, you know how True roll wit' that thing. Von walked up on the car, but it was a short conversation."

"You lucky as hell. What if them niggaz had butted heads?"

"It wouldn't have been my problem," Rhonda said flatly. "Don't neither one of them have no papers on this pussy." Rhonda patted her crotch for emphasis.

"Rhonda, you be playing dangerous games."

"They're only dangerous if you get caught slipping, and you know slipping ain't even in my character. Besides," Rhonda pulled a stack of bills from her purse, "sometimes the gains are worth the risk. Now bring your naïve ass on." Rhonda began walking.

Reese fought off the feeling of stupidity Rhonda had tossed on her and fell in step behind her.

14

Check, nigga," Larry said, wiping his forehead with his tank top.
"You sure are a glutton for punishment," Paul teased, dribbling
the basketball between his legs. "It's ten-six, me, and your ass is already
out of gas."

"It ain't over till it's over, punk," Larry responded, still trying to
catch his breath.

"Have it your way, old man."

Paul bounced the ball to Larry, who gave it back with an overly aggressive chest pass. As soon as Paul put the ball on the floor, Larry was
on him. He slammed his gut into Paul's back, trying to knock him off
balance, but Paul kept his footing. Larry tried to swat the ball away,
but ended up slapping Paul on the wrist. Paul dribbled out, then faked
right. When Larry bit, Paul went left. Thinking Paul was going in for a
layup, Larry darted into the lane. To his surprise, as well as the small
gathering of people watching, Paul stopped short. Giving Larry a
friendly wink, he put up a jump shot that went soundlessly through
the net.

"Game!" Paul announced, tossing the ball to a winded Larry.

"Man, fuck you. All you got is that punk-ass jump shot." Larry tossed the ball back to him.

"That jump shot just won me twenty dollars of your hard-earned money." Paul laid the Ball up.

"Ain't neither one of you niggaz got no skills," Jah informed them, stepping onto the court with one of his shifty-looking cohorts. They were both dressed in white T-shirts and long denim shorts.

"What's up, purse snatcher?" Larry joked.

"Still trying to get your girl to stop calling me." Jah smiled. "What's good, yo?" he addressed Paul.

"Ain't shit. Just teaching this lame dude how to hoop." Paul nodded at Larry. He went to dribble the ball, but Jah swiped it away.

"If you're done beating up on Jenny Craig rejects, I might be able to show you a thing or two." Jah tossed up a jump shot almost identical to Paul's, which fell through the hoop.

Paul smiled lovingly at his little brother. "So the student thinks he can challenge the teacher?"

"Only one way to find out," Jah answered, pulling his T-shirt off. "Me and my dude against you and Fat Boy."

"Watch you mouth," Larry warned him.

Jah winked. "You know it's said in love."

Paul watched the miniature version of himself disrobe in preparation of the matchup. He happened to glance down at the sagging waistline of Jah's shorts and noticed he had a gun holstered to his belt. "Don't you think that might weigh you down." Paul nodded at the nine.

"Call it a handicap." Jah adjusted his belt, but didn't bother to remove the gun. "We'll even let y'all have the ball first."

Paul stood behind the foul line, pressing the ball between his palms. He tried staring into his brother's eyes, but found that he had to turn away after a while. Though he and his brother were thick as thieves, he knew there were two sides to the young man. There was darkness in him, passed down from their father, that had skipped over Paul. The same darkness, Paul remembered, that had frightened him when he looked into his stepfather's eyes as a child.

He and Jah had the same mother, but different fathers. Jah's father was a rude boy named Prince, who had terrorized the neighborhood back in the late eighties, early nineties. Prince was a Jamaican cat who had snuck into the states to flee prosecution for the murder of two tourists, which he had committed in his native town of Kingston. Immediately after arriving in America, he took it to the streets. He was a notorious stickup kid and murderer who would bring it to anyone. Big or small, if Prince thought you were holding, he would put that iron to you. It was this same trigger-happy attitude that had gotten him murdered eight years prior. Jah had never really gotten to know his father, but they harbored the same evil in their hearts. Paul had heard stories about some of the gruesome deeds his brother had committed in the streets, but he loved him the same as he did when they were kids.

Jah was caught off guard by the speed his brother used passing the ball to Larry. The big man bypassed Jah's partner and put the ball in the hoop. The next time out, Paul hit Larry, who hit him right back. Before Jah could get his footing, Paul had scored. Underestimating Jah, Paul tried the pass again. This time Jah picked it off and hit his partner for the easy layup.

The crowd of onlookers on the sidelines increased to watch the competition. Jah hit his partner with the ball, then hit the paint and called for it. Paul immediately swooped in on him and tried to keep Jah from scoring. As Jah backed him down, Paul could feel the butt of the gun digging into his hip. In the moment it took for him to try and get his mind off the gun and back into the game, Jah had made a layup.

"Don't get tired on me now," Jah said, tossing the ball at Paul.

"It's kinda hard to D you when that fucking cannon is poking me in the side." Paul tossed the ball back. "Why don't you put that off on the side so we can play?"

"Man, that's like walking in the precinct and copping out to something I already got away with." Jah tried to go in, but Paul cut him off, forcing him to dribble the ball back out. "As soon as I lay my hammer down, a nigga gonna try to lay me down. You know we can't have that." Jah put up another jumper, but it bounced off the rim.

Paul grabbed the rebound and dribbled it out to the three-point line. "See, that's karma fucking with your conscience. You done did so much bullshit to people that you're always thinking somebody is out to get you." Paul tried to go in, but Jah swatted the shot and got the ball back.

"Big brother, you better act like you know. If it ain't the police, then its punk-ass niggaz that don't wanna see you shine. Either way, somebody is always out to get you." He hit a jumper.

"Man, y'all two niggaz is bullshitting." Larry walked over. "There's more talking going on that balling."

"Be easy, dawg. I'm just kicking the facts of life with my little brother," Paul said.

"Nigga, the only fact of life I know is survival of the fittest." Jah unclipped his gun and brandished it. Some of the people who had been watching the game ducked for cover seeing the young man pull a gun. Paul, however, just stood there, staring at his little brother.

"Why don't you put that thing away before you get us knocked." Larry looked around cautiously.

Jah held the gun out a moment longer, then returned it to the holster. "Nervous-ass nigga."

"Jah, why don't you be cool? This ain't the Wild West," Paul said.

"Try telling that to the niggaz who gave me this." Jah lifted his tank top, showing off the bullet wound just below his ribs. "It's a cold world, big brother, and you gotta always be ready to lay the heat to a nigga, straight cheese. These streets ain't nothing nice."

"You telling me like I don't know, Jah. I was running these streets since before you were thought about," Paul reminded him.

"I'll give you that, bro, but there's a big difference between running your mouth and busting your gun, ya heard? We gotta do this again sometime, fellas. One." Jah threw his T-shirt over his shoulder and started for the park exit.

"Yo, y'all niggaz ain't gonna finish the game?" Larry asked, throwing his hands up.

"You two have fun. Me and my man gotta take care of something," Jah replied, making his exit.

True stood in the tiny recording booth within the bowels of Big Dawg Studios, glaring at the people sitting on the other side of the soundproof glass. Don B. sat monitoring the instruments while Lex was rolling a blunt. Pain lounged on the love seat playing with a hunting knife. The heat that mixed with the thick veil of smoke within the small chamber stung True's eyes, but he didn't need to see the music sheet to know his verses. This was his sixth take.

"Let's try it one more time," Don B.'s voice came through the speakers.

True sucked his teeth and lit a clip of haze he had been smoking. "Come on, fam. Why we gotta keep doing this shit?"

"Because it ain't right yet," Don B. answered.

"My dude, I'm in here spitting nothing but heat. How we ain't got it down yet?"

"Because I said we ain't got it down yet. Do it again, True."

True and Don B. glared at each other from opposite sides of the glass. True felt he had just wrecked his verse of the latest Bad Blood song, "Never Without My Nine," but for some reason Don B. kept making him do it again. This frustrated True because he was used to doing his own thing in the studio. When the Asian engineer was behind the boards, he let True and the other members of the group do their thing, but Don B. was a different case. He wanted perfection.

Seeing young True's reluctance to do the verse over again, Don B. stopped the session. Cutting off the exterior speakers, he stepped into the booth with True. "Yo, what up wit' you, fam?"

"Ain't nothing up with me," True said, exhaling a thick cloud of smoke.

"It gotta be something wrong with you, son. We've been in here for hours and you still bullshitting on the verse."

"Ain't nobody bullshitting, Don, I think it's tight."

Don B. twisted his lips. "You don't even believe that shit, B. Your voice is mad flat, and I can hear you wheezing. You need to ease up on them cigarettes, yo."

"Man, it ain't the cigarettes," True said.

"It's gotta be something, fam. I'm paying too much money for this studio time for you to be in here playing, True."

"Don, you know I'll kick you something for the time."

"Money ain't the issue here, dawg. It's your performance that I'm having a problem with. True, do you know the difference between you and them niggaz?" Don B. asked, motioning toward Lex and Pain, who were getting high and playing with the console. When True didn't answer, Don B. continued. "They're street cats trying to be rappers, whereas you're a rapper still trying to be a street nigga. No disrespect to them cats, but I can't see them putting out no platinum solo albums. They're always gonna have the streets, but the crossover appeal ain't there."

"All we need is the streets," True said, as if he knew what the hell he was talking about.

"Wrong. True, believe it or not, we're gonna see most of our bread off them little white kids in the suburbs than we will from the hood."

"Don B., that don't make no sense. The hood has had your back since day one."

"Oh, I know, and I love the hood for that, but they ain't who's going to the record stores buying my shit. You know as well as I do that a nigga in the hood is more likely to spend five dollars on a bootleg than to go into a record store and drop thirteen dollars on a CD, myself included. On the other hand, you've got those white kids from suburban America climbing over each other to get to the Virgin Megastore to cop that new Don B. shit."

True sucked his teeth. "Fuck them crackers. They don't know nothing about what we do down here."

"That's my point, God. The only thing these white kids know about the hood is what they hear on records and what they read in books. Why do you think the major publishing houses are suddenly so interested in the urban-book market? They're making millions of dollars off a genre that they wouldn't touch a few years ago. It's all about marketability."

"Yo, Don, I ain't trying to be one of these niggaz out here rocking a shiny suit, you know that ain't my style," True said seriously.

"Ain't nobody asking you to change who you are, True. All I want you to do is realize who you can become. We make good money getting spins on BET, but we'll make more if we get spins on MTV. To get the type of paper that's due to us, we gotta put out a superior product. Understand where I'm coming from and do the verse over."

True stood there, finishing off his blunt while Don B. returned to his post behind the board. He understood what Don B. was saying, but at the same time he didn't. Niggaz loved their camp on the streets and they were making paper, but their paper didn't match up to Don B.'s. He was a wise young cat, and so far everything he had told True had been right on the money. The kid knew the business. If Don B. believed that the verse could be better, then it probably could. With this thought in his mind, True grabbed the microphone and did the verse over.

Don B. smiled at the newfound vigor that True used to attack the track. The lazy, smoked-out look in True's eyes was replaced with that fire Don B. knew still burned within the young MC. Pain and Lex even stopped what they were doing to admire their partner in the booth killing it.

Don B. kept all the members of the group on a short leash, but he was always hardest on True. The youngster reminded Don B. of himself when he was starting out. The difference was that while Don B. had to learn the game, True was born into it. In the eighties, his mother Gloria ran one of the busiest shooting galleries on Lenox Avenue. It was originally established by her brother Mack and his crew, but when he went to prison, she took over and ran it just as her brother had. With a warm smile and a cold razor game, all the hustlers respected Gloria.

In the summer of 1985, two things happened that would change Gloria's life. The first was she had gotten knocked, thanks to a snitch who was jealous of her wealth. The DA had a shitload of charges against her and the feds were trying to add their two cents to the mix to pin a RICO charge on the young woman. The second was she found out that she was pregnant with True.

Gloria suddenly found her life very complicated, with impending parenthood and fighting a case, but she was a soldier and was determined to handle it. Feeling the heat that was closing in around her, True's father disappeared, never to be seen again. It didn't make much of a difference because Gloria was used to holding herself down anyway. Running back and forth to court in addition to being pregnant forced Gloria to slow down, but she refused to close up shop. She'd be damned if her baby would come into the world with nothing. She herself had had enough hungry nights for the both of them, so it was something she couldn't see for her seed.

What it eventually came down to was the law wanting Gloria to give up her connect for a reduced sentence. Her response to the DA was "Kiss my ass," right before she spat in his face. For her reluctance to cooperate, Gloria received five-to-fifteen years in state prison. While out on bond and getting her affairs in order, she considered running, for fear of having her child in jail, but realistically, she knew that it would only make the situation worse. She had no life skills and the little money that the DEA hadn't snatched was dwindling. Thankfully, having a child in prison was not to be her fate. Three weeks before she was to turn herself in, she gave birth to a baby boy. She named the child True because that was the code she and her family had always lived by. Be true to who and what you are.

Gloria spent as much time as she could with the boy before turning herself in. The state wanted to take the boy, but she was able to find an aunt who would take him in for a small fee. While in prison, Gloria counted the days until she would be reunited with her child, but a beating from a CO who she refused to sleep with stole that chance from her. In 1991, Gloria died from massive head trauma, never getting to know her son.

Two years ago there were many unsolved murders committed in New York City, but two were of particular interest to True's crew. The first victim was a former corrections officer and the second was a washed-up dope fiend who was said to run with True's mother back in the day. The police conducted an investigation, but when it was all said and done, neither were really missed.

"That muthafucka spits," Lex said, passing the blunt off to Don B.

Don B. accepted the blunt and inhaled deeply. "Y'all niggaz need to take notes. I told you, listen to my direction and I'm gonna make you stars."

"I'm already a fucking star," Pain said arrogantly.

"Pain, shut the fuck up. You ain't gonna be shit but a number if you don't stop catching cases," Don B. told him.

"A nigga gotta eat."

"Eat? Don't I keep you niggaz well fed and fresh? Come on with that bullshit, Pain. I'm trying to give ya life a fucking purpose, so stop throwing fucking stones at the pen. These lawyers ain't cheap, and one of these days it's gonna take more than a slick-talking Jew and money to get your ass out of trouble."

"I ain't no stranger to a bid. If I was to have to do some more time, I'd just write like ten more albums," Pain said ignorantly.

"A nigga in a cage can't get no money," Don B. told him.

"Or no pussy," Lex added.

Don B. lit a cigarette and blew smoke rings into the air. "You niggaz need to stop running your mouths and go over your verses. We got a show tonight and I need you to be on point."

"I'm always on point, kid," Pain said.

"Nigga, stop fronting. You'll be the main one to forget your verse," Lex teased him.

"Fuck you, nigga. I'm the muthafucking freestyle king of New York," Pain boasted. "Yo, Don, what up wit' that freak y'all niggaz popped off this morning?" he said, changing the subject.

"Yo, shorty head game was fire!" Don B. recalled. "She even let Tone and them niggaz hit it."

"Damn, I'm tight I missed that one," Lex said.

"Don't sweat it. She's a neighborhood chick, so we'll bump into her again." Don B. grinned and went back to watching True in the booth.

"Yo, I gotta get up outta here," Pain said, looking at his watch.

"Where the fuck is you going? Dawg, we still got work to do," Don B. reminded him.

"I'm gonna come back and lay my vocals, but I got something I need to take care of."

"Pain, I know you ain't dipping out of a session for no pussy?" Lex asked, clearly not feeling Pain's early departure.

Pain smiled broadly. "Never that. I told my moms I would do something for her. I'll be back."

"Yo, Pain, I don't give a fuck what you gotta do, just make sure your ass is on time for the show tonight."

"My dude, I said I'll be back," Pain said as if he was catching an attitude. He walked out of the studio and anxiously tapped the elevator call button. His finger came away from the steel button leaving a sweaty fingerprint. Pain wiped his hands against his pants in an attempt to dry them. Just a short cab ride and I'm good, he told himself, stepping into the elevator.

15

"What do you think of these?" Yoshi held up a pair of fire engine red boots.

"The heel is too high for my taste," Billy grumbled.

"It's only two inches," Yoshi said, examining the price and putting them back. "I need to get something to wear to Exit tonight." Yoshi took another pair of shoes off the shelf and asked one of the employees to bring her a size seven.

"Why don't you wear something you already have?" Billy suggested.

Yoshi looked at her and twisted her lips. "Billy, you can't be serious. You know how many niggaz in there are gonna be holding? I can't show up in there looking half-ass. What you need to do is see if they got one of these in your size." Yoshi handed Billy a black dress with spaghetti straps.

Billy held the dress against her and performed a visual fitting. "Nah, this ain't really my style. Yoshi, you know I ain't trying to go to the club with my back all out."

"Billy, you need to knock it off," Yoshi said, snatching that dress from Billy and picking up one that was her size. "This dress would look hot on you and you know it."

Billy took the second dress and looked it over. "I can't front, this is a hot dress. I just be feeling some type of way about my weight lately. Look how big my ass has gotten." She turned around so Yoshi could see her onion.

"Billy, you sound like a white girl," Yoshi teased her. "Baby girl, ass is good. Guys love a woman with junk in her trunk. You see how these niggaz be jumping out the window over this?" Yoshi slapped her palm against her own onion, drawing a hungry look from a gentleman helping a fat woman into a wedge sandal. "See what I mean," she said and winked at Billy.

Billy glared at the employee, causing him to turn his head away. "Ain't none of these niggaz shit. When it's all said and done, they're all out for the same thing."

"Billy, why are you so fucking morbid when it comes to the subject of men? That's why muthafuckas think you a dyke."

"Please, you think I give a fuck what people think about me? You know I ain't no fucking dyke." Billy looked for Yoshi to agree with her statement, but only found a raised eyebrow. "What're you looking at me like that for? Yoshi, I know you don't believe that dyke shit."

"Billy, you've been my girl for longer than any of us have been hanging, so you know I ain't gonna bullshit you. I *know*."

Billy folded her arms. "You know what?"

"Do I need to say it?"

"I'd appreciate it."

"You got a little sugar in you, ma," Yoshi said flatly.

"You can't be serious. Yoshi, you know me and you know I've been with guys."

"Yeah, Billy, I know you ain't no virgin to dick, but I don't think you too much care for it. I ain't seen you with a nigga since, Sol, God bless."

"I've dated a few guys."

"Billy, dating and getting your fuck on are two different things. You and me have always been the prettiest of the crew. Rhonda and Reese couldn't never fuck with us, as far as clothes or looks. These niggaz used to be sick over you, ma. But now you on some other shit. I don't know if it was Sol's death, or some knucklehead nigga breaking your heart, but you gotta shake that shit off, Billy. The world is too big and there's way too much dick out here for you to have to go that route."

"Yoshi, you're just like them bitches Reese and Rhonda. All of y'all think you know some shit," Billy said, becoming very defensive.

Yoshi continued to stare at her seriously. "On the real, I know you've seen what the other half was like, but that ain't none of nobody's business but yours. I love you the same. I'm just wondering, what made you go there?"

Yoshi had definitely struck a nerve. Billy had always held her heart close to her chest, but Yoshi had known her for a very long time. "Yo, when Sol got killed, I was fucking up behind it. I mean . . . we were both young, but there was no doubt that we loved each other. During the time I was mourning him, I had niggaz offering me their condolences and shit, like they were sorry to see Sol go. He had blocked their game in life and was still doing it in death, because all them niggaz wanted to fuck and I was dead loyal to my man."

"Billy, I can only imagine how you must've felt," Yoshi said sympathetically.

Billy looked at Yoshi with partially glazed eyes and shook her head. "No, you can't. Sol wasn't just some nigga I was fucking, he was chosen. God put him here to be a Divine reflection of me, Yoshi. Not having him felt like someone had chopped off one of my limbs: sometimes you still feel it, even though there's nothing there."

Yoshi averted Billy's gaze when it fell on her. To see her so exposed made Yoshi somewhat uncomfortable. She was used to Billy being the hard, emotionally in control member of their group, but watching the tears well up in her eyes brought a lump to Yoshi's throat.

Billy absently thumbed the heel of a shoe someone had abandoned as she continued her sad tale. "He said he would be there for us against all odds. I guess a bullet didn't factor into the promise." Seeing the confused look on Yoshi's face, Billy decided to enlighten her. "I was six weeks pregnant the day Sol was killed."

"I didn't know," Yoshi said with watery eyes.

"No one did, Yoshi. I had just told him and we decided to keep it a secret until we decided what we were gonna do. When he died, the decision became clear."

"Billy, you had an abortion?" Yoshi asked in disbelief.

Billy looked at her friend very seriously. "What would you have done? Yoshi, I was a child myself at the time. With Sol and me together, we might've been able to do it, but just me? I wasn't gonna be out here on welfare, barely able to take care of mine like Rhonda. The choice to keep the baby would've been crueler than the one I made."

"You did what you had to do, Billy."

"I guess." She shrugged. "I always wonder what if, but I know I can't get either of those lives back. For a long time after I kept reinventing myself, trying to find somewhere to belong. I can't front, I've done some things that most of y'all might not agree with, but I'm still me when it's all said and done. Everybody running around thinking they know what's up with Billy, when Billy doesn't even know what's up with herself."

A heavy silence hung between the two friends, which Yoshi decided to break by asking, "So how many women have you slept with?" Both of them nearly fell over the rack of dresses laughing, drawing the attention of the store manager, as well as the rent-a-cop playing the front door.

"We better pay for our shit and go, before Roscoe P. Coltrane locks us up for shoplifting." Yoshi nodded over at the security guard. "Plus, we gotta head over to the electronics store to meet Rhonda and Reese."

"Ain't no need to rush. You know them hos ain't never on time," Billy said.

"I know. Reese is slow as hell and Rhonda is always getting caught up with her bad-ass kids."

"Cut it out, Yoshi. Them kids is all right."

"Billy, are we talking about the same kids? P.J. is sneaky-ass hell to be so little and Pooh is hardheaded. Alisha is another story altogether."

"She's a preteen, she's supposed to be feeling herself."

"Fuck all that, the little bitch is straight-up grown," Yoshi declared, placing the items on the counter. As she waited for the girl behind the register to finish ringing up her purchases, she noticed that a guy standing two registers down was staring at her. Yoshi, being who she was, turned around and looked him up and down in a stink way. He finished paying for his stuff and made his way toward her. She immediately dipped her hand in her purse to retrieve the razor she carried in case he wanted trouble.

"Excuse me," he said, slowing his approach. "I don't mean to stare, but don't we know each other?"

"I don't think so," she said, looking up at the six-three chocolate cat, who was built like he played for some pro team.

"Your name is China, isn't it?"

"Sometimes," Yoshi said suspiciously. China was the name she sometimes went by when she was dancing.

"I'm Nel," he said and extended his hand. "You probably don't remember me, but we met at Pussy Cat. I spent quite a bit of paper with you that night." He chuckled.

"The Pussy Cat is a big place, sweetie. A lot of people come in and out of there and drop paper on the kid. Was there something special about you that I should remember?"

"Guess not." His smile threatened to fade, but he held it. "Listen, I didn't mean no disrespect, love. I just wanted to extend a dinner invitation. You know, on some friendly shit."

"Nah, I don't think that's gonna work."

"Baby girl, don't be fooled by my appearance." He gestured toward his outfit, which consisted of jeans and sneakers with a white T-shirt. "I ain't no hustler, I work for transit. I just wanna get to know a nice young lady."

Yoshi looked him over and had to admit that he was fine as hell, but she knew it couldn't go down. "Nothing personal, boo, but I don't date guys I meet at the club." Yoshi picked up her bags and motioned to Billy that she was ready to go. When they had made it to the exit, he called behind Yoshi.

"So if we had met on the street you would've accepted?"

Yoshi stopped short and gave him a look that said, "I'd fuck the shit outta you," but replied, "We didn't meet on the street, so I guess that makes the question irrelevant." With a flirtatious wink, she left him standing there smirking.

Reese followed Rhonda down Third Avenue, in the Bronx, as she floated toward yet another store. They had been on the avenue for over an hour and still hadn't gotten to the spot where they were supposed to meet Yoshi and Billy. Reese stood by and watched Rhonda run through the bread that Von had given her, buying things not because she needed them, but because she could. There was a part of Reese that hated Rhonda for that. Here she was, trying to make ends meet the best way she could, and Rhonda was pimping niggaz as well as the system to live above the average.

"Rhonda, don't you think you've done enough shopping? We gotta meet Yoshi and Billy," Reese pointed out.

"I know, I know. I just wanna look in this store right quick to see if I can find me a shirt."

"You bought a shirt in the store we just left," Reese reminded her.

"Come on, Reese, I didn't come up here with you so you could rush me. I gotta make sure my fit is tight for tonight."

"Tonight? What's going down tonight?" Reese asked, clueless as to what Rhonda was talking about.

"Reese, have you been vacationing on another planet? The party at Exit is popping off. True and his peoples are performing. Don B. is footing the bill and everybody is gonna be there. Reese, how you gonna fuck a nigga and he ain't even tell you he was throwing the party of the summer the following night?"

"Oh . . . Don B. mentioned it to me, but it slipped my mind," Reese lied. "I already got my fit, but I do need to snatch some shoes. Come with me over here," Reese said, heading into the nearest shoe store. The two girls made conversation while Reese selected a pair of shoes for the party. She felt kind of dissed that Don B. hadn't invited her to the party, but she told herself that they were all too fucked up to think about it. She had had her fifteen minutes of fame and shame and was good on both, but Rhonda kept bringing it up. She knew that deep down Rhonda was jealous that she had fucked Don B. Sure, she popped off with True, but he wasn't the Don. Rhonda was used to having one up on Reese when it came to men, but this time the tables had been turned.

"I wonder what Yoshi and them is gonna wear to the party?" Reese said offhandedly.

"You know Yoshi like to have all the light on her, so she probably gonna wear some freak shit. And that bitch Billy will probably be wearing a suit from the Men's Warehouse," Rhonda said sarcastically.

"Why you always got some slick shit to say about Billy? You hang with her every day, but you stay talking about her."

"What you getting so defensive about? You act like you bumping cats wit' the bitch, Reese."

Reese snaked her neck. "Don't play with me, bitch. You know I only do dick."

"That's the same thing ya girl be saying."

"Rhonda, do you really think Billy is a dyke?"

Rhonda thought about it for a moment before answering. "Yo, you know I got mad love for Billy, but I heard some shit that's making me wonder if ol' girl really dines at the Y."

"What you heard?" Reese asked, not bothering to hide her anticipation to hear the latest hood gossip.

"Reese, if I tell you this, I swear to God, you better not open your mouth," Rhonda told her seriously.

"Come on, Rhonda, this shit is gonna stay between us," Reese assured her.

"Well, you know Billy been hanging with them dyke bitches since back in her varsity days in high school, as far as we know, on some cool shit."

"Yeah, that ho Jean and her peoples."

"Anyhow, this was supposed to have happened around the anniversary of Sol's death and you know how Billy gets all sad and shit around that time of year. She was supposed to have been getting bent with Jean and this bitch from the Lenox Terrace. I can't think of her name, but you know her when you see her. Real pretty bitch with long hair and—"

"Get on with the story, Rhonda!"

"Like I was saying, in the midst of all this drinking and smoking, the pretty bitch starts getting all touchy with Billy. It was supposedly on some old comfort shit, but you know how them bitches do. Well, this is just what I heard, but one thing was supposed to have led to another and they had a threesome."

Reese looked at Rhonda wide-eyed. "You need to stop lying!"

"I'm dead-ass! You know my brother Kelvin is a faggot, so he runs in those circles. He was supposed to had got the story from a girl who goes to school with Jean's little sister, who heard her telling someone on the phone."

"I knew it!" Reese jumped up and down. She drew some funny looks, but ignored them. "Ain't no way she was hanging with all them dyke hos and not getting down."

"If you ask me, I think her and Yoshi are eating each other's pussies," Rhonda continued. "Them bitches seem a little tighter than they should be."

"Nah, I don't think Yoshi get down."

"Baby, I don't put nothing past nobody. You know Yoshi be at them clubs around all that pussy. All them stripper bitches be dyke'n."

Rhonda and Reese continued walking down Third Avenue, window shopping and slowly making their way to the electronics store to meet their friends. Halfway down the hill, they spotted their counterparts coming across the busy street. Rhonda was the first one to smile and wave them to their location.

"Hey, bitches!" Rhonda said, hugging Yoshi, then Billy.

"What's up, Rhonda? What took y'all so damn long?" Yoshi asked, looking at her watch.

"Shit, I had to stop and pick up a few things."

"I thought the idea was that we were supposed to be shopping together?" Billy interjected.

"Y'all bitches shop at them skinny women stores. I gotta go where they cater to blessed women," Rhonda said, cupping her breasts.

"Well, me and Billy already got what we needed," Yoshi said, raising her multiple bags.

"Billy, what could you possibly need from a *women's* clothing store?" Rhonda asked sarcastically.

Billy sucked her teeth and cut her eyes. "Don't be funny, Rhonda."

"Talk that shit now, but when y'all see my girl in her dress, you're going to be all on her shit," Yoshi cut in.

Reese and Rhonda exchanged suspicious glances.

"What the fuck is that all about?" Billy asked.

"Bitch, stop being so paranoid," Rhonda said. "Y'all ready to go back to the city? I wanna get high."

"All you ever think about is weed," Yoshi said.

"And dick," Billy mumbled.

"At least I'm getting some," Rhonda shot back.

"Why don't y'all two knock it off? I wanna check one last store before we head back."

"Well, let's hurry up and do it, then. I still got shit to do before we head out." Rhonda brushed between Yoshi and Billy and started across the street. Billy gave Rhonda a disgusted look that Reese mistook for something else. As Rhonda's earlier accusations replayed in her head, she made it a point to walk behind Billy.

16

Slick was a man in his midthirties, but could still pass for twenty-something. He wore his hair in a short afro and you could never find him with a hair out of place. From his expensive clothes to his jewels, Slick was a man who prided himself on being fly. Everyone in the St. Nicholas projects knew him, but his weeded-out brain and supersize ego told him that he was an international nigga.

He was a nobody who always wanted to be somebody. Being that his uncles had been heavy hitters, he tried to build a rep off their name. Slick had established himself as a respectable hustler, but in essence he wasn't really built like that. Still, he was the nephew of two killers, so niggaz let him live, and eventually found a friendly respect for him.

Slick had never been a very good hustler, fucking up more money than he made. This all changed about two years back when fate finally swung in his favor. His uncles, with a friend of theirs, had robbed these white cats out of Long Island for some dope. They thought they were just putting the gorilla on some lame white boys, but one of them happened to be the son-in-law of a Mafia capo. The Italians tracked the brothers to where they were hiding in Connecticut and executed them. They searched high and low for the dope, but there was only one person outside the brothers who knew where it was stashed. When Slick hit the block, the fiends were falling out off his shit. Everyone in the hood wanted to fuck with Slick and his dope, but he only let select people into his circle, mostly his closest friends and members of his uncles' old crew. He had halfway gotten his weight up, but still didn't have the common sense to know how to really capitalize on his good fortune. His saving grace was the fact that he had steady clientele. No matter how much of a knucklehead he might've been, no one could deny the fact that he had good dope, and good dope always equaled profit.

On that warm summer afternoon, he found himself strolling through the projects, or his kingdom, as he liked to call it, chatting on his cell and flanked by his right-hand man, Keith, and a girl he had met earlier that day. He glanced at her long brown legs for the umpteenth time and licked his full lips. He was going to enjoy that sweet pussy, but he had arrangements to make first.

The whole hood was buzzing about Bad Blood's performance at Exit that night. They had performed at the spot before, but that was on the strength of Don B. and only short freestyles. This would be their first time performing at Exit since the release of their single. The club was sure to be lined with wall-to-wall pussy and Slick intended to be there.

He was yakking away on the cell with a chick he used to fuck with named Sondra. She had the good fortune of being the assistant to Don B.'s publicist. It wasn't the most high-profile position in his growing organization, but the perks were excellent. For an empty promise and a few dollars, she had agreed to get Slick into the VIP section after the performance. Of course, when he got there he was going to front like he got in on the strength of his own credibility. His spirits were high when she agreed to the favor, but suddenly that all changed when he spotted two dudes beating the hell out of one of his workers.

Ralph was a small-time hustler trying to make his way up the syndicate ladder. At five-eight and just over a hundred and fifty pounds, he wasn't a very intimidating sight, but let him tell it, he was gangsta with his. Ralph was a consummate schemer determined to blow up, but he didn't have the nuts or the smarts to really make a name for himself. The lack of these qualities didn't stop him from trying, though. His latest venture was going hand to hand for a cat named Slick, who moved dope in the projects. He wasn't making kingpin money, but dope proved to be far more profitable than crack.

"Hey, baby," Ralph called to a young lady who was wearing a pair of denim shorts that almost exposed her entire ass. When she ignored him, he got indignant. "Word, you can't stop? Well, fuck you then, bitch!"

"That ain't no way to talk to a lady," a voice called from behind him. Ralph turned around with intentions on getting fly with his mouth, but the words froze in his throat when he saw Jah and Spooky approaching.

"What's good, my dude?" Ralph extended his hand and mustered a fake smile. Jah looked at Ralph's hand, but didn't shake it.

"You," Jah replied, giving him an equally fake smile. "You got that for me?"

"Damn, I meant to hit you and let you know what happened, Jah. Don't you know, ya boy got a ticket for pissing in the street. Fucking police made me pay a hundred-and-fifty-dollar fine for that shit, son. I was tight."

"Word?" Jah said, clearly not believing a word Ralph said. "I know how these dicks can be wit' them tickets, fam, but ya ticket ain't got nothing to do with what I asked you."

"I'm gonna pay you, but I ain't got it right now. That ticket put me behind."

"Come on, Ralph, a buck fifty ain't nothing to a baller like you. My nigga out here getting money," Spooky added.

Ralph shot Spooky a contemptuous look, but didn't say anything. "Yo, as soon as I finish my shift, I'm gonna come see you with that," he said to Jah.

"Ralph, you told me the same thing when you ass betted me for the hundred dollars in the first place, then I didn't see you for two weeks. I ain't got time to chase you, duke. Just give me mine so I can get up outta here."

Over Jah's shoulder, Ralph spotted Slick approaching. Seeing his employer helped to build his confidence and changed the whole way he was coming at Jah. "Fam, I told you I ain't got it right now. I'll bring ya bread through later. Why you stressing me over a little hundred cash anyway?"

Jah looked over at Spooky, who was wearing the same puzzled look that he was. When he spoke to Ralph, his words were calm and even, but the fire that burned in his eyes made Ralph cringe. "Dawg, I'm not really feeling the way you're coming at me right now. You trying to be tough or something?"

Ralph sucked his teeth before answering. "Yo, come on, man, I ain't trying to get into it with you over no petty-ass hundred dollars. I'm on my grind right now, so I'll drop it to you later."

Jah's face suddenly became very peaceful. "Okay, I'll see you later then."

Ralph let go of the breath he was holding, thinking how fortunate he was to dodge the chaos that was sure to come his way. He opened his mouth to invite Jah to smoke a blunt with him, but never got the chance. Jah caught him with a right cross, immediately dropping Ralph. Jah followed with a kick to the face and a stomp in the gut, putting Ralph in a world he had no idea existed. In a swift motion he tore both the pockets off Ralph's jeans, sending loose change and a cell phone scattering on the ground. In Jah's fist, he now held several hundred dollars in crumbled bills of multiple denominations. The take was more than what Ralph owed Jah, but the rest would go for the "pain and suffering" incurred collecting the debt.

Jah brought the heel of his sneaker down across Ralph's nose, breaking it. "Don't never play your fucking self." Jah kicked him again. "I'm a gorilla on these streets!" Charging footsteps from behind caused Jah to spin around. Before he even looked to see who it was, he had his hammer drawn, freezing Slick midstride.

Slick had intended on rolling up and getting on some G shit, but seeing the angry young man with a big gun softened his approach. "Fuck is going on over here?"

"Be easy, my nigga. This ain't got nothing to do with you," Jah told him. He had taken the gun out of Slick's face, but still kept it pointed at him.

"You beating up one of my workers in my hood," Slick said, trying to keep his voice calm.

"Your worker shouldn't be ass betting niggaz," Jah shot back.

Slick looked from Jah over at Ralph, who was on the ground bleeding all over the ramp to the building. He knew that if Ralph had ass betted the young man, then he deserved what he had gotten, but he had to make some kind of showing in front of his man and the girl.

"I feel you, but that's my money you're taking, not his," Slick tried to reason.

"Listen, fam, possession is nine-tenths of the law. Nothing personal." Jah crammed the bills in his pocket and started backing out of the projects, flanked by Spooky.

Slick watched helplessly as the two young men backed out of the projects. When they were safely outside the black gates, Jah and Spooky took off running. They cut through the back of Lionel Hampton and disappeared up St. Nicholas Avenue.

Slick was fuming. Not only did the two men take off with only God knew how much of his work money, but they had made him look bad. Slick always boasted about how he was such a big man, but two young kids had snatched food right out of his mouth. Had he been alone, he might've let it go and just fucked Ralph up for bringing that kind of drama to his doorstep, but they'd done it in front of people. To save face, Slick would have to react.

"Yo," Larry answered his phone.

"What's up, lard ass?" Jah said playfully.

"Do you kiss your mother with that mouth?"

"No, but I kiss your girl with it," Jah replied.

"Okay, did you call me to snap or did you want something?" Larry finally asked.

"Yeah, I got some more bread to put with what we already got. Is shorty still gonna do it?" Jah asked.

"She said she was, but I'll know for sure later on tonight. I'm about to start getting ready for the party, so I ain't gonna have time to pick the money up from you."

"Don't worry about it, I'll hold on to it until like tomorrow or something."

"Don't spend it on weed and guns," Larry joked.

"Fuck you." Jah hung up the phone.

A part of Larry felt guilty for sneaking behind Paul's back, but it had to be done. The less he knew for the moment, the easier it would be for Larry and Jah to do what they had to do. Besides, if all went well, Paul was going to cake off lovely.

Pain stepped out of the taxi on 169th and Amsterdam Avenue. He gave the cabdriver thirty dollars and was halfway across the street before the cabbie could even peel off his change. Keeping his hands tucked in his pockets and his eyes peeled for trouble, he darted around the corner and up the steps of a brownstone. A young Hispanic boy who had been sitting on the stoop nodded at Pain in greeting and moved to the side to let him in the building.

Pain bounded up the three flights of stairs and knocked on a thin-brown door. There was some shuffling and words whispered in Spanish before the door was finally opened. A dark-skinned boy with dark curls stood behind the door, with a baseball bat clutched in his hand. Pain stepped in and submitted himself to a search before he was given the green light to proceed. He passed several doors on his way down the hall on the way to the living room. He had no idea what was in the closed-off rooms, nor did he have a desire to find out. His thoughts were purely focused on the reason he had come.

When Pain rounded the corner to the living room, there were several men present. The three men seated around the table he was familiar with, but the fourth man wearing the baseball cap was a new face. He glanced over his shoulder at Pain briefly, but kept his eyes on the several bundles of cocaine stacked on the table in front of him. After a brief exchange of words, the bundles of cocaine disappeared into a Macy's shopping bag and the man in the baseball cap got up to leave. His eyes lingered on Pain for a minute, trying to place his face, but he didn't stare. Nodding, the man in the baseball cap brushed past Pain and made his exit.

"Well, well, if it isn't the big rap star." The smallest man at the table smiled.

Pain detested the little man, but still managed to muster a smile. "How you doing, Paco?"

Paco was a big-head Dominican cat getting money uptown. He was born into a family of career criminals and cocaine dealers and carried himself as such. Paco was a vicious man who would kill or order murders on a whim and respected nothing other than a dollar. He was a loathed and feared man all throughout Harlem and, unfortunately, the remedy to Pain's problem.

"I assume you've come here today because you have my money?" Paco asked, leaning forward on his elbows.

"Paco, you know you're my nigga and I'd never shit on you." Pain smiled, trying to keep his hands from wringing together in anticipation.

"So where's my bread?"

Pain looked at the ground. "I ain't got it right now, Paco. But that's my word, I'm gonna have it to you within a week or two. I need you to look out for me this one last time, and I'll hit you wit' that. We about to get our first royalties from the single."

Paco closed his eyes and took a deep breath. The two gorillas sitting at his sides tensed up, but didn't move. "Pain, how long have you been telling me this shit? I don't wanna hear about your fucking royalties!"

Pain felt the chill of fear grip his heart, but tried to maintain his gangsta façade. "Stop acting like that, man. You act like I don't spend money with you."

In a flash, Paco was on his feet and in Pain's face. "Don't come in here telling me what the fuck you spend, little nigga. I get money up in this bitch twenty-four seven. You think that little punk-ass couple of hundred dollars you spend every so often means something to me? Don't be fucking funny, kid."

Pain wanted to knock Paco on his ass, but he was sure the bodyguards would cut him down for it. He had to play it cool until he got what he needed. "Paco, you know me and you too cool to be beefing over some short paper. I'll tell you what, hook a nigga up and when I get paid for this show I'm doing tonight, I'll come drop that bread off to you."

Paco was still breathing heavily in Pain's face, but some of the anger in his eyes had drained away. He motioned to one of the bodyguards, who tossed him a large Baggie. "Pain," he said, holding the Baggie between his fingers, "I'm gonna do this for you, but I want my money tomorrow. Not the day after, not when you get your royalties. I want it *tomorrow*."

"I got you." Pain reached for the bag, but Paco snatched it away.

"I'm not fucking around with you, man. You're deep enough in debt to me as it is, and I'm not comfortable with it. Pretty soon everyone is gonna think they can shit on me." Paco extended the bag and snatched it back again. "You take this package and the clock starts ticking, we clear on that?"

Pain looked at the bag hungrily and could almost feel the icy burn of the cocaine in his nostrils and throat. His rational mind told him not to take it, but the runny nose and hot flashes were telling him otherwise. Thinking of nothing but getting the monkey off his back, Pain took the package. "Yeah, we're clear."

"Dawg, you gotta roll," Larry urged Paul.

"I don't think so, man. I might just chill with Marlene tonight," Paul said.

"Come on with that shit, Paul, you can chill with Marlene tomorrow night. You need to be at this spot."

"Larry, you know I really don't do the club like that. All it's gonna be is a bunch of niggaz trying to holla at these chickenhead-ass broads. I don't feel like getting caught up in that."

Larry looked at Paul as if he didn't have a clue. "See, any other night you might be right, but tonight is different. Bad Blood is performing at the joint, kid. You know how many bitches is gonna be piled up in that joint?"

"Bad Blood? You mean them li'l niggaz that hang on Forty-second?" Paul asked. Paul knew of the group, but couldn't profess to know them very well. He had seen Jah with True a few times, but his own relationship with the young cat didn't go any deeper than an occasional "what's up." From what he remembered of them, the whole clique was composed of young knuckleheads throwing stones at the penitentiary.

"Baby boy, them little niggaz done came up. They got a single out right now that got the streets crazy."

Paul sucked his teeth and walked over to his closet. "There's probably gonna be a bunch of young hood niggaz up in there."

Larry strode over to where Paul was standing and began thumbing through his shirts. Paul wasn't really a dressy nigga, but he kept a few nice pieces from the days of his con game, which still fit.

"Come on, dawg, stop shooting hole all in the shit and roll," Larry said, eyeballing a green shirt of soft woven cotton. "You might even get some pussy 'cause you rolling with me."

Paul playfully shoved his friend on his way back to the small square that was designated the common area. He flopped onto his stool and reached for the clip that had burned out minutes prior. Examining the blunt momentarily, he pressed the coils of his flint lighter against it. The smoke stung his eyes, shoving a tear down the side of his nose. Paul held the smoke before releasing it into the air. His eyes took on a glassy look, then became very sharp. As if Larry wasn't even in the room, Paul turned to his easel and stared at it.

"Larry, you think you're the fucking man," Paul called over his shoulder, dipping a thin brush into a bit of violet goop. "I don't need you to get no pussy, my game is tight."

"Nigga, yo game is stale!" Larry shouted, grabbing a box of Timberlands from the top of the closet. "Paul, we used to kill these hos, but since you got all loved the fuck up, you be on some bullshit."

"Nigga, 'cause I'm trying to be good to my shorty my game is stale?"

Larry tossed the box and shirt on a swivel chair. "Ain't nothing wrong with being good to your girl, but you still gotta recognize your base nature. Treat yaself to a little fun, kid." Larry took the blunt from him. "You ain't married yet." Giving his buddy a wink, Larry began rummaging though the refrigerator for a beer.

"Now you got jokes," Paul said, accepting one of the two Heinekens that Larry had managed to scare up. "Just because I got a girl doesn't mean that I'm not the same dude, and it sure as hell doesn't mean I'm getting married."

"Paul, you my dude, I ain't mad at you. I'm just saying, you gotta live a little. You can't spend all your time up Marlene's ass."

Paul was tight, but he tried not to show it. Every so often the fellas would tease him about the amount of time he spent with Marlene. He enjoyed spending time with his girl, but he had to admit that he missed hanging out with his boys. It had been ages since he had been out anywhere other than local spots.

Paul sighed and grabbed the phone. "I'm not going to this party because you pressured me. I'm going because I feel like stepping out."

"That's what I'm talking about," Larry said proudly. "We gonna take it back to '96!"

"Larry, stop being such a fucking vulture," Paul said, dialing the phone.

"Who're you calling?"

"Marlene."

"Come on, man," Larry said and threw his hands up. "Don't check in with her."

"I'm not checking in. It's called a courtesy call. Maybe when you get a girl you'll learn to do the same." Paul ignored Larry and waited for Marlene to pick up.

Marlene stood barefoot on the tiles of her kitchen wearing a pair of sweat shorts and a tank top. Her hands expertly brought the small knife down in even strokes, chopping a lemon. On the stove a pot of hot water for tea whistled, but still went unattended as Marlene chatted away with Audrey on her cordless.

"Girl, I almost had to get black on this bitch in Target," Audrey informed Marlene.

Marlene shook her head as if Audrey could see her through the phone. "Audrey, you can't ever go anywhere without getting into it with somebody. What done happened now?"

"First of all, the line was long as hell. Now, if I was window shopping, there wouldn't have been anybody there, but the one time I wanna go in and pick something up, a thousand other people get the same idea. So I wait on the line for almost forty-five minutes and when

I get to the register, the little Puerto Rican bitch talking 'bout, 'Sorry, no more cash. Credit only.' Then when I tried to explain to her that I had been waiting for a long time, the little bitch had the nerve to catch an attitude, talking about it wasn't her problem."

"What did you end up doing?" Marlene asked, finally removing the pot from the stove.

"What do you think I ended up doing?" Audrey asked, as if Marlene shouldn't have had to. "I raised so much hell up in there that they finally got the manager to come out and handle my purchase. I tried to get them to knock something off the price for my trouble, but they weren't trying to go that far."

"Audrey why you gotta be so damn *black* all the time?" Marlene joked.

"Fuck that. She should learn some damn courtesy. If you don't like your job, find another one. Don't be giving the customers no attitude."

"I know that's right," Marlene agreed, making her self a cup of tea.

"So what you doing tonight?"

Marlene sipped the brew and frowned. "Nothing much," she said, adding two more scoops of sugar. "I'll probably kick back and watch a DVD."

"The story of your life. You need to come out with us," Audrey suggested.

"Where are you heifers going?""

"The marketing firm up the street from us is having some kind of function at the Hammerstein. I went to one of their events last year and it was off the hook. Let's go get drunk and talk about people." Audrey laughed.

"I don't know if I feel like partying tonight. Besides, I don't know if Paul is coming by or not."

"Marlene, you need to quit. You haven't been out in a while and you plan on spending your night sitting by the phone waiting to see if Paul calls?"

"I ain't waiting for him to call, but we were supposed to do something this weekend, we just haven't decided which day."

Audrey sucked her teeth. "Please, you know how niggaz do on a

Friday night. He's probably gonna go out and get drunk with his degenerate-ass friends looking at ass."

"You're so extra, Audrey."

"I'm not extra, I'm real. The weather is nice and it's mad parties popping off around the city. Paul spends time with you so he can build up his credit. If he spends a weekend with you when there's nothing going on, he knows he's free to go out on a weekend when it's popping. Marlene, men are like wolves, they're always gonna need time to prowl."

"Audrey, contrary to what you might think, Paul enjoys spending time with me," Marlene spat, "and furthermore, I know that I ain't gotta watch him like some of these muthafuckas."

"That's something that I could argue, but I'm not going to. Come out with us, Mar. We can hit the party for drinks, then go for a bite afterward. We can make a girls' night of it." When Audrey noticed that Marlene was still reluctant, she added, "Vincent is gonna be there." This got Marlene's attention.

Vincent Gold was one of the VPs at the Rothstein firm, which was the company hosting the party. He was six-five with hazelnut skin and caramel brown eyes. For the last year or so, he had been trying to get at Marlene, but she wasn't trying to take their relationship beyond a professional level. Not that it wasn't a tempting offer; he was gorgeous, gainfully employed, and about something. Any woman would've been lucky to have him. Marlene was loyal to Paul, though. He might not have been all the things that Vincent Gold was, but he was hers.

She composed herself and got back with Audrey. "So what, is that supposed to make me jump out the window and go? You know I got a man, Audrey, so don't go there with me."

"Whatever, Mar. So you gonna come out with us or not?"

Before Marlene could answer, the other line beeped on her cell. A quick glance at the number revealed that it was Paul. "Audrey, I'll call you back. My boo is on the other line."

"Whatever, sprung ass," Audrey said, hanging up.

"Hey, baby," Marlene answered when she clicked over. It only took a matter of seconds before her angelic smile melted into a frown. Paul had just broken the news to her that he and Larry were going out and she wasn't happy with it. Though Marlene was irked, she knew better than to let Paul know it. She was seasoned in life and had to maintain her composure at all times.

"Okay, baby, I understand," she lied.

"I knew you would, boo," Paul said. "I probably won't be out that long. Me and Larry are gonna go shoot pool and maybe have a few drinks. If you're still up, I might come out there when it's over."

"Don't inconvenience yourself over me," she said, a little sharper than she had intended. "I don't want you traveling all this way on the late night. Do you and we'll talk in the morning." Before Paul could respond, Marlene hung up.

For a little over five minutes, Marlene just stood in her kitchen staring straight ahead. Audrey's words replayed in her head and stunk like a hot pin. It wasn't the fact that she said it, but the fact that someone else could be allowed to put doubt in her mind. Marlene tossed her cup of tea in the sink, deciding that she was too far gone to be soothed by drinking herbs. Instead, she grabbed her pack of Bambu papers and walked toward her bedroom. As she thumbed through her massive walk-in closet, she decided what was good for the goose was good for the gander.

Part Two

One Hell of a Night

17

By the time the girls arrived at Exit, the line had already began to snake up the block. Teenage boys and girls hustled up and down the streets wearing Bad Blood paraphernalia and brandishing picket signs advertising their latest single "Slap Ya Self." The sidewalk was crowded with people of all ages and social statuses buzzing about the highly anticipated performance. It seemed like the hometown boys were gonna make good.

The girls were out to get it that night, dressed to turn heads. Rhonda wore a pair of tight-fitting jeans and a spandex shirt with the word "freak" stretching across her large breasts. Reese was also doing her thing in a denim dress and high-heeled shoes. Guys looked their way as they stepped onto the curb, but Billy and Yoshi were the real showstoppers.

The black dress that Yoshi had bought for Billy hugged her like a second skin. It dipped low in the front, exposing the tops of her breasts, and clung around the hips. Her hair was done up in a fresh wash and set, hanging straight down her back and slightly curled at the ends. As she passed a guy they knew from the block, he tried to holla, not even realizing it was her.

Yoshi was over the top, as usual. The tight leather shorts she wore hugged her ass and hips, showing just a little cheek at the bottom. The top she wore was completely see-through with floral patterns. The only thing that kept the whole world from seeing her breasts was the short leather vest she wore. Both guys' and girls' mouths hung open as she sauntered toward the club.

"You see all these muthafuckas out here?" Billy asked, trying to ignore the uncomfortable looks she was getting.

"Looks like everybody turned out for Bad Blood's performance," Reese said.

"I knew we should've gotten here earlier, fucking with your slow ass, Reese," Rhonda said with attitude.

"Me? If you didn't have me go home with you first, I wouldn't have taken so long to get dressed."

"Well, I ain't trying to wait wit' all these thirsty-ass niggaz. By the time we get in the open bar is gonna be over."

Yoshi scanned the front of the club until she spotted who she was looking for. "We might not have to," she said, heading toward the entrance. The other three girls followed closely behind.

Yoshi brushed past the people standing on the line as if she didn't even notice them. A few chicks shot her dirty looks. One girl with a bad weave even went as far as to say, "Who does that bitch think she is?" Yoshi ignored the bum bitch and continued toward the door, parting the rest of the crowd like the Red Sea. The way she carried herself, you could tell she was someone important.

A hulk of a man stood at the door, checking IDs and hurting the feelings of anyone who didn't fit the criteria of what they deemed acceptable by turning them away. When Yoshi and her crew approached, his face took on a hard edge, but softened when he made out the features of the light-skinned dime leading the pack.

"China, what's hood, boo?" He greeted her with a smile that lacked a tooth in the top front.

"Ain't nothing, Bear. How you?" Yoshi returned his smile.

"Can't complain. Say, I haven't seen you at the Wild West in a while."

"I stopped going since the crowd slacked off. All my regulars can catch me at the Lady."

"That's what's up. I gotta come through there and catch the show."
Bear finally noticed the girls with Yoshi anxiously looking at the front
door. "You girls going in?"

"Yeah, but the line is kinda long," Yoshi said, giving him the puppy
dog eyes.

Bear's crusty lips parted into a broad smile. "China, you know I
ain't gonna make you wait on no line, you and ya girls just go on in."
He unclamped the barrier and held it for them to enter.

"Thank you, Bear," Yoshi said, kissing him on the cheek. Giving
the cackling girls on the line a fuck-you look, she and her friends
walked past through the velvet rope.

No sooner than they'd gotten inside the club, they were assaulted
by the stench of musk and a god-awful heat. Even with it being almost
pitch black inside, the walls were still sweating. Quite a few heads
turned when the quartet stepped out on the floor. With some effort,
they managed to squeeze their way over to the bar. Rhonda bumped
and shoved her way into a corner, where they all flocked over and ordered their drinks.

"Yo, it's popping in here," Rhonda said, looking around at the
people assembled to support the local group. "I'm gonna get pissy
drunk and let one of these niggaz hold something."

"I don't think it's a nigga in here that ain't held your goods," Yoshi
said.

"Don't hate, bitch. Especially with the sign on your pussy that says
'Two-for-one on the weekends.'"

"Say what you want, but my bank account ain't never in the red,
welfare baby."

"Can't y'all two ever go anywhere without showing your asses?"
Billy asked.

"Oh, shut up, Billy. You think you're the shit in your little dress.
Hell, you almost look like a girl for once." Rhonda looked her up and
down.

"Rhonda, you know I ain't even the one," Billy said, giving her a
look that let her know it wouldn't take much for her to come out of the
heeled shoes she was wearing and get it popping. Before the argument
could escalate further, the bartender brought their drinks over. When

Billy went to tip, the bartender he waved her off, letting her know that the gentleman at the end of the bar had already taken care of Him. Billy looked in the direction in which he pointed and was surprised at who she saw making his way toward them.

"Damn, you see that guy?" Reese asked, watching the man approach.

"Do I? I'm about to make that nigga my next baby daddy," Rhonda said, adjusting her bra so her breasts stood up more.

The young man continued making his way in their direction. As the lights flickered, his chocolate skin seemed to melt in and out of the crowd. In the dim club you couldn't tell where his black silk Armani shirt ended and his skin began. With a hungry glare and a confident smile, he brushed his way over to where the girls were standing. When he had made it to their little clearing, Crazy Eight stepped in front of him.

"Ladies, what it is?" Eight said, tugging the collar of his JCPenney's suit.

"Oh, hell nah!" Rhonda threw her hands up.

"Crazy Eight, get your ass out the way." Reese shoved him.

He caught his balance and looked down at the girl. "What the hell is wrong with you? Didn't your mama ever tell you not to lay hands on a pimp?"

"So you're a pimp now?" Billy asked, already knowing that Crazy Eight was full of shit.

"I've been pimping since I was ten. My daddy was a pimp and my mama was a ho. Get it right."

Rhonda dipped her hand into her bra and took a step toward the man. "Eight, if you don't get your ass away from over here, you're gonna be a sorry yellow nigga."

Eight, not wanting to call her bluff, made his exit. "I ain't wanna be over here anyway, you hos ain't got no class," Eight called over his shoulder.

When Rhonda finally managed to get rid of Eight, she looked back in the direction that the stranger had been approaching from, but to her disappointment he was gone. She scanned the crowd frantically, but couldn't locate him. When she turned back around to express her displeasure to her crew, her stomach sank. The stranger had reappeared and was breathing heavily on Billy.

Jah moved swiftly around the corner, keeping his head low and his hands in the pockets of the light leather jacket he was wearing. Spooky was supposed to roll to the club with him, but had gotten caught up with some baby mama drama at the last minute. That was one of the many reasons that Jah was happy he didn't have any kids. The new chain he had bought swung heavily around his neck every time he took a step. A few chicks sized him up, but he wasn't trying to stop and kick game. The last thing he wanted was to be caught slipping on a dark-ass street. Once he was safely inside the club, he could really get his swerve on. When Jah got to the front of the club, he was immediately spotted by Bear. The bouncer gave him a distrustful glare and mumbled something under his breath. Jah gave one last look around and approached the club.

" 'Sup, shorty?" Bear said, looking down at the much-shorter Jah.

Jah watched a couple enter the club and turned his attention back to Bear. "Trying to get my swerve on like everybody else."

Bear looked Jah up and down and noticed that his shirt didn't set right on one side. He had been doing his job for too long not to know when somebody was holding. "You looking a little heavy there." He nodded at the very slight impression in Jah's shirt.

"Come on, Bear. Why you giving me a hard time?"

"Jah, you know damn well they don't want no hammers inside this joint. You trying to make me lose my job?"

"I would never jeopardize your job, Big Bear. Me and you too cool for that. I'm rolling solo tonight and you know how niggaz feel about me in these streets." Jah nodded toward two cats on the line who were trying to act like they weren't watching him. "Do ya boy this solid," Jah said, slapping Bear's palm and leaving a hundred-dollar bill in it.

The bouncer eyed the bill in his palm and pretended to be pondering the idea. "A'ight, li'l nigga, but you better not start clowning up in here."

"Bear, you know me better than that. I'm just trying to fuck with some of these bitches," Jah said, passing through the velvet rope. "Yo, come uptown and see me tomorrow and I'll give you a good deal on this watch I came up on."

"A'ight, but don't be trying to rob me on the price," Bear warned him.

"My dude, you just got me for a hundred cash. You got the best hand all day." Jah gave him a nod and disappeared into the crowd.

Bear grinned as he pocketed the hundred dollars Jah had given him. He felt like he had gotten over on Jah, but in actuality, the youngster didn't give a fuck. The hundred dollars had come out of Slick's pocket, so it wasn't like Jah felt it. Besides, with the way niggaz had been acting on the streets, the hundred dollars for the insurance policy under his shirt amounted to money well spent.

Slick and his crew rolled to the spot G-style. He was dressed in a black suit, with a V-neck silk shirt and hard-bottom Stacey Adams. For the event, Slick had rented a black Infinity truck, also black to match his outfit, with custom rims. It had cost him a grip, but you couldn't put a price on fashion. He jumped out of the backseat, looking every bit like a movie star coming out to greet his adoring public. The iced-out Jesus piece swayed from the end of his thirty-five-inch chain, in tune with his shoes clicking on the ground.

"Yo, it's mad bitches out here, kid," Rel said, coming around the truck to stand next to Slick. Rel was a nigga who was getting money back in the days, but habitually going in and out of the prison system. His inability to get a handle on his drinking and drugging, thwarted every attempt he made to get back on his feet. Common sense dictated that if you kept fucking up at something, then maybe it wasn't for you, but Rel wasn't known for his common sense. He was hell-bent on getting it by any means necessary and this is why Slick kept him around.

"You know Don B. and them niggaz attract the pigeons," Groovy said, joining the two men. Groovy was Slick's gunslinger. He was about nineteen years old and dying to make a name for himself in the game. His father was a spineless coward who served as an errand and whipping boy for Slick's uncles. Groovy used his father as an example of how he wasn't going to grow up, and went out of his way to insure he never wound up in that position. These two men were the core of Slick's crew.

"You niggaz just maintain your cool when we get up in there. We're on some VIP shit tonight, so let's act like it."

"You know I keep my cool at all times, Slick," Rel said. "I was the coolest nigga on the block back in the days. I kept a bad bitch and a fresh knot every time you seen me. I been away for a minute, but the hood still recognize. I'm going in there on some mack don shit, baby. Any bitch I choose to lay this game on tonight should consider herself lucky." He bust out into a snicker.

Slick laughed along with his friend and shook his head. Rel would go on like this all the time, reminiscing about his days on top. Slick never had the heart to tell him that the song was over, so he let him live in the moment.

"Yo, I got something on that kid who robbed Ralph's punk ass," Groovy remembered. Slick listened intently as he was given the run-down. "He calls himself Jah, at least that what Ralph knows him as. I asked around and his name is ringing off on some old Billy the Kid shit. He's a young boy, but he's carrying grown-man weight."

Groovy continued to tell Slick what he had learned about the young man named Jah and the more he talked, the bigger the ball of ice forming in Slick's stomach got. Thanks to Ralph, he had a problem he didn't need or want. He was sure that he had more guns and more soldiers than the youngster, and would eventually get to him, but how much would he lose in exchange? Knuckleheads like Jah didn't think like rational people. They were impulsive and acted without thinking. It was sure to be a headache, but he'd have to deal with Jah eventually. As they walked toward the VIP line, Slick weighed the pros and cons of his predicament.

"Name?" Bear asked, looking at the three men standing outside the rope.

"Slick," the leader said casually.

Bear glanced at his list. "Don't see your name up here."

"Maybe you missed it, player. Why don't you look again?" Slick said, a little more assertively.

"And what was your name again?"

Before Slick could open his mouth, Rel stepped up. "Yo, come on, man. This is Big Slick from uptown, stop acting like you don't know." His entire body language was hostile, changing the vibe of the conversation.

Bear tucked the clipboard under his arm and stepped to Rel. "Shorty, who the fuck do you think you're talking to? Yo duke, I'll pound you the fuck out!"

Seeing the situation about to get ugly, Slick stepped in the middle of the two men. "Easy, big man." He laid a hand on Bear's chest, which he slapped away. "We ain't come here for that, my dude. My homegirl Ariel invited us down, and I wouldn't let my peoples shit on her name by coming down here like that."

Bear slacked up a bit, but he let his angry glare linger on Rel longer than necessary. He looked at the list again and tapped a name with his finger. "Yeah, she put y'all niggaz under her comp. Give me twenty a piece," Bear told them spitefully.

Groovy frowned. "Twenty cash? I thought we was comped?"

"*She's* comped, you niggaz is guests." Bear folded his arms and waited for their next move.

Rel looked like he was about to start again, but Slick silenced him with a gesture. Slick dug in his pocket and reluctantly handed Bear sixty dollars. When they were being searched, the giant made sure he was extra rough with Rel, slamming his palm into his crotch and pushing him roughly when he was done. When the three men entered the party area, all the drama they'd gone through disappeared and there was only the stage.

18

Rhonda stood off to the side, looking like she wanted to be sick. This was hands down one of the finest men she had ever laid eyes on, but instead of her finding out how he liked his dick sucked, the stranger had passed her right by and was all up on Billy's dyke ass. She couldn't make the connection right off, but she headed over to where they were standing to find out.

Billy closed her eyes to make sure she wasn't seeing things, only to open them and find out she wasn't. His breath smelled like apple tarts and Billy found herself suddenly craving sweets. "How're you doing, Billy?" Marcus asked, standing close enough for Billy to feel his body heat.

"Hi," she said, trying to keep her nervousness from showing. Rhonda and Reese were staring at her, making the situation even more awkward. At the barbecue she had been confident, but in closed quarters she was choking.

He leaned in close enough to Billy's face to where their lips almost brushed. "Twice in the span of a few days has got to mean something."

"It means that the world is too small." She placed a hand against his chest to define boundaries.

"Marcus, get up off my cousin." Yoshi swatted his arm playfully.

"Yoshibelle, what's good?" He hugged the smaller woman. "Cousin, huh? I should've known that you two shared genes." He eyed Yoshi playfully.

Billy looked from Marcus to Yoshi, and her face flashed defensiveness. "You two know each other?"

"Marcus works over at Shooter's. You know I do them every other weekend," Yoshi said, as if she should've known that.

"Oh," Billy said, trying to hide her embarrassment.

"I should be asking where the hell the two of you met." Yoshi shot Billy an accusing look.

"At a barbecue," Marcus spoke up. "Billy and I had a mutual friend and some common interests."

"Billy, you ain't gonna introduce your peoples to your friends?" Rhonda butted in.

Billy shot her a look, but didn't press it. "Marcus, this is Rhonda and that's Reese." She nodded to Reese, who finger waved.

"Hello," he said politely, nodding at each girl. "So," he turned back to Billy, "since you haven't accepted my invitation to a drink at the club, could I buy you one here?"

"No thank you," Billy said, ignoring Rhonda, who was motioning for her to say yes.

"Damn, you're hard as nails," he said, frowning a little. "I don't want much from you, ma, just some conversation. As a matter of fact, bring ya homegirls. I got a table upstairs."

Billy looked at Yoshi, who nodded in approval. Reese just had a silly grin on her face, while Rhonda looked away. "A'ight, we'll come up for a minute."

Marcus smiled, reminding Billy of a movie she had seen Blair Underwood in. "Right this way," he said, parting the crowd for them.

"Come on, y'all," Billy said, following Marcus.

"Nah, me and Reese are gonna walk around for a minute, we'll meet you up there," Rhonda said.

"We are?" Reese asked, puzzled.

"Yeah."

Yoshi shrugged and followed Billy. "Suit yourselves," she called over her shoulder.

Reese watched her friends disappear into the crowd, on their way to having untold fun, and couldn't figure for the life of her why she was standing there with Rhonda. "What the fuck is your problem? I wanted to go to the VIP and get my drink on."

Rhonda jealously watched the backs of Yoshi's and Billy's heads as the handsome Marcus led them away. Her insides burned at the missed opportunity. Marcus was supposed to be her vic, and instead she took a backseat for Billy. Instead of going with the flow and backing her friend, she hated on her. "Fuck them bitches. I ain't feel like being no fake hos anyway. You see the way Billy was all over that nigga?"

"It looked the other way around to me," Reese admitted.

"Bitch, please, you didn't peep that shit. Thirsty bitch was all up in this nigga's space, rubbing on him and shit."

"Rhonda, I think you're just tight because you didn't get to try him."

"Fuck outta here, he wasn't all that. Besides, I ain't pressed for dick. Let's move around and see who's up in here."

Rhonda bumped her way through the crowd and Reese grudgingly followed. As they hustled across the dance floor, a sea of hands and arms reached out to detain them or just get a touch of their soft flesh. Though Rhonda and Reese weren't as pretty or fair-skinned as the other girls, that didn't mean they were tore up. They got their fair share of attention, too.

As Rhonda bopped to the beat, a warm hand reached out and clamped over hers. Rhonda was about to get fly until she saw who was holding her. He was a dude who appeared to be in his late twenties, with a heavy Jesus piece around his neck. His swagger said that he might be worth a few dollars, so Rhonda decided to dance with him. Motioning for Reese to jump on his partner, Rhonda went in for the kill.

Slick momentarily lost his balance when Rhonda backed her big ass into him. He didn't expect shorty to be so aggressive, but she came out ready to party. He grabbed her by the waist to bring her wild body movements under control and pressed his groin against her. Rhonda pushed him off and continued dancing. Several times Slick's hands tried to roam over her and she had to fend him off. A little friendly palming of the ass was okay, but he was trying to sample all her goods.

Reese wasn't faring any better with Rel. Not only was he like an octopus, grabbing her everywhere she didn't swat him, but he had absolutely no rhythm. His two-step was okay, but every time he tried to add something to the mix he ended up looking like the rusting Tin Man in *The Wizard of Oz*.

"Slow down, playboy," Reese told him, removing his hand from her ass.

"Come on, shorty, stop acting like that," Rel said, busting another stiff dance step. "We in here partying, act like you're trying to have a good time."

"Yeah, that's all good, but slow it up a little bit."

"Slow it up? Baby girl, life is too short to be slowing up, know what I mean? You gotta live in the moment, boo, and right now the moment is about us. A nigga know how to treat a lady. What you want, a little drink or something? Me and my niggaz is in here balling out of control, act like you know about us."

Reese stopped dancing. "Listen, I ain't really trying to hear all that balling-out-of-control shit. I'm telling you to watch your hands. You act like you just came home or something."

Rel looked at her quizzically. "Shit, I did. A nigga just touched down ten months ago, know what I'm saying? I'm back on the streets about to take my rightful place at the head of the table. You don't know who I be?"

"Whatever." Reese began walking away, not wanting to hear any more of his bullshit.

"Oh, it's like that?" Rel called after her. "That's a'ight, shorty, you just made the worst decision of your life. You keep on stepping and I'm gonna go find me another bitch. One who knows how to act when she's chose."

Ignoring Rel's ranting, she made her way back toward the bar area. Rhonda was doing her thing, so she left her to handle it. She just hoped that the guy she was dancing with had more class than Rel. She ordered a Hennessy sour and waited patiently for the bartender to bring her drink. After about ten minutes, the girl wearing the too-short miniskirt set Reese's drink down, along with her bill. When Reese looked at the total, she wished again that she'd gone with Yoshi and Billy.

A commotion erupted off to Reese's left, drawing the attention of everyone at the bar. Bright flashes of light danced throughout the dark room, while a few young girls shrieked. The crowd slowly began to part and snake a path in Reese's direction. Squinting against the effects of the flashbulbs and strobe lights cutting the darkness, Reese was able to make out a face. The face was familiar to her, but she couldn't think why. As he drew closer, with a small cluster of people in tow, Reese's brain finally clicked. It was Jay from Don B's suite.

Jay had traded in his fitted cap for a bandanna advertising Bad Blood's single. The platinum Rottweiler head, which was their crew's trademark, hung around his neck like a guardian. He waved someone to follow and Reese's heart began to pound because she knew who she would see momentarily. And big as life, there he was.

Don B.'s St. Louis Cardinals hat was pulled low over his eyes, exposing only his squared jaw and goatee. A baseball jacket of the same team hung lazily off one shoulder as he stopped to hug a chickenhead who had jumped in his path. He and his entourage were heading in Reese's direction, leaving her stuck like a deer in the headlights. Reese looked around frantically for somewhere to get low, but was boxed in by the people trying to catch a glimpse of Don B.

The ghetto star's eyes were masked by dark sunglasses, but Reese could've sworn he was looking right at her. Her heart began to race as Don B. closed the distance between them. Reese tried her best to look cool, but there was only so much cool she could muster standing directly in the entourage's path. When Don B. was standing directly in front of Reese, she felt like she wanted to fall out. She searched her mind for something to say to him, but ended up not having to. Without so much as a "hello," Don B. sidestepped her and continued on his way to the VIP section. Reese felt like a two-dollar whore watching his arrogant Harlem swagger carry him through the crowd and away from her.

19

Paul stood against the wall, sipping his drink and watching the scantily clad young ladies pass. He felt a little awkward, caught up in the crowd of partygoers, since it had been quite some time since he had been to a club. Larry was on the dance floor trying to make a baby with a dark-skinned chick wearing her hair in a twist. Busting into a series of moves, he proved that he was far more nimble than his size let on.

Paul continued to bop his head to the beat and watch his friend enjoy himself. The scent of Glow by Jennifer Lopez intruded on Paul's senses, taking him on a brief trip down memory lane. He had woken up to the scent of that mixed with sex on quite a few moments during a summer gone by. He only knew one girl who wore that fragrance and when he turned around, he found himself face to face with her.

"Oh, shit!" Paul blurted out.

Isabel was a short Puerto Rican girl with toned legs and a serious ass. She and Paul had had a one-night stand that lasted over a year right before he hooked up with Marlene. Whenever he and Isabel would hook up, they'd have wild drunk sex that was like nothing he had ever experienced. Isabel had a head game that a lot of chicks needed to study.

"Long time, stranger," Isabel said, brushing a strand of blonde hair from her face.

"What's good, ma?" He pulled her close to him. "I see you changed your hair color."

"That isn't all that's changed," she said, poking her chest out.

At first he was confused, but upon closer examination he realized that her breasts were different. Back when he was hitting it she was about a B cup, but since then she had stepped it up to a high C. Paul tried to keep from staring at her ass in the tight-fitting dress she wore, but the fact that he knew what she looked like under it made it hard not to.

"So who you in here with?" she asked, drawing his attention back to her exotic face.

"My nigga Larry Love," he said.

"You still fucking with that fat muthafucka?"

"You know that's my dude, so I don't know why you in here about to talk sideways about him."

"Because he's a big-mouthed piece of shit," Isabel stated. "Yo, my homegirl and her baby's father ain't been the same since."

Around the time Paul and Isabel were messing around, they had made the mistake of hooking Larry up with one of her friends. Paul was against it, because he semi-knew the girl's man and didn't feel comfortable with the setup. Still, they insisted and the girl gave Larry the pussy. He had the girl doing all kinds of wild shit and when the novelty died out, he stopped calling her. Had it ended at that, it wouldn't have been a problem, but it didn't.

It turned out that Larry and the girl's boyfriend were rivals from the streets and there was tension between them anyhow. They exchanged words on several occasions, but it rarely went beyond dirty looks. One night the both of them were in the bar getting hammered and ended up getting into a shit-talking contest. The kid said some real fucked-up shit about Larry and his hustle game, but the finishing blow was delivered by Larry. He made an offhanded comment about a tattoo the girl had gotten a week prior. It was a heart located just above her pussy so the kid knew there was only one way Larry could've seen it. Larry and the kid ended up having a nasty brawl in which Larry got cut right before he knocked the kid out. When the kid went home he proceeded to kick the shit out of his girl and tossed her into the streets with nothing but the clothes on her back. When Isabel and her friend approached Paul and Larry about the incident, Larry fell over laughing. Ever since then, the girl had despised the ground that Larry walked on.

"Hey, that was on y'all. I'm the one that said not to hook them up." Paul laughed. "So what up with you? You and your crew tearing it up as usual?"

"Please believe it." Isabel gave Paul a high five. "You only live once." "Don't live too much."

"Never that, just enough to keep me happy," she shot back, about to reenter the crowd.

Paul grabbed her hand gently and halted her departure. "Damn, I ain't seen you in how long and you're dipping off on me like this?"

Isabel smiled. "Paul, we've known each other too long not to keep it real. I know you've got a girl, and I ain't trying to come between that."

Paul was momentarily shocked. He hadn't seen Isabel in quite some time, so he was a little curious as to how she found out about his girl. He thought about lying, but knew Isabel would see right through it. "Yeah, I got a girl," he admitted, "but that doesn't mean we can't hang out on some cool shit. It's a party, right?"

Isabel thought on it for a minute. Seeing Paul brought back a lot of memories and for an instant she could almost feel him inside her again. No, she had to stick to her guns. Paul had issues and at this point in her life, her space was too small for unnecessary baggage. For as much as she would've loved to have said, "Fuck your girl!" and take him in the bathroom and let Paul pound her out, she knew it would only complicate things further.

"Paul, you know we've never been able to just hang out without fucking," she said and smiled flirtatiously. "Nah, for as much as I would like to catch up on old times, I'm in here trying to make moves. Maybe another time when the playing field is a little more even. Later."

Paul watched Isabel disappear into the crowd and felt the pang in his loins. Even though he and Isabel were fuck buddies, there had always been something more under the surface that neither of them would admit to. Not only did she have some bomb-ass pussy, but Paul enjoyed being around her. With Isabel he never had to worry about what he said or did. With her he could always be himself and that was something he greatly missed.

"Who was that?" Larry asked, slightly out of breath. Paul turned around a little startled because he hadn't heard Larry approach.

"I see you've decided to take a break, Twinkle Toes," Paul teased him.

"I was about to tell you that you needed to get out there and shake a leg with one of these bitches, but I see you've got everything under control. Now stop avoiding the question. Who was that?"

"Oh, that was Spanish Isabel."

"You mean shorty who had the friend?"

"Yeah."

"Man, I sure am mad I fucked that up. Shorty head was fire!" Larry declared.

"Yeah, and you probably could've still been getting it if you hadn't been so petty," Paul told him.

"Fuck that bitch and her man. It was fun while it lasted."

A girl wearing tight capri pants walked by and touched Paul's hand. She waved at him and disappeared into the crowd.

"I sure am glad I decided to come out tonight," Paul said, watching the girl walk away.

"I see you, ya thirsty muthafucka." Larry pushed him. "You got a bunch of tender young joints to experiment with and a guaranteed whorebag you can slide with. You're batting a thousand, my nigga."

"You know I ain't on it like that, Larry. I'm good with one girl, I don't need the headaches of multiple bitches."

"Bullshit, Paul. I see that thirsty-ass look in your eyes," Larry said seriously. "I knew that all it would take is one night for you to be back in your element before that dirtbag side of you resurfaced." Larry gave Paul a pound.

"Nah, man. I'm just trying to get my drink on and enjoy the night. I'm feeling good and can't nothing blow mine right now."

"I don't know about that." Larry gave Paul a smug smile and turned him around to see who was heading in his direction.

· · ·

"Was that Don B.?" Rhonda asked when she made her way back to where Reese was standing.

"Yeah," Reese said, trying to hide the shame in her voice.

"Did you say anything to him?"

Reese thought on it for a moment. "I spoke."

"You *spoke*?" Rhonda asked disgustedly. "Reese, what the hell is wrong with you? You're supposed to be glued to that nigga's side. He was our ticket to get into the VIP."

"Rhonda, did you forget you turned down our ticket into the VIP?" Reese reminded her.

"Please, that nigga they rolled in there with ain't nobody. Don B. and them are the niggaz we're supposed to be rolling with."

Rhonda went on and on and for the most part Reese drowned her out. She felt bad enough without Rhonda's annoying-ass voice adding to it. Rhonda had something to say about everything and everybody. The basis of her whole style revolved around scheming and complaining. Sometimes she wished her friend would just shut the fuck up. A brief glimpse of a profile to their left gave Reese just the way to shut Rhonda up.

"Ain't that Paul?" Reese asked, nodding in his direction. "Oh, who that li'l Spanish bitch he with?"

Rhonda looked around to see where Reese was pointing and found Paul posted up in the corner. He was smiling and talking to a pretty Spanish girl with long blonde hair. The way they were cooing and carrying on was enough to drive Rhonda insane. Something about the sight of a smile on Paul's face drove her berserk. Motioning for Reese to follow, Rhonda moved in her baby daddy's direction, thinking of what new drama she could heap into his life.

"Man, I don't know why y'all was even trying to press them sluts," Rel said, pounding on the bar to get the bartender's attention.

"Rel, shut yo ass up and get the drinks right!" Groovy told him.

"Watch how you speak to a vet, li'l nigga. I've been doing this since you was clinging to yo daddy's pant leg." Rel popped his collar.

Slick looked at him seriously and burst out laughing. "Duke, why you always talking shit? This ain't '89, and you ain't a captain no more. You a nigga out here trying to get it, like we get it."

Rel felt small, but he had to maintain his big man composure. "Slick, you talking shit? Nigga, at least when I had my crew out here I wasn't getting stuck up by juvenile delinquents. Picture one of these water-dick li'l muthafuckas running up on me." Seeing the embarrassment on Slick's face made him feel better.

Slick was about to come out of his mouth sideways, but seeing the bartender setting his drink down took some of the bite out of his mood. "That's a'ight," Slick said, careful not to let Rel know he was uptight. "When I catch shorty I can fix that problem. You, on the other hand, can't do nothing about the fact that you don't get no pussy," Slick remarked, laughing as he headed back through the crowd, leaving Rel at the bar feeling burnt.

At the site of his son's mother heading his way, Paul immediately felt his kill switch trying to flip itself into the on position. He thought that he'd be able to enjoy a nice night out with his right-hand man Larry, but seeing Rhonda threatened to jeopardize that. He thought about trying to slip away into the crowd, but knew it wouldn't be of much help. Rhonda had already spotted him and would be sure to track him for the entire night until she got her point across.

"Just be cool," Larry told him, seeing the irritated expression on his friend's face.

"I am cool," Paul lied.

"Paul, I know you. Don't let that girl goad you into causing a scene. We paid good money to get in here and have a good time, so let's do that."

"I hear you," Paul said, giving himself a mental pep talk.

"What's up, baby daddy?" Rhonda smirked as if she knew something he didn't.

"'Sup," he replied, not bothering to make eye contact with her.

"What the fuck is his problem?" Rhonda asked Larry.

"He's chilling," he said to Rhonda, but continued to look at Reese, wondering if her ass had been that phat the last time he saw her.

Rhonda frowned at his answer and turned back to Paul. "Drinks on you?"

"I ain't got it," Paul said shortly.

"You ain't got it? You must got it, 'cause you still ain't brought P.J.'s sneakers."

The devil in Paul screamed for him to pounce on her, but he chose a softer approach. "Rhonda, please don't start with me."

"Ain't nobody trying to start with you, Paul. It ain't even that serious," she said, giving him a stink look. "I'm in here trying to get my swerve on, not harass your maggot ass."

"Rhonda, why you always starting with that boy?" Larry asked.

Rhonda spun on him as if she was ready to fight. "Why don't you mind your fucking business?"

"You better watch your trump-ass mouth, I ain't Paul," he warned her.

Rhonda got ready to lay into Larry, but spotting True across the room talking to a big-butt female changed her plans. "Come on, Reese," she said, pulling her toward True's direction. "Fucking derelicts," she said over her shoulder as she passed Larry and Paul.

"I swear that bitch lives to make my life miserable," Paul said after Rhonda had gone.

"Shit, you're acting like you're just discovering that." Larry patted him on the back. "Tell you what, let's see if we can't get one of these nasty hos to suck on your little dick. A good shoot of head will make you forget about Rhonda."

Paul winked at his friend. "A good shot of head will make me forget about a lot."

"That's the Paul I know," Larry said, leading him to the bar.

20

The party at Exit was in full swing, with hundreds of people drinking and having a good time, but the VIP area was the official spot to be. Behind the black curtain there was an entirely different party going on. Celebs and big names from different hoods mingled, sipped expensive liquor and champagne, and were all trying to outstunt one another.

Marcus's table was situated toward the back, right off from the small bar area. Billy thought that he would be in the club with a bunch of his boys, but instead he was surrounded by women. Cat was also in attendance, with Rose and two other girls. She gave Billy hungry looks from time to time, but other than that she minded her manners, probably because Marcus made it a point to sit between she and Billy. Billy wasn't sure if he had done it because of his eagerness to make her comfortable, or the fact that he wanted her all to himself. Whatever the reason, she was going to keep an eye on him.

Billy had been apprehensive about joining him behind the black curtain, but he had proven himself to be a perfect gentleman. When they arrived at the table, he pulled chairs out for Billy and Yoshi and whenever the waitress came around he let them order first.

"Why are you staring at me like that?" Marcus asked, noticing the inquisitive look Billy was giving him.

"Wondering what you've got up your sleeve," she said bluntly.

Marcus rolled one sleeve and then the other. "Nothing but some skin and a few tats." Billy smiled a little. "You know, you're much prettier when you're not frowning," Marcus pointed out.

"You need to cut it out," she said.

"Cut what out?" he asked innocently.

"Trying to run game on me."

Marcus furred his brows. "Because a man gives you a compliment, he's gotta be running game?"

"As if you don't know how niggaz do."

"I don't know how niggaz do, 'cause I'm not a nigga. I'm a young man in search of a little understanding."

"Smooth, smooth," Billy said.

"Shorty—"

"My name isn't shorty," Billy corrected him.

"Excuse me . . . Billy, why are you giving me such a hard time? All I'm trying to do is get to know you. Is that such a bad thing?"

"Depends on your intentions for doing so. Nobody does something for nothing," she said finally.

Marcus just stared at her for a moment and said nothing. Billy had the face of an angel and the eyes of a lioness. She acted so hard, but Marcus could see the hurt lingering under the surface. He himself was no stranger to pain and this only made him want to know her more. To know what it was that made her so angry and try to help her get past it.

"Why are *you* looking at *me* like that?" Billy asked.

"Just wondering," Marcus said, still looking into her eyes.

"Wondering what?"

"What man was foolish enough to stomp your heart into so many little pieces?"

"What makes you say that?" she asked, a little surprised at how intuitive Marcus was.

"The kind of pain in your eyes don't come easy, love. You've got 'broken heart' written all over your face, and I was just wondering what I could do to help put the pieces back together."

"You can't do anything for me that I can't do for myself, Marcus."

"What makes you so sure, if you're not willing to let me try?"

"I'm good," she said, standing.

Marcus grabbed her arm and stopped her from walking away. "Damn, Billy, you act like I did something to you. I'm not the enemy. Whatever that chickenhead-ass nigga did to you can be undone."

Billy's eyes flashed a rage that Marcus couldn't understand. "You don't know shit about me." She snatched her arm away. "That 'chickenhead-ass nigga' you're talking about was the love of my life and that's something you'll never know anything about!" With tears beginning to well up in her eyes, Billy turned and ran from the VIP area.

Marcus stood to go after her, but was stopped by Yoshi's gentle hand on his shoulder. "Don't," she told him.

"Yoshi, I didn't do anything," he said, letting her know that he hadn't intentionally hurt her friend.

"I know you didn't. Guys are a real sore spot with Billy." Yoshi went on to tell Marcus the story of her relationship with Sol and how it ended. When her story was done, he felt like a world-class dickhead.

"I had no idea," he said, eyes cast to the ground.

Yoshi patted his cheek. "I know you didn't, boo. Let me go talk to her." Yoshi left the VIP area and went in search of her friend.

Rel sat at the bar, downing his fourth shot of Jack Daniel's. Slick and Groovy had hooked up with two freak-ass broads and were out on the floor doing their one-two. Rel, not wanting to be the odd man out, excused himself to the bar. There he sat, knocking back Jack and drinking Heinekens like they were going out of style. By the time he emptied his plastic cup, he was on his way to being fucked up.

A dark-skinned girl with short hair and glossy lips took a seat on the stool next to Rel, accompanied by her Puerto Rican friend. He tried to give the Puerto Rican girl the "what's good?" eye, but she ignored him and continued talking to her friend. Seeing that she wasn't with it, he moved on to the dark-skinned girl. He looked over her curvaceous thighs and full breasts and decided that she would be the one for the night. Seeing that she was unwilling to make eye contact with him, Rel got more aggressive with his macking.

"What's up, baby girl?" he half slurred.

"Nothing," she said, still not looking in his direction.

"That's a whole lot of junk in your trunk," he said, openly glaring at her ass. "I'm saying, though, you checking me and I'm checking you, let's make something happen."

"Checking for *you*?" she said, looking from Rel to her Puerto Rican friend. "You hear this nigga?"

Rel, seeing they were trying to play him to left, slipped into his cool shit. "Don't let the Jack fool you, baby. I'm that nigga. I be big Rel, been to hell and back just to make sure the devil had my trap," he rhymed. "The whole world know who I be, silk shirts and gators but still maintain my G." Rel folded his arms as if he had laid his A-mack game down, only to have both girls laugh in his face.

"Why don't you take your drunk ass on the dance floor and try to sweat it out," the Puerto Rican girl said.

Rel was just about to haul off and slap the girl when he noticed the big bouncer Bear watching him from across the room. He knew if he swung, security would definitely swoop in and open up a can on his ass, so he held his hand. Mumbling a curse under his breath, Rel slipped off the stool and slunk into the crowd.

Rel made several other attempts to holla at females in the club, but they were all failed ones. He reeked of liquor and couldn't walk without stumbling. The heat trapped within the club only added to his inebriation. A face loomed in the crowd that snapped Rel partially back to sobriety. His eyes zeroed in on the girl with the long black hair and his face glazed over in anger. Wiping his mouth with the back of his hand, Rel bumped his way through the crowd to settle an old score.

Yoshi bumped her way through the crowd, side-stepping dancing couples and swatting away curious hands. She tried to spot Billy, but there were so many people in the spot that she had a hard time of it.

She spied Rhonda off in the cut and thought about asking her if she had seen Billy. From the looks of it, the girl was exchanging words with True and some girl, so she left it alone. She could only imagine what kind of bullshit Rhonda was over there starting, but she wanted no parts of it.

Moving farther within the crowd, Yoshi spotted two of the regulars who came to the club to see her. They tried to get her to stop and have a drink, but she declined, explaining that she was looking for someone and promising to be right back. Yoshi moved from the center of the club to the bar and was about to make her way toward the bathroom when a voice stopped her.

" 'Sup, Yoshi."

As soon as she heard the voice, her skin began to crawl. Conducting most of her business in the dark had taught Yoshi to identify people more by their voices rather than their faces. Rarely did you get a good look at the face of a trick, dancing in the dimly lit VIP sections or turning tricks in a dark motel room. Already knowing who she would see, Yoshi turned around to face Rel.

"Small world," he said, teetering on drunk legs.

"What up, yo. I gotta make moves," Yoshi said, turning to move away from Rel.

"Hold on," he said, grabbing her arm, "you acting like you ain't got time for a nigga?"

"Rel, I was looking for someone." She tried to pull away, but his drunken grip held.

"Fuck all that dumb shit, ma." He fished around in his pocket and pulled out some bills. "I got a buck for you, let's get up outta here and do something."

Yoshi looked at the crumpled bills as if Rel were holding a fist full of shit. "Yo, I ain't got time for this right now, Rel," she said and jerked free, "I told you I'm looking for somebody!"

Rel suddenly became very angry. "You little freak-ass bitch, I know you ain't in here trying to stunt, like you don't know what it is!"

"Yo, Rel, if you start that shit in here, you're gonna be a sorry muthafucka!"

Rel stepped closer to her, causing Yoshi to step back. "You threatening me? I done laid niggaz down for less serious offenses. Bitch, stop acting like you don't know my résumé."

"Rel, I'm telling you—" Yoshi didn't get any further before Rel tossed his drink in her face. Liquor saturated her hair and dripped down her face and vest as she stood there shocked. The potent whiskey stung her eyes, making it hard to see, but Yoshi could make out a figure approaching behind Rel.

A fist came from behind Rel, hitting him square in his lip. His teeth struck against the interior of his bottom lip, causing blood to pour from his soup coolers. Rel turned around to defend himself, but was met by a left to the eye. That preceded a shot to the gut and a combo to the face. The crowd parted, allowing Rel to fall to the ground. The young drunk lay there counting sheep, while Jah stood over him, breathing like a wild man.

"Jah, what are you doing!" Yoshi shouted, grabbing him about the waist, keeping him from officially finishing Rel off.

Feeling someone's hands on him, Jah turned around, still ready for combat. When he saw that the hands belonged to Yoshi some of the fire burned from his eyes. Jah surveyed his surroundings and saw that the deck was stacked against him. From one direction, security bulls dozing their way through the crowd toward the scene and from the other, two young men were doing the same, cursing and knocking over people who got in their way. The guy leading the charge bore a striking resemblance to the dude Ralph was working for. Jah figured that a good run beat a bad stand any day and made his move.

"We gotta boogie!" Jah said, grabbing Yoshi by the arm and leading her through the crowd.

"Wait," she said, pulling away, "what about my girls?"

"We'll call them from outside." He reinforced the grip on her arm and continued pulling.

Yoshi stumbled along behind Jah, trying to keep from busting her ass in the heels she was wearing. A good Samaritan tried to block their path, but Jah removed him with a clobbering blow with the butt of his gun. The Samaritan fell back, leaving a clear lane to the door. Yoshi spared one last glance over her shoulder and the last thing she saw was someone pointing security in their direction as darkness stole her vision.

True was feeling himself after the reception he and his crew had received when they entered Exit. Passing the bar area, Jay paused and whispered something to Lex. They both laughed, looking in the direction of a girl who was standing by the bar. Upon closer inspection, True recognized the girl as one of Rhonda's crew. He couldn't help but wonder if she was the same girl Don B. and Jay had run a train on. Knowing how Rhonda's crew got down, it was very possible.

"True!" a young girl shrieked, trying to reach out and grab his shirt. Before he had a chance to react, one of the bodyguards/chaperones Don B. had assigned to them grabbed the girl about the waist and dragged her off. "I love you, True!" she continued to scream, even as the bodyguard dragged her through the crowd.

"We got these bitches going crazy and we ain't even touched the mic yet," Pain said, as if the girl had been calling his name.

"Stick to the script," Don B. said, joining his protégés. "We've got a show to do, so fuck with them bitches later. Business first." Without waiting for Pain's reply, Don B. disappeared behind the black curtain.

Pain glared at his back angrily. "Hating-ass nigga," he mumbled.

"Say it to his face," True prodded him.

"Ain't nobody scared of Don B.," Pain responded.

"I hear that hot shit. Pain, Don B. is trying to put us on the map, why don't you stop talking shit all the time?"

"I'll pop shit whenever I want," Pain said, putting on his tough-guy face. "I know Don B. put us on, but that don't mean I gotta suck his dick. That's your job."

"You better watch your fucking mouth, nigga," True said, preparing for battle.

"Y'all niggaz knock it off," Jay said, separating them. "We don't air our dirty laundry in public. You niggaz got a problem with each other, settle it with the gloves."

"Yeah, a'ight," Pain said, stepping through the curtains.

"Why that nigga always acting up?" Lah asked, careful not to let Pain hear his question. His yellow face was coated in sweat from the sweltering club.

"That's just how Pain is." True shrugged it off.

"True!" a feminine voice called. The voice belonged to a copper-skinned beauty who wore her hair in tiny boxed braids. She had an onion for an ass and breasts that looked like she was hiding two cantaloupes under her tight Lady Enyce shirt. The remaining bodyguard got ready to intercept the young lady, until True let him know she was good.

"Yolanda, what the deal?" True said, pulling her within the secured circle. Yolanda was a girl that True had met at Greek Fest. She was a fast young thing who had been seen on the arm of several of the city's most dangerous men. Though Yolanda was scandalous, she and True had a beautiful understanding. He could hit her pussy whenever he wanted, as long as she was taken care of for her services.

"You know I had to come out and show the hood love." She kissed him on the cheek.

"I know that's right." True could see the hunger and want for an introduction in the eyes of his crew, but ignored them. Yolanda was free to do who and what she wanted when he wasn't around, but when he was on the scene, it was all about him. There would be no trains run on his little bitch.

They chatted for a while, catching up on old times and things of the like, when a commotion broke out behind him. The wide-backed bouncer was standing directly in front of True so he couldn't see who the person was who was trying to break the circle. He could tell it was a female, but the way the women were acting that night there was no telling who it was. When the bodyguard moved, True spotted Rhonda about to be led away.

"Get the fuck off of me, I know him!" Rhonda said very indignantly.

"Sure you do," the bodyguard said, pushing her back.

True exhaled. He didn't want Rhonda fucking up his flow, but he knew if he didn't step in she was going to cause a scene. "It's cool, Rock. I know shorty." Rock looked from True to Rhonda and reluctantly let her pass.

"Told you, muthafucka," she said, pushing past the security

guard with Reese on her heels. "What's good, baby," she said, practically shoving Yolanda out of the way so she could stand next to True.

" 'Sup, Rhonda," he said, trying to act like he wasn't embarrassed.

"I've been thinking about you since you left my house!" she shouted in his ear. The blasting music made it hard to hear, but Rhonda was talking louder than she had to. If Yolanda had heard, or taken offense, she didn't show it.

"Rhonda, this is Yolanda," True said, ignoring her statement.

Yolanda mustered up a fake smile and extended her hand, but Rhonda looked at it as if it was something vile. "Yeah, I've seen you around before."

Yolanda thought about grabbing Rhonda by the hair and whipping her ass, but she knew that's the reaction that she had expected. Instead, she went below the belt. Leaning into True to whisper, she said, "I know it's been a while since we hooked up, but you could've just given me a call before you went out and started picking up strays. Come find me when you're finished with your charity case." Yolanda kissed True on the cheek again, then turned her attention to Rhonda. By the look on the girl's face, Yolanda knew she felt threatened, which only made the fact of knowing that she had nothing on her all that much sweeter. Chuckling under her breath, Yolanda sauntered back the way she came.

Seeing the smirk on True's face only pissed Rhonda off further. "What the fuck is so funny?"

"Nothing," he said, trying to hold back the laughter.

"I'll bet. What did that little bum bitch have to say about me?"

"She didn't say anything, Rhonda."

"True, you and these little bitches better stop playing with me. Don't act like I won't get it popping in here. I don't know what you're doing with that bitch anyway, with all the cum she's swallowed in Harlem."

"If that ain't the pot," True mumbled.

"What did you say?"

"I said it's mad hot." True fanned himself. "Yo, you want a drink?"

"Yeah, me and my girl will take some drinks," Rhonda said, pulling Reese over. "Get us two shots of Henny."

"Yo, y'all two niggaz come here," True called to Jynx and Lah. The two men walked over wearing confused expressions. "Here." True handed them some money. "Get these ladies some drinks and hold them down for me. I gotta go holla at Don B."

Rhonda started to say something, but True was already in motion. She called his name over and over, but he couldn't hear her over the loud music and the sound of his own laughter.

"No the fuck he didn't." Rhonda snaked her neck, watching True weave through the crowd. Reese tried to contain her laughter, but it ended up coming out anyway. "Bitch, I know you ain't laughing, when Don B. didn't even acknowledge your ass."

"Come on, Rhonda, the shit was funny," Reese said.

"Yeah, True is a funny muthafucka all right."

"So what are you ladies' names?" Lah asked, trying to make small talk with the women True had so graciously set them out with.

Rhonda looked at him as if he had called her a name. "Nigga, you can't be serious. Get the hell out of my face." Rhonda bumped past the stunned young man, with Reese following. They had only made it a few steps before the sounds of a scuffle sent people scattering.

Rhonda was almost knocked over by the crowd, which was trying to get as far away from the fight as possible. When something jumped off at the club, no one wanted to be crushed under the rush of bouncers or hit with a stray punch, so the sensible thing was to move away from the commotion. Rhonda, being who she was, charged head on into it to see what was popping. She broke through the crowd just in time to see the back of Yoshi's head disappear into the mix on the other side.

"I wonder what this bitch done started now?" Rhonda asked no one in particular.

21

Billy stood on the corner, smoking a cigarette she had bummed off some dude who was trying to rap to her. Smoking was something she had first tried hanging out with Rhonda and Reese, but quickly decided that it wasn't for her. But with everything going on, she needed a smoke to calm her nerves.

She felt like a complete ass for running out of the club like that. She cherished Sol's memory in a way that most people couldn't understand. He had been gone for a while, but she still couldn't seem to let go of the memory. Soon, she told herself, but not yet.

She felt horrible for treating Marcus the way she had. How could he have known about the tragedy of her lover? Billy was so caught up in watching for an ulterior motive that she never considered the fact that he might actually be a nice guy. All he had been guilty of was trying to get to know her and she had probably ruined that. The worst part about it was she was actually starting to feel him.

Marcus appeared to be the total package: handsome, respectful, and employed. In a sense, he was too good to be true. It had been a long time since she had kept company with a man, let alone entertained the idea of actually letting him in. Maybe if she ever ran into him again, she'd be a little more courteous.

Billy's thoughts were interrupted by the sound of the emergency door being flung open. Jah and Yoshi came spilling out onto the curb like they had the devil on their heels. Jah looked around frantically as if he couldn't decide which way to go, with a pistol dangling at his side. Yoshi's face was stuck somewhere between excited and turned on. Billy scratched her head, wondering what the hell was going on.

The emergency exit had led Jah and Yoshi to a small corridor. There was hardly any light, save for the dim illumination of the emergency bulbs. Yoshi slowed down to get her bearings, only to have Jah pull harder.

"Why don't you slow your ass down!" she shouted.

"I'll slow down when we're outta here," he said and continued to pull.

"I can't move that fast in these heels," Yoshi said, nearly twisting her ankle trying to keep up.

"Yoshi, I just stomped that nigga out and I'm packing," he said, raising his shirt. "Now, unless you wanna go to jail or risk that dude waking up and trying to tear ya fucking head off, you better keep moving."

After weighing her options, Yoshi kicked her shoes off and did as she was told. Something about watching Jah move through the dark corridor, pistol in hand, turned her on. It took a lot of guts for the youngster to run up on a dude like that in the club. Men had fought over Yoshi before, but never to defend her honor. If nothing else, Jah had gained her respect that night.

"Jah, what the hell was that all about?" Yoshi asked, tripping over something she couldn't quite see.

"That nigga threw a drink on you," he said, helping her to keep her balance. "He's lucky I didn't kill his ass for it."

"Jah, I appreciate you looking out, but I'm hardly worth you catching a body over."

"Why not?" he asked seriously. "Listen, Yoshi, I don't know what the deal was with you and duke, but I wasn't gonna fall back and let him do that. No woman deserves that kind of treatment. Especially my . . ." Jah stopped himself.

"Your what?"

"Nothing, let's just keep moving." Ignoring the questioning look Yoshi was giving him, Jah continued to the end of the hall. When they got to the fire door, he listened momentarily before opening it. When he was as sure as he could be that there was no one outside to ambush them, he pushed the door open and they were finally greeted by the night air.

"What the hell are you two doing sneaking out of the fire exit?" Billy asked, approaching Yoshi and Jah.

Yoshi sighed. "Girl, you don't even wanna know."

"Yoshi, I'm sorry I wigged out on your friend. Its just that—"

Yoshi cut her off by placing a finger tenderly over Billy's lips. "You don't have to explain anything to me, Billy. I talked to Marcus and he's cool."

"I still feel stupid. The first time I get around a good-looking guy, I go all psycho on him. I should go back in to apologize." Billy started for the entrance, but Yoshi stopped her.

"Another time, sweetie," Yoshi said, pulling her in the other direction. "The party is over."

"What the hell happened in there?" Billy asked.

"I'll tell you when we get in the cab," Yoshi said, pulling out her cell and placing it to her ear. "I'm about to hit Rhonda and tell her that we're getting the fuck outta here."

"You do that. But before I go anywhere, somebody is gonna give me an explanation."

"What?" Rhonda shouted into her cell phone. Bad Blood was about to go on and the crowd was hyped, so she had to move near the door to really hear. Even being far away from the stage, she had a hard time understanding Yoshi. "What you mean, y'all are ready to go? Yoshi, the show just started." She listened as Yoshi spoke, making faces at everything she said. "A fight with who? Look, bitch, I don't know what kind of shit you got yourself into up in here, but I ain't ready to go. The show hasn't even started yet." Yoshi said something else, but it went in one ear and out the other. "Whatever, Yoshi. I'll see y'all bitches on the block," she said, hanging up.

"What's wrong?" Reese asked, noticing the change in Rhonda's mood.

Rhonda sucked her teeth. "That bitch Yoshi, on her bullshit as usual."

"Yoshi? Where the hell did she disappear to?"

"Probably found a dick to fall on," Rhonda said humorously. "Her and Billy are outside trying to catch a cab."

"So are we leaving, too?" Reese asked, hoping Rhonda agreed so she wouldn't run the risk of seeing Don B. or Jay.

"Hell no. The party is just about to get popping and we're gonna shut this bitch down." Rhonda held her hand up for a high five.

Reese slapped it, but it was only halfhearted. Ever since she had seen Don B., she had wanted to crawl under a rock and die. She had been a fool to think that someone like Don B. could dig a girl like her, but she still let him and his crew hit it. She had played herself and knew it, but there was nothing she could do about it now. Reese followed Rhonda to the foot of the stage and watched nervously as Bad Blood came out to the roar of the crowd.

Paul stood off to the back of the crowd, sipping a vodka and cranberry. Someone had announced that Bad Blood was about to take the stage, throwing the crowd into a near frenzy. Paul didn't understand what all the hype was about. He had heard the group spit on mix CDs and thought they were good, but they were hardly the caliber of rappers people were trying to amp them up to be. Paul was from the era of cats like Rahkim and Big Daddy Kane, so this new generation of hip-hop didn't move him like that.

"It's about to go down, kid." Larry approached, handing Paul another drink.

"Damn, I haven't even finished this one," Paul complained, but accepted the drink. "You trying to get me fucked up?"

"Paul, stop whining like a little bitch. It's the weekend, my dude!"

"Larry, every day is the weekend to you." Paul downed the first drink he was holding and went to work on the second one.

"And that's why I'm easy like Sunday morning." Larry winked.

A girl with skin the color of milk chocolate and thighs made for adult magazines walked up and playfully bumped Larry with her wide hip. Paul half heard him say something to her, but couldn't make it out over the murmur of the crowd. The girl smiled and pointed off somewhere in the distance and motioned to Larry that she would be right back.

"Who's the chick with the big ass?" Paul asked, hungrily eyeing her exit.

Larry ran his tongue across the top of his mouth, "Oh, that was this little freak bitch I met about half hour ago. Her name is Portia or some shit."

"You get right to it, don't you?"

"Damn right! We paid fifty dollars to get in here, and I plan on getting my money's worth. And you wanna know the best part?" Larry asked, looking around.

"What?" Paul asked suspiciously.

In answer to his question, Portia returned with a friend. The second girl was dark, but not as dark as Portia. Her hair was feathered and split on one side. Glassy brown eyes went from Paul to Larry as the girl sized them up.

"Stacy, this is the kid Larry that I was telling you about and his man, Paul." Portia pointed to Paul, who was smiling goofily. She leaned in so only Stacy could hear her, "Told you he was cute."

Paul gave Stacy the once-over and felt himself becoming semierect. She was a slick young mud kicker who had blossomed nicely. Paul could see a hint of nipple beneath the sheer pink shirt, tied about the belly. Stacy noticed his stare and matched it. The way she held her mouth sent Paul's imagination racing with the endless possibilities. Yes, he could tell she was a fast bitch and had just enough hood in her to do some real nasty shit if the mood was right. Just how Paul liked them.

That wicked side of him that he had promised to put under wraps when he and Marlene became official beat his chest, demanding its due, and Paul wasn't sure how long he could be put off. He looked

over at Larry, who was smiling at him mischievously; that fat muthafucka knew just what he was doing when he selected the two hood rats.
He knew that the devil would come knocking and he was doing everything he could to make sure Paul answered the door.

Bad Blood had the crowd bugging. They performed "Slap Ya Self "
and had everybody in there losing their cool. They had only been on
the stage for three minutes and two fights had already erupted in the
crowd. The dance floor became like a battlefield and Rhonda loved
every minute of it.

"These niggaz is in here tripping," Reese said, stepping to the side
just in time to dodge a bottle dropped by a drunk partygoer.

"I ain't wit' all this elbow-to-elbow shit," Rhonda said, squeezing
toward the corner.

True was onstage doing his verse. His pants were hanging partially
off his ass, exposing his two-way. When he moved to the end of the
stage where Rhonda was standing she tried to get his attention. True
couldn't hear what she was shouting over all the noise, but even if
he could he wouldn't have responded. Rhonda was a good fuck, but
he didn't need her fucking up his groove that night. He was trying to
step his game that night and bag something exotic. Rhonda was local
pussy that he could tag whenever the mood struck him.

"I know this muthafucka hear me," Rhonda said to Reese.

"Rhonda, let that man do his thing," Reese said. She watched intently as Pain went into his verse in the song. Unexpectedly, Don B.
was heading in their direction. He was holding a microphone in one
hand and a towel in the other. Reese tried to back out of his line of vision, but Rhonda was pushing her closer to the stage.

"Bitch, watch out," Rhonda said and shoved Reese.

Reese stumbled and caught herself on the edge of the stage at the
exact moment Don B. reached down to get a bottle of water out of the
small cooler onstage. His tinted eyes landed on Reese, whose breath
caught in her chest. She couldn't see his eyes behind the glasses so
there was no way to tell if he recognized her or not. Reese tried to
think of something to say, but drew a complete blank.

"Don B.!" Rhonda shoved past Reese and tapped Don B.'s pant leg. He looked down at her and nodded. "It's Rhonda, Kelly's sister!"

No! Reese wanted to scream at Rhonda, who was waving her arms like a woman on fire, trying to get Don B.'s attention. Don B. glanced at Rhonda, but Reese was sure he couldn't hear a damn thing over the music. He smiled and said something back, but it was drowned out. It looked like Rhonda was about to try and climb on the stage, when Don B. was called back to do his verse in the "Slap Ya Self" remix. Once again, Reese had narrowly dodged a bullet, but how long could she keep it up? Eventually she would have to face her demons.

22

The ride uptown turned out to be a pleasant one for the two and a half fugitives. They made a brief stop at a diner and all picked up some takeout orders of bacon and eggs. Hearing Yoshi's recollection of Jah coming to her rescue tickled the hell out of Billy. It was the first time she had smiled all night and Yoshi was glad to see the change in her friend's mood. Sometimes she worried that Billy would let her grief drive her to do something stupid.

Billy got dropped off at her house, leaving Yoshi and Jah alone in the taxi for the rest of the ride. It seemed like as soon as she got out, a silence fell between the two. The only sound in the taxi was Patti LaBelle singing about good love on a lite-FM station. Every so often Yoshi would catch Jah looking over at her, but he'd quickly turn his head if she turned to face him. It was funny to her how a nigga who was supposed to have no fear couldn't look her in the eye. Eventually the alcohol and the chronic caught up with Jah and he dropped off to sleep.

Yoshi leaned against the door and studied Jah's profile by the murky lights of the streetlamps they passed. Even sleeping his face sported a slight scowl, but it was still the most relaxed she had ever seen him. For the first time, Yoshi realized how young Jah looked. His face was smooth as silk, with not even the slightest traces of hair. Gone was the hard façade of the street soldier, and in its place there was a sleeping little boy. She had to admit that Jah was a very handsome young man, but he was always so extra on the streets that a girl would never have a chance to appreciate his natural beauty. With strong features and full lips, Jah was very easy on the eyes.

She was still shocked at how hard he had gone for her. He wrapped Rel up without so much as a second thought as to what could've happened to him. He could've gotten locked up, or worse, Rel and his peoples could've did him dirty. Still, he was there when Yoshi needed him and she was thankful for that.

As a car passed, beeping its horn, Jah began to stir in his sleep. Yoshi started to reach out and touch his soft face, but he moved his hand closer to his gun, stopping her. The last thing she needed was this crazy little nigga having some warped dream and mistaking her for an enemy. For now she would adore him from a distance.

The cab coasted to a stop on 124th and Morningside. The street was empty with the exception of a group of young men loitering on the stoop. They eyed the yellow cab warily for fear that it might be the police in one of their many disguises. Jah must've felt the tension because he snapped out of his sleep and looked around.

"Where the hell are we?" he asked.

"This is where I live now," Yoshi said, fishing around in her purse for her money.

Jah looked at the building, which was a walk-up that had been recently renovated. His gaze fell on the curious young men in front of the building, bringing a scowl to his face. "You want me to walk you in?"

Yoshi looked at the men uncomfortably because she didn't know their faces. "I'll be okay," she said, more confidently than she felt.

Jah picked up on the uncertainty in her voice. "Nah, I'll walk you on. Yo," he turned to the driver, "hold on a second while I walk her in."

"Come on, come on. I already go out of my way coming to Harlem," the driver protested. "You make it stop, you catch another cab."

"Why you acting like a nigga ain't gonna pay you? I got money, duke," Jah said, showing the driver a knot.

"No, no. I already go too far out of my way!"

Jah looked like he wanted to do something to the driver, but Yoshi eased him with a gentle hand on his arm. "It's okay," she said, handing the driver thirty dollars. "We'll call you another cab, Jah," she said to the youngster.

Jah climbed out of the taxi and went around to the other side to hold the door for Yoshi. Taking her by the hand, he helped her to the curb. He looked back at the cabdriver, who was staring at him maliciously, and spat in his face. Thick phlegm dripped down the cabdriver's face and settled on his upper lip. In a rage he threw the door open, but was frozen by the sight of the cannon Jah now pointed at him.

"Go ahead, nigga," Jah said, aiming the pistol at the cabdriver's face. "You got some frog in you?" Nervously, the cabdriver sped off without bothering to close his door. "Bitch-ass nigga!" Jah shouted at his taillights. Yoshi just shook her head and allowed Jah to lead her to the building.

The gang who was posted up on Yoshi's stoop quickly got out of their way as they approached. One of the boys who had been staring at Jah quickly turned his eyes away when the young man looked in his direction. The rest of them just nodded as Jah and Yoshi walked into the building.

Yoshi's first-floor apartment was tastefully decorated in warm autumn colors. There was an auburn-colored couch that with the matching love seat formed an L in the living room and a big-screen television that took up a good amount of the wall. Yoshi also had a huge china cabinet filled with crystal glasses and figurines. Her hardwood floors were clean and polished almost to a mirrored shine. The apartment looked like it belonged to an older couple as opposed to a young girl from the hood. Jah had to admit it was hardly what he expected.

"Damn, you got a fly crib, Yoshi," Jah said, looking around in awe.

Yoshi tossed her purse on the couch. "What did you expect, some Section Eight shit with roaches running all over the place?"

"Nah, I didn't mean it like that," he said.

"I'm just fucking with you, Jah. Here," she said, tossing him a Dutch and a dime bag of weed she had gotten out of her purse. "Roll this and I'll call your cab when we're done smoking."

Jah popped the bag open and inhaled. "This is that killa!"

"Nothing but that good shit goes in these lungs," Yoshi said, walking toward the bedroom.

Jah cracked the blunt open and dumped the guts into a wastebasket. He skillfully rolled a blunt shaped like a baseball bat and dried it with the lighter. Picking up the round remote control from the table, Jah cut the television on. News 1 blasted from the television's speakers, startling him.

"You better not be out there breaking my shit up!" Yoshi called from the bedroom.

Jah was lounging on the couch watching *A Time to Kill* on cable when Yoshi came out of the bedroom. She had traded in her club clothes for a pair of red sweats and a tank top. Even in the baggy pants her ass still jiggled, nearly hypnotizing Jah as she passed by to get to her portable bar.

"You want something to drink?" she asked, placing two glasses on the bar top.

"Yeah, I'll take some Henny if you got it," he replied, lighting the blunt.

"I got Henny, but not the kind y'all be drinking," she said, pouring a dark liquid into the glasses.

"There's more than one kind?" he said, trying to hide his embarrassment about being so damn ignorant.

Yoshi gave him an amused look. Jah's naïveté only added to his appeal. Though he acted like he was the hardest nigga on two legs, she was beginning to see that he was really just a boy trapped in a man's world. Yoshi made her way back to the couch and handed him one of the glasses. She watched him as he sipped the potent liquor and screwed up his face.

"The initial bite is a killer, but it goes down smoother than regular Henny," he said, letting out a silent burp. "What kind of yak did you say this was?"

"It's called Privilege. Strictly for the grown and sexy," she said, sipping from her own glass.

"Then it's right up my alley," he boasted, draining his glass.

"Boy, please. You don't know a damn thing about being grown."

"Ah, but you didn't say sexy," he smiled broadly.

"Whatever, fool," she said, snatching the blunt from him.

Jah watched as Yoshi took a deep pull of the chronic and held it. She expertly let some of the smoke escape her mouth and inhaled it through her nose. The way she looked sitting within the cloud of smoke with her hair pinned up in the back made Yoshi look like an Aztec goddess to Jah. He knew how Yoshi got down, but that still hadn't done anything to slack his attraction to her. Most niggaz were attracted to Yoshi, but for the most part it was just physical. For Jah, it went far deeper.

"What's the funny look about?" she asked, catching him staring.

"Huh?" he asked dumbly.

"You heard me. You're sitting there looking like you wanna eat me."

"I might," he said, playfully.

"Jah, you play too much," Yoshi said, laughing it off. When she looked over at Jah, she saw that his face was serious.

Jah was uncomfortable with the way she was looking at him. He felt like all that was in his heart was suddenly written across his forehead. "Say, you think I could get a private show?" he said jokingly, holding up some bills.

Yoshi suddenly became very angry. "I should've known there was an ulterior motive behind all that bullshit you've been kicking in my ear. I think you need to go," she said, getting up and going to stand by the front door.

"Hold on, I was just joking," he said, moving to cut her off before she reached the door. He reached for her arm, but she jerked it out of reach.

"Joking, my ass. Jah, you think I don't know what these dumb-ass niggaz say about me? Hold on, better question: Do you think I care? Let me tell you something, little boy. I might do some foul shit, but

I don't just set my pussy out to anyone holding a few dollars. Your little knight-in-shining-armor front might've gotten you into my house, but it doesn't mean it's gonna get you into my bed."

"Is that what you think this is all about, me wanting to fuck you? Jesus, Yoshi, I know at least ten bitches I can call that would give it up if I asked, so why the hell would I come in here running game trying to hit it?"

"That's the same thing I'm asking myself. Jah, you and me have always been cool, so I don't understand why you would come at me like that."

Jah's tone was emotional when he spoke. "Yoshi, I haven't come at you like anything. I'm not trying to game you outta no pussy, it ain't that serious."

"I'll just bet," she said, turning her head so he wouldn't see the tears rimming her eyes. "You thought you were gonna come in here, hit it, and tell your little greaseball-ass friends how you've just added freak-ass Yoshi to your list of hits. You niggaz fucking disgust me."

"Look at me," he said, placing a hand on her shoulder. When she still didn't turn around, he stepped around to her line of vision. "Yoshi, I ain't like these niggaz," he said seriously. "I mean . . . yeah, I dig you, but not because you strip, sell ass, or whatever it is you do in the club. That shit don't mean nothing to me. I dig you because I think you're fly."

Tears flowed freely down her cheeks as she listened to Jah speak. She wanted to believe him, but there was no way a guy so young could be so deep, especially one as feared as Jah. His eyes held a seriousness that she had never seen in him before. Yoshi tried to turn away, but he held her fast. Though she was angry, Jah's strong hands soothed her a bit. He leaned in as if he was going to kiss her and she didn't stop him. Her mouth opened of its own accord to receive him, but it was not her lips he was aiming for. Tenderly, Jah kissed the tears away from her cheeks.

"Stop," she whispered, but leaned in closer to him. Everywhere Jah's lips touched sent a tingle through Yoshi. At that moment Jah ceased to be that little boy who Yoshi had watched toss firecrackers into Chinese restaurants and became a man, a man who wanted her. Not out of lust, but out of need. A need that she, too, had felt somewhere in the bowels of her womanhood. With a euphoric sigh, she gave herself to Jah.

23

R honda awoke to the sun shining through a dingy window, attempting to blind her. Her body was numb, but she was very aware of the fact that she was in pain. When she tried to lift her head, it felt like someone had clubbed her with a rubber mallet. Running her tongue along her teeth, she could taste the remnants of something she didn't want to identify. Rhonda stretched and when she yawned, she almost wretched at the taste of her own breath. It had truly been one hell of a night.

She looked around the room, trying to get some idea of where she was, but the fact that the room kept spinning made it difficult. Rhonda could make out a small wall-mounted television hanging over a doorway, and a cheap picture hung over the rickety dresser. She had figured out that she was in a motel, but didn't know which one. Her hand brushed a lump in the sheets beside her, causing her to jump almost completely out of the bed. Slowly peeling the covers back, she exposed the sleeping form of Slick. Suddenly it was all coming back to her.

After being snubbed by True at the club, Rhonda was beyond uptight. She immediately hit the bar and started throwing back shots. Sometime during the course of the night, Slick had ended up picking up the tab and making sure Rhonda had all the liquor she could stand.

Afterward, they dropped Rel off and the rest was somewhat hazy. From the looks of things, she had fucked Slick. Curiously, she pulled the covers farther off his body and was astonished to see how big his dick was. It was no wonder she was so sore.

Glancing over at the other bed, she made out two forms. One was that of Groovy, who was unconscious with his mouth open, and the other was that of Reese. Rhonda wondered if she had fucked Groovy, but being that she was still fully dressed, she doubted it. "Square-ass bitch," Rhonda mumbled, sliding out of the bed.

Like a cat burglar, she crept around the room, gathering her clothes. Noticing Slick's crumpled pants on the floor at the foot of the bed, Rhonda's scheming-ass brain began working. Careful not to wake Slick, she dipped her had into his pocket. He had about eleven hundred dollars, but Rhonda only took two. If he had been half as hammered as she had, he'd probably think he spent it tricking off. After jumping into her clothes, she began the task of trying to wake Reese.

"Reese," she whispered, shaking her sleeping friend. "Reese, get up." When Reese still didn't move, Rhonda shook her harder. "Reese!"

"Huh?" Reese popped up, sleepily. "What time is it?"

"Time to get your shit so we can roll," Rhonda said, snatching her shoes off the floor.

Sluggishly, she sat up and tried to get her bearings. Reese rolled out of the bed and rubbed the sleep from her eyes. Seeing the man in the bed next to her, Reese immediately checked for her pants. Thankfully, they were still buttoned as tightly as she had left them. After what she pulled with Don B. and company, she no longer trusted herself. Reese rolled out of the bed as carefully as she could and gathered her shoes. Before she had even placed the second one on, Rhonda was already halfway out the door. Taking one last look at the two sleeping men, Reese slipped out the door behind Rhonda, hoping she hadn't done anything too grimy to the men.

Marlene's rest was broken by the sound of her cell ringing. She had meant to turn the ringer off when she came in that morning, but had been so tired she fell out as soon as she came in. The cell phone finally stopped, only to have the house phone pick up where it left off. Fearing that it might be an emergency, she picked up.

"Hello?" Marlene rasped into the phone.

"Girl, I know you ain't still sleep?" Audrey asked, sounding way too bright-eyed.

"Yes, I'm still sleeping. That's what normal people do on weekends. What do you want, Audrey?"

"I wanna know what happened to you last night," Audrey said suspiciously. "One minute you're over in the corner running your mouth and the next minute you vanished on me. What's up with that?"

Marlene was fully awake now. "Oh, I was tired, so I left."

"Without telling me?"

"I hit you on your BlackBerry."

"Yeah, and I hit you back, but you didn't respond."

"I was probably already asleep, Audrey. You know I don't keep late hours."

"Umm-hmm."

"What's that supposed to mean?" Marlene asked defensively.

"Nothing. I just wondered if you and Vincent disappearing at the same time was some type of freak coincidence or not."

"Audrey, I don't know what you're insinuating, but I don't like it."

"Marlene, I'm not insinuating anything. Call it deductive reasoning," Audrey said, trying to be clever. "You and Vincent Gold spend the whole night examining each other's tonsils, then you both happen to vanish at the same time. Something you wanna tell me, Mar?"

"Oh, no you ain't! Audrey, I know you ain't trying to say me and Vince did something."

"I haven't said anything, Marlene. I'm just saying, if I finally got to jump the bones of somebody I had a crush on, I'd confide it in my best friend."

"Audrey, I do not have a crush on Vince."

"But you didn't deny fucking him," Audrey pointed out.

"Audrey, you know damn well this pussy has Paul's name on it," Marlene assured her.

"Oh, I don't doubt that. But that wouldn't stop the next dick from making a pit stop," she joked. "Anyhow, let me get to the real reason I called you. Where did Paul tell you he was going last night?"

"He said he and Larry were probably gonna go out and play pool, why?"

"I didn't know Exit had pool tables."

"Exit? Audrey, what are you talking about?"

Audrey smiled on the other end of the phone, pleased with herself to be able to spread new gossip, even if it might have caused a problem between her friend and her man. "Well, you know how every bitch from every project rolled down to Exit last night for Bad Blood's performance?"

"What the hell is a bad blood?" Marlene asked, not being up on the hip-hop underground.

"Mar, what planet are you from?" Audrey asked, as if Marlene was supposed to automatically know who she was talking about. "Bad Blood is these sexy little muthafuckas from out of Harlem. They're doing big things in the music biz."

"Audrey, please make a point if you have one," Marlene said, not bothering to hide her irritation.

"Oh, yeah. Well, my cousin Tammy and her girls took they fast asses down there, trying to score a baller, and saw Paul up in the joint."

Marlene sucked her teeth. "Audrey, you woke me up to tell me something your lying-ass cousin Tammy said? You know she wouldn't know the truth if it slapped her in the damn face. Remember the time when she said Puffy was taking her to Negril?"

"I know she be lying, but she swore up and down it was him."

"Bullshit. Tammy doesn't even know what Paul looks like."

"Yes, she does. You know you keep that picture of him on your desk and she's always looming around the office. She said he was up in there with some fat kid and these two stank-looking bitches."

"Is she sure?"

"She seems to be. Mar, I told you them young boys ain't shit. The first time you give them a little freedom, they out there chasing . . ."

Audrey continued to talk, but Marlene really wasn't listening. She just kept thinking about the fact that Paul had lied to her and what he was trying to cover up by doing so. When she had finally grown tired of hearing Audrey's voice, she told her that she would call her back after investigating Paul's story.

Marlene put the cordless back on the charger and rolled out of the bed. When she stretched, she felt a slight throbbing in her thigh. Hiking her nightgown, she noticed a bruise in the shape of a man's thumbprint beginning to form right on the muscle. "Shit," she said, rubbing at the bruise as if it would go away. She would have to put some ice on it and hope that it went down, if not away. It was way too hot to spend the next few nights sleeping in full-length pajamas.

Walking as if she was still asleep, Marlene made her way into the bathroom. She looked in the mirror and wasn't pleased at what she saw. Her eyes were puffy and bloodshot from drinking and there was a nasty-looking web of saliva that had dried on her cheek. Her hair was a mess, too, because she had forgotten to wrap it the night before. She ran her fingers through her hair to untangle it and watched tiny flakes of sand fall into the sink.

Paul leapt up and nearly fell off the couch when his cell phone rang in his ear. He had been a fool for sleeping with the thing right by his head, but he wanted to be able to hear the alarm when it went off. Seeing that it was one o'clock and he had set it for eleven, it hadn't done him much good.

Paul looked around, trying to pinpoint the noisy device and was immediately sorry that he had moved at all. His head felt like there was a game of Pong going on inside it and he was losing. Using more touch than sight, he located the phone under the cushion he had been lying on.

"Who this?" he said, not bothering to hide the fact that he was pissed off for being awoken.

"Paul, I know you can answer your phone better than that," Marlene said.

"Hey, baby," he said and yawned.

"Sounds like you had a rough night."

"A little something. You know when me and this fool get together we try to drink up everything in the place. We didn't get in until like four or five."

"The pool hall stays open late these days, huh?" she asked sarcastically.

Paul, immediately sensing that she was trying to trip him up, got his wits together. "We didn't stay at the pool hall all night. We went out for drinks."

"Yeah, how much they charging for drinks in Exit these days?" she asked, letting him know that trying to think up a lie would be useless.

"You spying on me, Mar?"

"No, I'm not spying on you. But when I try calling my man's house for over a half hour and don't get an answer, it makes me inclined to wonder."

"I didn't answer my phone because I'm not home," he said.

"I know that now. So where are you? Did you spend the night with one of those bitches you were all up on?"

"Come on, Mar, it's too early for this shit. Can we talk about it later?"

"No, we can't talk about it later. Where did you sleep last night, Paul?"

"I slept at Larry's, the same place I am now."

"What made you sleep at Larry's, don't you have a home to go to?" she asked as if she were conducting a cross-examination.

"We came here after the club and fell asleep. What's with the twenty questions?" he asked.

"Nothing, Paul. I'm just trying to find out how your night went."

"My night went the same as it always does when I hang with Larry. We got sloppy drunk and crashed at his pad."

"I hope you didn't get so drunk to where you would've done anything to jeopardize our relationship."

Paul had finally had enough. "Yo, what the fuck is your problem?"

"Don't take that tone with me, Paul."

"I can take whatever tone I want, because I'm a grown-ass man who's answering to his girl like she's his mother!" he barked.

"I'm not trying to be your mother, Paul, I'm just making sure you're not keeping me in the dark about anything."

"Jesus H. Christ! Marlene, I spend damn near every waking minute with you. When do I have time to keep you in the dark?"

"Men are sneaky, Paul. You can make time."

"Marlene, I told you, me and Larry came here and fell out. We ain't do shit but get twisted."

"I hope so, Paul. Anyhow, are you coming to see me today or do you guys have another party to go to?" she asked, changing the subject.

"Very funny," he said sarcastically. "Yeah, I'll be through there. I gotta go pick P.J. up first, though."

"Oh, that's good. I haven't seen him in a while. We can rent movies and eat popcorn."

"Sounds like a plan to me," Paul said, speaking a little more pleasantly than he had a few minutes prior. "So I'll see you later."

"Paul?"

"Yeah, baby?"

"I'm sorry I snapped at you. Sometimes I get a little jealous."

"Don't worry about it, Mar. You know I would never put us at risk. I'll see you sometime this evening."

"Love you, big daddy."

"Love you, too, li'l mama." Paul ended the call and lay back on the couch. He would get up and head home in a minute, but he needed a few more minutes of sleep first. No sooner than his head had hit the couch, a voice startled him.

"Guess you've got one hundred problems instead of ninety-nine?"

Paul popped up and looked over the side of the couch. Stretching her long legs was Stacy. She was naked except for a thin sheet covering her midsection. Paul looked down at his own body and noticed that he was wearing nothing but his boxers. Stacy smiled up at Paul, who could only mutter "fuck . . ." in response.

24

Reese exited the large brown building on 137th and Fifth Avenue with her head hung low. Her eyes were puffy and irritated from crying, and it seemed as if her nose wouldn't stop running. In one hand she held a wad of balled-up tissues that one of the nurses had given her and in the other she held a sheet of paper, with a prescription for penicillin on it.

A few days ago, she had noticed a funny smell coming from her vagina when she was using the bathroom. Thinking it was something cosmetic that didn't agree with her, she switched her brand of douche and feminine wash. To her surprise, the smell was still there. She had made an appointment to see the gyn on Monday, but when she used the bathroom that morning and noticed an off-color discharge, it added urgency. After leaving the hotel and shaking Rhonda, she made a bee-line for the STD clinic, which kept short hours on Saturdays. After filling out the necessary paperwork and getting swabbed, she was devastated to find out she had contracted the clap.

Reese was devastated by the news, so much in fact that she almost fainted in the nurse's office. Her mind whirled, trying to figure out how the hell it had happened or who could've given it to her. She counted off on her fingers the number of men whom she had slept with unprotected within the last week or two and was horribly embarrassed when it spanned both hands. There had been Teddy, a guy she fucked with named Nashawn from the Polo Grounds, and of course the cats from Big Dawg. There were so many that she had no way to pinpoint exactly who it might've been. She had heard stories about girls who had caught STDs from guys and always figured it couldn't happen to her, but it had. She was lucky the rapid HIV test came back negative, but she would have to be tested again in six months to be sure.

Reese collapsed on the steps of the building and placed her head in her hands. She had enough issues in her life already and getting burnt only made things worse. Feeling broken and defeated, she began to cry. Reese had gambled one time too many with her pussy and lost.

"Willamina Jefferson, I know you hear me calling you!"

Billy wearily pulled her head out from under the pillow and looked around as if she were trying to figure out where she was. The dress that Yoshi had bought her was crumpled and dropped in a corner near her dresser, and the shoes were nowhere to be found. "Hell of a night," she muttered.

"Willamina," her mother said, barging in, tired of waiting for an invite, "girl, I've been calling you for the longest. What in the hell are you still doing asleep at three o'clock in the afternoon?"

"Three o'clock?" Billy asked, looking over at her digital clock to make sure her mother wasn't bugging out.

"Yes, three o'clock," she said, tossing the cordless phone on the bed. "Rhonda is on the phone. Damn girl has been calling all morning," she said, slamming the door as she left the bedroom.

Billy stretched her arms to the heavens and listened as various joints crackled and popped. She looked at the phone for a long minute before even thinking about reaching for it. She had had a rough night and really didn't feel like hearing Rhonda's bullshit, but she knew if she didn't get on the phone, Rhonda would just keep calling, or worse, come over.

"Yeah?" she said as she yawned into the phone.

"What was with that bullshit you and Yoshi pulled last night?" Rhonda said in a nasty tone. "Y'all leaving us in the club like that was real fucked up."

Billy held the phone away from her ear and looked at it as if it were malfunctioning before responding to Rhonda. "First of all, its too damn early for you to be calling my house talking outta your ass. Yoshi had to dip because she and Jah go into it with some kid who disrespected her. I was ready to go from the gate, so I bounced, too. I thought Yoshi explained this to you?"

"Yoshi was trying to tell me something like that, but that don't explain why I didn't hear from you."

"Rhonda, the last time I checked my mother's name was Regina. I don't have to report my every move to you, so check yourself before it be something," Billy warned her.

"Whatever," Rhonda said, then clicked her gum. "What you doing today?"

"I don't know yet, I'm just waking up. What's on your calendar?"

"It's too damn hot to do anything right now, but I'll probably be on the streets later. Maybe I'll give Reese's silly ass a call."

"What's she up to?" Billy asked.

"Oh, I forgot you didn't know. That little hot-in-the-ass bitch gave Don B. some ass," Rhonda said gleefully.

"Get the fuck outta here!" Billy was now wide awake.

"I'm dead-ass. It was supposed to have happened the night you disappeared."

"That little slut. So was she all up on him at the club last night?"

"See, that's the funny part," Rhonda continued. "Had I been the one to bag Don B., there's no way in hell that I wouldn't have been drinking like a queen and a few dollars heavier at the end of the night. This bitch acts like she's scared to say two words to the nigga."

"What was up with that?" Billy asked, not really understanding Reese's actions. Reese wasn't as scandalous as Rhonda, but she was a sack chaser in her own right.

"I don't know, but had it been me, I would've been on my bullshit," Rhoda said. "Something is funny with her story and I'm gonna get to the bottom of it."

"Speaking of stories, a little bird told me that a certain rapper was spotted coming out of your building," Billy said.

"Damn, muthafuckas always clocking me."

"So did you fuck him that day, or before then?" Billy asked smugly.

"Why do I have to have fucked him, because he was coming out of my building?"

"No, because I know your trick ass." Billy laughed.

"Fuck you, Billy," Rhonda said, good-naturedly. "You damn right I gave him some pussy. That li'l nigga is on his way to being a star."

"That's my girl, always looking for a come-up," Billy said sarcastically.

Rhonda said something, but the beep on the line muffled it. "Hold on, I got another call." The line momentarily went silent and Rhonda was back. "I gotta go. That's Paul on the other line. I'm about to bark on his ass for trying to stunt the other night."

"The drama in your life never ends," Billy replied.

"Whatever, bitch. 'Bye!"

"Get out the mirror, son. Your eye don't even look that bad," Groovy said, flicking the thumb sticks on the PS2 controller.

"Man, I'm gonna kill this nigga when I catch him!" Rel said, angrily pressing the ice pack against his cheek. He hadn't really felt it the night before, but when he woke up he felt the effects of Jah's blow. His cheek, just below his right eye, was swollen and a blood vessel was busted, leaving a nasty red web on the white of his eye.

"I still don't see how you let ol' boy catch you slipping like that," Slick said, thumbing his own stick.

"Fuck you mean, you don't see how? That nigga snuffed me. Yo, on everything I love, if he hadn't snuck up on me, I'd have laid his ass down in the club. On the real, these niggaz be acting like they don't know what it is wit' ya boy, know what I mean? I'm about to get back on my tough-guy shit, son."

"That tough-guy shit is what got yo ass punched in the eye in the first place," Groovy reminded him. "If you hadn't been trying to play gorilla with that bitch, duke would've never decked you."

"Yo, how the fuck you sound right now?" Rel asked seriously. "A nigga get a lucky snuff off in the club and you're making jokes? Yo, if anything you supposed to be helping me figure out how we gonna catch this nigga and put his lights out."

"Go ahead with that fake gangsta shit." Groovy waved him off.

"Nah, Rel is right," Slick said. "First these little niggaz rob the spot, then a nigga snuffs Rel in the club. Niggaz is acting like we ain't 'bout our shit. We gotta tighten up, fellas."

"The only thing I'm gonna tighten up is that bitch Yoshi," Rel declared.

"I told you that bitch was a snake, son. If you ask me, it was probably a setup," Groovy said.

"Word," Rel agreed, convincing himself that that was actually the case. "Yo, when I spring the trap on these muthafuckas, my justice is gonna be swift. If you don't believe nothing else, you better believe that."

"Don't worry, Rel, you know I ain't gonna let this shit go unpunished. After we deal with this thieving muthafucka Jah, we're gonna find out who laid hands on you. But until then, what we doing today?"

"Getting money," Groovy said.

"We get money every day, my dude. I'm talking about recreationally. It's mad hot out and I know these bitches is gonna be on the streets in full force."

"While y'all silly muthafuckas is sitting here playing video games, we need to be on the streets. Let's go up to Rucker Park and see what's popping."

"Yeah, lets do that. But first let's get this fool some sunglasses. Him running around with his shit all broke up is gonna make us look soft."

"Fuck you." Rel scowled at Groovy. He went back to the mirror and continued dabbing his eyes with the ice. "Had it been you, your ass would've probably ran. Fake tough guy." Groovy thought the situation was funny, but Rel didn't see it like that. Not only had Yoshi dissed him when he tried to pour his heart out, but she had been the cause of him getting knocked out in the club. Hundreds of people had seen or heard about the incident and it wouldn't be something that Rel would live down anytime soon. His pride might've been hurt, but he was still a gangsta. The next time he bumped into Yoshi, he would show her just how *'bout it* he was.

"Man, fuck these little niggaz," Groovy said, tossing his joystick to the ground. "If you're really that uptight about the shit, let's go handle it!"

Rel looked from Groovy to Slick, who just shrugged. He hadn't expected Groovy to call him out like that, but the glove had been thrown. If he didn't respond properly, any hope he ever had about regaining his G status would go permanently out the window.

"Fuck it," Rel said, walking out the front door, followed by Groovy.

Slick just sat on the chair and shook his head. It seemed as if Groovy and Rel were always out trying to prove who had the biggest dick, when all he wanted to do was make money. Still, they were his team, and he had to ride out. Removing his P89 from the dresser drawer, Slick followed his boys onto the battlefield.

About an hour after Rhonda hung up with Billy, there was a knock on her door. She tied the strings of her bathrobe but left enough slack to show her entire thigh. If you looked close enough, you could see that she wasn't wearing any panties. With a larcenous smirk and a Newport balanced between her lips, Rhonda opened the door for her baby's daddy.

Paul stood in the hallway wearing a white T-shirt and denim shorts that stopped just above the line of his ankle socks. Though he tried to maintain his straight-edge composure, she could see the hungover sway in his stance. He nodded in greeting and stepped into the apartment. When he passed her she could still smell faint traces of alcohol seeping from his pores, partially masked by a sweet fragrance that she didn't recognize. Probably something his bitch bought him, she thought to herself.

"Well, hello to you, too," Rhonda said, locking the door.

" 'Sup, Rhonda," he said, helping himself to a seat on the couch. His eyes were red from the night before, but Paul's face was slack and serious.

"Look, don't be coming through here with no attitude." Rhonda walked into the living room and stood directly in front of him.

"Rhonda, regardless of how you spend your time, my every waking thought isn't based around making your life difficult."

"Whatever, nigga," she said, dipping her hand into the pocket of her robe and handing Paul an envelope. "This came for you a few days ago."

"Shit, I don't know why people still send me shit here," Paul said, reading the return address.

"Must be a sign," she said, sitting next to him on the couch.

"Don't flatter yourself," he said, chuckling.

"Paul, you need to stop fronting. Don't act like you miss hitting this," she said, slapping her thigh, causing it to jiggle.

"Rhonda, that shit is yesterday's news," he said, looking away from her.

"Yesterday's news can be tomorrow's headlines, you better act like you remember what it is."

"Rhonda, all I remember is two people who couldn't sit horses. I ain't fucking with you."

"You know you were always stuck on yourself. Ain't nobody trying to break up your little make-believe life. I had you before the swagger, nigga."

Paul looked at her and laughed. "You know, it kills me how you sit around and try to act like being with you was a great boon for my life. The best and only thing you've ever done for me was give me a beautiful son, who I love with all that I am. Other than that, you were a fucked-up dream."

"Maybe, but I'll bet it was a wet one." She spread her legs a bit, letting Paul get an eyeful of her bush.

Paul looked from Rhonda's exposed pussy to her scheming eyes. Her hand slowly made its way down her chest and stomach before it came to rest on her vagina. Using her index and ring fingers, she spread her pussy lips and began massaging them with her index finger. A low hissing came from somewhere deep within her, causing Paul to shudder.

"Whatever you're selling, I ain't buying," he said, standing up.

Noticing the slight bulge in his shorts, Rhonda pressed her attack. "Paul," she said, slithering off the couch, moving next to him, "why you acting like that? It's been a long time since you let a bitch taste that." She grabbed for his crotch.

"Keep your hands to yourself," Paul backpedaled.

"Ain't nobody here but us. I won't tell if you don't." She reached for him again, but Paul caught her about the wrists.

"Where's P.J?" Paul asked, his tone making it clear that he wanted no part of what she was offering.

Rhonda's eyes flashed hurt and then anger. "He's in the park." She jerked away from him. "You didn't see him when you came in?"

"If I'd seen him, I'd have never come upstairs in the first place. Later, Rhonda." Paul headed for the front door, but Rhonda stopped him.

"That bitch really got you trained, huh?" she asked, smirking as if she couldn't believe he'd turned her away.

Paul smiled as if she didn't have a clue. "It ain't about being trained. It's about knowing a once-in-a-lifetime opportunity when it comes your way, and having the good sense not to fuck it up over a leftover piece of pussy. Peace." Paul left the apartment leaving Rhonda stuck on stupid.

After dressing, Billy made her way into the living room where she found her mother hard at work on the laptop. Regina worked downtown at a large corporation as a financial analyst. The title was much more glamorous than the pay, but it kept the rent from falling behind and food on the table.

"Must you always bring your work home with you?" Billy asked playfully.

Regina looked at her daughter over the rims of her wire-rim glasses. "I don't see nobody else trying to keep the lights on."

"Jesus, what's gotten into you this morning?" Billy flopped on the couch near Regina's desk.

"This job is driving me crazy." Regina hefted a thick envelope for Billy to see. "These white folks work me like a dog and reap all the benefits."

"Mommy, if you hate your job so much, why don't you quit?"

"Sure, and depend on you to take care of us?" Regina said sarcastically. "Don't think so, sweetie."

"I work," Billy said defensively.

Regina stopped her clicking on the laptop and looked at her daughter seriously. "Billy, that part-time job you've got at Marshalls ain't work."

"So you're saying because I don't work for somebody's fancy firm, my job doesn't measure up?"

"I'm not saying that at all, Willamina. To be gainfully employed in this day and age is a blessing, with the economy being the way it is. Most folks have to take work wherever they can find it. What I *am* saying is, as smart as you are and as hard as I've pushed, you shouldn't have to settle."

"Come on, Mommy. I'm really not in the mood for speeches. Do we have to go there again?"

"Billy, the truth is a painful elixir. Ever since your father was killed, I've busted my ass to make sure you'd have the opportunity to be something better. You were always good with books and there isn't a man that can touch you on the basketball court. You had the best of both worlds, and I've had to watch you try your best to piss it away running the streets with trash."

"Mommy, I'm gonna pull it together," Billy told her.

"That's the same thing you've been telling me for the last few years, darling. 'I'm just taking a semester off, Mom. I'll go back.' Remember that one?"

"I don't really wanna hear this," Billy said, standing to leave.

"Well, you're gonna hear it!" Regina shouted, slamming the heavy folder on the desk. The look she was giving Billy froze her in her tracks. "Billy, there were so many things that I wish I could've done with my life, but I missed my chance. It isn't too late for you."

Billy folded her arms. "Mommy, why are you pressing me?"

"Because there was no one around to press me and I nearly wasted my life. You were the only thing I ever did right." Regina came from around her desk to stand in front of Billy. She placed her hands on her daughter's cheeks and looked into her eyes, eyes that were much like her own at that age. So young and full of life. A lone tear rolled down her cheek, but she kept the rest at bay. "Willamina, all I want is for you to do the right thing while you still can. Don't wake up one day and find yourself a welfare mother, wondering how it happened."

"I won't, Mommy," Billy said, pulling away. Making hurried steps, she left the apartment.

"I hope so," Regina said to the space where her child had been standing only seconds prior. "I hope so."

Billy moved through the clean lobby of her building, gasping for air. It felt like the walls were closing in on her and she needed to be away from the source of her deprivation. Exiting the building, she took a deep breath and appreciated the muggy New York air.

Regina always knew how to strike a nerve in her only child. Billy knew that her mother meant well, but she also didn't understand the ways of the new world. She thought that if you had a college degree then you automatically were given a good job and stability. This was hardly the case. Billy knew plenty of people who had graduated from college and still found themselves stuck in dead-end jobs or miserable lives. Even if she had gone back to school and played college ball, there was no guarantee that the WNBA would come calling. No, she had to do whatever it was that made her happy, and she just hadn't found anything as of yet.

Her cell phone vibrated in he pocket, startling her. She pulled the small phone out and glanced at the caller ID. Not recognizing the number, she contemplated whether she should answer it or not. She started to return it to her pocket, but decided against it. For all she knew it could've been important, so she picked it up.

"Hi, Billy. It's Marcus," the caller said.

"Marcus? What the hell?" she said, pretending to be annoyed. She was actually glad he called. She had been thinking about him since she met him and wondered what he was really all about.

"Wait, wait. Please, don't hang up. Just give me five minutes of your time and I'll leave you alone."

"Okay, I'm listening." She glanced at the call timer.

Marcus took a deep breath, "First, I want to apologize for what I said to you in the club. I had no idea what you've been through, and I felt like a dickhead for coming at you like that."

"You'll get no complaints from me," she cut in.

"Are you gonna let me finish or what?"

"Sorry, go ahead."

"Billy, I don't wanna complicate your life, I just wanna get to know you. I know you're cautious about your heart, and as God is my witness, I'd never intentionally hurt it. I just want a chance. One dinner, Billy. If you still think I'm an asshole, then I'll get out of your life. Just give me a shot."

Billy paused, as if she were contemplating his offer. She was glad that it was a phone call so that Marcus couldn't see the silly grin that had spread across her face. Her mind still told her to tell him to go to hell, but her heart told her to give him a shot. She couldn't live her life mourning Sol, and though she didn't intend to fuck Marcus, he could be the first step in helping her let go.

"Okay, Marcus," she said, in a tone that suggested she had a million things she could be doing other than talking to him on the phone. "I'll give you your one dinner, but I'm warning you, if you try some fly shit, it's off wit' your head. We clear on that?"

"Crystal," he said, trying to hide the joy in his voice. "Are you free tonight?"

"I might be," she said, teasing him. "What did you have in mind?"

"A light dinner. I know a good Italian restaurant in midtown that we can hit."

"Sounds good."

"Great! You can meet me at the club tonight and—"

"Hold on, par. I'm not really trying to sit up in no strip club," she told him. "You said dinner."

Marcus chuckled. "Baby, you got the wrong idea already. I have to work there until about ten, but the rest of the night is ours. Come down about nine-thirty and have a drink until my shift is over. Don't worry, I won't let the girls get at you," he joked.

"Very funny. I'll be there, but I'm leaving at ten on the dot, whether you're done with your shift or not."

"Fair enough," he agreed. "So I'll see you tonight."

"Wait a second," she said. "If you don't mind me asking, how did you get my cell number?"

"Yoshi gave it to me," he answered, as if she should've already known.

"It figures. I'll deal with that bitch later."

"I hope you're not mad?" he asked.

"Nah, it's cool. You just remember what I said. Ten, and not a minute later."

"I got you, Billy. Ten it is."

"Later." She ended the call. Billy's spirits were immediately lifted at the thought of having a nice dinner with Marcus's fine ass. She could've cursed Yoshi out for giving up the number, but she knew if Yoshi didn't think Marcus was on the level it wouldn't have happened. Billy made a U-turn and headed back toward her building. If she was stepping out, then she would need something to wear.

25

"Yo, I'm telling you, son, I got the hottest shit on the block right now. You need to stop playing and fuck with me, duke." Crazy Eight was on the block, trying to hustle his CDs as usual, doubling as block entertainment for Jah and Spooky.

"Nigga, why you always out here trying to push them CDs, knowing damn well nobody wants 'em?" Spooky asked, eyeing one of the CD cases comically.

"'Cause this is the new movement, God," Eight said seriously. "Don't you realize the power of the spoken word? Music is the universal message, my dude."

"I got a message for you: Get the fuck up outta here with them bootleg-ass CDs."

Eight's eyes took on a semimurderous glint. "Duke, you ain't gotta dis me. Just say you don't want it."

Spooky didn't like Eight's tone and decided to teach him a lesson. "Well, I don't want the shit!" Spooky said, sending the CD floating through the air.

Eight watched helplessly as his CD hit the street and got crushed by a speeding car. Eight looked from the shattered pieces of his CD to

Spooky. Fire burned behind the young man's eyes as he sized Spooky up. The look made Spooky so uncomfortable that his hand moved to the gun he had tucked on him.

Jah gave Spooky a look, letting him know that he didn't approve of what he had done. He dipped into his pocket and handed Eight a twenty-dollar bill. "Here, this is for the CD asshole broke, and let me get one for the crib."

Eight's eyes softened a bit when he took the money from Jah. "Good looking out, fam. Let me get your change."

Jah stopped him. "Don't worry about it. Go get me a Dutch from the corner store and we'll call it even."

"A'ight, my dude," Eight said, mounting his bike. "I'll be right back." He pedaled off to the store, leaving Jah and Spooky alone.

"Why you do that shit, fam?" Jah asked, his face screwed up.

"Man, fuck Crazy Eight." Spooky spat on the ground. "Why do you give a fuck about a derelict-ass nigga like him?"

"It ain't the point of him being a derelict, Spooky. Come on, man, Eight is from the hood. How many fucking years we knew that cat?"

"Fuck him, homeboy ain't wit' us, and if you ain't wit' the team, you ain't shit," Spooky said with conviction. Spooky had been Jah's right-hand man since grade school, but they had very different views on life. Jah was a gangsta, meaning he was down for whatever to put food on the table, but he was reasonable about most things. Spooky was a cat who didn't see logic. If you were weak, you were a victim.

"You need to get a grip, Spook," Jah told him.

"The only thing I need to grip is my dick and my nine." He grabbed each to get his point across. "Yo, how was that party last night?"

"It was a'ight," Jah said, silently remembering it.

"Duce and them niggaz from Thirty-seventh was up in there. They said it was wall-to-wall hos."

"Yeah, they was definitely in there trying to get it popping," Jah said, instinctively looking up and down the block for trouble.

"I know you popped something, 'cause when I called ya phone, I didn't get an answer." Spooky looked at him, waiting for an explanation.

"Nah, I was on some tired shit," Jah lied.

"You paid all that money to get in there and didn't try to slide nothing? That ain't like you, my dude."

"Man, I ended up having to jet up outta there. This bitch-ass nigga was coming at me sideways so I had to lace his boots." Jah threw phantom punches.

"Where was he from?" Spooky asked.

"I don't know, but I think he runs with that kid Ralph was working for, 'cause I seen them trying to creep after I laid homeboy out."

"Yeah, that nigga Slick." Spooky thought on it. "I heard some shit about him. He's supposed to be holding the projects down on some heroin shit. Thinks he's a real big man."

"Is he gonna be a problem?" Jah asked.

"He's got a few niggaz behind him, but he ain't no killer. The boy is really just living off his family's rep. That scary-ass nigga don't want no static."

Jah nodded as Spooky talked. He felt better knowing that Slick wasn't some wild-out killer, but he would still keep his eyes peeled for danger. Spooky was taking the whole thing lightly, but Jah wasn't the type to underestimate anyone. A scared nigga was the most likely to pop you.

After giving it some thought, Jah said, "I'm still gonna do some digging on him to find out exactly what duke is about. In the meantime, we might wanna consider putting Ralph to sleep."

"Ralph? What the hell for?" Spooky asked. "He for damn sure don't want none of us."

"Oh, I know and that's all the more reason I'm thinking about rocking this punk. We disrespected him and he's too afraid to retaliate on his own, so it makes sense to think he'll probably gas this nigga Slick to try and come at us. Ralph ain't about shit, but he knows us. He knows our habits and where we be, and that information could prove to be dangerous. This is how we're gonna play it with duke . . ."

While Jah was running the plan down to Spooky, Yoshi was getting out of a cab on the other side of the street. She was still tired from the night before, but she had business that needed to be handled. She had been so caught up with the drama on the streets that she had neglected her pockets. Her rent was due in a few days and she needed to get on her job. A local cat who she had been dealing with wanted to see her, which meant he was willing to come out of his pocket. Everyone that fucked with Yoshi knew that every second of her time was worth a dollar and that's how she lived her life.

The spot they agreed to meet was at IHOP on 135th and Seventh Avenue. She got out of the cab on Lenox and decided to walk to Seventh. She enjoyed a cigarette and the weather on her stroll. When she got halfway up the block, she noticed Jah and Spooky posted up in front of a small building directly across from the YMCA. She tried to act like she didn't see him, but her eyes acted of their own will and rested on the young dude who had aged five years in her bed. Jah spotted her and gave a nod.

Just seeing him, even at a distance, made her feel in a way. The night/morning they had had together was like nothing she had ever experienced with a man, and Yoshi had been with quite a few. For as hard as Jah was on the streets, he was a pussycat between the sheets. He had tenderly placed kisses over every inch of her body, causing pleasure in waves. When he went down on her, she thought she would pass out from the sheer bliss of it all. The real kicker was when he ran up in her. Jah might've been on the short side, but he had a giant stroke. Several times throughout the course of their lovemaking she thought that he had hit a vital organ.

When it was done, there was an uncomfortable silence between them. Neither had meant for it to happen, but they couldn't deny the fact that it was magical. They both agreed that they'd keep their romp quiet for the time being, not exactly sure where it would go from there. The last thing they needed were wild rumors circulating through the hood that could potentially fuck up a good thing. For as much as she wanted to run to him and kiss his face, she knew she couldn't blow it up. Instead, she returned his nod and kept it moving.

"Damn, I'd love to fuck that bitch," Spooky said, watching Yoshi walk up the block. Jah just remained silent, his eyes fixed on Yoshi. "Yo, I heard she do something real strange for a little bit of change." Spooky, thinking he had said something clever, reached his hand out for a pound. Jah just stared at it.

"Sometimes you talk too much," he told Spooky.

"That ain't nobody but freak-ass Yoshi. Stop acting like that, Jah."

"See, that's the reason you don't get no pussy. Everything that comes out of your mouth about a bitch is derogatory," Jah said. "How long have we known Yoshi and you're over here talking about her like a dog?"

Spooky raised an eyebrow. "Jah, since when are you worried about me shitting on a bitch? Nigga, you're just as foul as I am, and you out here on your women's lib shit? Let me find out you feeling that ho. A-ha." he suddenly chuckled, *"Jah's in love with a stripper,"* he sang, mimicking T-Pain's single.

Anger flashed across Jah's face, but he checked himself before responding to Spooky's accusation. "Dawg, how long you known me and you acting like you don't know my style. My heart is cold as a December morning, so don't press me on no sucker-for-love shit. All I'm saying is that I don't always feel like hearing that shit." Jah turned away.

"Sprung-ass nigga," Spooky mumbled.

About then, Crazy Eight had come back with the Dutch Master and a twenty-two-ounce bottle of St. Ides wrapped in a plastic bag. "Yo, you want some?" Eight asked, trying to hand the beer to Jah.

"Nah, I'm good." True pushed it away. "Yo," he turned to Spooky, "let's go smoke that in the park."

"Why we can't smoke it right here?" Spooky asked, splitting the blunt open and dumping the guts all over the front steps of the building where they were loitering.

"Because I don't want these old folks who live here tripping about us ignorant-ass niggaz fucking up their stoop with our drug paraphernalia. Not to mention we're two doors down from a funeral home and half a block from the precinct."

"True," Spooky said, trying to kick away some of the mess he had made. As he made steps toward the park across the street, he noticed Crazy Eight was following. "Where the fuck do you think you're going?"

"We about to get high," Eight said, continuing to push his bike.

"Nigga, you ain't smoking wit us."

"Yo, I went to the store and can't get high?"

"Eight, you're good," Jah cut in.

"Yo, Jah, I ain't trying to get high with this crazy nigga," Spooky protested.

"Then roll yourself a personal blunt," Jah said, continuing across the street with Eight on his heels.

"How long are we gonna ride around, man?" Groovy asked, turning left on 135th and Eighth.

"Till we spot the little muthafucka. Why, you got somewhere to be?" Rel barked.

"Fam, watch how you talk to me," Groovy warned him. "All I'm saying is that we've been riding around the same ten blocks for the last hour and we still ain't seen the cat."

"Ralph, you sure this is where he hangs?" Slick asked the man in the backseat, who was fidgeting uncomfortably. After leaving the house, Slick and his men had tracked Ralph down and pressed him about information on the kid Jah. After comparing notes about the robbery and what the streets were saying about Rel's run-in, they discovered that the perps were one in the same. This only added urgency to their quest to find Jah.

"Yeah, man," Ralph said, looking as if he was trying to sink into the seat. When they had approached him about info on Jah, Ralph was more than willing to give it to them. But when they insisted that he come along for the ride, things got complicated. He knew that if word got back to Jah about him running his mouth, the clock would start ticking on his life.

"If you're so goddamn sure, why the hell haven't we bumped into him yet?" Rel snapped.

"Why don't you chill out?" Groovy said, lighting a cigarette. He took a long drag and tossed the smoldering match head out the window.

Rel looked at him, frowning. "Chill? This little muthafucka robbed us and tried to split my shit. Word to mine, son, I'm ready to tear this kid's head off."

"Rel is right. We can't let this li'l nigga slide," Slick agreed.

The men continued to talk among themselves, while Ralph tried to remain calm. The task proved to be harder than he'd hoped as his hand kept sweating and he felt like he had to take a shit. Just then he looked across the street and saw Jah leading Eight and Spooky into the park.

"There he is!" Slick said, pointing in their direction.

"Yeah." Rel checked his revolver. "Roll up on this nigga so I can pop his ass."

"Be easy." Slick waved him back. "Groovy," he addressed the young driver, "pull up alongside of them. We'll creep slow and lay his ass down."

Groovy slowed the car to a crawl, while Slick rolled the passenger's side window down. Gripping his P89 with both hands, Slick leaned out the window and tried to draw a bead on Jah. Hands shaking nervously, Slick tried to keep the sight trained on the back of the young man's head. He had shot at people before, but couldn't say for sure if he'd ever hit anyone. His hands were sweating so fiercely that he feared he might drop the gun as soon as he licked a shot off. Without even looking at them, Slick could feel the eyes of his team watching him judgmentally. He was their leader and had to show and prove that he was fit to be such. Taking a deep breath, he wrapped his finger around the trigger and prepared to handle his business.

Yoshi walked into the IHOP and her mere presence demanded the attention of every man in the room. She paused near the entrance and surveyed the eatery. Toward the back, already seated and sipping orange juice, was the man she had come to meet. Eyes hungrily watched as she stalked through the room on the way to the rear booth. A waiter who had been paying more attention to Yoshi than where he was going tripped over a WET FLOOR sign and dropped his entire tray of food. Yoshi just shook her head as she took the seat opposite Red.

"Damn, you always could make a nigga fall and bump his head." He smiled up at her. Red was high yellow, with auburn hair and a baby face. Once upon a day he had played football for Kennedy High

School, but somewhere along the line he lost his way. Had he applied himself, Red could've played D-1 ball, but once he had moved his first pack he decided that he'd rather be rich than educated.

"Just another thirsty-ass nigga," she said as if it was nothing. "So where the hell you been hiding?"

"You know me, Yoshi," he said with a smile. "I be in, out, and around. I just came back from NC."

"Get that money, baby." Yoshi smiled.

"You know I ain't never been one to sit around broke, ma." He sipped his coffee. "So what've you been up to?"

Yoshi fidgeted with her napkin. "Trying to keep my head over water, baby."

"You still working the clubs?" he asked, looking her directly in the eyes.

"A girl has gotta eat."

"Indeed," he replied.

The waitress came on the scene to take their orders. Yoshi went with two eggs and a side of bacon, while Red went with the two pancakes and bacon. For a moment neither of them said anything. Yoshi busied herself with checking the time on her phone, while Red just stared. His hazel eyes made Yoshi feel like they were burning a hole in her. She had always been a sucker for his eyes. Soft, yet cold.

"So let's cut to the chase. I'm in town for a minute and I'm trying to have some quiet time with you. Maybe we can dip out to AC or something. You wit' that?" Red asked.

Yoshi's face reddened ever so slightly. "Look at you." She smiled, letting the sun bounce off her perfect teeth. "Trying to get me to skate on a whim. I gotta work and I have a life. I can't just cancel all my plans and dip off with you."

"I don't see why not. Come on, ma, you know I don't get to see you that often. I gotta check for that when I come through town."

"Tell me anything, nigga." Yoshi said it like she didn't believe him, but she knew full well what effect her pussy had had on Red. His stroke was decent, but it all went out the window when she was on her job. She could always get a whimper out of him if she worked her vaginal muscles the way he liked. Red had done everything, from licking her ass to her feet. Yoshi knew she had a good shot, and every time a nigga like Red came out of his pocket the claim was strengthened.

"For real, Yoshi. You be having a nigga thinking about that, so it's only right that I come check on it," he said.

"I hear you talking." She sipped from the glass of water the busboy had set in front of her. "You and me have always had a beautiful understanding, but you know how I do it."

"Of course," he said as if she needn't have even hinted. "You know I always take care of you, boo."

"Okay, as long as we understand each other," she said.

Red chuckled. "You know, I've never gotten you, Yoshi."

"And that's supposed to mean . . . ?"

"You're smart, fine, and have ambition. A nigga could make you a winner."

"I'm winning already, cat daddy," she said slyly.

"I could never dispute that, but I mean going about it the right way. You ever think about chucking all this shit and letting a nigga make an honest woman out of you?" he asked seriously.

"And depend on someone else to take care of me? Never and a day, boo. I'm a bitch that's always gonna go out there and get it for myself. It's not even my style to gamble my well-being on someone else's dime."

"Nah, I don't mean lay up on a nigga. I'm talking about going half on something. Yoshi, if you were to just get your priorities in order, you could make some lucky cat real happy."

Yoshi twisted her lips and said, "Red, I do things the way I do for a reason. Affairs of the heart can make the game too complicated. Besides, a dude that sells poison for a living can't give me advice on morality."

He laughed at that. "Good one, ma."

The waitress had now returned and began placing their meals in front of them. Yoshi looked at her food and hoped Red wouldn't think she was a low-class ho after seeing what she was about to do to her meal. Jah had sapped her of all her strength and she hadn't had a chance to eat since yesterday afternoon. When she lifted the fork to cut into her eggs, she heard a shot.

• • • •

Jah walked ahead, twirling the Dutch between his fingers, while Eight and Spooky continued to bicker behind him. He was so engrossed in his own thoughts that their voices sounded like overlapping murmurs. Missing a beat, the Dutch slipped from Jah's fingers and hit the ground. Just as he bent down to pick it up, something whistled over his head. He felt the shot more than heard it as he dove to the ground and came up holding his .40.

A black minivan was coasting, with two shooters hanging out the window. Jah made out the stunned face of Slick, as well as that of Rel firing wildly from the rear window, but not hitting much of anything other than parked cars. Spooky was a trained soldier, so there was no need for Jah to shout a warning or even look in his direction. By the time Jah got off his first shot, Spooky had already let off three.

The windshield exploded in a spray of glass, causing both Rel and Slick to duck. Spooky was trying to lay down everyone in the car while Jah shot for the tires, trying to stop the vehicle. Slick and his crew had underestimated the youngsters and found themselves in a gorilla-type firefight. A bullet grazed Groovy's cheek, spooking him into stepping on the gas. Even as the car sped away, Jah and Spooky continued firing on it, riddling the minivan with holes. As the vehicle bent the corner, they could make out Ralph's face staring out what was left of the back window.

"Punk-ass niggaz!" Spooky screamed, waving his gun. "Yo, you seen how fast them niggaz got outta here, son?" When Spooky didn't get a response, he turned around looking for his homeboy, fearing the worst.

The front of Jah's shirt and part of his face were spattered with blood. He was kneeling, breathing heavily as if he had been running. Beneath him, Crazy Eight lay on the ground twitching with two red dots in the middle of his shirt.

"Damn fool went and got himself hit," Jah whispered.

"Man, we gotta go," Spooky said. Seeing that Jah still hadn't moved, he grabbed him by the shirt and lifted him to his feet. "Jah, that nigga is meat. We gotta get the fuck outta here before one-time shows up."

Jah nodded but continued staring at Eight. When the shooting had started, Eight had tried to run with his bike and took one in the gut. Even shot, he was still trying to pull that raggedy-ass ten-speed to safety. The second shot hit him in the chest, flipping the young man backward. He was twenty-two years old when the lights in his eyes were dimmed forever.

"Yeah, kid. That's how you lay a nigga down!" Rel boasted.

Groovy sucked his teeth. "You didn't even hit Jah."

"Yeah, but I hit his man." He hoisted his still-warm pistol. "You seen the way that boy folded?" He tapped Slick.

Slick looked at Rel as if he'd woken him from a peaceful dream. "Shut up and put that hammer away."

"Groove, turn this joint around so I can get another crack at him," Rel said anxiously.

"What are you trying to do, get us knocked?" Slick asked. "Groovy, we're dropping Ralph off and dumping this hot-ass car. Yo," he turned to Ralph, "you straight?"

"I'm cool," Ralph said nervously. His stomach was flopping so much that he thought he was going to shit himself.

"Ralph, you're a part of this team and I protect my own." Slick placed his arm around him. "Don't worry about nothing. Stay the true cat that you are and leave Jah to us. We're gonna handle this nigga," Slick assured him.

Ralph nodded dumbly like he was digging everything Slick was saying, but his thoughts were already on where he was going to relocate. They had tried to hit Jah and missed, which changed the arrangement drastically. Paul's baby brother was a relentless dog. He wouldn't stop coming until he had killed all of them, or fallen to a bullet himself. Ralph didn't intend on sticking around to find out how it played out.

Jah and Spooky tore around the corner of 134th like they had the devil on their heels. The police hadn't arrived on the scene yet, and there was actually no telling how long it would take them. Considering that the closest precinct was only a block and a half away, you'd think they'd have been on the scene at the first sound of shots. Unfortunately, this wasn't the case with the NYPD. When it came to matters in the hood, they tended to take their time.

Jah stopped unexpectedly at a corner payphone. Spooky shouted for him to come on, but he ignored him and punched in some numbers. "Nine-one-one emergency, how may I help you?" the voice came through.

"Yeah, a white dude got shot coming out of the funeral home on 135th." Without waiting for the operator's response, Jah took off running up the block. He couldn't give Eight his life back, but at least he could make sure he didn't have to lie in the gutter any longer than he had to.

26

Marlene sat on the edge of her bed with the television tuned to the Cartoon Network. P.J. sat on a stool, between her legs, as she cornrowed his hair. The boy's locks were so soft that she had to do some braids over as they kept coming out. Normally kids his age never sat still for anyone to do their hair, but she had made sure to supply him with a bucket of Gummy Bears to keep him occupied.

Her cell ringing gave Marlene's tired finger a break. "Hello?" she said, cradling the phone between her ear and shoulder. Her face twitched once, then resumed its cool demeanor before telling the caller she couldn't talk.

"Who was that?" Paul asked, entering the room. He was dressed in a white T-shirt and blue jeans.

"Audrey. I wanna finish P.J.'s hair before I get caught up on the phone with her talking ass," Marlene said, snapping a rubber band on the end of a braid.

"Daddy, we going outside today?" P.J. asked, popping another Gummy Bear into his mouth.

"Yeah, we can hit the streets in a hot one, smell me?" Paul rubbed the boy's head.

"Paul, I wish you wouldn't do that," Marlene told him.

"Do what?" he asked.

"Talk to P.J. like he was one of your boys. Do you want him to grow up using improper grammar?"

"Marlene, the li'l nigga is only three. He ain't gonna remember this shit when he's older."

"Watch your mouth! Don't you know that kids are like sponges at this age? It's bad enough that his M-O-T-H-E-R is ignorant as all H-E-L-L, but he doesn't have to end up that way."

Paul snatched P.J. off the stool and twirled him in the air. "You crazy? My little man is gonna be president or some shit like that!"

"Not with a potty mouth," Marlene said, tapping the plastic comb against her thigh. "Now, could you please put him down so I can finish doing his hair?"

Paul placed the little boy back on the stool. "I got this, boo," he said, and kissed Marlene on the forehead.

"And while I'm thinking about it, where are you going? We're supposed to be spending the day with P.J."

"Oh, I'm gonna run out for about an hour or so. Larry is coming to scoop me," he said, as if it were no big deal.

"Larry doesn't even have a car."

Paul just shrugged. "I didn't ask how he was getting here. Don't worry, baby, I won't be gone that long."

"Paul, you didn't get here until this afternoon and now you're leaving again?"

"Baby," he said, and planted a kiss on her neck, then her lips, "I'm just gonna go take care of this thing with Larry right quick and I'm coming back."

"If that fat friend of yours gets you into trouble, don't call me," she said to his back as he disappeared. Marlene had a few choice words that she would've slung his way, but luckily for Paul, she didn't want to harm little P.J.'s ears.

"What's the matter, Mar?" the boy asked, looking up at her with caramel eyes.

She forced a smile to her lips. "Nothing, baby." Marlene's attention was drawn to her cell as it rang for the second time. She peeked out the bedroom doorway to make sure Paul wasn't around before picking it up. She was relieved to see Audrey's name flashing on the screen.

"Yeah," Marlene answered.

"What's going on, Mar?" Audrey asked.

"Just braiding P.J.'s hair."

"Oh, y'all got him for the weekend?"

"Yeah. You-know-who decided she wanted to play nice."

"Probably so she can get her freak on," Audrey remarked.

"More than likely, but who she's sleeping with isn't my concern. She can do what she wants as long as she doesn't bring it around P.J."

"You never can tell with a bitch like that. Them kids are probably exposed to all kind of bullshit staying over there. You know, Paul is a pretty smart dude, and if he could manage to stop running the streets with stupid muthafuckas like Larry, he might actually make you a half-decent husband. I still can't figure out for the life of me what made him fuck with Rhonda like that."

"Girl, you don't know how many times I've asked him that question. Let him tell it, he wasn't really fucking with her like that before he got locked up. Then he comes home and he's a daddy."

"So Paul's first time meeting P.J. was when he came home?" Audrey asked, obviously leading up to something.

"Yeah, P.J. was almost one, I think."

"Umm-hmm."

"And what's that supposed to mean?" Marlene asked.

"Well, we all know how bitches like Rhonda get down, so I was just wondering if Paul ever found out for sure if he was P.J.'s father."

Marlene got very quiet. It was something she had often wondered about, but had never really pressed. She thought she could see parts of Paul in P.J., but P.J. looked so much like his mother that she couldn't be sure. The thing was, P.J. had straight hair and fair skin, which neither of his parents had. Though it could have come from an earlier strain of one of their families, something told Marlene it hadn't. Then when you threw in Rhonda's rep as a jump-off it raised a few questions. She thought about bringing it to Paul's attention, but didn't want to rub a sore spot.

"Audrey, whatever went on in Paul's life before me doesn't concern me," Marlene said.

"Well, it should," Audrey replied. "Mar, what if you go through the motions of playing stepmother to little P.J. only to find out that he isn't Paul's?"

"Audrey, that's ridiculous. And even if through some fluke the K-I-D turned out not to be Paul's, I'd love him the same."

"Marlene, you're full of shit. You mean to tell me that you wouldn't be the least bit bothered if you went through eighteen years of this bullshit with Rhonda for nothing?"

Marlene shivered at the thought. "Well, what would you have me do, ask Paul to submit to a DNA test?" she asked sarcastically.

"Hell no. Do it behind his back. All you gotta do is call Dana and ask her to look out." Dana was a friend of Marlene's who worked at the same DNA testing center that was featured on talk shows. A while back, Marlene had helped her baby's father out of a jam, so the girl owed her a favor.

"Audrey, I don't even like what you're suggesting. I'll talk to you later." She ended the call. Audrey had some nerve, asking Marlene to do something so underhanded. She was sure P.J. belonged to Paul . . . wasn't she?

Marlene shook her head to clear the foolishness from her mind. She would not follow up on Audrey's bullshit. Besides, even if she did decided to call her girl Dana, how would she get the samples to be tested? Marlene brushed Audrey's idea off and continued parting P.J.'s hair. As she plucked the loose strands of hair from the comb, an idea suddenly began to form in her head.

"Nigga, that was some bullshit," Paul said as soon as he got in the car.

"Fuck is you talking about, my dude?" Larry asked, pulling away from the curb.

"Yo, how you gonna let me run up in shorty?"

Larry gave him a wild look. "I let you? Paul, I ain't got no control over what your dick does. You fucked Stacy, not me, at least not the first round." Paul snickered.

"I'm glad you think this shit is funny," Larry said seriously. "P, I wish you could've seen yourself last night. You were a little stiff at first, but once we threw back a few shots you was doing you, kid. Stacy came at you like she was seasoned, and you handled that freak bitch. I'll bet that pussy was crack!" Larry raised his hand to give Paul a pound, but Paul just looked at it.

"I'm serious, man. You know I'm trying to keep it funky wit' Marlene, so as my man you should've checked me when you saw me going there," Paul told him.

"Duke, I tried to slow you down, but you wasn't trying to hear it. Then when you and shorty started popping E pills . . ."

"E pills?" Paul asked in disbelief.

"Yeah, we all took 'em. You had your tongue so far down Stacy's throat that I thought you were gonna come up with a tonsil. The funny shit is, when we got to the house, y'all started getting it on right in front of me and Portia. On the real, when you was hitting that phat ass from the back, I almost lost my cool. Next thing you knew, me and shorty started popping and we all ended up in a pretzel on the floor. Dawg, I wish I had a video camera 'cause niggaz didn't believe it when I told them!"

Paul placed his head in his hands. "I don't believe this shit. Son, if Marlene finds out . . ."

"She ain't gonna find out, so stop crying about the shit. Don't nobody know but me and you."

"And the million other niggaz you told," Paul said.

"Man, those is hood niggaz. What are the fucking chances that one of them is gonna have a conversation with Marlene, let alone blow you up. You did ya thing dawg, enjoy the moment."

Though he couldn't remember everything, there were occasional flashes of his night with Stacy. Her warm mouth and moist pussy would be etched in his brain for a long time. Paul felt like shit and Larry's nonchalant attitude wasn't helping. He really wanted to be good to Marlene, but it seemed like every time he turned around he was fucking it up. She had been a good chick and didn't deserve to be shitted on. The damage couldn't be undone, but he would make sure it didn't happen again. Or so he hoped.

"So where the hell are we going anyway?" Paul asked, noticing that Larry hadn't gotten on the Queensborough Bridge.

"Just be cool, my nigga. I wanna show you something." Larry cut under the tracks of the 7 train and turned into Silver Cup Studios. The young black dude manning the security booth nodded and waved them into a parking spot. Paul looked around at the hangar-type structures and wondered what the hell Larry was about to get him into.

"What up, Seth?" Larry got out and gave the security guard a pound. "This is the dude I was telling you about." Larry nodded toward Paul, who was still in the car.

"Cool, cool. Come on, we gotta do this quick," Seth said, heading for the main building. Larry followed and motioned for Paul to do the same.

They entered the building, getting second looks from some of the employees but no one bothered them. After walking the length of a winding hallway they found themselves standing in front of a fire door. Paul opened his mouth to say something, but Larry waved at him to be quiet. When Seth popped the door, he led them onto one of the small sets located within Silver Cup.

"What do you think?" Larry asked Paul.

"Think about what?" Paul asked, confused.

Larry sucked his teeth. "The space, fool."

"I guess its okay. What do you plan on doing with it?"

"I'm not doing anything with it, but you are. Seth is gonna fix it so that we can use this place for a night to put on a little exhibition. You're finally gonna get a chance to showcase your work!" Larry said proudly.

Paul's eyes got as big as saucers. "Larry, are you bullshitting me?"

"Man, I wouldn't even play with you like that, knowing how you feel about your work. This is official tissue. The chick I fuck with downtown is tied in with some rich crackers. She gonna invite some of them down here to get a first look at the works of Harlem's latest sensation. I didn't wanna say anything until I was sure we could pull it off."

"I don't believe it!" Paul said, grabbing Larry in a bear hug. "If you was a chick, I'd kiss you on the mouth!"

"You do and I'll knock you the fuck out," Larry joked, breaking loose. "You think you can have your shit ready in less than a week?"

"Damn right I can. Yo, I'll never be able to thank you enough."

"You wanna thank me, get this art shit popping and get your life in order, my dude."

Larry felt good about seeing his friend smile. Paul had been down a rough road and his luck was long overdue to change. Putting the whole thing together had been no easy task. The girl he'd slept with for the hookup was a mud duck, but she had some very powerful friends. The hardest part had been getting the bread together to make it happen. Larry worked and hustled on the side, but he still hadn't been able to put up the money to rent the set and kick out all the bribes it would take to get everybody onboard at Silver Cup. Even though Seth had the security hookup, there were still people who would have to be taken care of. This is where Jah came in. When Larry came to him and revealed his idea, Jah was more than willing to do his part and then some. For the last few months he had been pulling capers and dropping the bread into Larry's lap. If it hadn't been for him, they'd still be trying to get it up. There was a lot about Jah that Larry didn't like, but he had to give the little dude his props. When it came to looking out for family, he would go through hell or high water.

P.J. had finally gone to bed for the night, leaving Marlene some much-needed quality time. She was beat from chasing him around all day. P.J. was a good kid, but children that age required a lot of attention. They had played, watched movies, and baked cookies before the youngster finally dropped off to sleep. Marlene was going to make herself a cup of tea and take a nice hot bath. No sooner had she put the pot on the stove, than she heard her house phone ring.

"Hello?" Marlene said, not recognizing the number.

"Yeah, can I speak to Paul?" Rhonda said, as if Marlene wasn't supposed to be answering her own phone.

Marlene looked at the phone, not believing the nerve of the little ghetto bitch. "He's not here, and P.J. is sleeping."

"I figured P.J. was sleeping, that's why I asked for Paul," Rhonda said in a borderline stink tone. "Look, when he comes in, just tell him that I'm still waiting for P.J.'s sneakers and I'm gonna need some money to pay Verna to do his hair."

"I'll relay the message about the sneakers, but I braided P.J.'s hair this afternoon," Marlene told her.

"How sweet," Rhonda said sarcastically. "Anyhow, tell him he can drop the money off when he brings P.J. home." Before Marlene could respond, Rhonda hung up.

"Fucking bitch," Marlene mumbled to the dead phone line. It was moments like those that Marlene regretted giving Rhonda the green light to call her house. She did it as a courtesy because P.J. spent nights there, but Rhonda used it as an excuse to irritate her. Paul's baby's mother was a royal pain in the ass and Marlene was getting tired of her shit. If Paul didn't have the balls or the desire to do something about her, Marlene was going to take matters into her own hands.

Walking to the supply closet in the hall, Marlene removed a small Ziploc bag and an envelope. Next she picked up the comb that she had been using on P.J.'s hair and Paul's brush. One way or another, Rhonda's bullshit was going to come to an end.

Part Three

A Vicious Cycle

27

"Yo, kid, I'm bored as hell," Groovy said, flicking through the channels on the television.

"Me, too, yo," Rel agreed, pouring some Hennessy into a plastic cup. "Man, we need to be on the streets."

"And risk that little nutball muthafucka Jah creeping on us?" Slick said from the wooden chair he was lounging on. "Nah, we're gonna keep a low profile until we resolve this shit."

"Yo, I'm feeling like a real sucka-ass nigga just sitting around, Slick. That young nigga ain't built like that," Rel said, downing his cup. "That's my word, we can get it popping wherever we see duke!"

"Man, I'm wit' Rel on this one, Slick." Groovy dropped the remote and sat up. "I know we beefing wit' the niggaz from the other side, but Jah ain't nobody. We're acting like we getting it on with some heavyweights. We got the guns and the soldiers, man, ain't no need for us to get low."

"Groove, I dig where you're coming from, but you gotta dig where I'm coming from. Right now we're banging out with some niggaz we really don't know too much about. We don't know how deep Jah's crew is, or exactly who he's with. Anytime one of us leaves here, we're gonna have to take a hammer and with his getting it on so close to the precinct, the streets are on fire. You gotta think about this logically." Slick was putting up a front like he was going at the situation logically, but he was really nervous.

Anytime he had gotten into a major beef in the past, his uncles or someone out of their crew would handle it. Now he found himself in some serious shit. A young man had already died because of it, and more death would surely come of it, all over some pack money and egos. If it was the last thing he did, he was going to make sure his life wasn't among those lost in the feud, and if he had to keep a low profile to do it, that's what he was going to do.

Rel picked up the bottle. "Y'all can do what you want, but I'm going out to try and get some pussy. Fuck Jah!" He took a long swig directly from the bottle.

"Yo, I think Shooter's on Thirty-eighth is popping tonight," Groovy said.

"Yeah, they always got some fine bitches up in there that'll fuck for some paper." Rel grabbed his crotch. "I'm wit' that."

"You coming, Slick?" Groovy asked, picking up his gun.

"Nah, y'all niggaz do y'all. Just be safe out there," Slick told them. He watched his crew leave, thinking how they were asking for trouble. Slick might not have been the toughest hustler in the streets, but he was damn sure one of the smartest. While Groovy and Rel continued to stick their heads in the lion's mouth, Slick would let it come to him.

"Why don't you slow down with that shit?" Lex suggested, watching Pain snort line after line of cocaine.

"Stop clocking what I do," Pain said, sniffling and snorting. "I'm a grown-ass man."

"You keep putting that shit in your brain and you probably won't live to see old age," True added.

"Nigga, I know you ain't talking wit' all the powder Don B. sniffs.

I guess 'cause that's your boss it's okay for him to do it," Pain said venomously.

True stopped rolling his blunt and moved to stand directly in front of where Pain was hunched over. "I'm getting real tired of the way you be coming at me."

Pain stood to meet his challenge, his eyes glassed over from all the cocaine he had snorted. "My dude, don't be raising up on me like you built like that. Don't let the shit these punk-ass magazines write about you go to your head. Bad Blood is a group, not a one-man show."

True matched Pain's stare. "Nigga, don't tell me about a group. I'm down for my niggaz all day, kid. You be the one acting all funny and shit. That coke be having you moody."

"Why don't the both of y'all relax?" suggested Jay, coming out of the bedroom. "Pain, every time I turn around, you arguing with one of these niggaz. We supposed to be a group, so let's act like it."

"*We?*" Pain made a face. "Nigga, you run errands for Don B. You ain't even a member of Bad Blood." This broke the tension and drew a laugh from all the young men in the room. Pain's cell phone started ringing, but he just looked at the caller ID without picking it up. It was the third time he had done it over the last hour.

"Fuck you keep looping?" Lex asked.

"Just this little chickenhead that can't get enough of daddy's dick," Pain lied.

"Well, why don't you call that bitch so we can all bust ass?" True said.

"Fuck outta here, you don't ever share your bitches, so why should I share one of mine?"

" 'Cause we a group." True tried to put his arm around Pain, but he brushed it off.

"Man, let's go outside. Its crazy hot in here," Lah said, fanning himself.

"Shut up and stop complaining," Pain said. "Matter of fact," Pain said, and tossed him a bag of weed, "roll that."

"Leave the little nigga alone, yo," Jay cut in. "He's right, it is mad hot in here. This project has always got some rat bitches running around trying to get their heads popped off. Let's go see if we can find some." They all agreed and filed out of the apartment in search of a good time.

The weather had dropped so Yoshi had changed into jeans and a short leather jacket. Her heeled leather boots clicked on the ground beneath her, making a strange melody accompanied by the rumbling of the wheels of her small rolling case. Her cell vibrated, causing her to reflexively slow up.

"Speak on it," she answered.

"What's good, informer?" Billy asked jokingly.

"Hey, Billy. Listen, I hope you're not tight about me giving Marcus your number?"

"Nah, it's cool. I was glad to speak to him."

"That's good. Marcus really is a nice guy."

"I guess I'll find out for sure tonight. I'm supposed to meet him at the club," Billy admitted.

"You freaky little heifer!" Yoshi squealed.

"It ain't even like that, bitch. I'm just meeting him there. He's taking me out for a nice Italian dinner."

"That's what I'm talking about," Yoshi said proudly. "Some niggaz try to jump straight for the pussy before they spend some dough. Knowing Marcus, he's probably gonna take you somewhere nice. Why can't all these niggaz move like that?"

"Well, I'm not making him out to be Superman just yet, but so far he's on the right track."

" 'Bout time you get out and date. I'm happy for you, Billy," Yoshi said honestly.

"It feels kind of funny, ya know. I've spent so much time trying to avoid dudes that I probably won't know how to act around him tonight."

"You'll do fine, Billy. I'll be at the club by the time you get down there so you make sure you check me before you slide out."

"A'ight, Yoshi. I'll see you tonight."

Yoshi tucked her phone back in her purse and continued toward the club. It was a modest little joint with blacked-out glass doors and a green awning with its name printed on it. Yoshi nodded at the young man smoking out front and continued through the entrance.

The inside of the club wasn't packed, but there were people sitting at the bar drinking. A few of the less attractive girls were on the pole doing their thing. They were out of shape and had skin marred with stretch marks, which was reflected in the light sprinkling of tips laid at their feet. The big spenders hadn't gotten there yet, but when they did, the real bitches would come out.

Passing the bar and a few patrons who tried to get her attention, Yoshi snaked through the hallway to the dressing room. The room contained about a dozen or so lockers and several vanity tables. Several of the girls were putting on their costumes while some sat around smoking blunts and sipping. Yoshi nodded, but for the most part she never got too friendly with the girls she worked with.

Sitting at the vanity table at the other end of the room, Yoshi sat down and began going through her case. As she was getting her first outfit of the night together, a girl they called Scar came over. She was a beautiful chick who was at least five-foot ten and built like a track star. She got her name Scar because of the tribal marks on her face. She was from some country in Africa, but Yoshi could never remember which one.

"What's up, China?" Scar asked in a slight accent.

"Another day, another dollar," Yoshi said, continuing with her task.

"Say, I've got some killer green." Scar produced a rolled-up joint from her halter top. "Real good shit my guy gets from Panama. You wanna blaze?"

"I'm good for right now, thanks."

Scar sat on the bench a little too close for Yoshi's taste. "What's the matter, China, you don't like me?"

"We cool, but if you don't move back a taste that might change," Yoshi said, with a sharp edge to her voice.

"Scar, get your hot ass outta here and leave China alone," a voice called from behind them. Cat strolled over, dressed only in a thong and white thigh-high boots. Even without a top, her perky breasts stood at attention.

"My bad, Cat," Scar said, gracefully sliding off the bench, "I didn't know she was one of yours."

"Whether she was one of mine or not, you keep sniffing around stray pussy and you're liable to get scratched." The look she gave Scar was one of warning. The taller girl took the hint and headed back to the other side of the room. "Some bitches," Cat said and shook her head.

"I don't know what it is with bitches hitting on me lately," Yoshi said.

"Can't say that I blame them." Cat eyed her.

"Don't play wit' me."

"I'm only joking, Yoshi. So I hear my brother has a date with your friend tonight."

"Damn, did he put it on the Internet?"

"Come on, Yoshi, I'm his sister. He seems to really like her," Cat admitted.

"I hope so. If he disrespects my friend, I'm gonna get in his ass," Yoshi warned.

"Yoshi, let me tell you something about my brother." She sat in the spot Scar had vacated. "Regardless of what you might think, he ain't like that. Yeah, Marcus used to be a dog just like the rest of him, but his rabbit got a hold of a gun."

"What?" Yoshi asked, confused.

Cat laughed. "He got played. Marcus had hooked up with this chick and fell head over heels for her. The boy was even thinking about moving in with her. Come to find out, she was fucking some out-of-town niggaz for hits of dope. That shit crushed my brother, and since then he's been really funny about the type of girls he dates. Trust me, he ain't gonna play no games with Billy's heart. If he's trying to holla, then he genuinely digs her."

"And why should I take your word for that?" Yoshi challenged.

Cat just shrugged. "Billy already made it clear to me that she doesn't do pussy, so I stand nothing to gain from trying to sabotage it. See you out on the floor." Cat got up and grabbed her top before heading out to the main floor. As she passed, Scar gave her a look, but kept her mouth in check.

28

Yo, I don't believe I let that clown-ass nigga hit it," Rhonda said, filling her plastic cup with Long Island iced tea.

"I thought you said he had a big dick," Reese said, sipping from her cup.

"Oh, from what I can remember the sex was good, but he ain't really got nothing to offer. I asked my brother about him and he told me that Slick ain't no heavyweight."

"So what, you bust a nut and hit the nigga for a few dollars. If anything, you came out on top."

"Baby, life ain't always about a few dollars and a nut. I'm looking for the big score," Rhonda told her. "Speaking of big score, what's up with you and Don B.?"

"Ain't nothing up," Reese said, her thoughts going back to her test results.

Rhonda gave her a funny look. "Reese, why don't you come clean? What really happened with Don B.?"

"I already told you, we fucked, I got dropped off, and that was that," Reese said.

"You a better bitch than me, 'cause I'd have been all up in that nigga's ass." Rhonda took a gulp of her drink. "On another note, where the hell is Billy?"

"Oh, you ain't know Ms. Thing had a date?"

Rhonda looked as if she couldn't believe it. "A date? With who?"

"Dude from the club. Yo, you should've seen Billy when she stepped out. Our bitch was killing 'em."

"I don't know what she got all dressed up for. She ain't gonna give him no pussy," Rhonda hated.

Reese's attention was drawn by the sound of male voices coming from her left. Under the dim streetlights she could make out the shapes of five men coming their way. Squinting, she could see the faces of True, Pain, Lex, and the little light-skinned one from the group, Lah. When the fifth face came into focus Reese, cursed under her breath.

"Is that True?" Rhonda looked in the direction in which Reese had been staring. "Yeah, that's him. Good, 'cause I got a few choice words for that nigga."

"Rhonda, please don't start," Reese pleaded.

"I ain't gonna start, I'm just gonna speak my mind."

Reese sighed, because she knew when Rhonda said she'd "speak her mind," she really meant she'd embarrass them. When the five men noticed Rhonda and Reese sitting on the bench, they altered their course and headed over to them. There was something about the look on Jay and Pain's faces that made Reese uncomfortable.

"Rhonda, what's good?" True asked, spreading his arms for a hug.

"Oh, now you wanna act like you know a bitch," she said, backing away. "That was some real foul shit you pulled in the club last night, True."

"What you talking about?" he said, trying to fake ignorance.

"True, how you gonna leave me with ya people so you can run around the club and whore yourself? You know me and you is cooler than that, so all you had to do was keep it funky."

True gave her a high smile. "My bad, ma. I got caught up with the show and shit and never had a chance to get back with you. What can I do to make it up to you?"

"I'll think of something," she said flirtatiously.

"Shorty, don't I know you?" Jay asked Reese, taking a drink from the bottle. From the way he was glaring at her, she could tell the liquor had him feeling himself.

"Do you?" she asked with an attitude.

"Shorty, stop acting like that," Pain said, wiping his nose with the sleeve of his shirt. "You know what it is."

"Excuse you?" Reese snaked her neck.

"You gotta pardon my dude. Sometimes he doesn't know what to say out of his mouth," Jay said in his best pimp voice.

"Well, you need to check him," Reese said.

Jay took another deep swig and rocked a bit. "Pay that nigga no mind. What I'm trying to find out is what's popping for the night?"

"I couldn't tell you. I've got plans of my own."

"You think you could include me and my niggaz in your plan?" Jay asked, putting his arms around Pain and Lex, who were eyeing Reese like fresh meat.

"Nah, I'm good." Reese turned away from them to hide her nervousness.

Jay took her slight as a green light to go in for the kill. "I know you're good. That was probably the best pussy I had in a long time, and that's why I'm trying to let my niggaz see what that's about."

"No the fuck you didn't." Rhonda got in his face. "Don't be coming over here trying to disrespect my homegirl."

"Shit, she did that on her own," Pain said and snickered.

"What?" Rhonda spun on him.

"She ain't tell you she blazed the whole Big Dawg squad?" Pain fell out laughing at his own "joke."

Reese felt like her whole body had caved in on itself. Everyone who had been listening was shocked, except for Pain and Jay, who were doubled over with laughter. The very thing she had been trying to keep on the low ended up coming out because a drunk nigga didn't know how to hold his tongue.

"Reese, is this nigga telling the truth?" Rhonda asked seriously.

"Rhonda, I . . ."

"Man, it ain't even go like that. Shorty ain't fuck the whole Big Dawg," Jay cut in. For the briefest of moments, Reese thought that Jay might have a shred of decency in him and had come up with a clever lie to save her reputation. Hearing his next words, that thought flew out the window. "She just fucked me, Don B., Rob, Cool, and Liza," he said, smirking.

"Oh shit, that's the chick y'all ran a train on?" True asked, shocked.

"Yo, heard shorty give it up," Pain said mockingly.

With a feral shriek, Reese charged Pain. The man was caught totally off guard when her nails raked down the side of his face. Reflexively, Pain hooked Reese in the gut, folding her. He went to move in for the kill, but Jay and Lex grabbed him.

"Be easy, my nigga. You can't be beating on no female," Lex said.

"Bitch, is you crazy? I'll leave your ass out here!" Pain raged, trying to break the hold they had on his arms.

"Dawg, you tripping," True snapped at Pain, helping Reese up off the floor.

"Fuck that bitch, son. If she's a fucking jump-off, then she's a jump-off. I know one thing, if these niggaz wasn't holding me, I'd stomp a mud hole in her ass." He made another attempt to break free, but his boys kept him in check.

"Youse a fucking punk, putting your hands on a female!" Rhonda shouted from behind True, sending Pain into another fit of trying to get loose.

"Rhonda, don't make it worse," True said. "Y'all get this nigga up outta here," True told his boys while he walked Reese and Rhonda to the building. Pain cursed and ranted for an entire block, while his boys dragged him to the car.

"You need to check your friends, True," Rhonda said angrily.

True threw his hands up in surrender. "Fuck did you want me to do?"

"You could've checked him about his mouth."

"Rhonda, you know how niggaz is. Your girl put herself out there and got called on it."

"Fuck you!" Reese said sourly. "Ain't none of y'all Harlem niggaz about shit anyway."

"Jay is from Yonkers," True said sarcastically. "And don't get mad at me 'cause you got exposed. I ain't have a nickel in that dollar. You brought this on yourself, ma."

"See, now this is all starting to make sense. You were avoiding him because you knew you played yourself," Rhonda said, proud that she had figured it all out, but completely disregarding her friend's feelings.

"Rhonda, I know you ain't over here passing judgment?" Reese folded her arms.

"Bitch, don't come at me sideways. At least if I had fucked a bunch of niggaz I'd have caked off. Your stupid ass ain't get nothing."

Reese was so angry that she started getting sharp pains in the back of her head. Rhonda was bombing her, as if she didn't already feel like shit. She wanted to punch her and True in their mouths, but they weren't lying. She went there and it blew up in her face.

"Fuck the both of y'all," Reese said, walking off.

"Don't take it like that, baby. Ain't nothing wrong with a little crew love!" True mocked her.

"Shut up, True," Rhonda told him. "Reese," she called after her friend, "you on some real bullshit right now, but you still my bitch!" Rhonda beat on her chest for emphasis. "Call me tomorrow!"

Reese ignored Rhonda's shrieking voice and kept moving toward the avenue. She was so angry that she had to concentrate to make her body cooperate with her mind. A few times she thought her legs were going to give out, but she managed to make it to the corner without incident.

Though Reese was heated, she was more hurt than anything. She had done some whorish things, but she knew she wasn't a true whore. She had gotten in the Hummer that night because she liked Don B., and the foolish little girl in her said that if given a chance she could make him feel the same way about her. In the end she went out the back, letting Don B.'s crew run through her, and gotten a dose of chlamydia. With the word out about how she got down, a man would never take her seriously. People wouldn't be able to see past the freak move she pulled in order to get to know who she really was.

At that moment, she hated them all. She hated Don B. for twisting her feelings, Jay for blowing it up, and Rhonda for being so damn judgmental. But as much hate that burned within her heart for them, she felt twice as much hate for herself for going out like that.

29

By the time Billy made it to the club it had just started to pop. Girls were being dropped off at the door by the vanload and the fellas were beginning to come out. Billy told the bouncer who she had come to see and was allowed in without having to pay the cover charge. She drew quite a few stares as she crossed the main floor on her way to the bar.

Before she left the house she had Reese come over and help her with her outfit. The girl might not have been very book smart, but she had an eye for fashion. She was rocking a pair of green parachute pants and brown suede boots balanced on inch-high heels. She had to practice walking around the house in them for about twenty minutes before she was sure she wouldn't bust her ass in the street. Her hair hung down her back, with bangs brushing her arched eyebrows. The silver hoop earrings dangling from her lobes played tricks with the light and swung against her lightly blushed cheeks. That night was supposed to be the beginning of her starting over, and she wanted the world to know it.

Glancing at her watch, she saw that it was only 9:35. She still had some time to kill before Marcus finished his shift, so she decided to order a drink. The bartender, though fully dressed, radiated sex. She was a shapely girl with full pink lips, rocking her hair in thick goddess braids. No sooner had she gone off to make Billy's drink than a party crasher was up in her space.

"How you doing, love?" he asked, trying to be sexy. His breath smelled of mints, but Billy could detect the stench of cheap liquor beneath it.

"Not interested," Billy said, not bothering to turn around to address him.

He moved around to her line of vision so she could see the imitation shark-skin suit he was wearing. "Don't act like that, baby girl. I'm just trying to buy you a drink."

"Thanks, but I can pay for my own drink."

"You yellow bitches kill me," he said, getting indignant. "Always acting like your pussy is sweeter than the next ho's because yo skin is lighter."

"Bitch?" Billy spun around on her stool. The movement was so swift that the wannabe pimp jumped back. "You got me fucked up with one of them weak-minded bitches you got working for you. Nigga, don't you know I will cut your fucking face?" She grabbed a bottle off the bar.

"No need for that," Cat said, grabbing Billy's arm from behind. She was dressed in a long robe, covering her entire body except her hands and face. "He was just about to leave, weren't you?" she asked the faux pimp, who looked at the bottle still clutched in Billy's hand and scurried away.

"Some niggaz ain't got no class." Billy placed the bottle back on the bar.

Cat shrugged. "What do you expect in a place like this? Marcus should be down in a second, he's in the office. He shouldn't be too long, but in the meantime I'm about to go onstage. Why don't you enjoy the show; you might change your mind about me." Cat winked and sauntered off to the stage stairs.

The lights in the club went dim when the DJ announced Cat was about to take the stage. The bass of hip-hop was replaced by African drums. The spotlight went on and Cat came out under it. Her eyes scanned the crowd as if she were hunting for someone in particular. Slowly, she began swaying back and forth, jerking in tune with the beat. The heat in the room seemed to skyrocket as Cat did her thing onstage. Dropping the robe, Cat exposed the tiger stripes painted onto her thighs, arms, and breasts. Her muscled legs stretched out into a split, and she bounced twice before popping back up. Every man in the house damn near salivated on themselves as they heaped cash at Cat's feet. By the time it was over, you couldn't see the stage floor through all the singles spread on it. Billy had to admit that Cat knew how to move.

"Enjoying the show?" A feminine voice brought Billy out of her trance. She turned from the vision onstage and had to blink at the one standing in front of her. Yoshi was dressed in a white bikini top that had stars covering the nipples. Her sarong clung to her hips, only exposing the top of her white thong.

"You look stank," Billy joked.

"Go to hell." Yoshi pushed her playfully. "I see Cat got y'all ready to trick off the rent money."

"Cat ain't got me wanting to do nothing, don't play with me, Yoshi."

"I see you eyeballing her."

"I was not!" Billy faked offense. "I can't front, she can damn sure work that stage."

"Billy, your rainbow flag is showing." Yoshi snickered.

"Every time I see you two you're talking about somebody." Marcus walked up on them. He was wearing a white button-up shirt and gray slacks.

"Why don't you make some noise when you walk?" Yoshi punched him in the arm.

"Hello, Billy." Marcus turned to her. His warm smile made her blush a little, which tickled him. "You look nice."

"You, too. Nice shirt." She gently touched his collar and stroked the material. "Italian?"

"French," he corrected her. "You ready to go, or did you wanna stay for the next act."

"Let's not end the date before it begins," Billy teased him. "I'll see you later." She hugged Yoshi. Taking Marcus's extended arm, she allowed him to lead her to the exit.

Yoshi leaned against the bar and watched her best friend be escorted out of the strip club with one of the finest men she had ever had the pleasure of meeting. She was happy that her friend had found someone who would hopefully know how to treat her. Seeing them together made her think of Jah.

They hadn't spoken since the night of their lovemaking, but she knew they would have to confront the issue eventually. She never saw herself falling for Jah, but she couldn't deny the butterflies he gave her. She just hoped that if she ever came to a point where she could lay her heart in someone's hands that they would be his.

Marcus led the way as he and Billy navigated the growing crowd inside Shooter's. It seemed like they couldn't move three feet without someone stopping Marcus. The DJ even shouted him over the PA system. They really show love to the bartenders at Shooter's, Billy thought.

When they had almost made it to the door, Marcus was sidetracked by one of the girls who absolutely had to speak to him. Feeling a twinge of jealousy, Billy kept waking. Coming out of the exit, she literally bumped into five men coming in. She recognized two members of Bad Blood, but couldn't call them by name. She tried to sidestep them, but the ugliest of the group blocked her path.

"What's good, ma, you leaving off work already?" Pain asked, glaring at Billy's breasts.

"Please, I don't work here. Excuse yourself," she said, pushing past him.

"Hold on, yo." Pain grabbed her by the arm. "Why don't you come inside and keep a nigga company for the night?"

"Because she'll be otherwise occupied," Marcus said, grabbing Pain's wrist. The two men exchanged challenging glares, which resulted in Pain letting go of Billy's wrist.

"Marcus, what's good, my dude?" Jay came over, breaking the tension.

"Chilling," he said to Jay, but kept his eyes on Pain. "I know y'all didn't come down here to cause trouble?"

"Pardon that." Jay nodded in Pain's direction. "My dude didn't know shorty was with you."

"Well, he does now. Y'all go in and have a good time, but keep that nigga in check." Marcus had a chill in his voice that served as a warning to anyone within earshot.

"You got it, Marcus. We'd never disrespect your club," Jay said, leading his team inside.

Billy waited until the men had passed through the entrance before speaking. "What was that all about?"

Marcus shrugged his wide shoulders. "Wasn't about nothing. I seen duke grab you and I stepped in. What kind of dude would I be if I didn't?" He acted as if he didn't see the suspicious look Billy was giving him. "Shall we?"

"Yeah, okay," she said and took his arm, "but you and I are going to have a serious talk this evening."

Marcus gave her a heart-melting smile. "I wouldn't have it any other way."

The two of them strolled off arm in arm like two lovers. It was nice, but short-lived as Marcus's Lexus GS300 was parked a few feet from the club. It was a 1993, but he kept it in mint condition. The car was fitted with wooden panels and modest twenty-inch rims. Billy reached out for the passenger door, only to have him step around her and do the honors. Billy smiled through the windshield at Marcus as he walked coolly around to the driver's side. She had to remind herself to thank Yoshi for the hookup.

Yoshi lounged at the bar, sipping a Long Island iced tea. There were some crumpled-up bills in the net purse she carried around the club, but it was nothing to write home about. She had made a few dollars doing lap dances, but the fish weren't really biting just yet. The patrons who had been there for a while were borderline shit-faced and broke, but dudes had been pouring in for the last half hour or so. New faces meant new money and she was damn sure gonna get her share.

"Hey, pretty lady," Black Ice said, taking the stool next to Yoshi's. He was dressed immaculately in a black shirt and matching slacks. His black gators were polished to a mirror shine, as was the gold buckle.

"Hi, Ice," she said in a very uninterested tone.

"Not yet, but I will be." He flashed his diamond-studded teeth. "How these tricks treating you tonight?"

"Can't complain. You know I handle mine."

"And that's the problem." Ice leaned in to whisper in her ear. "You're handling yours instead of letting the best man for the job take care of it."

"And I'm guessing that would be you?" she asked sarcastically.

"Who better than Ice, the ladies' vice, 'cause he handles their business oh so nice?" he sang. "Yoshi, my game is already approaching orbit and it's about to be out of this world. You know just as well as I do that your fine ass don't wanna miss the mother ship when it leaves. *Can't you see I'm trying to put you up on what's happening? You need to choose a nigga and quit napping."*

"That was cute." She chuckled.

"Cute is for monkeys and puppies, doll, and I ain't either one. I'm just trying to put you up on this pimpin'."

"First of all, what the fuck do I look like, working up in joints like this at all hours of the night? To give the next man my paper? I don't fuck wit' no pimps, and even if I did, why the hell would I choose you?"

"Because I'm the most qualified cat to play this game since a square nigga wit' a grudge put a bullet in my daddy's brain. I was bred for this shit, baby, so ain't nowhere for me to go but up. The question you need to ask yourself is, do you really wanna be stranded down here with the squares or partaking in the finer things with the players? When you decide you're tired of letting a nigga paw you for pennies, give me a call and let's bathe you in some dollars." Ice dropped a business card on the table and headed back through the crowd.

"China, you're on next!" Claudia shouted from behind the bar.

Downing the rest of her drink, Yoshi got up and prepared to take the stage. Before she walked away she picked up Ice's card and tucked it in her bag.

• • •

"That nigga was gonna push your shit back," Lex teased Pain.

"He wasn't gonna do shit. If duke tried to get fly, I'd have let him have it!" Pain boasted.

"With what, when we left the guns in the car?" Lah cut in.

"Shut up, Lah. You lucky we even letting you hang out with us tonight. You're True's bitch," Pain accused.

"I ain't nobody's bitch." Lah poked his chest out, but when Pain looked in his direction he shrunk back a bit.

"Stop fucking wit' the little nigga." Jay threw his arm around Pain. "At least Lah shows up to the studio on time."

Pain pushed Jay's arm off his shoulder. "Fuck you, and this limp-dick little nigga. Let's snatch a table and get pissy."

"Finally something we can agree on," Jay said.

The five men made their way through the club, which was damn near crammed. Half-naked women were strutting around, drinking or offering lap dances while the men gladly gave up their singles. All throughout the room cats were saluting Bad Blood. When word got out that they were in the house, the girls turned it up. It was nearly ten minutes before they were able to commandeer a table in the far corner.

"See that there, my nigga?" Lex asked, throwing his arm around Lah. He turned the youngster toward a chocolate thing with an ass that looked like two Halloween pumpkins. "That's what you call a two-pump chump."

"A two-pump chump?" Lah asked, not catching on.

"Two pumps in that big ol' ass and you bust," Pain explained.

"Like a stone chump!" Lex added.

The men exchanged laughter and filed into the booth. They were barely seated for two minutes when a waitress came over to take their orders. She was scantily dressed in a black skirt that barely covered her ass. She greeted them all with a warm smile, knowing that the young rappers would tip nicely. After taking their orders, and ignoring the fact that Pain kept touching her ass, the waitress went off to get their drinks.

"I'd fuck that bitch," Jay said.

"True story," Lex agreed.

Pain talked shit among his boys and watched the girls while they waited for their drinks. Again his cell phone rang and he didn't answer it. "Fuck you," Pain mumbled. His hungry eyes scanned the room, mentally sampling the variety of girls who were in attendance that night, wondering which one he was going to take home.

"For a bartender you carry a lot of weight around that spot," Billy said suspiciously.

"What do you mean?" he asked, cutting off another piece of his steak.

"I mean the way people treat you at Shooter's. Everybody seems to think you're the shit."

"Guess I'm just a lovable guy," Marcus said and smirked.

Billy sniffed the air. "I smell bullshit. Seriously, what do you really do at Shooter's?"

Marcus looked at her as if he were thinking of what to say. "Real talk?"

"Real talk."

"Okay, I've got a little money tied up in the spot," he admitted.

"So all this time you've been screaming you're a bartender and you're the owner?" Billy asked, with a note of disappointment in her voice that he'd duped her.

"Part owner," he corrected her. "Me and Shooter got an understanding."

"See, you're already starting off on the wrong foot by lying." She folded her arms.

"Technically, I didn't lie; I omitted part of the truth," he pointed out. "I do tend bar and help out around the spot. Just because I'm upper management doesn't mean things don't need to get done.

"Billy, I know you're feeling in a way, but I had several good reasons for not telling you right off the back. If I had told you I owned the club, you'd have just thought I was out here trying to recruit more girls. A better reason is because I wanted you to get to know me as a person, not a club owner who's sitting on some bread."

"Oh, so I strike you as the kind of girl that's out here on a paper chase?" she asked defensively.

"Not at all, but I don't always trust my first instincts. I tried that once and got myself burned for it."

"Oh, sorry to hear that," Billy said, as if she didn't already know his history. "Well, if it'll make you feel better, I'm not on it like that. There's nothing a nigga can do for me that I can't do for myself. I go out and work for what I need."

"And that's one of the things that attracted me to you. Billy, from the first brief conversation we had at the barbecue, I knew you were a girl about her business. You don't find that much these days. Most chicks are just out for a come-up."

"Just like most niggaz are out for a nut," she shot back.

"There are always exceptions to the rules."

"That's what I'm trying to tell you."

Marcus smiled at her wit. "You've got a response for everything, don't you?"

"Pretty much," she replied.

"So now that my secret is out, do you think I'm a filthy liar who you never want to see again?" he asked, looking at her with puppy dog eyes.

Billy wanted to laugh at the face he was making, but kept it in check. "Maybe, but I won't make such a rash decision just yet. Before we go any further, is there anything else I should know?"

"Just that you have the most breathtaking eyes." He blinked like a swooning schoolgirl.

Not being able to hold it any longer, Billy burst out laughing. "Boy, you are too much."

"For most women." He placed his hand over hers. "But for someone like you, I'm just enough."

30

Spooky sat on the edge of his queen-size bed, checking the chamber on a brand-new Ruger. Jah was standing in the middle of the bedroom, practicing his draw in the mirror. He would snatch the .40 from his belt and aim it at the mirror, each time trying to best the previous. He loved the little gun and it had been with him for years.

"Man, why do you still have that thing?" Spooky asked.

"Because it's a good gun." Jah continued his routine. "This shit ain't never gave me a problem."

"That's because you ain't never been stopped with it," Spooky pointed out. "Jah, how many muthafuckas you done shot with that?"

"A few." He retucked the gun.

Spooky shook his head. "You carrying that hot-ass piece like we ain't got more iron." Spooky reached under his bed and slid out a wooden box. Inside the box there were two handguns and some clips. Snatching a Glock from the box and checking the clip, he handed it to Jah. "Try that. It's about the same weight, and brand new. Take that hot-ass forty and toss it in the fucking river."

Jah examined the gun from butt to barrel. Balancing the Glock in one hand and the .40 in the other, he noticed that the Glock was slightly heavier and had a slightly longer barrel. Though it wasn't as pretty or as proven as his .40, it would put a generous-size hole in something.

"It's a'ight," Jah said, tucking the Glock in the back of his pants and putting the .40 back in his belt holster. "Yo, I gotta go take care of something right quick, but I'll hit you in a little while."

"Fuck is you going? We gotta plan our counterattack," Spooky said.

"We'll handle that later. Let me go do this thing right quick and I'll be back."

"Jah, I know you ain't putting off a rider mission for no pussy?"

"Come on, Spook, you should know me better than that. Would I put splitting a nigga's shit on the back burner for some pussy?"

"Hard to tell these days," Spooky mumbled. "Do what you gotta do and hit me back. Make sure you're careful out there."

"All day." Jah gave Spooky a pound and left.

When he made it outside Spooky's building, he felt as if a weight had been lifted. Spooky was without a shadow of a doubt Jah's best friend and crime partner, but there were some things that Jah wouldn't ever share with him. He had been trying to shake his comrade all day to handle more pressing business. Punching in a number on his cell, Jah placed the phone to his ear and waited. He had been thinking about making the call all day, but hadn't yet found the time. Between Spooky's shit talking and the walking dead men who tried to hit him up, his day had been pretty full. Still, the thought lingered in his mind. Even during the shootout he kept thinking that if he died he'd never be able to tell her how he really felt.

After about five rings it went to voicemail. Jah started to hang up, but figured if he did he would'nt be able to build the courage to make the call again. Sucking it up, he left a voicemail.

"What up . . . ah . . . this is Jah. Um . . . listen, I was just calling to see what was up. 'Bye." Jah hung up abruptly. He immediately wished that he'd just hung up and not said anything. He must've sounded like a complete ass. The damage was already done, so there was no sense worrying about it. All he could do now was wait and see if Yoshi would call back. In the meantime, he had a grand old idea to occupy his time.

• • •

"Yo, it's so many hos in here I don't know what to do with myself," Groovy said, leaning against the bar sipping his drink.

"You ain't never lied, my dude," Rel agreed.

"I'm glad we came out instead of kicking it in the crib with Slick."

"Yeah." Rel downed his glass of cognac. "We supposed to be one of the livest crews in Harlem, and we're playing commando with a kid that's barely old enough to drink. That nigga Slick is on some other shit that I can't get with."

"True." Groovy nodded. "You think we'll get another crack at Jah?"

"More than likely. See, let me run down to you what I learned in this game, youngster." Rel put his arm around Groovy. "People like Jah are creatures of habit. They get comfortable with a certain geographical area or routine and that's what they stick to. When he think the heat has died down, he'll be right back up to his old tricks, and I'm gonna put a bullet in his head."

"Rel, you stay talking some movie shit," Groovy teased him.

"Nigga, my life is a movie. You know how much dirt I've done and gotten away with?" Rel boasted. "I done laid down way harder niggaz than Jah. Slick is my nigga, but he ain't got no spine for war. That's why I should be in charge."

Groovy raised an eyebrow. "You?"

"Muthafucking right, me. I got twenty years invested in this game, son. I ain't supposed to be no lieutenant, I'm a fucking general."

"All that shit sounds good, Rel, but this ain't the eighties. These cats play by a different set of rules than you're used to."

"That's why the game is fucked up now. The art of drug trafficking is supposed to be a gentleman's craft, but you got little know-nothing muthafuckas changing the rules and making shit harder on everyone else. I'm telling you, my dude, I'm gonna bring the game back to what it was."

"Whatever, nigga." Groovy waved him off and went back to watching the girls move about the floor. Seated at a table in the back, he noticed a familiar face. "Yo," he said and tapped Rel, "ain't that Jay and them from Bad Blood?"

Rel squinted in the direction his friend was looking. "Yeah, that's them niggaz. Fake-ass rappers."

"Yo, let's go holla at them niggaz, son. I know Pain from my old hood."

"Come on, man, I ain't trying to jump on nobody's dick."

"How are we dick riding when I just wanna say 'what up' to my dude?" Groovy asked.

"Fuck them niggaz." Rel spat.

"Man, bring your hating ass on," Groovy said, heading in their direction. Rel sucked his teeth and followed.

"Pain, what's good, my nigga?" Groovy approached the table.

"Oh shit, li'l-ass Groove!" Pain shouted over the music. His speech was slurred from the drinks they had consumed. "I ain't seen you in a minute. Where the fuck you been?"

"I'm making moves in Harlem now," Groovy told him. "Yo, I hear y'all niggaz is getting crazy spins on the radio."

"You know how Bad Blood do it," Pain said, giving Lex dap. "Sit down and have a drink wit' us, my dude," he told Groovy.

Groovy eagerly took a seat. "Yo, this is my dude, Rel." Groovy pointed at his partner, who was still standing.

"What up?" Rel said dryly. The men at the table exchanged snickers, peeping Rel trying to play the strong silent type.

"Take a seat, my man," Jay told him. "All are welcome here." Rel reluctantly sat down. "Yo, we got two more bottles of Moët on the way, but y'all niggaz order whatever you want to drink. It's on Big Dawg!"

"What do you mean, you've gotta go? Where the hell are you going?" Valerie asked.

"I told you, I gotta bounce for a few weeks," Ralph replied, tossing a pair of jeans into his duffel bag. "I gotta take care of this thing, but I'll be back."

Valerie looked at him as if he was foolish for even attempting such a weak lie. She had been with Ralph for three years, so she knew his character better than he did. "That's a load of shit and you know it. Ralph, tell me what's going on!"

"Woman, I ain't got time to explain it to you right now!" he shouted, drawing the strings on the duffel bag.

"Oh, you're gonna tell me something," she said and sat on the bag, "or you ain't going nowhere no time soon."

Ralph wanted to belt her, but he knew a run-in with the police was the last thing he needed at that moment. Telling Valerie the truth was his best option of getting the hell out of Harlem before the wolves came out.

"Listen, some shit went down with me and my niggaz and somebody got killed," he finally admitted.

"Killed? Did you have something to do with that boy that got killed on One thirty-fifth?" Valerie asked.

"Ma, I was there, but I didn't have nothing to do with it. I rode with Slick and them niggaz to hit Jah and—"

"Jah? I thought y'all was friends?"

"Man, that nigga put his hands on me about some bullshit paper I owed him, so all that friend shit went out the window. All I did was show Slick and them where he be at, but I swear I didn't shoot anyone."

Valerie just sat for a long time, never saying anything. She looked at Ralph as if she was trying to process what he had just told her. It started out with her lip quivering, then tears rolling down her cheeks, then the next thing Ralph knew, Valerie was bawling.

"Val, what're you crying for? I told you I didn't shoot anybody."

"That's not why I'm crying," she said, sobbing.

"Then what the hell is your problem?"

Valerie wiped her eyes with the palms of her hands and cleared her throat. "Ralph, me and you done been through some shit, but for the most part we've had a wonderful relationship. I never thought the day would come when I was embarrassed to be your girl."

"Embarrassed? What the hell did I do?" he asked.

"What did you do?" she asked, as if it was a stupid question. "Ralph, you're a rat!"

"What? Bitch, is you crazy? You're only a rat if you cooperate with the police."

"Ralph, you can't be that dense. You gave someone up for your own selfish reasons. I don't give a shit if it's the police or the competition, the code of silence always comes first. To make matters worse, you had the goddamn nerve to point him out."

"Well, what did you expect me to do?"

"You could've handled it like a man. Jah bleeds just like anyone else. If you had a problem with that man, then you should've handled it, not duped someone else into doing it. That's some snake shit."

"Fuck that, it was him or me." No sooner had the statement left Ralph's mouth than a wad of phlegm left Valerie's mouth. It smacked Ralph dead on the cheek and slowly dripped down his face. He started to jump on her, but froze when he saw she had produced a very large pair of scissors.

"You know, those were the exact same words that came out of my cousin's mouth when he gave my baby brother up to the feds. You're so worried about your own selfish pride that you ain't even thinking about how this affects the people around you. It's because of ignorant-ass niggers like you and Slick that the ghetto is the ghetto. Y'all are so reckless wit' ya shit that you probably killed an innocent man and the police are gonna be hot on your asses. Not to mention that Jah is still alive. Youz a sad muthafucka, Ralph, and I just pray that he doesn't catch you before you make it out of town because Jah is surely gonna carve you up for what you've done. Get the fuck outta my house!"

Ralph was fuming, but he just nodded, took his stuff, and left. As he walked to the elevator, he got dizzy thinking how a woman he had loved for years had reduced him to nothing in a matter of seconds. He knew he was a lowlife shit for putting the finger on Jah to be hit, but his survival instincts kicked in, overriding his honor. New York was over for him.

After a few drinks and several dirty jokes, Rel had dropped his tough-guy persona and was having a good time with the cats from Big Dawg. They proved to be a group of cool cats who knew how to have a good time and didn't mind spending paper. The DJ announced that China was about to take the stage, drawing the men's attention. When Yoshi stepped out, Rel's eyes went wide.

"Damn, pick your lip up, homey," Pain teased.

"That's a bad bitch up there," Lex said, hungrily eyeing Yoshi.

"Fuck that slut," Rel said.

"You know her or something?" Jay asked.

"Yeah, a li'l freak bitch from the hood," Rel said, reclining in his seat, trying to look cool. "Me and one of my niggaz ran up in that not too long ago."

"Get the fuck outta here," Pain said, sitting up.

"True story, kid. Shorty is a prime freak, into all kind of crazy shit. She used to like me to get rough with her and act like I was taking the pussy," Rel lied. "For a few dollars, she'll even take it in her shit box."

"Yo, our paper is crazy long!" Jay boasted.

"Since you know the bitch, why don't you set it up?" Lex suggested.

"Yeah, I might be able to do that," Rel said coolly.

"Well, get your ass up and go holla at the bitch, son," Pain ordered.

"Nah, we can't do it like that. She'll get in trouble with the niggaz that own the club if they get wise to her turning tricks. When she gets done onstage, I'm gonna hit her on the jack and put it together."

"Damn, you might be good for something after all." Pain slapped Rel on his back.

Rel grinned like a fool as he accepted praise from around the table for the potential jump-off. He looked over at Yoshi and smiled sinisterly. He had put himself out there for Yoshi and she had shitted on him, a slight he hadn't forgotten. Rel rubbed his hands together in anticipation of payback on the bitch who had stepped on his heat.

Before stepping around the corner to where the elevators were, Ralph peeked out cautiously. His .25 was secured in his boot, but he still didn't feel safe. Before even pressing for the elevator, Ralph called a cab and the operator confirmed it'd be there in three minutes. Covering all his bases, Ralph pressed for the elevator.

Ralph had only been waiting for a few seconds, but it felt like forever. He was so nervous that he felt like he would shit his pants if he didn't get out of Harlem soon. Finally, the elevator chimed and the rusty doors began to slide open. Ralph took one step and light exploded in his eyes. He slumped against the wall, feeling the blood begin to run from his nose. Struggling to open his eyes, Ralph almost fainted when he saw Jah standing over him, smiling.

"Oh shit!" Ralph said with his eyes bugging out of his head.

"Shit is right, and when you rode out with them niggaz against me and my people, you stepped in a whole pile of it."

"Yo, Jah, it wasn't like that. Let me explain!" Ralph pleaded, scrambling backward until he hit the wall.

Jah reached down and grabbed Ralph by the front of his shirt, snatching him to his feet. "Fuck can you explain to me, how youse a sucka-ass nigga, or why Crazy Eight died in the fucking gutter? Nah, don't explain it to me, explain it to the devil when you meet him, bitch-ass nigga!" When Jah cleared his .40 from the holster, Ralph made one last attempt to save his life and lunged for it. For this he was rewarded by a shot to the chest. As he stumbled around, trying to stop the flow of blood, Jah gave him one in the face. "You rat bastard." Jah laughed before stepping back onto the elevator.

Valerie jumped when she heard the gunshots. The retort was too loud to be coming from outside, so it had to be coming from somewhere in the building. Instinctively, she grabbed the phone to call the police, but when her hand touched the receiver, she paused. Though it pained her to do so, she sat back on her bed and did nothing. There would be no police or ambulance called to try and save Ralph, which she doubted was possible at that point anyhow. Though she loved him, Ralph was a rat and got dealt with accordingly. She would mourn her man, but for as much as she loved him, she knew he had brought the terrible fate on himself.

31

Mar!" Paul called out, bursting through the front door. "Where are you, baby?" Not getting an answer, he proceeded to search the house for her. P.J. was sound asleep in the guest bedroom, with the Cartoon Network still playing on the twenty-inch television set. Watching P.J. sleep reminded Paul of a happier time in his life, a carefree time when he didn't feel the weight of the world on his shoulders. Stroking the sleeping child's face, Paul vowed that he would never have to suffer. Clicking off the television, he kissed his son on the forehead and left the room.

Paul searched the kitchen, bathroom, and master bedroom, but there was still no sign of Marlene. He knew she had to be there somewhere because she would never leave P.J. in the house alone. That was the kind of move Rhonda pulled. He was just about to call her cell phone when he heard voices coming from the downstairs studio. Careful to make as little noise a possible, Paul crept down the stairs. He could hear Marlene whispering on the phone, but couldn't make out what she was saying. When he reached the bottom of the stairs, she was standing off to the side with her back to him.

"Marlene?" he called.

Marlene spun around with a fright. The movement was so sudden that she almost dropped her phone. "Hey, baby," she said, trying not to look like she got caught with her hand in the cookie jar. "Audrey, I'll call you back," she said, ending the call before getting a response.

"What're you doing down here using the phone?" Paul asked suspiciously.

"Oh, I didn't want to wake P.J.," she said.

"Then why not just go in the bedroom?"

"Baby, you know how loud Audrey and I can be when we're on the phone." She kissed him on the lips. "I didn't expect you back this early."

"I told you I'd be right back."

"Yeah, but your 'right backs' can sometimes last until damn near the next day."

"Whatever, Mar. Do you wanna hear what he wanted or not?"

"Of course I do." She grabbed him by the hand. "You can tell me all about it upstairs," she said, leading him back to the main level of the house. "So," she began, entering the kitchen, "what did Larry's fat ass want?"

"Marlene, don't talk about my friends," Paul told her.

"I was only kidding, Paul. You know Larry is one of the few who I can tolerate. So what hair-brained scheme has he cooked up now?"

"Nah, baby, this ain't no scheme. Larry has set something up that may be just what we needed."

"And what might this be?" she asked suspiciously.

"An art exhibit." Paul went on to tell Marlene of Larry's under-the-table deal with the security guards at Silver Cup and how he planned to help Paul host an art show on one of their sets. Marlene listened, emotionless, until Paul was finished. "So what do you think?"

Marlene thought on it for a minute and said, "I think the both of you are crazy."

"What?" he asked, not believing she couldn't dig the idea.

"Paul, how do you and Larry plan to hijack a film set in order to host an art exhibit?"

"We're not hijacking it, Mar. Seth is gonna fix it so we use the set on a night when there's no one filming at Silver Cup. We'll be in and out before anyone even knows we were there. What could go wrong?"

"Well, for starters, someone could find out about your little bootleg exhibit and call the police. Trespassing is still a crime in this state."

"Marlene, why do you always have to punch holes in shit?" he asked heatedly.

"I'm not punching holes in anything, Paul. I'm just trying to make sure you don't get yourself into trouble messing with Larry and his little plan."

Paul gripped the sides of his head. "Goddammit, Marlene, this isn't some little plan. My best friend has busted his ass to try and help me out and all you can do is find flaws in it. What the fuck is your problem?"

"Well, since you asked, I'll tell you. I'm tired, Paul. Tired of waiting for you to wise up and get a regular job. Tired of your sickening-ass baby's mother and tired of wondering if I'm gonna wind up an old maid. Baby, you know I'm totally supportive of you and your dreams of becoming an accomplished painter, but we have to be realistic about this. You can't keep living day to day waiting for your big break. We can't live on hope."

"You know what, I ain't even trying to hear this shit." Paul turned to walk away.

"Don't walk away from me when I'm talking to you!" she shouted, roughly grabbing his shirt. To her surprise, Paul spun around with a maddened look in his eyes. A snarl emitted from somewhere deep in his gut as he lashed out. Marlene braced herself, waiting for the blow to land on her chin, but instead Paul put his fist through the cabinet door.

"Keep your fucking hands to yourself!" he snapped. "You don't have to believe in my plan, Marlene. Hell, you don't even have to be supportive of it, but for the love of God, don't tear it down. I'm sleeping downstairs tonight." Paul stormed down to the basement, slamming the door behind him.

Marlene stood in the middle of the kitchen trembling. For a minute she actually thought he was going to knock her out. She had known that kind of man in the past, but had never seen Paul's dark side before. Now that she had, she wanted no part of it.

• • • •

Yoshi sat on one of the long benches in the dressing room, counting her take. She had made just six hundred dollars for the evening. Not bad for a few hours of work. Changing from her costume to her street clothes, she repacked her rolling case and prepared to leave for the night.

"Yoshi, you need a ride home?" Cat asked, slinging her bag over her shoulder.

"Nah, I'm straight. I'm gonna walk to Forty-second and grab something to eat. I'll take a cab from there."

"A'ight, baby girl. It's late, so you be careful out there," Cat warned.

"Please, with all the police running around Times Square, I'll be safer out there than I will be in the car with you," Yoshi joked.

"This is true." Cat winked. "See you later, boo."

After securing her case, Yoshi made her way to the street. The walk to Times Square was a brief one, allowing Yoshi to check her voicemail. One was from Rhonda saying something about Reese sleeping with some dude, and the other was from Jah. She swooned when she heard his voice, remembering the night they had shared together. He was so cute trying to be cool, but tripping over his words. She had given quite a bit of thought to the whole situation and wondered what was stopping them from taking a chance. She was feeling the young boy and it was obvious that he was digging her. She decided that she wouldn't call him back that night, but the following day she planned to confront him.

Pain was so twisted that he knocked over several bar stools on his way out of Shooter's. He and his crew had had a blast with the two hustlers from uptown. And to make it sweeter, they were scheduled to get a piece of that fine light-skinned bitch who had been onstage. At first he thought Rel was full of shit and wouldn't be able to pull it off, but he had sat there and supposedly watched the young man make the call.

"I don't believe I'm going through all this for a piece of pussy," Lex said from the passenger seat of the truck.

"I told you, man, shorty likes to role-play. When I spoke to her on the jack she said she was gonna give all of us the time of our lives," Rel said from the backseat.

"Yeah, I'm dying to get a piece of that fine pussy, too, but this is some weird shit," Jay admitted, snorting a line of cocaine out of a dollar bill and handing the tray to Pain.

"Hey, man, if you don't want none of this trim, you can take the faggot way out like ya man," Rel told him, referring to Lah, who had opted to pass on the pussy and go home.

"Watch ya mouth, duke. You don't know me well enough to be calling me out my name," Jay warned.

"Both of y'all niggaz shut the fuck up. I'm trying to bust ass and head back to the hood," Pain growled.

The men in the car went back and forth for the entire ride uptown. Groovy stayed silent. Every now and again he would shoot Rel a dirty look, which Rel pretended not to see. He wanted to fuck Yoshi, too, but didn't particularly agree with the way his man was going about it. Though he had gotten in the car with them, he wasn't sure if he was ready to take the ride.

By the time Yoshi stepped out of the cab in front of her building, she was dead tired. After shaking her ass for the majority of the night, all her strength seemed to have fled her body. She wasn't even sure if she would stay awake long enough to eat her food.

Thankfully, there was no one in front of her building when she got there. She didn't knock the young dudes who hustled on her block, but sometimes they made her uneasy. She was standing on her stoop, fumbling for the lobby key, when she felt a presence behind her. She spun around to find herself staring into the drunken eyes of Rel. He was flanked by three other men and they didn't look like they had come to pay a social visit.

"What's popping, bitch?" He grinned.

That was the last thing Yoshi heard before pain exploded in her cheek and everything went black.

32

Billy was roused from her slumber by the sound of her cell phone's message alert. Cracking one eye, she looked at the screen and saw she had five missed calls. Figuring they could wait, she tossed the phone to the foot of the king-size bed and rolled over. It was at that moment that she remembered she didn't have a king-size bed.

Billy leapt up so fast that she was almost airborne. Her eyes frantically looked around the room, trying to figure out where the hell she was. The room was decorated with an expensive bedroom set and plush carpet, but Billy didn't recognize it. Tossing the covers back, she was relieved to see that she was still fully dressed, with the exception of her boots.

"Don't worry, your virtue is still intact," Marcus said, leaning against the bedroom door. He was dressed in a pair of gray sweats and a tank top, showing off his tattooed arms.

"How did I get here?" she asked in a raspy voice.

"On the wings of gossamer," he said, sitting on the edge of the bed. "No, but seriously, you fell asleep last night during the movie."

Billy shook the fog from her brain and recalled the events that led to her winding up in Marcus's bed. After dinner they had gone out for drinks at a lounge uptown, where they danced the night away. Afterward, Marcus had invited her back to his place to watch *Imitation of Life*. Normally, she wouldn't have gone back to a guy's house on the first date, but she felt safe with Marcus. Besides, she had called Jean and given her his license plate number before they'd left the restaurant. Marcus had gone out of his way to make sure she had a good time and she was greatly appreciative of that. It had been quite some time since she had gone out and had a genuinely good time, especially with a man. He scored big points in her book.

"You better not have been in here trying to grope me in my sleep," she said as she stretched.

"Wouldn't dream of it. When I grope you, I want you to be wide awake," he teased her. "By the way, someone has been blowing your phone up all night. I hope you don't have a crazy boyfriend that's gonna try to run up in here and pop off."

"Knock if off," she said, picking up her phone. The calls were from 212 numbers. Each number had the same prefix, but the last four digits were different. They looked familiar, but she couldn't place them.

"Something wrong?" he asked.

"I hope not," she said, dialing her voicemail box. Billy listened as the first message played.

"Hello, this message is for Willamina Jefferson. This is Nurse Donna Reid at Harlem Hospital, calling in reference to your sister Yoshibelle Johnson. Please give me a call back at. . . ."

"You cool?" Marcus asked.

"I don't know," she said nervously. "It was someone from Harlem Hospital calling about Yoshi."

"Is she okay?"

"I'm about to find out," she said, dialing the number Nurse Reid had left on the message. After telling the operator who she was trying to reach, Billy was put through. "Hi, this is Willamina Jefferson, you called about my sister?" she asked, praying nothing had happened.

"Ms. Jefferson, I'm a nurse at the rape center at Harlem Hospital," Nurse Reid informed her.

"Oh my God, rape center? What's happened to Yoshi?" Billy asked frantically.

"Ms. Jefferson, your sister was brought in this morning. She was found raped and beaten outside her apartment building."

"God, please don't let this be happening. How? Who?"

"Ms. Jefferson, we really don't know much right now. The police came to question her, but she was still too shaken up to be much help. She just requested that we contact you."

"I'm coming over there right now," Billy said, ending the call.

"Billy, what's wrong?" Marcus asked.

"Yoshi was raped last night," she said, searching for her other boot. "I don't know much yet, but I'm on my way over to the hospital to find out. Can you call me a cab?"

"Fuck a cab, I'm driving you," he said, grabbing a hoodie and his car keys. She opened her mouth to protest, but he waved her silent. It was obvious she wouldn't be rid of him that easy. The two of them made a mad dash out of the apartment and headed into Harlem to find out what the hell had happened.

Slick sat on his bed with his mouth hanging open. On his lap was a copy of the Sunday paper, with an article telling of a young man murdered not even three buildings away from him. They found Ralph slumped in the hallway of his girlfriend's apartment building, shot multiple times. The police said that when they questioned his girlfriend she simply said, "He went out to get a pack of cigarettes and never came back." Though Valerie wasn't yet a suspect, the police didn't quite believe her story. It seemed odd that Ralph would've been "just going to the store" carrying all his worldly possessions. Not needing to read any more, Slick tossed the paper into the corner.

The police deduced that Ralph had been murdered over a drug beef, but they were only partially right. The way Slick figured it, Ralph had gotten spooked by the botched hit and tried to hightail it out of town. Apparently, Jah had caught him before he was able to make his escape. It was just as he'd told his boys, never underestimate your enemy.

Grabbing his P89 from the dresser drawer, Slick walked to the window and scanned the projects. Ralph's murder had changed the rules of the game considerably. If Jah had gone out of his way to murder Ralph, he would surely be coming for Slick somewhere down the line. When that time came, he would be prepared.

"Damn, I'm starving!" Pain said, taking another forkful of his scrambled eggs. "Wrecking a bitch's pussy takes a lot out of you." After their romp with Yoshi, him, Jay, and Lex had gone to the diner to grab some breakfast.

"Yo, shorty had some good pussy," Jay added. "Lex, you missed out, kid."

Lex took a sip of his orange juice. "Man, that shit was too intense for me. First Rel clocks the bitch on some wild-man shit, then he's fucking her like she kicked his dog. Y'all say what you want, but I don't think she was having as much fun as the rest of y'all."

"She was loving that shit, nigga. You hear the way the bitch was moaning," Pain said. "You and that nigga Groovy stayed outside like some little faggots."

In the beginning, Lex was just as down to run a train on Yoshi as the rest of them, but something about it didn't feel right. The story Rel fed them about her liking to role-play and reenact rapes was a weird request, but Pain knew some chicks who were like that. He used to fuck with this Jamaican chick who would demand that he slap her face until she bled during sex. In this day and age, all kinds of new fads were popping up. He had expected Rel to shove her around or shake her up as part of the game, but he was totally thrown off when he hit her. Shorty looked scared shitless, but Pain and Jay were so coked up that neither of them seemed to notice. The men took turns fucking the girl in her ass and pussy while ravaging her breasts. When Lex saw blood, he excused himself from the scene.

"Son, I was gonna try and crack for some head, but this stupid-ass nigga kept that fucking T-shirt wrapped around her mouth," Pain said, snorting from the leftover coke that was dripping in the back of his throat. "I need another shot of that freak bitch."

Lex became very serious. "Let me tell you something, my man, ain't none of us ever going near that freak bitch again. Y'all can believe that bullshit Rel put in your heads about role-playing if you want, but that shit was straight-up rape."

"Man, we ain't no fucking rapists. She wanted it," Pain tried to convince him.

"My dude, you can't be that fucking stupid." Lex shook his head.

"Fuck that rape shit y'all niggaz is talking. We caked up out this bitch!" Jay declared. "If shorty tries to get on some funny shit, we'll just pay her off."

"Whatever, man," Lex said. His attention was drawn to Pain's cell phone rattling on the table. Pain looked at the screen and sucked his teeth, but didn't answer. He had been looping someone all night, and Lex was starting to think that it wasn't a female like he'd told them.

"Who the fuck keeps ringing your phone?" Jay asked.

"Nobody important," Pain said, wiping his mouth with a napkin. "Let's get up outta here." He stood, dropping a fifty-dollar bill on the table.

The three men made their way out of the diner and into the morning sun. It was almost twelve o'clock, so the sun was nearly at its highest point. On their way back to the truck, a black Lincoln pulled to a stop next to them. The back doors opened up and three Spanish cats stepped out, holding pistols at their side. By the time the group even noticed the men, Paco was coming around from the driver's side.

"What's up, Pain?" Paco said with a smile.

Pain's eyes got as wide as saucers. He looked from his crew to Paco and the men carrying the automatic weapons and was mad at himself for leaving his gun in the car.

"I've been trying to call you since yesterday," Paco said, standing directly between the trio and their car.

"What the fuck is this shit about?" Jay asked, trying to hide his nervousness.

"Oh, you ain't know? Your boy here owes me a grip and I want it. You got my money, Pain?"

Lex couldn't believe what was about to go down. He always told Pain that his habit was going to get him into some shit, but he never imagined getting caught up with him. He tried to gauge the distance from where he was standing to the truck and wondered if they would gun him down before he made it.

"Paco, I ain't got it all, but—"

Paco waved his hand for silence. "Save it. I told you when you took my shit that the clock was ticking. Time's up."

The world suddenly began to move in slow motion. Pain saw his partner Lex fall before he heard the shot. Paco had drawn a weapon and blasted Lex twice in the chest. The aspiring star spun and collapsed to the ground. His body heaved one last time and the life drained from his body. Jay made a move, giving Pain fleeting hope that someone would stand with him in the battle for his life, but to his surprise Jay took off running. He had almost made it to the corner when one of Paco's people gunned him down. Jay took four shots to the back and fell face-first into the street. Pain found himself alone, staring down the barrels of several automatic weapons.

At that moment, Pain's entire life flashed before his eyes. He was about to become one of the biggest rising stars in hip-hop, but the little greaseball Spanish cat standing in front of him was threatening that. In a last attempt at saving his life, Pain lunged for Paco. Before he had even gotten within arm's length, a slug tore through his side. He was so coked up that he didn't even realize he had been shot until the second bullet hit him. He tried to run off, but received two more slugs to the back. Pain lay on the floor, kicking his legs as if he were still trying to run. As he watched Paco standing over him, gun trained on the middle of his forehead, all he could think about was how he was never gonna make it onto MTV.

"Yo, kid, you made the papers!" Spooky exclaimed, showing Jah the article about Ralph's murder. "You pushed that boy's shit smooth back."

"Why don't you say it a little louder, I don't think the people on the fifth floor heard you," Jah said, breaking up a block of weed on a magazine.

"Fuck these square-ass niggaz!" Spooky shouted. "They know who the fuck we be. Our murder game is superofficial."

"Spooky, don't be saying that shit too loud. The block is on fire right now and I ain't trying to get knocked with this thing on me." Jah exposed the butt of his .40.

"Jah, why the fuck do you still have that thing, didn't I just give you another gun?"

Jah sucked his teeth. "Spooky, stop sweating me."

"Yo, you been on some real moody shit since the night of the party. What's good with you, duke?"

"Nothing, I just got a lot on my mind right now," Jah told him.

"You know what," Spooky said and sat beside him on the stoop, "I think the problem is your ass is backed up. You need to get yaself some pussy instead of always running around plotting on a dollar."

"Nigga, when I'm plotting, your ass be right alongside me."

"True," Spooky said, then laughed. "But on some real shit, your head ain't been in the game lately. I might pop a lot of shit, but I love you like my own blood. If something is on your mind, you know you can talk to me about it."

Jah looked over at Spooky to see if he was bullshitting, but to his surprise his friend's eyes were sincere. "Dawg, if I run this shit down to you and you try and play me, it's on!" Jah said seriously.

"My dude, I wouldn't even do it to you like that. Holla at ya boy."

Jah paused for a minute, contemplating if he could go through with it. "A'ight. I met a chick," Jah finally admitted.

"I knew you din't have that sick puppy look in your eyes for nothing!" Spooky punched him in the arm. "Do I know the bitch?"

"Nah, you don't know her, and she ain't no bitch, foul-ass nigga. We was on some cool shit at first," Jah continued, "then one thing led to another and we ended up fucking. Now the shit is all awkward."

"Awkward? You got yourself a shot of pussy. What's awkward about that?"

Jah looked at him, not believing his ignorance. "It ain't about the pussy, man. I mean, don't get it fucked up, the pussy was the bomb, but feelings got involved. I mean, I'm trying to fuck wit' shorty like that, but I don't know if it's a wise move."

"Why not, is she all fucked up or something?" Spooky asked.

"Oh, nah, shorty is bad, but she 'bout her scratch."

"So you paid for the pussy?"

"Hell no!" Jah assured him. "I just mean she's high maintenance."

"Oh." Spooky nodded. "I'll tell you like this; you already know better than to be letting a bitch be out here climbing in your pocket, so we ain't even gotta touch on that. We're soldiers on these streets, so we always think as such, but at the same time we're men. You could blow every bitches back out from here to D.C., but ain't nothing like having that one shorty that makes you feel whole. A chick that makes you always want to be yourself, smell me?"

"Yeah," Jah said, seriously taking in Spooky's words. "You're right, my dude. I'm just gonna lay it out for shorty and let the cards fall wherever they fall."

"That's what I'm talking about." Spooky nudged him. "And when you speak to Yoshi, ask her if she's got a friend."

"How the hell . . . ?"

"Jah, you're like my brother. I know you." Spooky gave him a wink.

33

Billy made hurried steps through the entrance of Harlem Hospital's K building. The guard sitting behind the desk tried to stop her to check her ID, but Billy ignored him and kept going toward the elevators. The portly man in the company-issued blue suit made to pursue her, but Marcus interceded. After a brief explanation, and a once-over of Marcus's identification, the guard returned to his post and troubled them no further.

During the elevator ride up, Marcus tried to offer Billy words of encouragement, but they went in one ear and out the other. Seeing the pain in her eyes, he wanted nothing more than to reach out and comfort her, but he didn't want to overstep his bounds. Before the doors had completely opened on the third floor, Billy was sliding between them and sprinting down the hall. Marcus found himself almost having to jog to keep up with her.

When Billy reached the nurses' station, she gave the young Trinidadian woman Yoshi's full name and was directed to room 322. Keeping her speedy pace, Billy moved down the hall to locate her friend. When she found Yoshi's room, she paused outside the door for a minute. Not really knowing what to expect, she had to gather the courage to go in. Marcus offered to go with her, but Billy declined. This was something she had to do on her own. Taking a deep breath, Billy pushed the door open and stepped into the room.

Yoshi lay on a bed, with the side of her face bandaged and her left arm in a cast. Her eye was swollen and her lip looked like it would burst if you touched it. Yoshi's whole body was covered in bruises and scratches from the ordeal. Tears streamed down Billy's cheek when she saw the mess the attacker had made of her friend.

"Yoshi?" Billy called to her, slowly approaching the aluminum bed.

At first Yoshi was still, but gradually she began to move. Stirring from her drug-induced slumber she looked at her friend through her good eye, which had a red web running through it. She tried to raise her arm, sending pain racing through her body.

"Billy?" she whispered through her swollen and dry lips.

"I'm here, baby," Billy said, rushing to her bedside and taking her good hand. "It's gonna be okay."

Yoshi tried to manage a smile, but only ended up wincing in pain. "I'm sorry," she said, sobbing through a distorted voice.

"It's okay, baby." Billy embraced her. "Who did this to you?"

"It was Rel and those guys from Bad Blood," she confessed. "When I went home from the club they were waiting from me." Yoshi's body shook from the sobbing. "I tried to fight them, but I couldn't make them stop. Billy, they hurt me so bad."

"Shhh." Billy stroked her forehead. "It's over now. No one is gonna hurt you again." The fury that burned inside Billy made her feel like she was sitting in a sauna. She had heard horror stories about victims of rape and her heart had always gone out to them, but having it hit this close to home hurt her beyond words.

Though Billy had asked him to wait outside, Marcus crept to the doorway and observed from afar. Watching Billy comforting her battered friend almost brought him to tears. A man who would violate a woman in such a way was beyond the scum of the earth. Though he hadn't known Yoshi very long, his sister stripped, too, making the offense feel too close to home. He could only imagine what he would do to someone if it had been Cat. Taking one last look at the tragic scene, Marcus left the women to their privacy.

When Rhonda entered her mother's apartment, the first thing she smelled was chicken. Someone was in the kitchen frying the hell out of a bird and it had Rhonda's stomach cramping up on her. She hadn't eaten since that morning and all the weed she'd smoked since then had her ribs touching. She licked her lips in anticipation as she rounded the corner to crack on her mother for a piece of chicken, but her pleasant mood changed when she saw her sister Kelly sitting at the kitchen table.

"Hello, Rhonda," Kelly said, in a tone that made Rhonda feel like it was a task to speak to her.

"What's up," Rhonda replied, matching her tone. For a minute the two sisters just stared at each other without speaking. Though they had been born and raised in the same house, the two of them shared a less-than-sisterly affection. Rhonda rolled her eyes and opened up the refrigerator.

"So have you come to get your kids?" Kelly asked.

"Excuse you?" Rhonda paused from her rummaging.

"Your *children*," Kelly repeated. "The two little people you pushed out of your ass."

Rhonda folded her arms. "Why do you wanna know? I don't remember leaving them with you."

"No, but you left them on Mommy, once again."

"Kelly, don't start with me. Mommy wasn't complaining about it."

"And how would you know, not that you listen when people talk anyway. Rhonda, did it ever occur to you that she might not feel like baby-sitting your bad-ass kids after working a twelve-hour shift?"

"Bitch, don't be talking about my kids," Rhonda warned her.

Kelly adjusted her glasses, which were sitting atop her head. "Rhonda, you act like you don't know your kids are bad-ass hell. When I was getting off the bus, Pooh and those little nappy-headed kids from down the street were throwing rocks at the winos in front of the liquor store."

"Please, them niggaz ain't nothing but some alcoholics," Rhonda said, as if she didn't run at least a pint a day through her liver.

"That isn't the point, Rhonda. Those are still grown men and Pooh should learn to respect his elders. And we're not even gonna speak on Alisha. Did you know that I found her ass around the corner all up in some boy's face? When I checked her on it, she had the nerve to suck her teeth and act like I was intruding on her time."

"I'm gonna knock the hell out of that little bitch when I catch her," Rhonda assured her.

"For what, emulating what she sees?" Kelly asked. "Rhonda, your problem is that you think whipping those kids' asses is the answer to everything. Granted, they could use a good ass kicking, but that isn't gonna solve your problem."

"So what would you suggest, Ms. Know-It-All?" Rhonda asked sarcastically.

"For starters, you could watch what you expose them to. When you're constantly doing and saying ignorant things around children, they're eventually going to pick up on it."

"So now you're calling me ignorant?"

"I don't have to call you anything, your actions speak for you," Kelly said venomously.

Rhonda closed the refrigerator and glared at Kelly. "I'm 'bout sick of your shit. All you ever do is look down your nose at people like your shit don't stink. You act like your life is so perfect, but I could point out a thing or two with you and your bullshit."

"Such as?" Kelly challenged.

"How 'bout the fact that the nigga you've been fucking for the last six months has a wife you have to share him with," Rhonda spat out, stunning Kelly. "Don't look so surprised. Just because I don't run in your little snooty-ass circles doesn't mean that my ear ain't to the streets. Acting like you're the queen bitch, but you ain't nothing but another man's mistress."

"How dare you, you little black bitch!" Kelly jumped up.

"Bitch?" Rhonda began, removing her earrings. "I got your bitch, you saditty ho!"

Rita came into the kitchen wearing a flowered bathrobe and a purple scarf over her hair. A cigarette dangled from her mouth, bouncing on her bottom lips as she spoke. "Hey, hey, what's all this noise about?"

"Mommy, you need to tell your ghetto-ass daughter to calm herself," Kelly said, cutting her eyes at Rhonda.

"You got one more name to call me and I'm gonna bust you right in your fucking mouth, bitch!" Rhonda told her.

"Jesus, Rhonda, why is your mouth so nasty?" Rita asked.

"Because she got me tight, Ma. Every time you turn around she's got something to say."

"Mommy, all I did was tell her the truth. She's always dropping her kids off with somebody so she can go out and shake her ass. She needs to find something to do with herself other than drink and smoke."

"Fuck you, Kelly. I'm grown and I ain't fucking nobody's man for my habits."

"Of course not, you're sleeping with them for Happy Meals," Kelly taunted.

Rhonda was so angry that she could feel the sweat beads beginning to form on her head. The next thing she knew she was lunging across the table at Kelly. Being caught totally off guard, Kelly caught the blow flush to her face when Rhonda threw it. She staggered back, almost falling, but the stove held her up. Rhonda tried to get at her again, but Kelvin grabbed her from behind.

"What the hell are you doing?" he asked, not knowing what had just gone down.

"Get off me, Kel!" Rhonda shouted, still trying to break his grip. "I'm gonna kill that bitch."

"Y'all bugging out in here, fighting in front of Mommy," Kelvin told them both.

"I don't give a fuck, Kel. I'm tired of that bitch trying me."

Rita looked from daughter to daughter and shook her head. "Lord, does the bullshit never end with you damn kids."

"You need to tell this hood rat something," Kelly said, holding her cheek where Rhonda had clocked her.

"Keep running your mouth and I'm gonna give you just what you've been asking for," Rhonda warned her sister.

"Dammit, Rhonda, how come every time you come over here you starting something?" Rita said.

"Me?" Rhonda couldn't believe she had been singled out. "She started it!"

"But you dragged it on. You've got three kids, Rhonda, when are you going to grow up?"

Tears began to spill from Rhonda's eyes. "You know what, y'all have been doing this to me for years, so I should be used to it. Every time something goes down, I'm to blame. It doesn't matter who started it, but your precious Kelly could never do any wrong."

"That's not true. I've always been a loving mother to all of you," Rita defended.

Rhonda's eyes went blank, then back to alert again. "Loving? You can't be serious. Ever since we were little all you ever cared about was your twins, and when Kelvin came out of the closet, he went on your shit list, too."

"Rhonda, you need to stop telling that bullshit lie. All you're doing is trying to get attention," Rita said.

"You can't even spell 'attention,' " Rhonda shot back. "All my life you've made me feel like I was more of a burden than a daughter. Everything I do is wrong! I can remember a time when I was twelve and I told you that your boyfriend had been touching me. Do you remember what happened?" Rhonda asked, staring at her mother, who wouldn't meet her gaze.

"Rhonda, that's enough." Kelvin tried to place a reassuring hand on Rhonda's shoulder, but she knocked it away.

"Nah, Kel, let's lay it all on the table." She turned back to her mother. "You slapped me in the face and called me a lying little whore. You even had the nerve to accuse me of trying to come on to that dirty old son of a bitch. Bet you felt like shit when they locked him up for raping that little girl on Eighth Avenue."

Rita covered her ears. "I don't have to listen to these lies."

"The truth is always a hard pill to swallow." Rhonda chuckled. "The saddest part about all this is that no matter what you did to me, or turned a blind to what other people did, I could never bring myself to hate you. Too bad you couldn't feel the same way about me."

Rita, too, was now crying and shaking her head. "You're a liar and a thorn in my side. Get out of my house!"

"With pleasure," Rhonda said, storming through the kitchen doorway. As an afterthought, she turned to Kelly and added, "When you bring your fake white ass outside, it's on and popping." Holding her head up triumphantly, Rhonda went outside to gather her children.

Rhonda shoved the door to her mother's apartment open so hard that it chipped the paint when it bounced off. She frantically pressed for the elevator that seemed like it was taking forever to come. When she finally made it on, she broke down into a fit of crying.

Growing up in her mother's house was like a living hell to her. Rita had never been the greatest mother to any of her kids, but she seemed to go out of her way to be mean to Rhonda. Maybe it was her rebellious spirit, or the fact that her father didn't stick around for very long after her birth. Whatever the reason, Rhonda was always the object of spite. Nothing Rhonda did was ever good enough for Rita. The day she moved out on her own was the happiest of her life. She thought that it would finally free her from the tyranny of her mother's judgments and the ridicule of her sister, but there was still pain by association.

Getting off the elevator, she paused in the hallway to gather herself before stepping out in public. Though she was no longer sobbing, tears still ran freely down her face. She couldn't go out onto the stoop and appear weak to the other ghetto birds. She was mad enough to put her fist through the drywall of the lobby walls, but more hurt than anything. Her cell vibrating in her purse gave her something else to focus on.

"Hello?" Rhonda placed the phone to her ear. When she heard the voice of the caller, she started to make a snide comment, but her face went blank when she made out what the girl was saying. "I'm on my way!" Rhonda assured the caller and ended the call.

"Yo, Rhonda!" Kelvin called, bouncing down the steps. "I need to holla at you for a second."

"Not right now, Kel, I gotta make a move," she told him, tucking her phone back in her purse.

"Listen," he began, "that thing with Mommy . . . well . . ."

"Kel, that shit has been going on since before you and your bitch of a twin came along, so I don't know why I ain't used to it. You were her favorite, so you couldn't understand where I'm coming from, but that's been your mother for a lot of years so you know how full of shit she can be. As far as I'm concerned, her and Kelly can both go to hell and I wouldn't lose a damn bit of sleep."

"Rhonda, I know you're mad, but they're still your family," Kelvin told her.

"Kel, if that's what family is like, then I don't want no part of it," she said seriously. "But it ain't nothing, baby brother. We'll always be cool." She hugged him.

"I know that's right." He smiled.

"Baby brother, you wanna do your sis a big favor?"

"I knew you were being nice for a reason," he teased her. "How much do you need?"

"I don't need money, stupid ass. I just want you to take Pooh and Alisha to my house and sit with them until I get back."

Kelvin wrinkled his face. "Rhonda, you know damn well I ain't gonna baby-sit for you while you go out and shake your ass."

"It ain't like that, I got an emergency," she said honestly. "Billy just brought Yoshi home from the hospital, so I'm gonna shoot over there."

"Hospital? Is she okay?" he asked in a concerned tone.

"I don't know the details yet," she lied. "I'll explain it to you when I get back." Rhonda tossed him the keys and headed for the door. "Thanks again, Kel," she yelled over her shoulder without waiting for an answer.

34

Jah had been calling Yoshi for the last day and a half and hadn't gotten an answer. His emotions constantly bounced between anger and regret, knowing that he was about to pledge his heart to a stripper and she didn't even have the common decency to call him back. To make matters worse, he found himself sitting across the street from her building, watching it like some crazed stalker. "Playing myself," he mumbled, getting off the bench and heading up the block. He was so engrossed in his thoughts that he literally bumped into Billy coming around the corner.

"Oh shit!" She jumped back, startled. "My bad, Jah."

"Nah, it's my fault. I should've been watching where I was going." He smiled weakly.

"What're you doing down this way?" Billy asked suspiciously.

Jah hesitated. "Ah . . . well, to be perfectly honest with you, I was looking for Yoshi."

"Yoshi? Why are you looking for her?"

"It's kind of personal." Jah looked at the ground.

"Well, Yoshi isn't feeling well, so you'll have to see her another time." Billy walked past Jah.

"I really need to speak to her," he said and walked alongside her.

"Jah, I don't know what kind of arrangement you and Yoshi worked out, but now really ain't the time for that bullshit. Like I said, speak to her another time," Billy said, marching up the stairs to Yoshi's lobby.

"I love her," he blurted out.

Billy froze in her tracks. She slowly turned around, knowing that she had heard him wrong. "You what?"

Jah put his head down as if he was ashamed of his feelings. "I don't know how or when it happened, but I do," he said softly. Jah couldn't explain why he was about to jump out the window and expose himself to Billy, other than maybe he just needed to say it out loud. Love is a blessed thing, but it can also be a heavy burden to carry. Jah went on to tell Billy of their friendly flirtation that had become something more, not omitting a thing. He told Billy of his sleepless nights swooning over memories of a shared moment, which almost brought her to tears. When it was all said and done, Billy was in a state of shock.

"I'm not out here chasing, Billy. I just wanted to tell her how I felt, while I still had the nerve to do it," he said sincerely.

When Billy looked at the fire in Jah's eyes, her heart couldn't help but go out to him. Here was a dude who she had never seen as more than a young reckless nigga who'd probably end up in jail sooner than later. Hearing what he had to say made her question her assessment of his character. When Jah spoke of loving Yoshi, his voice had the same passionate pitch that Sol's used to. There was no faking that.

"Jah," Billy began, "I don't know if I should even be telling you this, but if you're keeping it a hundred about what you've told me, you might just need to know. I just need your promise that you won't wild out and make the situation worse."

"Billy, what are you trying to tell me?" he asked.

"Yoshi was raped the other night." Billy told him the full story of what had happened to Yoshi, just as she had told it to her, leaving out the names of the culprits. She had to stop a few times and compose herself, as even recounting it hurt. By the time she got to the end of the story, Jah's face was stained with tears.

"How? Why?" he asked, barely able to get the questions out.

"I'm not gonna go into details with you, Jah, because I know how you are. Just know that the matter is gonna get handled."

"Billy, can I see her . . . please?" he pleaded.

She thought on it for a minute. Yoshi was still broken up about the whole ordeal—physically and emotionally—and not really ready to receive anyone but her girls and her family. The only reason she even tolerated Marcus was because he was footing the bill. Still, Jah was a man in love and chances might've been that Yoshi felt the same. It was a good possibility that seeing Jah might help with her recovery process.

"Jah, if I take you to where Yoshi's staying, do you think you can keep from upsetting her?"

"Word to everything I love," he said. "Yo, all I wanna do is make sure she's okay. I just wanna see her for a minute and I'm gone, Billy."

After grabbing a few things from Yoshi's, Billy and Jah hopped in a taxi and headed out to Queens. Marcus had a two-bedroom apartment he kept out that way but hardly stayed in, and he'd offered it to Yoshi while she recovered. It was in a secluded area and the grounds were patrolled 24/7. Even if Marcus hadn't been hovering over the girls like a mother hen, they would've been safe.

Billy paused just outside the apartment door to give Jah some last-minute instructions. "When we get inside, you don't say a fucking word. I'm gonna go in the back and tell Yoshi that you're here. Don't get your hopes up, though, because there's no guarantee that she'll even want to see you."

"If she doesn't feel up to it, I'll bounce," he assured her.

Letting herself in, Billy led Jah through the foyer to a carpeted living room. There wasn't much furniture in it, with the exception of a sofa bed and a large television that had an Xbox hooked to it. Marcus, who had been playing Madden, glared up at Jah. Billy tapped Marcus's leg and led him into the kitchen, where they spoke in hushed voices. A few moments later they came back out. Billy's face was indifferent while Marcus's was just suspicious.

"Jah, I'll be back," Billy told him, disappearing into the bedroom and leaving the two men alone.

Marcus waited until he was sure she had gone before addressing Jah. "So you know Yoshi from the block?"

"Something like that," Jah said. Though Marcus wasn't coming at him sideways, something about his posture made Jah's hand move closer to his gun.

"Listen, my dude, I don't want you to take this the wrong way, but I feel like I gotta say it. Billy says you're good peoples, but I don't know you well enough to go on the word of a female. Yoshi has been through a lot, probably more than you can imagine. She's in a very fragile condition right now, so I would appreciate if you kept that in mind when you go back there. I couldn't see her hurting any more than she already is, smell me?"

Jah peeped the underlining threat in Marcus's statement, but forced himself not to try and tear the kid's head off. "I dig where you're coming from, so we won't have any misunderstanding about that there. I got nothing but Yoshi's best interest at heart."

"Cool." Marcus nodded and went back to playing the game.

Jah stood by the front door looking everywhere but at Marcus. Something about the man's cockiness made him want to punch him in the face. Luckily, he didn't have to wait around too long because Billy came walking out of the back, with Rhonda on her heels. Jah watched her face, trying to read it.

"I heard Billy say it, but I had to see it with my own eyes," Rhonda said, giving Jah a pound. "What wind blew your ass this way?"

"I needed to see Yoshi," he answered.

"For what? When did you two become all buddy-buddy?"

"It's a personal matter," Jah said, becoming irritated that Rhonda was keeping Billy from speaking. "So?" He looked at Billy.

"Okay, she'll see you," Billy said. Jah was so excited that he tried to go in the back, but Billy grabbed him by the arm. "Hold on, speedy. She still needs her rest, so don't excite her and don't stay long."

"You have my word," he said seriously, making his way down the hall. The walk was a short one, but it felt like the green mile. Jah waited outside the bedroom door, trying to figure out what to say. There was no scripted speech that he could give that would make the pain any easier to handle, so he opted to just speak from his heart. Jah slowly pushed the door open and went in to face Yoshi.

"Hey," Yoshi said from her elevated position on the bed. Her face was black and blue and the swelling in her lips still hadn't gone down. She tried to smile at him, but he could tell it pained her to do so.

"Oh my God," Jah whispered.

"I guess I'm having a bad hair day." She tried to joke, but her pain and embarrassment at her physical state was obvious.

Jah moved to the side of the bed and knelt beside her. The lump in his throat was so big that he almost couldn't speak. Yoshi tried to turn her head away, but he gently turned her face back toward him. "What did they do to you?"

"Punk-ass niggaz got at me," she said, trying to sound tough, but she was unable to hide the emotional turmoil. "I'm sure Billy already told you what happened, so there's no need to go over it again."

Jah felt like screaming, but didn't want to upset her. "I'm so sorry." He pressed his cheek against her hand and enjoyed the warmth.

"It wasn't you fault." She touched the back of his head. "It was my own fault. If I hadn't—"

"You stop right there," he cut her off. "No woman deserves this, I don't care who she is or what she does. Them niggaz is wrong, and I'm gonna show them the error of their ways!" he said heatedly. "Just tell me who did this to you and I'm gonna smoke all they asses."

"No, Jah," she said, surprising him. "All that's gonna do is make things worse. I don't want you getting into trouble over a filthy whore like me." She suddenly began to sob.

"Yoshi, you'll never be anything other than an angel in my eyes." He wiped the tears from her cheek, careful not to hurt her.

This brought another weak but genuine smile. "Jah, I appreciate you trying to make me feel better, but I'm not ashamed of what I am."

"Yoshi, a whore is someone who sleeps with men for money with malicious intent," he explained to her. "You're just a girl that's made some poor choices. Baby girl, you're one of the most beautiful people I've ever met. Do you know how special you made me feel the other night?"

"Jah, everyone feels special when they're busting a nut," she said and turned away.

"Baby, a nut ain't nothing new to me so I ain't tripping over no pussy. That night was special to me, real special. That's why I'm here."

Yoshi looked at him as if he had lost his mind. "Jah, I know damn well you didn't come here to crack for no pussy?"

"Hell no!" he said seriously. "I came here to tell you how I felt." He lowered his voice. "I've never been the most emotional cat, but you stirred something in me that I didn't even know was there." He paused to compose himself. "Yoshi, I'm feeling you and that's the real deal."

"I'm flattered, but what exactly are you trying to tell me?" she asked, figuring she was reading the message wrong.

A million thoughts ran through Jah's mind at once. He tried to speak, but the words came out tangled. Taking several deep breaths, he said finally, "Yoshi, when I say I'm feeling you, I mean I wanna fuck with you on some exclusive shit."

The look Jah gave her when he said it took Yoshi's breath away. Her state could only be described as speechless. Many a man had tried to acquire Yoshi as his main lady, but there was always something to be gained on his part, or something lacking. She didn't see that in Jah. In his eyes she saw not a killer's edge, but the gentleness and innocence of a child that the lonely side of her wanted so badly to cling to. At that moment, all she could think to do was hug him close to her and loose the floodgate of tears that she had been holding back, but she hesitated for fear of corrupting what was left of his innocence with her sin.

"Jah," she said and looked down at her hands. "When I was a little girl I used to watch these TV shows and dream of the day when a guy would come along who would help me carry this pain around. When I got older and bore witness to my own truth, I realized there wasn't no princes in the ghetto. I gotta get it how I live, same as you, because that's the only way we know how."

"Unless we find a different way together," he said.

"Touché," she said and tried to smirk. "Seriously, though, I don't want you talking out your ass because you see a bitch all laid up. I'm broken right now, and it ain't nothing that won't be fixed with time and work, so please don't treat me like a charity case."

"I wouldn't," he told her. "This is a sincere plea for some understanding."

"We'll see, Jah." She patted his hand. "I've got a lot of self-repair ahead of me, so I'm not trying to rush anything."

"And I'm not asking you to. All I want is to be your crutch, and eventually your strength," he shot back. Against his better judgment, Jah leaned in and kissed her softly on the lips. He tried to be as gentle as possible, yet still let her know how serious he was, through that one tender act.

"Where're you going in such a rush?" Rhonda asked Jah, who was making moves toward the front door.

"Just need to get a little air," he said over his shoulder.

Billy watched dumbfounded as the young man stormed out. Marcus caught the look in Jah's eyes when he passed. He was no stranger to pain, so he knew Jah was going through a thing. Again, his thoughts went back to his sister and how he would react if something similar had happened to her. He had promised Billy that he wouldn't get directly involved, but he never said anything about adding his two cents. Grabbing his cell phone, he excused himself to the kitchen.

Rhonda gave a cautious look around before following Jah out the door. When she got in the hallway, she was surprised to see Jah with his head leaning against the door. A deep sobbing erupted from the young man as his shoulders went up and down in tune with his grief. For as long as Rhonda had known Jah, she had never seen him this broken up. Though she hadn't been in the room with them, she was still a woman and had an idea that there was more to him and Yoshi than people had picked up on.

"Jah," she said and placed a hand on his back. To her surprise, his sobbing got worse. "What's the matter, little brother?"

"Do you see what they did to her?" he asked without turning to let Rhonda see his tears. "They fucked her up crazy bad."

"Yeah, them niggaz did some sucker shit," she agreed.

"I asked her who they were, but she wouldn't tell me. I swear to everything I love, I'd track them dudes down and blast them all!" He punched the elevator door.

Rhonda couldn't help but to feel fucked up for Jah. He was reacting to the sight of Yoshi much the same as she had, but what burned in Jah was pure evil. Rhonda remembered then how she begged God to give her a means to teach Yoshi's attackers a lesson, and here he was . . .

"Jah," she said, leaning in to whisper in his ear, "I know who did this, but if I tell you, you can't say where you got the info from."

Jah spun around so fast he scared her. "Rhonda, if you know something, don't keep me in the dark."

The mad glare in his eyes told Rhonda that the tidbit of information she held meant the lives or deaths of several men. She reveled in her godly powers for a long moment before setting the wheels in motion. "It was Rel and them niggaz." Pulling Jah closer to whisper, Rhonda went on to tell him the full story of Yoshi's rape, including the details that Billy had omitted earlier. By the time Jah left, Rhonda was thoroughly convinced that she had set a mad dog loose in the streets. She smiled triumphantly and waited for the other shoe to fall.

35

You just gonna sit there and get high all night?" Elaine asked, placing one hand on her hip. She was a piss-yellow dime that Spooky had on-and-off-again relations with. He dug her on a level above just being a fuck thing, but he couldn't deal with her mouth. Like Rhonda, who was straight reckless when it came to knowing what to say out of her mouth, she could get a nigga tight to the point where he wanted to jap her.

"Pretty much." Spooky exhaled a dark cloud. He was draped lazily over his recliner, half playing a game of Major League Baseball.

"I swear, you're the laziest muthafucka." She bumped the recliner as she passed it.

"Shut up and bring me something to drink!" he yelled to Elaine. "Crazy-ass broad," he mumbled.

"I heard that shit. Don't make me fuck you up!" she called from the kitchen.

"Fuck are you, part bat?" Spooky whispered. Swinging himself into an upright position, Spooky began concentrating on the game. As soon as he got into it, someone knocked on the door. Spooky ignored it, but they knocked again. "You hear every damn thing but the door, huh?" Spooky called to Elaine.

"How the hell am I supposed to be getting you something to drink *and* answer the door? Put the game on pause and see who it is, with your lazy ass!" she called back.

"Bitch," Spooky mumbled, going to the door. Once he was certain it wasn't an enemy, he unlocked the door and went back to the game without bothering to open it.

Jah came in and locked the door. He nodded a greeting to Elaine, who just finger waved. He walked into the living room and took a seat on one of the dining room chairs. His face was grim, but his eyes said that something was on his mind.

"Okay, spill it," Spooky said, noticing the look on Jah's face.

"I'm in a bad way right now, my nigga," Jah admitted. "I got some shit on my plate and I really ain't sure how I wanna handle it."

"Holla at ya boy," Spooky said, putting the joystick down.

Jah glanced toward the kitchen. "It's kinda personal."

Spooky nodded in understanding. "Elaine!"

"What, nigga?" she snapped, coming out of the kitchen with his drink in her hand.

"Watch ya mouth," he warned. "Go in the back and occupy yourself while me and my man talk." He held his hand out for the cup.

She thrust the cup in his hand so roughly that Pepsi splashed on his tank top. "Spooky, don't be in here trying to talk to me like your name is Ron O'Neil because this nigga Jah is here. I'd hate to have to fuck you up."

"You ain't gonna do shit but go back there and wash your hot-ass little box, so I can hit you wit' this pipe." He slapped her playfully on the ass.

"I'll wash my snatch when you wash your dick," she said, heading toward the bedroom. "Cheesy-dick li'l nigga!" she called over her shoulder.

"Y'all two are off the chain." Jah laughed.

"Yeah, that's my boo, but I can't fuck with that bitch," Spooky said. "So what's on your noodle, my dude? I know you didn't come down to the mouth of madness to shoot the breeze. Tell me whose throat it is so we can make moves," Spooky said, cutting to the chase.

"Yo, it's about Yoshi." Jah went on to tell Spooky what had happened to Yoshi several nights prior. Though it still pained him to talk about the whole ordeal, being able to talk about it made the load easier to carry. When he was done with his story, all Spooky could do was shake his head.

"That's some punk shit. I got sisters, so I know how I'd react if it happened to one of them. This shit needs to be handled."

Jah nodded. "I know it, my dude, and I'm gonna take care of that. I just came by here to let you know what was popping and to snatch that vest, then I'm gone."

"You ain't going nowhere without me," Spooky told him.

"Spook, this ain't about business, this is a personal vendetta over a broad. I'd never even ask you to get caught up in this crazy shit. You know when I go in, I'm going for body count, and you don't need that kinda heat on you."

"Jah, I keep telling you that you're my fam, duke," Spooky explained while tying his Timberlands. "These niggaz already violated by trying to do us in, now they raped a chick we fuck wit'. These niggaz gotta be taught the error of their ways." Spooky slid an assault rifle from under the couch. "Let's go show these cats how gorillas move."

Marlene sat at her desk within her small home office, the phone pressed tightly against her ear. She listened intently while the caller spoke. Her face bore a look of shock at the information she had just received. In response to the date, all she could say was, "Are you sure?" The caller confirmed the facts and Marlene nodded. "Okay, fax it to my home office," she said and hung up the phone. The whole conversation left her in a state of shock.

"Mar, I'm about to drop P.J. off at his mom's house," Paul said, sticking his head into the office.

"Paul, we need to talk," she told him.

Paul sighed under his breath. "Mar, I really ain't in the mood to argue. I'm dropping my son off and I'll see you later."

"Paul, I don't want to argue, but we need to talk."

"Mar, I said not right now. I've gotta lot of stuff to do," he told her.

Before she could offer comment, his cell went off. "Hello?" he answered in an irritated tone.

"Paul," Marlene said.

"In a minute, Mar." He waved her off. "What do you want, Rhonda?" he said into the phone. "I'm brining him in a little while. Come on, don't put me through this shit right now 'cause I'm not in the mood. What?" He looked at the phone. "Watch how the fuck you talk to me! You know what? 'Bye Rhonda," he said and ended the call.

"You know, I think that girl has got radar. Every time we're in the middle of a conversation, her ass is on the line."

"What can I say? My baby's mama is a professional pest. Let me get up outta here before she starts blowing my phone up." He headed for the door.

"Well, I've got some things I need to get off my chest before you skate out," she told him.

"As soon as I get back we can argue all you want, but right now I gotta go."

Marlene slammed her hand against the table. "Paul, why is it that you have time for everyone except me? Not communicating is going to hurt our relationship more than help it."

"See," Paul said as he ran his hands over his face, "this is the kinda shit I be talking about. I told you that I'm trying to cram a whole bunch of shit into a small window of time. After I drop P.J. off, I gotta get the pieces ready for the show. I need a clear head for that, and going at it with you ain't gonna help."

"But Paul . . ."

"I gotta go, Mar." He ducked back out of the office.

Marlene started to get up and follow him, but decided against it. She was in a very emotional state and didn't trust herself not to do or say something rash. Instead, she sat back down and fumed. She wanted nothing more than to throw a tantrum and wild out, but the grown woman in her kept her rooted to the chair. Placing her hands in her head, Marlene began to cry.

Paul didn't understand how much he hurt her when he closed himself off that way. It made her feel like her needs weren't as important as his. She was in his corner about any and everything, but she didn't feel he was giving the same of himself. What he failed to realize was that Marlene was a woman in her golden years and needed more attention than the average female. She had gone through the days of angry walk-outs and not speaking when she was in her twenties and didn't have the strength to repeat the process with Paul. Some serious changes would have to be made if she intended to go all the way with him.

Marlene didn't know how long she had been sitting there, but by the time the doorbell rang she had a splitting headache. At first she thought it might be Paul, but he had a key and therefore would have no reason to ring the bell. Audrey wouldn't come over without calling, so she wondered who it could be.

As quietly as possible, she made her way to the front of the house. She peered through the curtains and saw a young Mexican man standing on her doorstep. He was dressed in a gray uniform and holding a cardboard tube and a rectangular box. Marlene opened the door and gave him a "what do you want?" look.

"Delivery," he said in a heavy accent, holding out an invoice bearing her name.

Marlene handed him a five-dollar bill and accepted the packages. Strolling to the kitchen, she shook the tube, trying to figure out what it could be. There was a low, shifting sound, but it still didn't reveal the contents. Placing the box and tube on the counter, she opened the envelope that held the card. There was no signature, but the note read:

Thank you for a wonderful evening.
Look forward to seeing you again soon.

Marlene didn't need a signature to know where it had come from. She placed the card down and opened the tube. Inside was a rose the color of blood on a stem that extended nearly two feet. Sniffing its sweet fragrance, Marlene smiled. The rose was beautiful, but what was inside the second box was the kicker.

It was a necklace made of sterling silver and woven to look like two snakes wrapping around each other. The centerpiece was a sapphire so clear that Marlene could see her hand on the other side. Marlene held the necklace to her neck and the sadness she had been feeling a few minutes prior faded a little. She was still pissed off at Paul, but her new gift took some of the bite out of it. With the way he was acting and what she had learned on the phone testing her strength, she wasn't sure how long she could take it. Though she loved the young man, she refused to sell herself short. Sadly, it was like her mother had always told her about Michael: "One man's trash is another man's treasure."

"Yo, you seen this shit in the paper?" Groovy walked up, flashing a copy of the *Daily News*. The evening air was soothing, so Rel and Slick decided to play the benches. Though they were out in the open, they hadn't forgotten about their beef with the elusive Jah. Rel had a hammer tucked in his Crunch 'n Munch box, and Slick's P89 was in the bushes beside them.

"Fuck is you talking about?" Rel asked, sipping Henny from a plastic cup.

"Mo money, mo murder." Groovy tossed the paper on Rel's lap. When Rel began reading, his jaw dropped.

"Up and Coming Harlem Rap Stars Murdered," Rel read the headline out loud.

> *Police arrived at the scene of what turned out to be a slaughter yesterday morning. Two drug crews turned the front of a popular Manhattan diner into the Old West, in a gun battle where as many as fifty shots were fired. Witnesses reported the young rappers Terrence "Pain" Pane and Raheem "Lex" Stewart of the group Bad Blood and an associate Jason "Jay" Brown got into a verbal exchange with a group of unidentified gunmen that turned deadly when a shot was fired. The rappers, whose gangsta anthem "Slap Ya Self " is quickly climbing the charts, had just come out of the diner when they were approached by the rival gang. Sources reported seeing one of the rappers pull a gun, which sent bullets flying from both sides. When the smoke cleared, two of the group's six members and Brown lay dead in the streets. No one knows exactly what sparked the shooting, but some say it may have been a dispute over drug turf.*

"If that ain't a crock of shit." Slick sucked his teeth.

"We was wit them niggaz just before that shit happened!" Groovy recalled.

"Lucky y'all left when you did," Slick said.

Rel shook his head. "Yo, that's some wild shit, son. On the real, if we had been there it wouldn't have gone down like that, word to mine. But see, that's what happens when you wanna be the man," Rel said, as if he was schooling Groovy. "I could tell them niggaz wasn't built like that, it's just sad they had to get their food ate to prove it."

The blood of young black men had been spilled on the streets yet again, and Rel was talking out of his ass. Slick had finally had enough. "Yo, why don't you shut the fuck up!" he barked. "All you ever do is talk about how you do, and how someone else is built. What the fuck are *you* built like?"

"Son, how you gonna get mad at me for telling my truth?" Rel defended. "Niggaz know who I be and what I represent, so my hood stripes could never be in question, you underdig me? I ain't trying to shit on they character, they went out like straight Gs. That's how I wanna go out, kid, word up."

"Rel, you can't be that fucked up." Slick gave an insane chuckle. "Those three cats was about to make it up outta this shit." He motioned at the projects around them. "And now they asses is stretched out. What the fuck is so glorious about dying in the gutter?"

"On some real shit, son, you need to fall back with all that Pastor Mase shit you're talking. Them niggaz knew what it was when they hit the block, fam," Rel said seriously. "Slick, I love you like my fam, but you ain't got no understanding of this here."

Slick gave him a puzzled look. "How the fuck you figure? Ain't I out here holding it down right along side you? When your gun go off, do mine ever stay quiet?" Slick asked seriously. "Don't try to downplay my street credibility, son."

"See, that's just what I'm talking about. I would never question your G, but your schooling was different," Rel pointed out. "You've always had your uncles, so you were able to learn the game under some true soldiers, but you didn't really have to put in no work. You think on shit too much, instead of acting on animal instincts. Me and

Groovy," he pointed at his partner, "we ain't never had shit. We come from straight fucking trash, and that's why we think like goons. Everything we know about the game came from hands-on education. Niggaz know Rel is a solider, 'cause I was a beast in my day."

"Well, this ain't ya day, and the beast has gotten a lot uglier," Slick shot back. "You keep running around with the fucked-up mind-set that your name is gonna protect you and somebody's gonna wake you up from that little dream." Slick got off the bench and walked away.

"Sensitive-ass nigga," Rel mumbled, finishing his cup.

True sat within the darkened recording studio thinking. An unreleased track from their album played softly through the speakers. Haze wafted from his nose and swirled around his head like a ghostly crown. He took another swig from the fifth of Jack Daniel's that was dangling at his side, but could only feel its burn as it went down. The potent whiskey had paralyzed his taste buds an hour prior. With his eyes closed, it felt like he could feel the darkness caressing his face as a lover would, and he welcomed it. At that moment, he felt like the absence of light mirrored his own existence.

True had read the bullshit *Daily News* article, and he knew the cat who had written it had no idea what the real deal was. Lex had given up robbing when he joined the group, and had gone harder than all of them when it came to making songs, so it was highly unlikely that he had beef with anyone. Jay was a notorious asshole, but didn't have the guts to piss off anyone who might've killed him. No, this had to be a result of Pain's bullshit. If he guessed correctly, it was over drugs. In that case, it was the only thing they'd gotten right.

True's lips moved along with Lex's verse as he spit on "Draw Arms," which was slated to be their next single. Almost his whole team had been taken out in one shot. Pain, Jay, Lex, they were all gone. Not only were they the core of the group, they were his family. True had his differences with all of the members, but they were still like his brothers. It would be hard to do without them.

A sliver of light coming from the door caught True's attention. With the details of his comrade's deaths still unclear, he wasn't taking any chances. In a less-than-fluid motion he grabbed his .45 off the floor beside him and drew on the door. When Don B.'s face became illuminated, he lowered it.

Don B. was startled when he noticed True huddled in the corner holding a gun. "Fuck is you doing?" he asked, turning on the lights. He looked at True and was a little disturbed by his appearance. His eyes were rimmed red and swollen. Even True's clothes were ruffled as if he had been sleeping in them.

"Sorry, I didn't expect nobody to come through here." True sat back on the couch. "What you doing around here this time of night?"

"Looking for you, kid." Don B. took the seat beside him. "Ain't nobody heard from you in like three days. What da deal?"

True shrugged. "I've been here, man. Writing." True nodded at a stack of papers in the corner. He must've written about fifty songs sitting up in the studio. "Thinking and trying to make sense of it all."

"Looks like you've been letting yourself slip." Don B snatched the bottle away from him. "True, what the hell are you trying to do to yourself?"

"I ain't trying to do nothing to myself that God ain't already done to me, Don," True slurred. "The whole click is gone, my nigga, our team!"

"True, I'm fucked up about this shit, too, but I ain't letting myself fall to pieces over it. Business still gotta be handled."

"How're we supposed to go on like this?" True sobbed. "Don B., we only half a unit."

Don B. put his arm around the weeping man and spoke softly. "True, we were strong as a unit, but our strength came from our individual gifts. Our niggaz is gone, but that don't mean we gotta forget them. We're gonna honor their memories and still push forward with this music thing."

True laughed insanely. "Dawg, Lah, and Jynx ain't no fucking rappers, they two candy-ass niggaz you snatched on some marketing shit. Me, Pain, and Lex was the fire behind it. How the hell are we gonna honor their memories?"

"By you shaking this shit off and stepping up!" Don B. smashed the bottle against the ground. "True, now is the time for you to be the leader I always knew you would, and carry the torch."

"Don B., that's a heavy load to carry."

Don B. chuckled. "Little brother, you were always the heart of the group. Since day one, people have always looked at you as the front man, so just continuing doing what you do best." He patted True on the back and smiled broadly. "Shine, my nigga, shine."

By the time Yoshi had finally dropped off to sleep, Billy was almost out on hers. For the last few days, she had been up almost constantly, either worrying about Yoshi or making sure she was comfortable. Her job let her take the take time off, but she had to do it without pay. The loss hurt her, but she sucked it up. Her friend's well-being was worth more than the few dollars she would lose.

Marcus was on the couch, snoring away. He had his head tilted at an awkward angle and the joystick was still resting on his lap. She couldn't help but admire how peaceful he looked at that moment. He had been by Billy's side through the entire ordeal. While she was sitting by Yoshi's bedside, he was the one on the streets doing what needed to be done. Whether it was going to the pharmacy, or making dinner runs, he held Billy down. The past few days she had spent with Marcus had given her a chance to see what he was really about.

Marcus must've felt her standing over him because his eyes immediately popped open. He glared at her for a minute as if he didn't know who she was, but his eyes softened when recognition set in. "Hey," he said groggily.

"How ya doing?" she said, sitting down beside him.

"A little stiff," he said, leaning his head from side to side. "How long have I been sleeping?"

"A couple of hours."

"Shit, I din't mean to fall out. I'm 'bout to get out of here." He started getting up.

"It's already late," she said and touched his arm. "It's cool if you crash here tonight and go home in the morning. Your ass is sleeping on the couch, though." She hit him playfully with one of the pillows.

"Girl, don't you know I was the pillow-fighting champ in '89," he said and hit her with the other pillow. Before long they were giggling like schoolkids and hopping around swinging pillows.

Billy tripped on the coffee table, sending her into an awkward spiral. Marcus caught her midfall, but the momentum sent them both crashing to the floor, with Billy on top. When the two of them locked eyes, time seemed to slow. The sound of their separate heartbeats melded together to make a strange symphony. Marcus started to say something, but she placed a finger over his lips. The moment was so perfect that words would've ruined it. Her insides felt as if God had laid a warm hand on her heart and melted the ice away. In a sense, it was as if he was telling her it was okay to love again.

Marcus was pleasantly surprised at Billy's aggressiveness. Initially, he had tried to put some distance between them, but she pressed her body closer to his. Billy kissed Marcus so deeply that his breath felt short when it was broken. Her pleading eyes said what her mouth would not and Marcus honored her request.

Flipping Billy onto her back, he began to pull her T-shirt over her head. Erect nipples taunted him through the fabric of the sports bra she was wearing, causing a throbbing in his groin. Using both hands, he pulled the bra up over her breasts and admired them. Billy had breasts the color of honey and nipples like milk chocolate. His mouth sucked at them greedily as she purred under the sensation.

Neither of them were sure when it happened, but at some point they both ended up on the floor as naked as the day they were born. Wild hands explored nude flesh without pattern or destination. She reached down and pulled on his dick, appreciating the hardness and length.

"Be easy. I haven't had sex in almost two years," she warned him.

"I will," he said. Marcus ran his fingers across her pussy and they came up soaked. Not being able to hold back, he attempted to enter her, but Billy stopped him.

"Aren't you forgetting something?" She looked down at his unprotected penis.

"My fault," he said, rolling off her. Marcus snatched a condom from his pocket and reassumed his position. He rolled the condom on, careful to make sure it was done correctly to lessen the chances of it breaking. Using his thumb to navigate, he tried to penetrate Billy. Just getting the head in was like trying to fit an elephant into a doghouse. She hissed in his ear and dug her nails deep into his back, but never asked him to stop. When he finally managed to work his penis in, it was pure heaven. He could tell she wasn't bullshitting about not having had sex, because the pussy was way too tight for her to be fronting. His forced entry was halted when he looked down and saw tears in the corners of her eyes.

"I didn't mean to hurt you," he whispered.

Billy reached up and touched his face. "Baby, these tears ain't got nothing to do with pain." Billy pulled Marcus back down on top of her and they made passionate love. It had never once occurred to them that Yoshi might come out of the bedroom and catch them. In truth, it didn't matter. That night the balance was restored to two lives.

36

When Paul got off the elevator the first thing he heard was the loud music. The walls were damn near vibrating from the bass coming out of Rhonda's house. Rounding the corner, he found himself engulfed in a cloud of weed smoke. Kelvin and some dudes Paul didn't recognize were standing in the hallway, passing a blunt.

"Uncle Kel!" P.J. squealed, running to the young man.

"What up, li'l dude?" Kel rubbed his head. "What's popping, Paul?" he addressed Rhonda's former lover.

"Chilling," Paul said. His tone was neither friendly nor hostile. He and Paul had never been the best of friends, but they always had a mutual respect for each other. Paul didn't knock him for being gay, and Kel didn't hold a grudge for Paul leaving his sister. They both understood Rhonda's character well enough to know it was bound to happen. "Your sister in there?" Paul nodded at the door.

"Yeah." Kelvin let out a cloud of smoke and passed the blunt to the kid standing closest to him. Paul nodded and walked his son inside.

The interior of the house didn't smell as strongly of weed as the hall did, but the air was rank with cigarette smoke. Rhonda seemed to be having a party of sorts, and it was a packed house. People were either sitting at the table playing cards for money or lounging on the couch drinking. In the center of it, running her mouth, was Rhonda.

"What's up, baby daddy?" She raised her glass. Paul just nodded. "You want me to pour you a drink?"

"Nah," he said, looking around at the assortment of grimy-ass men and women scattered throughout the house. "I just came by to drop P.J. off, 'cause I got some shit to do. These people gonna be here all night?"

"I can't call it, you know how parties can get." She toasted Reese, who was sitting next to her, wearing a spaced-out look on her face.

"Well, you might wanna think about shutting it down early tonight, being that your children are here," he pointed out.

"Please, they love to party just as much as their mama. P.J., show your daddy the dance you learned." The little boy bust out into the latest rap video move, drawing applause from the crowd. "That's my boy!"

"Rhonda, is that what you spend your time teaching our son?" Paul was clearly irritated.

"Stop acting like that, Paul. He's just a kid," Reese said, adding her two cents.

"I don't recall ever fucking you, or us having a seed together, so mind your fucking business."

"Y'all knock that shit off in front of P.J.," Sheila said. She was a brown-skinned girl who lived next door to Rhonda. "Paul, why don't you have a drink and hang out for a minute?" she suggested, trying to defuse the situation, but of course Rhonda wouldn't let her.

"Paul, don't come in my house disrespecting my company," Rhonda defended Reese.

"Then keep your puppy in check," he snarled.

"Who the fuck you calling 'puppy'?" Reese acted like she wanted to get up, but the look Paul gave her changed her mind.

"Paul, we in here having a good time, so don't start. You've dropped P.J. off, so you can go now," she said, as if continuing the conversation would stop her from doing something important.

"I don't even have the strength to do this tonight," he mumbled under his breath.

"Nigga, you ain't gotta do shit. Your son is home safely, so you can excuse yourself," she said, giving Reese a high five.

"Rhonda, don't be in here stunting like I won't bust ya head for you," Paul warned her.

"Please, you ain't shit to me, so you ain't got no reason or right to put your hands on me!" she said, way louder than she had to.

"Everything okay over here?" Von walked over. He had a half-empty Corona dangling from his hand. He was staring at Paul like he was trying to decide if he was going to frog up or not.

Paul tried to keep his voice calm when he addressed him. "My dude, this ain't got nothing to do with you, so just go on back in the cut and finish your beer."

Von screwed his face up. "I'm saying, I see you over here getting loud with my shorty, so I gotta figure it's something that requires a *man's* attention."

Paul looked from Von, who was flaring his nostrils, to Rhonda who was wearing a smug grin. The old Paul was banging against his chest, begging to be loosed upon the big-lipped kid and his chickenhead baby's mother, but looking at his son's confused face, he knew he couldn't wild out.

"Your shorty?" Paul gave him a sad look. "Whatever, my man. Like I said, this is between me and my son's mother, so fall back."

By now, someone had turned the music down and everyone was watching. Von knew he couldn't go out without making a show of it. "Duke, you don't know me well enough to be telling me what I should do."

Paul saw that diplomacy was getting him nowhere, so he changed his tactic. "Sheila, could you please take P.J. next door for a minute?" he said in a voice that was entirely too calm.

"Come on, Paul, let me just walk you to the elevator," Sheila pleaded, seeing the glare in his eyes. She had known Paul for quite a number of years, so she knew the ugliness when it was about to make a guest appearance.

Paul smiled at Sheila as if everything was cool. "Don't worry, baby, I ain't gonna wild out. I just got some things I want to say to Rhonda and I don't like to argue around P.J."

Sheila looked from Paul to Rhonda and knew that there wasn't much she could do to stop the storm that was brewing. "Come on, baby," she said, leading P.J. by the hand to the door. When she looked back at Paul over her shoulder, he was smiling broadly.

Paul waited until P.J. and Sheila were out of the house before addressing the situation at hand. "Listen, big boy," he said as he turned to Von, "I don't know what kind of arrangement you and my son's mother have, but when it comes to my seed, don't put your mouth in that," Paul said in a deadly tone.

"Fuck you think you're talking to?" Von swelled up. "Son, I eat niggaz food for a pastime!"

Von smiled triumphantly, but his moment was short-lived. Paul fired a right hook that snapped Von's head back and sent spit flying on Reese. Before Von could recover, Paul followed with a left to the side of the head. Von tried to fall, but a knee to the gut kept him on his feet long enough for Paul to lace his boots with an uppercut. Von bounced off the wall and slid down on his ass.

"No the fuck you didn't!" Rhonda shouted, charging Paul. She got within three feet of him and received an open-hand slap that busted her lip.

One of Von's boys caught Paul from behind with a jab to the back of the head. Paul quickly shook it off and fired with a right and a left, landing both on the man's chin. Another cat came rushing out of the bathroom with a knife in his hand. Paul caught his arm in a vise grip and twisted it, elbow facing up. With a downward strike, Paul popped the joint loose. By then, Von had recovered enough to bash Paul in the back of the head with a beer bottle. Paul staggered, but kept his feet under him.

Using the moment to his advantage, Von swooped in. He hit Paul with a barrage of punches, not really allowing him to get his bearings. When Paul finally did manage to get a good shot off, Von's boy who had caught the two-piece rejoined the fight. Paul was backed into the corner, trying to fend off multiple attackers. Von had just pulled his razor when a clicking sound halted everything.

Kelvin stood in the middle of the living room with a nine pointed at Von. "It ain't even going down like that, my dude. Not in my niece's and nephews' house. Party is the fuck over."

"Kel, how you gonna side with this nigga over me?" Rhonda barked.

"Rhonda, it ain't about taking sides. It's about you allowing niggaz to disrespect where my little ones lay their heads. This is some real chickenhead shit."

"Fuck you, Kel! Since you wanna side with this piece of shit, you can get the fuck out, too!"

"You a'ight, my dude?" Kelvin asked Paul, who nodded. "Let's get up outta here."

Paul stood up straight and flexed his jaw. His face was sore, but it didn't hurt as bad as it should've from the blows Von's punk-ass friends caught him with. The worst of his injuries was the bump on the back of his head, but there was no skin broken. The three battered men glared at him menacingly, but he matched all their stares. Von was nodding his head as if to tell Paul it wasn't finished yet. Paul nodded back, and cracked him in the jaw. The others moved for Paul, but the sound of the armed man clearing his throat froze them.

"You a real punk-ass nigga, Paul!" Rhonda said, rubbing her cheek. "This is the last muthafucking time you're gonna put your hands on me."

"Eat shit and die, you lowlife bitch!" he spat as he passed her. The crowd parted like the Red Sea when the strange duo passed. Paul looked over his shoulder at Rhonda and saw a look in her eyes that could only be described as pure hatred. He chuckled to himself, thinking how he fixed her and her little boyfriend, but Paul had no idea of the lengths that a woman scorned would go to for revenge.

"One day your sister is going to make me kill her," Paul said, pressing the first-floor button of the elevator as if he hadn't done it five times already.

"Paul, I don't even know why you keep feeding into it when you already know how she is," Kelvin said.

"I'm telling you, I can't do this anymore," Paul declared.

"My dude, you've got to start using your head," Kelvin told him. "Rhonda is gonna be the way she is for the rest of her life. I mean, I love my sister, but sometimes I feel fucked up for those kids. P.J. is lucky enough to have two parents, so don't deny him that by letting her bullshit get you into trouble." The elevator stopped on the fifth floor and Kelvin stepped off.

"Where the hell are you going?" Paul asked.

"I left something down here earlier that I gotta pick up. Be easy, my nigga." Kel hit Paul with the peace sign and let the elevator door close.

Paul got off the elevator on the first floor, glad to be free of the piss-smelling box. He hit the lobby door and stepped out into the cooling night air. Rhonda had pissed him off beyond belief and a brisk walk was just what he needed. Paul had just made it to the mouth of the projects when a police car cut him off. Two officers, one chubby and one thin, got out and approached him from opposite sides, both keeping their hands close to their weapons.

"What's going on?" Paul asked nervously.

"You live around here?" the chubby cop asked. He was looking at Paul as if he were trying to decide whether to hit him in the face first or the gut.

"Nah, I was visiting my son," Paul said, trying to keep at least a few feet between himself and the cops.

"Let's see some ID," the thin cop demanded, looking Paul up and down. Paul slowly reached into his pocket and handed his license over. They studied it as if it might've been written in a foreign language. "Where're you coming from?"

"I told you I was visiting my son, he lives in that building right over there." He nodded toward the building.

The chubby cop clicked his walkie-talkie. "Central, can we get a location and name of the perp on that disturbance." The walkie-talkie squawked something in response that caused the officers to share a suspicious look. Paul suddenly felt very queasy.

"Sir, can you please place your hands on the car?" the thin cop asked in a demanding tone.

"What's the problem?" Paul backed up.

The chubby cop drew his weapon and trained it on Paul. "Sir, if you run, I'll be forced to fire."

Paul's hands shot straight up. "Hey, man, ain't nobody running, be the fuck cool."

"Stop resisting!" the thin cop barked, twisting Paul's arm roughly behind his back.

"Yeah, that's him!" Rhonda shouted, coming out of the building. She was holding an ice pack on her jaw and had a small gathering of people behind her for dramatic effect. "Lock that nigga the fuck up."

"Please step back, ma'am," the chubby cop said, blocking her path, but he still kept his gun pointed in Paul's direction.

"Rhonda, you called the fucking police on me?" Paul asked in disbelief.

"You're damn right. I told you I was gonna fix your ass for putting your hands on me," she said smugly.

"This is some bullshit! Rhonda, you know I was just defending myself, your little boo tried to get at me," Paul declared.

Rhonda shot Paul and evil glare and smirked. "I don't know what you're talking about. All I know is you came into my house and started swinging on me, and I've got a bunch of witnesses to vouch for that." She motioned to the people behind her.

"You lying little bitch!" Paul struggled. "That's a fucking lie," he addressed the thin cop. "Rhonda, tell them what really happened!"

"That's the story as I know it," she said coolly.

"You lying little bitch!" Paul tried to wild out, but the cop prevented him from getting to Rhonda. "Someone tell them this bitch is lying." Paul spoke to the crowd, but no one came to his defense. "I can't go to jail, I've got an art exhibit tomorrow night."

The thin cop had trouble restraining him, so the chubby one lent a hand. "If you're lucky, you'll have seen the judge by then." The two cops wrestled Paul into the back of the car and slammed the door.

"Let's see that snooty bitch Marlene get you out of this one," Rhonda said and laughed. "Your little fairy-tale life ain't looking too good, is it?"

"Fucking bitch!" Paul shouted from the backseat.

"Don't worry, baby daddy, I'll put some money in your account when I get my check!" Rhonda taunted as the police took Paul away.

Marlene lay in her bed, trying to get into her Jackie Collins novel with little luck. It was three o'clock in the morning and she still hadn't heard from Paul. She tried calling his cell phone, but it kept going to voicemail. She wanted to cry, but figured it wasn't going to do her a damn bit of good. She would just have to accept the fact that Paul wasn't ready to be an adult just yet.

She reached under her bed and retrieved the journal Paul had brought for her on their one-year anniversary. The inscription on the front read, "Thank you for twelve months of happiness." She got all choked up for a minute, thinking about how their relationship had been before the bullshit came into play. It seemed like the more of her heart she gave him, the more he neglected her. She understood his problems within life and God knew she didn't blame him for Rhonda, but how much of a toll was carrying the weight of everyone else's bullshit and neglecting her own needs going to have on her? Marlene wasn't getting any younger and she had had about enough of twisting Paul's arm.

Picking up her house phone, she dialed Audrey. When she picked up, Marlene said, "Audrey, I might be going away for a few weeks, so I'm gonna need you to do something for me."

37

Reese knelt over the toilet, puking for the third time that morning. She had been going through this since a day or so prior. At first, she thought it was the combination of alcohol and penicillin, but when her mother had made a comment about her skin glowing a bit more than usual, paranoia kicked in.

When she was just about sure that nothing else was going to come out, she pulled herself up from the toilet. The face that stared back at her in the mirror was an unattractive one. Her eyes were red and speckles of vomit were on her chin. Taking a cold cloth from the side of the sink, she proceeded to wash her face.

"What the hell is going on with me?" she asked her reflection. She waited for a minute, but getting no response, figured she was on her own. Now came the moment of truth. Her nausea and her mother's comment had sent her scrambling to Duane Reade to get a home pregnancy test. She had peed on the stick before the vomiting started back up, but she was stalling. After getting burned, punched, and dissed, she was deathly afraid of what she mind find out next.

"Suck that shit up, Reese. You can do it," she told herself. Reese's hands trembled as she picked up the little white stick and held it to eye level. When she saw how many lines had appeared, she flopped down and placed her forehead on the side of the sink. She tried to scream, but found that she no longer had a voice. All she could do was weep silently.

Groovy came out of the liquor store, cradling a bottle beneath his arm like a football. He and Rel had had the good fortune of meeting two little sack chasers on the ave who were out looking for a good time. They had planned to get the hos high and drunk and fuck their brains out.

No one had seen or heard from Jah and his man in a minute, so Groovy was inclined to believe they were hiding somewhere, licking their wounds. It was like he and Rel had said from the beginning, the two youths didn't wanna play with the big boys. Slick was still acting funny, but things were business as usual for the two hoods. He had looked up to Slick as sort of a mentor, but his actions of late made him question his faith in the older man. Much like Rel, Groovy wasn't big on thinking, so he believed in taking a more hands-on approach to everything. Slick and all his strategizing was making him feel soft and he didn't like it.

Rounding the corner, Groovy literally bumped into someone. The bottle had almost slipped from his hands, but he managed to maintain his grip. He looked up, ready to bark, but paused. Something about the kid wearing the black stocking cap looked familiar, but Groovy couldn't place him right off. When the young man smiled it all began reaching Groovy's mind and it clicked. Spooky was quick on the draw, but young Groovy was quicker. Smashing the bottle against Spooky's face, Groovy took off running in the other direction.

His cheek hurt from where the bottle had struck him and his eyes burned from the liquor running in them, but it didn't stop Spooky from chasing Groovy. The young man zigzagged through the pedestrians on the sidewalk, making it hard for Spooky to get a shot off, for fear of hitting innocent bystanders. Groovy had no such reservations and proceeded to fire his Glock.

Chest heaving and almost out of breath, Groovy rounded the corner and tried to make a break for St. Nicholas Avenue. He knew if he reached the park, he could lose Spooky and come back another day. Sparing a glance over his shoulder, he saw that he had the man by at least a block. Seeing that he still might live through this gave him added speed as he burst out onto St. Nicholas.

When Groovy tried to cross the street, he was cut off by another man on a dirt bike. "Oh shit!" was all he could say as Jah hit him in the chest with the .40. Groovy rocked to one side and lost his footing. He almost hit the ground, but managed to steady himself with his hand. Just as he tried to get up, Jah blew his kneecap off, putting him on his back.

"Where you going, Jumping Jack Flash?" Spooky asked, finally catching up to Groovy. "You hit me in the face with a fucking bottle." Spooky stomped on Groovy's ruined knee, causing him to shriek.

"You muthafucka!" Groovy rolled on the ground, holding his knee. "I'm gonna kill you niggaz!"

"You ain't gonna do nothin', you raping piece of shit." Jah kicked him in the face, breaking his nose. "Even on my thirstiest day, I ain't gotta take the pussy."

Groovy looked at Jah as if he didn't understand, but as realization began to kick in, he started laughing. "Is that was this is about, a bitch?"

"Watch yo mouth." Jah kicked him again.

Groovy yelped and went back into his fit of laughter. "And here I thought you niggaz had come to handle your business on some official shit, and you out here popping off over some bitch." He spat blood on he ground. "Well, fuck y'all and that bitch. You should've heard the way she screamed when my nigga put his dick in her ass," he taunted.

"That's funny?" Jah asked emotionally.

"Nigga, that shit is beyond funny." Groovy's laughter got louder. Suddenly, the sound of gunfire drowned out his laughter. Jah started at his shins and worked his way up Groovy's body. It wasn't until his clip was spent that he allowed Spooky to pull him away.

"Rel, you're so funny," Sunshine said, pawing him. She was a short chick with cocoa skin and large breasts.

"Yeah, I know, baby. I always said I should've been on Def Comedy Jam," he said arrogantly.

"So you really run this whole project?" Scar asked, as if she was really interested in hearing him talk about himself further.

Rel popped his collar. "This *my* hood right here. I got the block on smash, boo, you ain't know?"

Scar and Sunshine continued to listen to Rel's ranting, wondering how much longer they'd have to put up with it. When the news of what had happened to Yoshi had reached Shooter's, all the girls took it hard, but none more so than Scar and Sunshine.

Since Sunshine had started working at Shooter's six months ago, Yoshi was one of the few girls that had been nice to her. Yoshi was like the big sister she'd never had, schooling her to the game of stripping and making sure she was okay. There were even times when Sunshine couldn't make tip-out and Yoshi had gone into her own money to make sure Sunshine was good.

Scar had a much more personal stake in it. When she was a child living in Africa, she had been a victim of rape. A group of local thugs had caught her coming home from school one day and took turns violating her then-virgin womb. When it was done, they beat her and left her for dead in an alley. Luckily, an old beggar woman found her and made sure she got to the hospital. The scars of what had happened had been with her longer than the tribal markings on her face. Her heart went out to victims of rape and she wished a pox on the offenders, hoping that they all burned in hell. When Marcus approached her with the plan he was piecing together with Jah, it provided her with a means to send one more on his way.

Rel was so caught up with trying to impress the two girls that he almost didn't notice the shadows begin to move. At first he thought his eyes might've been playing tricks on him, but when two male figures holding weapons detached themselves from the darkness, he knew that they weren't. It was on! Rel tossed Sunshine from his lap and pulled his gun from under the bench. He tried to raise it, but to his surprise, Scar slapped it out of his hand.

"Bitch, what the fuck are you doing?" Rel asked in disbelief.

Scar was no longer looking at him with the fluttering eyes of a schoolgirl, but with the murderous glare of a predator. "That girl you raped was a friend of mine, you worthless piece of shit," she said as she pulled a razor. "When you die, I'm gonna dance on your grave."

Scar swung the blade in a crossing motion, trying to cut Rel's face. He weaved from the attack and caught her on the chin. He expected the blow to fold the tall woman, but she remained standing. Scar came back with a double swing, catching Rel across the gut. His white T-shirt began to turn red at the bottom from the blood that was now trickling from his stomach.

Rel couldn't believe what the fuck was happening to him. A minute ago, he was waiting for his man Groovy so they could get some ass, but now he found himself leaking with two assassins closing in on him. He weighed his options and figured a good run was better than a bad stand any day.

38

"That nigga trying to run!" Jah shouted.

"I got him," Spooky said, trying to draw a bead on Rel's fleeing back. He fired two quick shots, missing with both bullets.

"Damn, you missed him," Jah said, jogging ahead of Spooky.

"Why don't you pop off instead of running your mouth!" Spooky shouted back.

Rel was tearing through the projects, screaming like a girl. He ran in zigzag motions, trying to avoid the flying death that was at his back. After hopping a fence, his building was finally in sight. He banged on the lobby door, but none of the people waiting for the elevator bothered to let him in. Rel had been terrorizing the St. Nicholas projects since he came home and frankly, the residents were tired of his shit.

Rel turned to seek an alternative escape route and his shoulder exploded. The fire shot from his neck to the tips of his fingers, putting Rel in a world of pain that he had never imagined he would visit. He was in so much agony that when he opened his mouth to scream it came out as gibberish. As he lay on the floor bleeding, he prayed for God to save him.

"God ain't gonna do nothing for a worthless sack of shit like you," Jah said as he walked up. He was out of breath and tired as hell from the chase, but seeing Rel leaking gave him added stamina.

"Yo, what the fuck is y'all niggaz doing?" Rel asked, scooting closer to the lobby door.

"What you think we're doing?" Spooky asked him, as if the question was a stupid one to begin with. "Time to answer for what you've done, Rel."

"Man, it wasn't my bullet that killed that boy. I swear it wasn't!" Rel tried to tell them.

Jah doubled over with laughter. "You silly muthafucka, this ain't about Crazy Eight. This is about you touching something that didn't belong to you."

Rel looked back and forth between the men, trying to figure out what was going on. He assumed that Jah was riding on him because of the botched hit, but he was telling him something different. He had done so many grimy things to people that there was no way to tell what Jah was talking about.

"Don't look around like you don't know what's going on, you fucking rapist." Jah kicked him in the face, knocking out his two front teeth. "That girl you and your homeys raped is someone very dear to me."

Hearing the word "rape," it all began to make sense. "Jah, I didn't know she was your girl. Yo, when them niggaz started tripping, I'm the only one that tried to stop them," Rel lied.

"Do I look stupid to you?" Jah placed his gun to Rel's eye.

"Please don't shoot me, man. I'll tell you where Slick is hiding," Rel tried to bargain.

Jah grabbed him by the shirt and pulled him to his feet. "Not to worry, my dude, we already know where your man is hiding, and I ain't gonna shoot you."

"You're not?" Rel asked, thinking it was a trick.

"Not at all, my brother. We've got something special for you," Jah said, frogging him into the building while Spooky covered his back.

Scar watched from the bench, smiling, as the two men dragged

Rel off into the building. What she had done was wrong, but no worse than what Rel had done. The way she figured it, the scales were now balanced. Tapping Sunshine to let her know it was time to leave, Scar made hurried steps out of the projects and hopped into a cab.

"This is some bullshit," Rel said, standing on the roof of the projects ass-naked.

"What you talking 'bout, fam, you should be comfortable naked in your own house. This is your hood, ain't it?" Spooky taunted him.

"Man, I thought y'all said you wasn't gonna kill me?" Rel looked around nervously.

"I said we weren't gonna shoot you." Jah tucked his .40. "Your ass is about to get your first flying lesson."

"Come on, son, don't do me like this," Rel pleaded. His eyes kept going from the fourteen-story drop behind him to the gunmen.

"I know damn well you ain't begging? Spook," he said and turned to his partner, "is this nigga begging?"

Spooky shook his head shamefully. "Sure sounds like it."

"I can pay y'all. I got about two hundred grand stashed at Slick's house. If you take me down to get it, it's all yours."

"Oh, we're gonna take your money, but your ass is still out," Spooky told him.

"Come on, man. Don't do me like this," Rel pleaded, with tears running down his face. "I got kids!"

Out of nowhere, Jah slapped him across the face. "Fuck yo seeds, nigga! Did you give a fuck about your seeds when you were fucking Yoshi?"

"Yo, Jah—"

Jah slapped Rel again. "I don't wanna hear shit you gotta say. Blue sky's are calling." Jah nodded toward the ledge. "You better get going."

"My dude, I can't jump off no roof," Rel said.

"You'll jump, or we're gonna put so much lead in you that they're gonna need a metal detector to find you," Jah assured him.

Rel looked from the ledge back to Jah. Though being shot would be a most painful experience, it probably failed in comparison to falling from the top of a building. For the second time that afternoon, Rel found himself weighing his options. If he was going to die, he wouldn't go without a fight. Using the element of surprise, he dazed Jah with a right to the chin. Spooky tried to help out, but Rel caught him with a two-handed strike to the gut. When he tried to run, Jah shot him in the leg.

Walking over to the now crawling Rel, Jah grabbed him by the arm and yanked him to his feet. He wrapped one hand around Rel's neck and gripped his testicles with the other. "You've got big balls," Jah said to Rel, who was whimpering in pain. "And I'm not saying it to flatter you."

"Mercy," Rel croaked.

Jah's face contorted into a mask of hatred. "Mercy is for the weak, and I don't know nothing about being weak." Tired of toying with Rel, Jah tossed him over the ledge.

The scream that pierced the quiet afternoon caused Slick to drop the bowl of cereal that he had been eating. He made it to the window just in time to see what he thought was a garbage bag streak past. Peering through the bars, Slick saw that it wasn't a garbage bag at all. He threw up all over the floor at the site of his partner Rel lying on the ground below. The impact had shattered his skull and left a nasty mess.

It didn't take Slick long to figure out what had happened. Moving like a man possessed, he began throwing clothes and cash into a laundry bag. He had no idea if his stalkers knew where he was hiding, but if they'd tracked Rel down, they probably did. Grabbing his gun, he headed for the front door. He would call to check on Groovy later, but right then he had to get the fuck outta the projects.

Just as he was about to touch the doorknob, someone knocked. Rel was dead and Groovy had a key, so whoever it was couldn't have meant him any good. Being that he was only on the second floor, he thought about jumping out the window, but that wouldn't have gone well for him if someone was covering the front of the building. Slick knew he only had one option. Dropping the laundry bag, he aimed his gun at the front door and emptied the clip.

Jah and Spooky walked fast, but didn't run up Eighth Avenue. Over Jah's shoulder, he held a laundry bag containing over two hundred thousand dollars in small bills, and the guns they had used to murder the St. Nick hustlers. Rel wasn't shit in life, but he did turn out to be useful for something in the end.

When he tossed Rel off the roof, he and Spooky headed downstairs to finish Slick. Spooky suggested they do it another time, as the police were surely on the way, but Jah wouldn't hear it. He was determined not to let another night go by with debts still to be paid.

The initial knock on the door was met by gunfire, as Jah suggested it might. Slick was so scared that he emptied the whole clip and didn't kill anything but the apartment door. While he was preoccupied, Jah made his way around the back of the building and climbed the few feet to the bathroom window. Slick never even saw it coming when the youngster clocked him in the back of the head with his pistol, knocking him unconscious.

When Slick woke up, he was ass-naked and tied to his bed. Jah questioned him about the rape, but Slick insisted he didn't know what Jah was talking about, which he didn't. He continued to try and tell them that they were about to kill an innocent man, but Jah didn't give a shit. Whether he took part in the rape or not wouldn't have saved his life. His innocence in the rape didn't change the fact that he had tried to murder Jah and he had to go. They didn't toy with him like they did Rel, but his death was just as painful, if not more so, as it took him a few minutes to die even after Jah had blown his shithole out.

Jah felt weary after the hit. He had shot plenty of cats in his day, but it was never like this. The times he had killed before had been about survival or a dollar, but the murders of Slick and his crew were about something else. Jah had killed those men because he hated them. When he squeezed that trigger, he poured every bit of hate and self-loathing he could muster into the deed. Now that they were dead, the hate was gone, leaving a feeling of accomplishment and closure.

"How much you think we made off with?" Spooky asked.

"I don't know, and we damn sure ain't gonna stop to count it right now. We gotta get low," Jah told him. "Check it, take this," he said and handed Spooky the bag. "Stash the guns and we'll dump them when the heat dies down."

"You're finally giving up that old forty-cal?"

"I'm giving up a lot of shit, Spook," Jah said with a seriousness that Spooky wasn't used to hearing from him. "Man, I've put in so much work this summer that I feel like I've been holding a nine to five."

"Go ahead with that stupid shit." Spooky waved him off and flagged a cab. "I know you ain't talking about getting out after all the muthafuckas we just dropped?"

Jah laughed. "Spook, you're my ace boon from the womb to the tomb. I'd never leave you high and dry. I'm still down for my nigga and always will be, I'm just thinking that with all the heat that's gonna come down on the streets, it might not be the smartest thing in the world for me to be running around acting all crazy. I'm just saying I might not wanna be so visible for a while."

"I feel you, but if we lay up, what are we gonna do?" Spooky asked seriously.

Jah placed his hand on Spooky's shoulder. "We ain't rich, but we ain't broke, either. My dude, we got money in the stash and on the streets. We're running around out here putting in work because we enjoy it. You're always telling me about your auntie in D.C. that's got your daughter. Why don't you go down and visit her?"

Spooky thought on it for a minute. "I do miss my baby girl."

"You should, being that you ain't seen her in months." Jah playfully mushed Spooky. "Take a few weeks to relax and get some out-of-town pussy."

"That doesn't sound like a bad idea," Spooky agreed. "What are you gonna do?"

Jah winked and started walking in the other direction. "Help a young lady I know get back on her feet."

"I always knew you was a sucker for love!" Spooky joked, as he got in the cab and pulled off.

The first uniformed officer that entered Slick's apartment lost his lunch at the sight that awaited him. Slick was on his stomach with his arms and legs duct taped to the bedposts. His back had been sliced repeatedly with a kitchen knife and there was a gaping hole where his asshole used to be. From what they could tell, Slick had been tortured before he died. Later that night, the coroner would deduce that the cause of death was someone sticking a high-powered handgun up Slick's ass and pulling the trigger.

39

Rhonda sat on her love seat, smoking a blunt and watching videos. Though most of the mess from the party had been cleaned up, the floor was still sticky and the house reeked of sin. After the police had carted Paul away, Rhonda resumed the party to celebrate. P.J. had spent the night at Sheila's, so she had no restrictions on how hard she went. She took Von in the bedroom and fucked him for an hour and a half as a reward for him standing up for her.

During their romp, she went on and on about how much of a G Von was and how he was killing the pussy, but it was all a prerehearsed script. What was really on her mind was how Paul had wigged out. When she had met him, Paul was a pure street nigga. He was like an older version of Jah, yet far more poised. His lawless attitude was one of the main things that attracted her to him. Those were the good old days, but since Paul had come home from jail, he was on a totally different page.

She had heard stories about cats going to jail and getting scared straight, but she didn't believe that about Paul. When she had asked him about it, he simply said, "Parenthood ages you ten years." He tried to sound all philosophical about it, but Rhonda didn't believe that shit. She had three kids and still felt like she was twenty-one. No, it wasn't the birth of P.J. that had changed Paul, it was his new bitch.

When Rhonda first started hearing stories about her baby's father having a new shorty, she already made up her mind that she didn't like her. She was nice to P.J. and seemed to have her shit together, but she reminded Rhonda too much of Kelly to even consider understanding her. To Rhonda, the greatest threat that Marlene posed was the fact that she had been able to manipulate Paul's heart. She did it under the guise of trying to help him grow up, but Rhonda felt that she was really just a controlling bitch.

"You gonna pass that or let it burn?" Rhonda asked, nodding at the blunt in Reese's hand, which sported a head of ash almost as long as the blunt itself.

"Shit," Reese yelped as the heat nicked her finger. "I was so caught up in this article that I wasn't even paying attention," she said, holding up the *Daily News* piece on violence in Harlem.

"This is some sad shit," Rhonda said, shaking the newspaper. "They found that nigga Rel, butt-ass with his whole skull caved in. First that silly muthafucka Pain, and now Rel's old rapist ass. Yo, this is the only summer I've ever seen where every greaseball muthafucka is getting what they deserve."

"Rhonda, that's some fucked-up shit to say." Reese gave her a disgusted look. "I wouldn't wish death on anyone, not even Pain."

"Bitch, then you must be stupid. Them niggaz not only put you on front street, but Pain tried to tear your head off. If it had been me, I'd be glad to see his ass rotting in the ground."

"Well, it ain't you, Rhonda," Reese shot back. "Yeah, Pain and Jay were both assholes and I'd have loved to see them get whipped out, but dying? Nah, I can't bring myself to wish that on anyone. Rhonda, you're my girl, but you ain't got no shame."

"I know you ain't talking about shame?" Rhonda raised her eyebrow. "I wasn't the one who let Don B.'s crew run through me. The crazy shit is that I'm not mad at you because you let them niggaz do you like a freak. I'm mad at the fact that you ain't even have the good sense to get some paper out of it. That not only makes you a freak, but a dummy, too."

"Fuck you, bitch!" Reese snapped. "All you do is sit around and criticize people. If I didn't know you, I'd think you had a perfect life, but I do know you, so we know that's far from the case. While you're busy putting everyone else's life under the microscope, why don't you try taking a look at yours?"

"What about my life? Ain't shit wrong with my life," Rhonda insisted.

"Ain't shit *right* with your life," Reese countered. "Your days consist of smoking weed and talking on the phone. The only time you get out of bed before twelve is on check day."

"Reese, don't come up in here acting like you get up and go to work every morning. I might only have a state income, but at least I got my own crib. Can't nobody come in here and tell me shit. Unfortunately, you can't say the same."

"And so what if I live with my mother, I ain't got no kids. Let me ask you a serious question. Have you ever thought about how the way you move affects your kids?" Rhonda gave no answer. "You run around yelling about how Alisha is too fast, but where do you think she gets it from?"

Rhonda waved her off. "Please, what I do ain't got nothing to do with her little ass being grown. That little bitch just needs a slap in her mouth."

"Look at how many slaps in the mouth Rita gave you, and you still ended up pregnant before we were out of high school," Reese pointed out. "Rhonda, those kids need more than a slap in the mouth. They need to know that it's not normal behavior to sit around and wait on the mailman to bring them a check. Instead of trying to beat niggaz in the head and trying to figure out how to get Paul back, you need to take a more active roll in what's going on in your kids' lives." By the look on Rhonda's face, Reese could tell she hit a sore spot. She hadn't meant to come across so harsh, but it needed to be said.

Rhonda thought about blacking out and punching Reese in the face, but if she did that then she would know she had struck a nerve. She looked at Reese coolly and said, "You know what? I might get a check from the state, and yeah, my kids might even be a little rotten, but dammit, I got my self-respect. You'd never catch me letting a bunch of dirty-dick niggaz like Don B. and his crew taking turns stretching my pussy out and walk away empty-handed. Instead of trying to preach to me, you need to be down at the clinic making sure your ass is all right."

Rhonda's words hit Reese like a physical blow. Her mind had almost blocked out what had happened at the hotel, but Rhonda had reopened the wound. No one knew that she had been burned, but the statement hit too close to home. Of all the girls she hung out with, Rhonda was the best at getting under her skin.

"Rhonda, you're crazy foul," Reese said, getting up and heading for the door.

"That's right, bitch, run away like you always do," Rhonda called after her. "One day you're gonna come across a problem that you can't run away from and then what're you gonna do?"

Reese ignored Rhonda and held back the tears that were trying to fall. Rhonda was speaking out of anger, but her words were ringing very true. Things were coming up left and right that were complicating the hell out of her life. Since she'd been a little girl, she always ran from her problems or acted as if they didn't exist. At some point in her life, she would have to take a stand. The fact that she was now pregnant and had no idea who the father was told her it would come sooner than later.

After three days of bologna sandwiches and being elbow to elbow with the same sex, Paul was finally a free man. When he had gone before the judge, she'd informed him that he was being charged with assault, disorderly conduct, and trespassing. Paul tried to explain that he had only tried to defend himself, but the female judge automatically sided with Rhonda. He felt sick when she set his bail at twenty-five thousand dollars. He was barely making ends meet and had no way to raise that kind of bread. Even putting up the ten percent for bond seemed like an impossible task. He had come to grips with the fact that he might be sitting up for a while when one of the guards informed him that he had posted bail. He knew he hadn't called anyone to tell them he was locked up, so he figured it had to be a mistake, but he wasn't going to tell them that. He took the blessing and was quietly processed out.

When he walked out of the Tombs, the early morning sun nearly blinded him. He had only been behind the wall for a few days, but his now light-sensitive eyes made it feel like far longer. He smelled like a cabdriver and was in dire need of a shave, but when he walked out of the Tombs and took a whiff of the stale New York air, none of it mattered.

Paul was glad to be free, but his anger at Rhonda still lingered. Never in his life had he felt so violated by a female. For years, he had been nothing but good to Rhonda, even when she went out of her way to be a bitch. He had held her and her seeds down and as payment now he'd be running back and forth to court, fighting his new case. Of all the fights they had over the years, she had never gone to those extremes, but apparently the gloves were now off.

Rhonda was playing the role of the victim when she was wrong all the way around the board. She was not only pressing charges, but had tried to put the wolves on him. He had seen the kid Von around before, but really didn't know who he was or what he was about. Knowing Rhonda, he was a low-class hood who Paul would have to be on point for in the future. The first thing Paul was going to do when he got back uptown was go by Spooky's and get a hammer.

Paul had been out of the loop for three days, so there was a lot to be done. Marlene was probably going to kill him when she caught him because he hadn't bothered to call her when he got knocked. With her being a defense attorney, she should've been the first person he called, but Paul chose not to play that card. The last things he needed was Marlene worrying and talking a hole in his head about Rhonda's bullshit and his quality of life. He had gotten himself into it, and he would get himself out.

Nothing that had happened over the past few days sat well with Paul, but what he felt the worst about was missing the exhibit. Larry had gone through a lot of trouble to set the event up, and Paul hadn't even showed. It hurt him to know that he had probably missed the opportunity to finally get his career off the ground, but what made him feel like shit was knowing that he had let Larry down. He had gone out of his way to try and help Paul out and because of his lack of self-control, he flushed it down the toilet. He would apologize to his friend later, but at that moment the most important thing to him was getting the hell away from Center Street.

By the time Audrey came out of the courthouse, Paul was already gone. She had planned on approaching him when he was released, but she didn't expect him to be processed out so quickly after she'd posted the bond. She looked up and down the street, but saw no sign of him, and being that there were multiple train stations in the area, she had no way to know exactly which way he had gone. She sighed and thought on her next possible point of intercept.

40

When Jah walked into the apartment, he was thoroughly surprised at what he saw. Yoshi was sitting at the table, chatting with Marcus and sipping herbal tea. She had taken her weave out and let her real hair breathe. It was flipped and pinned up in the back, with one side hanging down to cover the spot where Rel had hit her. Her face still bore scrapes, but the worst of her bruises were fading.

"Hey," Jah said, coming into the kitchen with Billy on his heels.

"What's up, Jah?" Yoshi got up and hugged him. She closed her eyes and allowed herself a moment to enjoy his scent.

"I see you're feeling better." He squeezed her once more before letting go.

"A little bit, even if I don't look it," she said and shrugged.

Jah kissed her forehead tenderly and pulled her close to him. "You're beautiful to me, ma."

"I don't think I'll ever get used to that," Billy whispered to Marcus.

"I heard that." Yoshi tossed a balled-up paper towel at Billy. "Don't act like we're the only ones in here hugged up."

Marcus pinched Billy's thigh playfully. "Funny the way things play out, isn't it?"

"Sometimes." Billy smiled. "And I'm glad this is one of them."

"Can you guys excuse us for a second?" Yoshi got up and took Jah by the hand. "I need to talk to Jah for a minute," she told them as she led him into the bedroom.

"Don't be in there fucking on my sheets!" Marcus joked.

"What's up? You feeling up for a quickie?" Jah joked. Yoshi's face remained serious. "Sorry, I was just playing."

"Jah, I know what happened," she told him.

"Huh?"

"Billy and Marcus tried to hide the newspapers from me, but I guess they didn't expect it to come on the TV news. I know what happened to Rel and the others."

Jah's heartbeat quickened, but he didn't let his face reveal what his mind was thinking. "Yeah, I heard about what happened to them dudes. Karma is a muthafucka, ain't it?"

"Jah, don't give me that karma shit!" She raised her voice a little louder than she meant to. "Baby," she said, calming herself, "I need to ask you a question and I need the absolute truth."

He didn't like where the conversation was going. "Okay."

Yoshi took a deep breath. "Did you do it?"

"Did I do what?" he said, faking ignorance.

"You know what I mean, so stop playing. Jah, if we're gonna keep it funky with each other, then let this be the starting point. Did you kill those men?"

Time slowed for Jah as he pondered the question and how best to answer it. He cared very much for Yoshi and wanted to try and establish something with her, but how would the knowledge of what he'd done affect that? Looking into her brown eyes, he saw a bleeding desire to know the truth, but at the same time he knew she might not be strong enough to handle it. Jah knew there was only one way he could answer the question.

"Nah, I ain't have shit to do with it," he lied.

Yoshi threw her arms around Jah and hugged him as tight as she could. "Thank God," she sobbed. "Jah, we've just found each other, please don't let this street bullshit cut our time short."

"I won't." He hugged her just as intensely. "I'm gonna be in your corner for as long as you need me." As Jah held Yoshi in his arms, he knew it would be a while before he went back to running wild in the streets. He was in no way saying that he would retire from the hustle, but he was sure as hell taking a long vacation.

Paul found himself riding the Harlem-bound 3 train in a very distraught state. When he hit Harlem, the first stop he had made was to Spooky's. He wasn't home, but after Paul fed Elaine the story about him having to get something for Jah, she allowed him to come in and scour through Spooky's arsenal. Paul sifted through a variety of handguns before he finally found a black .40 inside a plastic bag. The gun looked worn, but he was sure they wouldn't hold onto it unless it worked.

Originally, he was going home to shower, but a very disturbing voicemail Marlene had left him altered his course: "Paul, this is my fifth time calling you and I'm feeling like a real chickenhead right now. You know what? As far as I'm concerned, you can stay wherever you are. I'm through. Have a nice life with one of those bum bitches you love so much and try not to let her flush your life down the toilet all at once." If he wasn't sure before, he was damn sure now that she was pissed off.

Paul decided he should call her and get a sneak preview of what he was in for. He punched in her cell number and got the automated service telling him that the number was no longer in service. He tried it again and got the same message. Paul even called her house phone, but the result was the same. As a last resort, he tried her job and was told that Marlene had taken a leave of absence. Frantic, he spent most of what he had left in his pocket and took a cab to her house.

Paul rushed up to the front door and tried his key. It slid smoothly into the lock, but wouldn't turn. He tried banging on the door and shouting her name, but no one answered him. Looking up at the window, he saw that the curtains were all drawn and there was no sign of movement anywhere in the house. Marlene had just up and vanished.

The ride back into Manhattan was less than pleasant. There were no seats on the bus, so he took the subway, which was sweltering without air-conditioning. He had racked his brains, trying to figure out where Marlene could've disappeared to, but he came up blank. She didn't have many friends and her parents lived in a different state. He could barely keep himself from panicking as the possibilities of something possibly having happened to her kept popping into his head.

He got off the train and walked hurriedly to his building. He still looked like walking death and really didn't want to see anyone. He had planned on going home to take a shit and a shower and continue working on the mystery of Marlene's disappearance. As Paul neared his building, he was very surprised to see who was waiting for him.

"It's about time you got here," Audrey said, clearly irritated.

"Audrey, what the hell are you doing here?" he asked, thoroughly surprised.

"Going against everything I believe in to help a friend out." She tossed him the envelope.

"Marlene sent you?"

"Who the hell else do you think would've put the bail money up for your ass? Rhonda?"

"But how did she even know where I was?"

Audrey shook her head as if even talking to Paul was a task. "She's a lawyer, remember?"

"Shit, she must be pissed," Paul thought out loud.

"Pissed?" She looked at him as if he were insane. "Little boy, that's the understatement of the year."

"Audrey, you don't have to keep throwing insults at me," he told her.

"You're lucky that's all I'm throwing at you after what you did to my friend."

"I didn't do shit to Marlene," Paul insisted. "I know she's probably mad at me for getting arrested, but it wasn't my fault. That bitch Rhonda lied to the police," he tried to explain.

Audrey just shook her head. "You don't get it, do you? This ain't about you getting arrested, Paul, it's about you being a fucking loser with the best thing that's happened to you."

"Yo, why you coming at me like I shitted on Mar? All I did was get locked up and you're acting like I've been fucking around on her."

Audrey slit her eyes at him. "Paul, my ear is always to the streets, so don't even go there with me. I just don't take the shit I hear about you and your friend Larry to Marlene because I ain't no homewrecker, but don't act like your ass is Ward Cleaver. You know, I used to think that you were an okay dude, but apparently you're just as fucked up as every other nigga running around trying to find his dick."

"Fuck you, Audrey. You don't know me to judge me," he said angrily.

"I don't have to know you, Paul, I know your type," she said. "Marlene has been trying to reach out to you, but you're too caught up with your silly-ass baby's mama to see the writing on the wall."

"Audrey, I've had a very trying couple of days and I really ain't got time for riddles or games. If you've got a contact number for Marlene, give it to me."

"She doesn't want to hear from you," she said flatly. "Marlene is going away for a while to try and rinse you out of her system."

"Away? Where?" he asked frantically.

"I don't know, and even if I did, I wouldn't tell you," she said spitefully. "You've done some bonehead shit in the past, but this latest batch of bullshit turned out to be more than my girl could take. Maybe in a few years you'll be wise enough to look back at all this and realize what a treasure you really had."

"Audrey, fuck this dumb shit you're talking. I need to talk to Marlene and get some answers," he said.

"That envelope should have all the answers you need." She nodded toward it. Paul looked down at the envelope he was holding as if he had momentarily forgotten it was there. He held it up to the light, but couldn't make out its contents. He looked at Audrey, who motioned for him to open it. There was something about the smug look on her face that made him hesitate. Paul started to just tuck the envelope away and open it when he got upstairs, but curiosity got the best of him. Careful not to tear the contents of the envelope, Paul ripped it across the top and removed two sheets of paper. The first one was a letter, folded over, and signed in Marlene's familiar handwriting. The second one was some sort of printout from a medical center, the name of which had been blackened out.

"I don't understand," Paul said, reading the printout over and over because he couldn't believe what it said.

"Harlem niggaz never do," Audrey mumbled. "That sheet of paper is from a DNA testing center. The little number on the side means that there is less than a one percent chance that you're P.J.'s dad."

"Wh . . . what?" Paul stuttered.

"It's like Billy Jean, baby: the—kid—is—not—your—son! Take care of yourself, Paul," Audrey said dryly as she headed back to her car.

The whole world suddenly began to spin for Paul. His eyes transmitted the information to his brain, but it was still caught up in the processing stage. Before he even realized he was moving, he flopped flat on his ass. P.J. had been his son for as many years as the little boy had been on earth. He loved him so much that he refused to believe that science was right. He needed answers and there was only one place he would get them.

Jah and Yoshi had gone out to the movies, leaving Billy and Marcus alone in the house. Billy had protested that her friend was going out too soon, but Yoshi insisted. She felt like she was hiding by staying cooped up in the house. Finally, Billy realized if getting out would help her friend on the road to recovery, she shouldn't stand in the way of that. Besides, she knew Yoshi was in the best of care with Jah. It was a strange love affair, but if it made Yoshi happy, then Billy was all for it.

"Can you believe those two?" Marcus asked from the couch where he was lounging. "Darling, I love you so," he said, doing a poor impersonation of Jah.

"You need to quit." Billy flopped on the couch and nestled herself in his chest. "I think they look cute together."

"The '06 Bobby and Whitney," Marcus joked.

"I ain't gonna tell you about cutting on my friends no more," she said, pretending to be serious.

"Nah, but I'm happy for them," he admitted. "Everybody needs somebody, wouldn't you agree?"

"In some cases," she said.

"I hope this is one of them."

"Sure feels like it." She kissed him just below the jaw. "Marcus, I don't think I ever had a chance to thank you for all the trouble you've gone through."

"No need to thank me, Billy. I'm doing it out of love, not in search of gratitude. I've got a sister and a mother and I wouldn't know what to do with myself if something like that happened to one of them. Besides, had I not been hanging around here all damn day and night, I might not have had the chance to find out what a wonderful person you are."

"Aw, you're so sweet." She patted him on the cheek. "I might have to let you taste this again."

"I'm serious, Billy. I think you're a real special lady, and I ain't trying to let you go no time soon," he said seriously. Marcus was staring at her so intensely that she cringed a little.

"Marcus, I know you mean well, but a girl like me comes with a lot of baggage; you might not be ready for me," she teased him.

"Baby, I ain't no stranger to baggage, I used to work at the airport," he said, matching her wit. "You need to stop playing so we can walk these dogs, ma."

"Walk these dogs?" She looked up at him. "That is so 1997." She craned her neck and kissed him. Who says there's no such thing as a happy ending? was the thought that passed through her mind.

41

During the short cab ride to Rhonda's house, Paul was going to go stark-raving mad. The printout shook violently in his hand as he read it for at least the hundredth time. "Less than one percent?" he said out loud. P.J. was his boy, his flesh. There was no way he could've come from someone else, it was impossible. This had to be a ploy by Audrey to try and worsen the situation with him and Marlene. If he hadn't been so hell-bent on getting to Rhonda's, he would've forced the truth out of her.

Just holding the printout in his hands was driving him nuts, so he decided to read the letter. Whatever Marlene had to say couldn't be any worse than the bomb Audrey had dropped on him. As soon as he removed the folded piece of paper, he recognized it as coming from the journal he had bought Marlene. When he opened it up and read it, his day got considerably worse.

My dearest Paul,
I know that writing you a letter as opposed to confronting you
personally might seem like a cowardly thing to do, but honestly, I
couldn't face you. I no longer have the strength, largely in part

because I gave all mine to you and never got anything in return. If you only knew how long I dreaded writing this letter, but somewhere in my heart, I knew I'd have to and that's why my words now flow so freely.

Paul, I've tried to express myself to you time and again. I've dropped hints, and said out loud what I wanted and what I needed, but you never seemed to hear me. All Paul is concerned about is what's best for Paul. It takes more than one person to have a successful relationship, and I guess that's why ours didn't work.

I always said that if I ever felt like I wanted to step out of the relationship, then I would end it all together, and that's the reason for this letter. While you were out running the streets and sleeping with chickenheads, I was left to sit at home and wonder if you were okay. When I needed to be comforted, you weren't there, so someone else stepped to the plate.

I never intended for it to happen, God knows I didn't, but when it did, it opened my eyes to the fact that I don't have to settle. This man, who had been right under my nose the whole time, showed me things that you couldn't or wouldn't. We made love in the sand under a pale moon. I know that's probably not what you want to hear, but I think you need to. Those are the kinds of things that make a woman feel special. Paul, I love you to death, but you have a lot to learn about what it takes to please a woman. There's more to keeping her around than just good dick.

I've tried to understand and be patient, Paul, but how long would I be forced to wait in the wings until you and Rhonda decided to get your shit together? It troubles me to know that the children who we will one day entrust our society to have parents like Rhonda as examples to follow. It's a sad cycle, and I only hope P.J. doesn't get caught up in the madness. No matter who fathered him, I'll always remember him as the son I got to have for a little while.

Paul, please don't hate me for what I've done, but try to understand me like I've tried to understand you. I needed to be loved, Paul, and you just weren't willing to do it the right way. Don't take this letter as a putdown or a scorn, but as a lesson learned in life. The next time you get a good woman, try to appreciate her more so that you never have to receive another letter like this one.

Love always,
Marlene

Paul's whole body shook. Though he wasn't crying out loud, tears ran down his face. The love he had held in his heart for Marlene withered and was reborn as a ball of hate. She had gone out of her way to take his heart and completely stomp on it. If she had been sitting beside him, there was no doubt in his mind that he would've broken her jaw. When a woman gets her heart broken, it hurts, but when it happens to a man, the pain is tenfold because his pride and ego is so much bigger.

He thought Marlene would be the one true love of his life, but she had turned out to be as sneaky and trifling as the next bitch. He cursed himself for not listening to Larry and keeping it as a fuck thing. This was the second time he failed to heed his friend's advice and it blew up in his face. Not knowing what else to do, Paul laughed hysterically and cried for the rest of the ride.

Rhonda sat at her usual post on the far end of the couch with her TV tuned to BET. She had finally gathered the strength to finish cleaning her house. As a reward to herself, she was going to get sky high and drunk. She was just about to crack open another Corona when someone knocked on the door.

"Alisha, didn't I tell you to take your fucking key when you left this house!" she shouted. Angrily, Rhonda made her way to the door and snatched it open. To her utter shock, it wasn't her daughter standing on the other side.

"Hey, Rhonda," Paul said in an all-to-calm voice. His eyes were bloodshot and held more than a slight glint of madness.

"Paul, what the fuck are you doing here? I've got a restraining order out against you!" she reminded him.

"I just came to see my son," Paul said.

"P.J.'s not here, so you can leave." She tried to close the door, but he caught it with his foot.

"That works, too, 'cause we gotta talk." He invited himself in. He crossed the living room with Rhonda on his heels.

"Paul, I hope you didn't come over here to start no shit, 'cause if you did . . ."

"Is P.J. my son?" he blurted out.

Rhonda was stunned by the question, but being a skilled schemer, she recovered quickly. "What kind of stupid-ass question is that?"

"Just answer it!" he barked.

The tone of his voice made Rhonda nervous. She had seen Paul enraged, but the state he was in was totally different. There seemed to be something terribly off kilter about him that day.

"Of course P.J. is your son. I ain't got no reason to lie," she told him.

"Good, then maybe you can clear this up," he said, handing her the printout.

Rhonda cautiously took the paper from Paul's outstretched hand and read it. When she got to the bottom, the blood immediately drained from her face. Though she was no medical technician, she got the gist of what the printout was trying to say. She looked over at Paul, who was watching for a reaction.

"What's the matter, cat got your tongue?" he said in a harsh tone.

"Paul, where the fuck did you get this shit from?" she asked, wheels spinning, trying to piece together a story.

"Doesn't matter where I got it, what I wanna know is is it true?"

Rhonda could've guessed where he got the paternity test, but she knew off the back it was Marlene. She had the resources and the motive to do some underhanded shit like that. When Rhonda caught her on the streets, it would be on and popping. Rhonda saw the seriousness in Paul's eyes and couldn't think of what to say. She could continue trying to convince him that it was all bullshit, but you couldn't argue with scientific proof.

"Paul, let me explain," she finally said.

"So its true?" he said, looking very unstable.

"Paul, when I got pregnant with P.J., I was fucking around on you, but I really believed he was yours. When he got older and didn't look anything like you, I started having doubts, but after seeing the two of you together and how you interacted with him, I knew he had to be yours. If you hadn't gotten the paternity test done, I'd still think he was yours."

"How could you do this to me?" he asked, placing his head in his hands. "All these years I thought he was mine and it was a lie."

The more Rhonda talked, the harder Paul cried. How do you tell a child who you've been taking care of and interacting with like father and son that it was all bullshit? All Paul wanted to do was take a minute to breathe, but Rhonda was lingering in his space. It was as if her being in the same room with him was sapping his strength. He needed to be away from Rhonda before he lost his cool.

Rhonda risked moving close enough to the sobbing man to place her arm around him. "Paul, you're the only daddy P.J. has ever known, so I don't see a reason to change that now. You can keep on being his daddy and we can sweep all this under the rug," she said, trying to convince him. Her voice in his ear sounded like the buzzing of an insect house, driving him further into madness. With a warrior's cry, Paul snapped.

He backhanded Rhonda in the mouth so hard that she flew to the other side of the room and landed in the corner. She tried to scramble to her feet, but he was on her again. He delivered two more vicious slaps to Rhonda's face and tossed her roughly on the couch.

"All these years and it was a fucking lie!" he raged.

"Don't touch me!" Rhonda screamed. "Somebody help!!!"

"Lying bitch." He slapped her again. "Dirty lying whore!" He kicked her in the thigh. "How the fuck could you do this to my life?" he asked, leaning down so she could hear his hoarse whisper.

"Paul, I'm so sorry," she said, smashing her Corona bottle against his head.

Paul staggered twice and tipped over. When he hit the hard floor, the .40 he'd stolen from Spooky's crib came loose and clanged to the floor. Rhonda tried to scramble for the gun, but Paul grabbed her by the leg and dragged her back. She tried to fight him off, but the punches she was landing didn't do much to stop him. Paul was too far gone. Rhonda managed to wiggle loose and make one last lunge for the gun. This time she got it. Just as Paul was pouncing on her, she was rolling over, holding the pistol. They tussled around on the ground and eventually ended up with Paul on top of Rhonda with the barrel of the gun pressed against his chin.

"Oh, you gonna shoot your baby's daddy?" he asked, as if it was all a game to him. Paul struggled to get the gun away from Rhonda, but she had a death grip on it. "You better let this gun go before we have an accident."

"Paul, you're bugging. Get off me." She struggled as he slowly bent the barrel in her direction.

"Fucking lying bitch," he snarled, dripping spit on her. "You put me through all this and the kid wasn't even mine. I'm gonna put an end to your shit, once and for all."

"Paul . . ." She twisted the gun at his chest. "Stop it. You're gonna—"

Rhonda's words were drowned out by the gunshot. All was still for a moment, but when the smoke cleared, another young life had been lost.

When the police arrived at Rhonda's apartment, the furniture was overturned and blood was all over the living room floor. They found Paul huddled up in the bathtub, babbling and clutching the printout. They tried to ask him what had happened, but he seemed incapable of coherent speech. It didn't matter, though, the scene in the living room told the entire story.

Rhonda was stretched out by the window, with a bullet hole in her throat. Her lifeless eyes stared vacantly at the detectives and plain-clothes officers who were moving through her house. Oddly enough, she would come to meet her end by the same man she sought so diligently to reclaim; just as she had always said, she "loved him to death."

The police called it a crime of passion: "The scorned lover who had come to settle old scores with his estranged son's mother." At least that's how the papers would write it.

When they tested the gun, they linked it to the murders of Groovy, Slick, and several other unsolved homicides. The police took Paul in and charged him with every last body.

Sometimes It Goes Down Like That

Everyone in the hood turned out for Rhonda's funeral. It was amazing how someone who had pissed so many people off could've touched so many lives. Whether it was good or bad, everyone had something to say about Rhonda's crazy ass.

Sometime during the course of the funeral, True had slipped in. He was dressed in a dark suit and shades so black that you couldn't see his eyes if you were standing right in front of him. Though neither of them would've ever admitted it, there was a special connection between True and Rhonda. No matter how much of a hood rat she might've been, something always seemed to draw him back to her. Whether or not they could've ever coexisted as more than fuck buddies was a question that would never be answered. Some of the chickenheads had tried to press True for autographs, but he rudely dismissed them. He was grieving and the limelight had no place in his darkness.

"Hey, True," Rita said, placing a hand on his shoulder.

"How you doing, ma?" He placed his hand over hers.

"Hanging in there." She shrugged. "It's gonna be hard, but I'm strong. Damn, I'm gonna miss my baby." When Rhonda died, Rita had been destroyed. She ran up and down the street screaming and pulling her hair out. She had treated Rhonda horribly all her life and now that she was gone, there would never be a chance to make it right.

Little P.J. came darting past, almost stepping on True's shoe. True grabbed the youngster and tossed him into the air as he scolded him for running in a funeral home. Rita looked at the two of them interacting and her breath caught in her chest. She had never seen the two of them together, so she never saw the resemblance between True and P.J. She had known Rhonda had doubts about who P.J.'s father was, but she never mentioned True as a candidate. They were dealing with each other at the time, so it was possible, but there was no way Rita could know for sure. It was just another secret Rhonda took with her to the grave.

Since the murderous summer of '06, things hadn't been the same in the hood. The police were riding around shutting all the hustlers down, trying to bring the end to the crack era in one swoop. They didn't have much luck, but as long as they kept their feet knee deep in black asses, the mayor was happy.

With all the tragedy surrounding her, Reese had finally woken up to the fact that she was wasting her life. She had her mother take her down to enroll in BMCC, where she would complete her GED and study business. With a baby on the way, she needed to put together a solid game plan and finishing her education was a damn good place to start. She had made it all the way to the abortion clinic and had gotten cold feet, decided to take that stand. She would keep her baby and raise it as best she could, father or not. She was a woman, and therefore possessed the strength to do so.

Billy also resumed her education, enrolling at LIU. She had to take out an asshole full of loans and still have her mother call in a favor, but they made it happen. Regina's faith in her daughter was slowly coming back. Marcus had remained a constant fixture in Billy's life. Between him, work, and school, Billy kept her hands full. This suited her fine because it kept her mind off the past. She would miss the people she had lost, but she had learned her lesson about carrying around ghosts.

Jah and Yoshi had moved into her apartment together. It took a while before she was comfortable enough to sleep there again, but having Jah's crazy ass by her side made it easier. Billy was skeptical about the move, but as it turned out, Jah and Yoshi got along famously. She had stopped stripping and gotten a job doing wardrobe for music videos. It was a gig True had hooked her up with. It was the least he could do, considering what his boys had put her through. Yoshi eventually let go of her demons and started looking forward to tomorrow.

Jah took what happened to his brother extremely hard. He had made the difficult decision to go to the police and tell them it was really his gun, that Paul had nothing to do with the murders. He couldn't sit on the sidelines while his big brother spent the rest of his life in jail. He would get a good lawyer, turn himself in, and put it in God's hands. A life without Yoshi was one he didn't look forward to living, but he couldn't sacrifice his brother like that, not even for her.

Oddly enough, Jah never had to act. Not long after Paul had been taken to Riker's Island, he slashed his wrists. As he bled out in the prison shower, he painted a mural on the wall in his own blood. It was the rough smear of a man who had a gaping hole in his chest. When Marlene left Paul, she took his spirit with her. Even before he died, there hadn't been much more than a shell of the old Paul left. Jah took this as his wake-up call to get out of the game.

Marlene and Larry Love completed a lovely three-week cruise, where they made love every sunup and sundown. Marlene found it ironic that all this time she'd thought that Larry was the problem, but he was actually the solution. They both felt bad about sneaking behind Paul's back, but it was just something that had happened. Larry happened to be there at a moment Marlene needed comforting and he was happy to oblige. Paul was his man, but he had no idea what to do with someone like Marlene. Larry was an expert on bitches, and would make sure she was handled properly.

When they got back to New York and found out what had happened to Paul, they both felt like less than shit. While they were away having wild sex on Marlene's dime, someone who loved them both dearly had lost his freedom and his life. The worst part was he had gone through it all alone. They would have to live with the fact of knowing that they each played a part in what finally happened to Paul.

Six months into their relationship, Marlene woke up to find her car missing and one of her bank accounts totally depleted. Larry had disappeared with her heart and almost all of her savings. Paul's best friend, who had rocked her to sleep, had in the end shitted on her. Marlene took an L because she went out like the very same kind of person she was always looking down her nose at . . . a hood rat!!!!!

THE HOTTEST BOOKS ON THE STREET
ORDER NOW!

Qty	Selection	
___	**Eve** • K'wan • 0-312-33310-2	$14.95
___	**Hood Rat** • K'wan • 0-312-36008-8	$14.95
___	**Hoodlum** • K'wan • 0-312-33308-0	$14.95
___	**Street Dreams** • K'wan • 0-312-33306-4	$14.95
___	**Lady's Night** • Mark Anthony • 0-312-34078-8	$14.95
___	**The Take Down** • Mark Anthony • 0-312-34079-6	$14.95
___	**The Bridge** • Solomon Jones • 0-312-30725-X	$13.95
___	**Ride or Die** • Solomon Jones • 0-312-33989-5	$13.95
___	**Criminal Minded** • Tracy Brown • 0-312-33646-2	$14.95
___	**If I Ruled the World** • JOY • 0-312-32879-6	$13.95
___	**Nasty Girls** • Erick S. Gray • 0-312-34996-3	$14.95
___	**Extra Marital Affairs** • Relentless Aaron • 0-312-35935-7 . .	$14.95
___	**Inside the Crips** • Colton Simpson • 0-312-32930-X	$14.95

TOTAL AMOUNT $_____
POSTAGE & HANDLING $_____
($2.50 for the first unit, 50 cents for each additional)
APPLICABLE TAXES $_____
TOTAL PAYABLE $_____
(CHECK OR MONEY ORDER ONLY—PLEASE DO
NOT SEND CASH OR CODs. PAYMENT IN U.S. FUNDS ONLY.)

TO ORDER:

Complete this form and
send it, along with a **check
or money order,** for the total
above, payable to V. H.P.S.

Mail to:
V.H.P.S.
Attn: Customer Service
P.O. Box 470
Gordonsville, Va 22942

Name:_____

Address:_____

City:_____ State:_____ Zip/Postal Code:_____

Account Number (if applicable):_____

Offer available in the fifty United States and the District of Columbia only. Please allow 4-6 weeks for
delivery. All orders are subject to availability. This offer is subject to change without notice. Please call
1-888-330-8477 for further information.

*California, District of Columbia, Illinois, Indiana, Massachusetts, New Jersey, Nevada, New York, North
Carolina, Tennessee, Texas, Virginia, Washington, and Wisconsin residents must add applicable sales tax.

 **St. Martin's Griffin**